LITTLE
TOWN
BLUES

LITTLE TOWN BLUES

A NOVEL

DAVID GONTHIER, JR.

atmosphere press

To my wife, Caron, and daughter, Shelby

"The nice thing about living in a small town is that when you don't know what you're doing, someone else does."

—Immanuel Kant

"A *rising star* in a little town might very well be just a *falling star* outside of that microcosm..."

—Maygyn-Daved (from their memoir: *This is the Strangest Life I've Ever Known: Waterfalls, Ghosts & Gender Euphoria)*

"These *little town blues* are melting away..."

—Fred Ebb & John Kander (from the song, "New York, New York")

AUTHOR'S NOTE

This story occurred in 1984. The year the first Apple Macintosh computer went on sale. The year TED Conferences, LLC began. The year an X-class solar flare erupted on the sun. The year the prime minster of India, Indira Gandhi was assassinated, followed by the Sikh Massacre. The year Hong Kong returned to China. The year the Soviet Union boycotted the Olympics. The year U.K miners went on strike. The year Mississippi finally ratified the 19th Amendment. The year Crack cocaine was introduced in Los Angeles. The year HIV was discovered, which identified the AIDS epidemic. The year Ingmar Bergman's internationally acclaimed *Fanny & Alexander* won the Oscar for Best Foreign Film. The year *Amadeus, Beverly Hills Cop, The Karate Kid, Red Dawn, The Terminator, Ghostbusters* and *Gremlins* became Hollywood blockbuster sensations. The year the Detroit Tigers beat the San Diego Padres in the World Series. The year Van Halen's "Jump" and Madonna's "Like a Virgin" hit number 1 on the music charts. The year actress Scarlett Johansson, musician Katy Perry and Facebook CEO Mark Zuckerberg were born. The year George Orwell warned us about...

MAY 1984

S	M	T	W	R	F	S
		1	2	3	4	5
6	7	8	9	10	11	12
13	14	15	16	17	18	19
20	21	22	23	24	25	26
27	28	29	30	31		

CHAPTER 1

GÜNTER'S MILLYARD
AND NIAGARA TWO

Fryebury Falls was so small that whenever anyone mentioned the town to outsiders, they would ask: *Where's that?* To them, it might as well have been another planet. Aside from the fact that it was so close to Boston, it *was*, in a lot of ways, *another planet.*

It was an old mill town that, like its neighboring Massachusetts towns, Amesbury and Newburyport, did business manufacturing hats, carriages, and clipper ships during the Industrial Revolution of the early twentieth century. In the center of this otherwise menial place existed a little haven of sorts, named after Fryebury Falls entrepreneur Alexander Günter, a German American who made a killing in some new business in the 1950s that manufactured soap and vitamins. Günter fronted the money to build what he eventually called *Paradise Park* around the remarkable and mysterious waterfall, which, according to him, was the nucleus of this little town. Someone once called the waterfall *Niagara Two,* and the name always seemed to stick.

The waterfall was apparently the result of some underwater phenomenon. Legend has it that a native of Fryebury Falls named Roderick William Hayes Gorman, an eccentric old scientist, philosopher (or "geophilosopher," as he liked to call himself), inventor and politician in the 1920s, concluded the following: "The waterfall was created by a spontaneous underwater geologic reaction. Something to do with subduction. Like Niagara Falls, only not nearly as epic in nature. Underneath the Merrimack River some time ago, an earthquake must have occurred. It was like a 'Big Bang' from below. Very strange indeed, especially for this part of the country. Some say forces from *beyond* created it. Something *supernatural*."

Legend also has it that Gorman frequently reported strange goings-on down at the waterfall throughout his lifetime. He even said the waterfall talked to him. As the story unfolds, you'll see that this old buffoon wasn't as crazy as people said he was.

In addition to Niagara Two, Günter's Millyard contained a number of noteworthy spectacles, all products of the entrepreneur's *Paradise Park*: rows of weeping willow trees; red, white and blue brick and gravel paths; finely-crafted pine benches, also representing the colors of the American flag; a black and white stone wall surrounding a fantastic greenhouse where exotic, tropical-looking plants and flowers inexplicably grew all year long; and a theater-in-the-round modeled after Greek and Roman architecture, replete with marble stairs, pillars and other gaudy, abstract artifacts and sculptures, including a column made of granite that resembled the crystal monolith in *2001: A Space Odyssey*. Incidentally, nobody ever put on any formal productions in this theater; the space was merely used as a sort of picnic ground, which outraged Mike Melanson's wife Julie who had dedicated her life to the performing arts, and always insisted that this theater should have been utilized solely for the plays of Euripides, Sophocles, Aeschylus and Aristophanes.

There were two ways one could enter Günter's Millyard. The first way would be to come in from Main Street in the downtown area; that's where most of the folks would enter. The other way was through the woods by way of a small stretch of forest that contained a variety of dirt paths; each path was a trail leading from Günter's Millyard to all the major dead ends off of Baker Street, Fryebury Falls' longest and least traveled avenue.

All the aforementioned people would conveniently enter Günter's Millyard by using one of these trails.

CHAPTER 2

DEAD ENDS OFF
BAKER STREET

It is no wonder that all of this forthcoming drama unfolds on three dead ends, for these characters' lives, as you'll soon discover, *were* dead ends. Each of the cul-de-sacs ran perpendicular to Baker Street and although they were within a mile of one another, they were – peculiar as it might have appeared – their own separate microcosms ("The Triumvirate" or "The Three Milieus," as old Gorman the "geophilospher" had called them).

The so-called middle class lived on Brown Ave. All eight homes, which were unbearably close to one another, were well-maintained split-levels. Each home was more or less a replica of the others; they were either all white, all gray, or a combination of both colors. And the dark green lawns were well-kept, short like turf, as were the flowerbeds surrounding the houses on all sides.

It looked like a Norman Rockwell painting in Levittown!

Take the Stevens family, for instance; they were one of the eight families who resided here. Ronald Stevens was a manager at the Seabrook Nuclear Power Plant just fifteen miles west of town, and Jean Stevens was a homemaker who worked a few hours a week at the very small Fryebury Falls Elementary School. They had two kids named Timmy and Michelle.

Another family – the Melons – lived right at the head of the cul-de-sac, the closest home (one of the white and gray ones) facing the woods. They had two beautiful daughters named Jessica and Meredith. Dick Melon was a banker: *the bank dick* as Timmy Stevens and his buddies would grudgingly call him. And his wife Lois had an advertising position at the Museum of Fine Arts in Boston. Rumor had it she made twice the money he did.

Nice folks, simple folks.

But the neighbors in question here were Moira Davis and her daughter Maygyn, and Jack Cleary and his boy, Jack Jr. – J.J. for short.

Moira was a voluptuous green-eyed redhead who looked like one of those classical *femme fatales* from the film noirs of the 1940s: someone like Lauren Bacall, Ida Lupino, Gene Tierney or Veronica Lake. Those wicked sirens of the silver screen all had similar characteristics: mysterious sleepy eyes; hard-boiled dispositions; and masculine-sounding voices from smoking too many cigarettes. Moira, too, had one of those smoker's voices. Not as hideous as Lucille Ball in her twilight years or Suzanne Pleshette in her *Bob Newhart* years, but definitely in the running. She was a five foot-three, thirty-two-year-old singer-songwriter with breasts as round and firm as cantaloupes, and although her face looked as though it had been slapped around continuously by the hand of hard life – she had crow's feet and dark circles around her eyes making her look perpetually comatose – she still somehow passed through life as one of the beautiful people.

Moira's daughter Maygyn – who physically resembled her (this must have been what Moira looked like when she was a teenager) – was not in the least bit like her. Although barely a teenager when all these events occurred, she fancied herself a literary girl: she dug those "real" writers like Kate Chopin, Charlotte Perkins Gilman, Fyodor Dostoyevsky, George Eliot, and Henry James. Her father, whose introduction is forthcoming, turned her onto this world.

Then there's Jack Cleary who lived next door. He was a big fellow – husky and broad-shouldered – standing at about six-foot-three. He may have appeared to be overweight to someone upon first glance, but he was really just a mass of oversized muscle. His face, although not good-looking or homely (and actually quite boyish) resembled an overgrown bulldog.

That's how Mike Melanson's wife referred to him, anyway.

Jack's son was even more bulldog-like, but not boyish in the least. The teenager actually had the face of a premature old man – wrinkles and all. His face literally looked as though it had been caved in; his eyes and mouth almost appeared to be attached to his nose, as if someone's massive hand clawed his face and the features permanently stayed there. Plus, he was beginning to lose his long, black, stringy hair.

J.J. stood for John Jeremy. He was his father's namesake: John Jeremy Cleary, Jr. J.J. was big boned, practically as tall as his father, and his droopy eyes were perpetually bloodshot and crossed from the accident. Four years earlier, when he was twelve, one of his peers, a known bully at the time (who mysteriously disappeared not long after the accident), pushed him off a four-story building, causing him to be permanently brain damaged. Consequently, J.J. was in a coma for three or four months.

Stagecoach Road, the so-called "Beverly Hills" of Fryebury Falls, was where the police chief Mike Melanson and his family resided. The reason why he lived *here* was because of his wife: she had *millions*. The Melansons lived in one of the three mansions on this road – and, incidentally, the only three mansions in town.

One of their neighbors was the incomparable Dr. Mark Porzio, a proctologist who had a house full of servants and no family. He worked at Massachusetts General Hospital and was rarely at home. One day, as the boisterous, three-hundred-pound surgeon was getting into his Jaguar, he said to Mike, "I've got half a dozen assholes to look into today, Melanson. How's tricks at the FFPD?"

Once, Dr. Porzio, after voicing his opinions about Thurber and his lifestyle, said to Mike, "Thurber should be the next asshole I fix – but I wouldn't touch *that* asshole with *your* prick, Melanson." And the fat old homophobic doctor laughed hysterically for ten minutes afterwards.

The other neighbor, Ross Thurber, who lived at the end of the road, was an arrogant five foot-four actor, writer, producer and director who made a living as an independent filmmaker. At that time, he was working on a character-driven series about gay yuppie life in Boston called *Beacon Street*. Apparently, he was close friends with New Yorker Andy Warhol and his then partner Jon Gould, a vice president at Paramount Pictures, as well as Velvet Underground's Lou Reed.

Mike Melanson was a big guy all the way around. He was a balding man of thirty-eight who was married to one of life's most eccentric beauties who called herself "Miss Julie." At six-foot-four, Miss Julie had at least two inches on her moderately tall husband. This Amazon came equipped with a perfectly proportioned hourglass-shaped body that existed only in magazines, long dark hair that draped over her perfectly shaped behind, and olive-colored skin, a product of her Armenian heritage. And their son Adam was a beautiful little boy who shared his mother's genes.

Running parallel to Stagecoach Road was Pine Street, a trailer park for lower-income families. It was a cul-de-sac, just as long as Brown Ave and Stagecoach Road were, but infinitely more congested. The street contained more than a dozen mobile homes, each one practically adjacent to one another. This neighborhood gave new meaning to the term "thickly-settled." A number of folks like Sonny Willis, Tony Pearce, David Henderson, and Jennifer Madsen all worked at the nuclear power plant with Ron Stevens, but a majority of the residents were schoolteachers.

Nancy Deleuze, for instance, was a biology teacher who lived with English teacher Jackie Bamford.

James Taplan taught Algebra at the high school and worked part time at Greg's Variety, a hole-in-the-wall convenience store located right in town. He was once a tackle for the Dallas Cowboys who permanently injured himself after the second or third game of his first season playing. Teaching was something he fell back on, he always told his students, but regardless of this attitude he was still what many considered a gifted and enthusiastic educator whose love for the number i, the quadratic formula and conic sections went unequaled, even when compared to other math teachers. Apparently Taplan (he always told his students to call him by his last name, like his fellow football buddies did) had been married years earlier (to a Dallas Cowboys cheerleader some have said) but as long as he lived in Fryebury Falls – which had been well over a decade – he was always the town's most eligible bachelor.

Then there were the Gibsons: David and Rebecca. They taught high school Chemistry and English, respectively. David Gibson was the hardest teacher in the school, but after taking his class you knew your stoichiometry, orbital notations, and electron configurations inside out. And Rebecca (who had an uncanny resemblance to Morgan Fairchild during her *Flamingo Road* days in the early 1980s), despite the fact that she had an overtly frigid disposition, was a moderately decent English teacher.

And then there was Travis Bread. He had a wife and five kids. He was an adjunct professor of Creative Writing, Film Studies, Theatre Arts and get this – Oceanography – at five or six different colleges near and in Boston. He got paid peanuts per course. No benefits. Luckily, his wife, Deandra, made a decent living in day care and she wrote children's books. Her novel *The Worst Night Ever*, about a group of kids who go to a haunted house on April Fool's Day, was a candidate for the Newbury Book Award.

At the end of Pine Street – in a mobile home furthest away from all the others – lived the Pearson brothers. George was a former biology teacher and high school baseball coach who had gone slightly out of his head when tragedy hit him. This was *his* home, which was already paid for when his younger brother Sam moved in a couple of years earlier. And George was Chief Mike Melanson's best friend from childhood.

Sam Pearson was presently his older brother's caregiver of sorts. Like George, he had taken a step or two back in life. At one point in time, he was a moderately successful writer. His novel *Another Life*, the story of a Greek immigrant who moved to Boston in 1901 only to commit a gruesome string of politically charged murders, reached Best Seller status for a short while.

Sam was Moira Davis's husband – Maygyn's father.

Moira and Sam were separated from each other, but they had not divorced.

And now, the story of *Little Town Blues...*

CHAPTER 3

ELLEN MORGAN'S
YOU-KNOW-WHAT

Miss Julie could not find a thing to wear. This was not an uncommon dilemma for her even though she had a closet the size of a master bedroom.

It was four o'clock in the afternoon on Thursday, May third, and the local TV celebrity was trying to decide which article of clothing would best suit her for her six o'clock spot on *Scandals on the Stars* (*S.O.S.*), a show that she created for the town's cable station, F.F.T.V.

She treated this as if she were dressing for the Oscars.

To Miss Julie Melanson, like Shakespeare had said, the entire world was a stage.

"M&M!" she screeched from the walk-in closet (The balcony viewers needed to be taken into consideration.)

She yelled again, this time in a different voice, a raspy one. She was impersonating Rosalind Russell from *Auntie Mame*.

"M&M!" she screamed his name so rhythmically – practically musically – as if she were singing. She continued: "Where the *hell* is my Saks Fifth Ave blouse, the one with the large zipper on the back?"

Mike Melanson jumped up when he heard the commotion. He had been napping downstairs on the leather recliner. He heard his name again, then sighed.

Oh, it's only Julie having another one of her conniptions, he thought to himself. *Conniption* was one of those words he remembered his grandmother had often used to describe someone's hysterical behavior.

He walked away from the recliner, wiping a bit of drool from the side of his mouth, and made his way up the staircase, which was carpeted in a thin, textured, exotic jewel-toned fabric, something his wife imported from Greece or Italy.

He moved robot-like as he ascended the stairs, his lower back and joints still aching from before. He had taken the day off from work, nursing one of those twenty-four-hour bugs that attacked him every few months or so.

"It's from all that damn coffee and those repulsive cancer sticks – *and* that insomnia of yours," his wife would say, admonishing his habits.

Miss Julie was convinced that her body was a temple to be worshipped: she ate only natural foods and exercised regularly. That's how she kept herself beautiful and fit.

In addition to consuming excessive amounts of coffee, smoking Marlboro Reds and eating fast foods, Mike had a sleep deprivation problem that began in childhood. And he never did anything to improve upon it either – no sleeping pills and no cardiovascular exercise, *which* his wife informed him would be the cure to all his ailments.

"Michael – you alive dahlin'?"

"I'm coming, Jules," he said hoarsely. He had the sniffles, and he was out of breath.

"What's with the *Jules*?" she reprimanded. She stood there half naked.

"Sorry. Miss Julie." He yawned, his eyes finally meeting hers.

"Forgiven," she retorted coldly, then cracked a smile.

How could he have forgotten *already* that not a week earlier, his wife, Julie Jill Najarian-Melanson of the prominent Najarian family in New Haven Connecticut, the moguls of New England's boldest coffee (Najarian Dark Roast), had taken on a new name? The former high school drama queen wanted to be called "Miss Julie" after the name of the classic play by August Strindberg that, like Ibsen's *Hedda Gabler*, portrayed women as independent creatures of passion. Sure, Miss Julie killed herself at the end of the play – so did Hedda Gabler for that matter – but to this aficionado of drama, the suicides were merely metaphors for the women's power to escape from their respective repressed patriarchal microcosms. On her night table, she kept a Gloria Steinem sticker with the following words: "Dying seems less sad than having lived too little."

Mike, never one for drama or the arts in general, once asked her who Strindberg was. "Wasn't that the guy who flew to France or something? They kidnapped his baby?"

Miss Julie was not amused.

"You are such a *low-down townie* with no concept of the real world," she would say to him from time to time, especially after ignorant questions like this one. "We need to instill some culture in you, m'boy!"

Frequently Mike would wonder: *What is this sexy, strange, smart and cultured woman doing with me?* So did the rest of the world, for that matter. He knew that he wasn't particularly attractive, not in a traditional sense, anyway. Or moderately intelligent, for that matter – not when it came to the arts, the things his wife knew so much about. Mike Melanson knew baseball, a thing or two about local police work and maybe as much about what made an automobile run. Once he asked his wife what she could *possibly* see in him, to which she replied in a tone that couldn't have been more authentic: "What kind of question is that? You're my handsome M&M, *that's why.*"

Mike and Miss Julie met at a Fourth of July picnic at town manager Gary Wyckoff's house in Amesbury, a town that neighbored Fryebury Falls near the Massachusetts/New Hampshire border.

Gary, a childhood buddy, fellow golfer and occasional beer drinker, was, like Mike, a small-town sort of guy who just so happened to be a savvy politician, even if it was only on the local level. Mike jokingly referred to him as "Mr. President."

Over the years, Gary befriended the New England coffee mogul David Najarian, who had his family – wife Rosemary and nineteen-year-old daughter Julie – at the annual Independence Day barbeque.

It was at *this* get-together, back in 1971, that the twenty-five-year-old rookie cop (he wouldn't become the police chief until another eight years or so), after downing a few of Gary's homemade brews, began a rather menial conversation with the beautiful young Armenian goddess. Mike hadn't seen anyone quite so drop dead gorgeous in his entire life – she looked like a model! Nevertheless, she had a certain down-to-earth charm that made her approachable. And by the end of the day, the girl had asked the good-natured policeman (whom she found to be refreshingly unlike the immature teenage boys who stalked her) out on a date. In fact, Julie had fallen so hard for Mike, who in those days was much thinner and athletic looking, that she even sacrificed her acting career (*temporarily*, she said) to marry him eight months later.

Three years later, Adam was born.

It hadn't been until recently – two years or so – that she landed this rather inconsequential spot on the local cable channel. Hosting a celebrity tabloid program was *her* idea; it was merely a way to pass the time, she insisted, until her acting career would officially take off.

"A show like this will be great for this humdrum little town," she'd tell the manager. "People eat this shit up. It'll be great for ratings. *I'll* be great for ratings."

Miss Julie possessed the beauty, the charisma, the wealth and the persistence to convince the most inept cable manager, Billy Ashburnham, that Fryebury Falls needed this program – if not to boost ratings (as if the station had an ongoing fan base!) then surely to add variety to the pathetic programming that already existed: high school dances; basketball games; holiday parades; and unsophisticated talk shows, hosted by Billy himself, where he would interview guests about town events or what new books were being donated to the almost non-existent library.

Miss Julie loved the joke about the *theft* at the Fryebury Falls library where "someone stole the book."

These digs against the town, which were frequent and always scathing, were directed toward her husband, or so he thought – and kidding or not, this made him wonder: If she hated little towns so much, then what in God's name was she doing *here* in the small town of small towns?

"It doesn't matter where anyone lives," Miss Julie would say. "If you have what it takes to make it large, then things will happen for you no matter *where* you are. A house is only a place to sleep. The *world* is our home! Plus, I hate Boston – and don't get me started on New York! *Puteo!*"

"I don't get you," Mike would tell her. *So contradictory!*

"I'm not meant to be *gotten*, M&M. That's the gypsy in me, m'dear."

"M&M," Miss Julie said softly. "Where is my Saks Ave blouse? I'm having a bitch of a time finding the confounded thing!" The word *blouse* was pronounced *blouse-ay*.

When Mike once asked her what a *blouse-ay* was, she called him a *low-down townie* with no concept of the real world.

"It's not in there?" he asked, poking his fat head into that closet that reeked of her perfume. *American Beauty Garden*

Fragrance it was called. Supposedly a cosmetic of the rich and famous, second only to her favorite perfume, *Oscar de la Renta*, which she loved mainly because of the product's following tagline: "Experience the Power of Femininity."

"*It's not in there?*" she mimicked. She had his nasally, squeaky voice down to a tee. She often reprimanded him for speaking through his nose.

"You need to speak from the diaphragm," she would say, cupping her hand and sliding it gracefully from her midregion up through her cleavage, pretending to be some famous drama coach like Stella Adler or Uda Hagen.

Mike thought: *Isn't a diaphragm a contraceptive?* But this he wisely kept to himself.

"You didn't throw it in the laundry, did you? That gets professionally cleaned, m'dear. And I need it for the show tonight. Black is my color. It brings out the *macabre* in me. Plus, it's a wonderful fit around my girls, don't you think?" She cupped her breasts, then squeezed her nipples.

Mike didn't answer, continuing to rummage through the forest of clothes.

"Are you watching the broadcast tonight?" she asked, almost sheepishly.

"I wouldn't miss it."

She smiled, looking into his eyes. It had taken her a while to get used to his gaze because the way his eyes were crossed made it seem as though he were looking in another direction when he was, in fact, facing her directly. This trait was absolutely disarming to the woman. "Adorably cute," she would tell him. "Like Marty Feldman and Peter Falk."

Mike knew Peter Falk – he was that charming actor who played Columbo (he could easily imagine the actor's voice saying, "Just one more thing, Mam!"), but he never realized, until his wife informed him, that the actor had a glass eye.

"It's last week's show," she reminded him in a singsong voice.

She redirected her attention toward her clothes, pawing frantically through the wardrobe the way a hamster would burrow through its pine bedding.

Suddenly he began coughing and sniffling.

"You better take care of yourself," she said.

"I'll be okay."

"Have you stopped that *abysmal* smoking yet?" He shrugged. "*Disgusting!*"

There was a short silence.

She gave him one of those glances – the kind mothers give to their sons after they have talked back or cursed.

She continued looking for that *blouse-ay* of hers, but after another minute or so, she gave up. "This one will have to do," she said, grabbing another black blouse with a zipper on the back. Mike coughed again. "You better get well soon, old man," she said, fitting her head through the neck of the blouse. "What would this little town do without you?" She snorted.

At times, Mike felt like his own father Lucien, a kind, gentle, introverted veterinarian who was married to the oversized, dominating Wendy, twelve years his senior and practically double his size. Mike remembered watching him sitting hopelessly in that old yellow recliner in their home on Baker Street like Walter Mitty, saying nothing as his wife loomed over him like an elephant, reprimanding him about his personal habits and his inefficiencies. It was actually quite comical looking back on it now. But was it really? Did Mike Melanson, fitting some sort of Freudian stereotype, marry a woman just like his own mother?

The one difference between the two women, however, was that Wendy Brown Melanson was *no* pin-up girl!

Mike's parents had since passed on. Both of them died from rare aggressive cancers at age forty-nine. Another reason why Miss Julie detested her husband's habit so much.

Then suddenly –

"What was it I read in *The Falls Monitor* the other day?" Miss Julie asked as she put her pants on. "That one of your boys – Dexter Crowley, was it? – saved – let me get this straight – a *cat*? Is that true? He saved a *cat,* and it made the paper?"

Mike nodded.

"A *cat*? A fucking *cat*?" The questions were phrased more like statements. Then she began to chuckle.

"Right. A cat." He cleared his throat. "Ellen Morgan's cat."

"And you remember her name? How sweet." She took a moment to prepare her next words. She opened her eyes widely, in a way that somewhat frightened Mike, and waved her hands through the air, and in her *S.O.S.* voice said, "And now this. Reporting live from *Scandals on the Stars*, it's Miss Julie. Tonight, an *exclusive* story. The infamous...the notorious...the sexy...and let's not forget the controversial...Ellen Morgan!" She cheered. "*Her* story." A dramatic pause, then her hands stopped moving altogether; they remained frozen in mid-air. She stared into her husband's crossed-eyes that appeared to be looking right at her (he *must* have been having a hard time facing her) and waited another beat before saying: "Learn how a group of police officers, under the stark command of Chief M&M, earned their wings in law enforcement today when they" – she stopped, giggled like a school girl, and then her left hand made its way to her crotch – "found *Ellen Morgan's...you know what*...and gave it back to her. Let me tell you the *inside* story."

With this line, she dropped down on the bed and began kicking her feet; she held her stomach because the laughing made it hurt: "Let me tell you the *inside* story – *the inside story*! Oh, no – that's too much!"

Mike stood there, half smiling, half grimacing, watching his wife who was still giggling like a madwoman on the bed. As he watched her, he pictured her as a cartoon character and then a moment later he conjured up a cartoon version of himself and before long the two cartoon characters were doing things to one another that could only be drawn with a pen.

Miss Julie finally stopped; she was spent, out of breath. After a few moments of resting on her back, she suddenly looked at her watch, sat straight up and said, "Whoa! I'm on at six. Gotta fly!"

She jumped off the bed, licked him on the nose, meowed, let out a snorted laugh, then darted out of the bedroom and sprinted downstairs, tripping on the last step (this was not the first time she did this – nor would it be the last). She picked herself up, turned around and cursed the stairs, then eventually made it out the front door.

Mike stood motionless and sighed, craving a cigarette he now had the opportunity to have.

CHAPTER 4

BLOOD IS THICKER THAN WATER

In the distance, along a foggy beach road, a chorus of a dozen or more droning female voices echoed in unison; half of them created the notes to a B chord and the other half produced an F chord. It was somehow both beautifully melodic and unbearably dissonant and sinister-sounding. As the voices increased in pitch, volume and tone, so did the breathing and rapid eurhythmics.

A figure with blond hair was running down the deformed, labyrinthine, dune-like road that pulsated as if it were a beating heart. It was expressionistic looking, like cardboard cutouts on a stage, like something out of that old German horror film, *The Cabinet of Dr. Caligari*.

She kept appearing and disappearing every few seconds or so, and each time she reappeared amidst the fog, the singing voices would skip, like a broken record, on the same sounds.

Then the fog enveloped the road as if it were smoke looming over a house on fire.

The figure got closer and closer – disappearing and reappearing with greater frequency – like experiencing a montage in slow motion. The observer, who was on the side of the road smoking several cigarettes at once, watched the oncoming figure with the utmost repose.

A flood of light, and what sounded like an explosion caused by an aircraft breaking the sound barrier, gave way to another image of the figure: she was naked and covered with blood. And there was something else attached to her, too. Something...slimy. A thick translucent fluid of sorts. It looked like egg whites.

The terror in her face intensified with each slow, strobe-like movement of her bloody thighs. The singing faded.

The observer was a man who barely had a face. The eyes had no pupils; he had no mouth; and his "nose" looked as though it were carelessly stitched onto a piece of fabric.

All was quiet except for the piercing sound of a breeze; it sounded like someone was whistling through a microphone. The observer turned away, looked upward and saw a black mass that at first took on no real shape, but then turned into a menacing phantom. The shadow then transformed into the blond figure again...she was in the sky looking down at him. He shrieked, the eurhythmics were bouncing like a drum roll; then he collapsed to the ground and into a fetal position, sucking his thumb as if it were a nipple; then a liquid, similar to that of egg white fluid, gushed out of his mid region.

He attempted to scream. No sound. Then the heartbeats subsided and there was an overwhelming sound of screeching tires, burning rubber and breaking glass. The observer looked, and the figure was quickly approaching him, disappearing and reappearing every second. She was holding something in her arms. From the way the light was hitting the girl in the fog, it looked as though she had a bundle of firewood.

Closer. Closer.

The observer began shivering. A foul smell that reminded him of what the color yellow must have smelled like made him gag. A greenish fluid spewed from his mid region. *What was she carrying?*

Get it away! Get it away!

He closed his eyes, but this only made the image clearer. He was finally able to scream; it sounded like a rat whimpering in its cage.

Get it away! Get it away!

He scrunched up his face and experienced the inevitable. He knew what she was carrying now. He kept screaming...rat whimpers.

The figure was draped in what looked like a kimono made of blood, gore, and that slime. She was carrying...

Get it away! Get it away!

A dead child.

It was mutilated beyond recognition.

The observer started to cry.

He opened his eyes not a second later, and it was daylight. No more darkness or fog or that...that figure with that thing in her arms.

But now there was something else approaching him. *Get it away!*

The image was locked in the white light that became more in focus with each step. Finally, he could make it out. It was a little girl dressed in a dark purple dress. She had flowing golden blond hair and piercing blue eyes. A gold-colored aura glowed over her head. The closer she got, the brighter the aura.

When she was at arm's length, he could make her out completely. He knew her well.

"Abbie-girl," he said as he gulped.

Heartbeats.

She walked closer and closer toward him until she disappeared inside him.

He gulped again.

Tears rained down his face and he couldn't breathe.

The girl's voice echoed throughout his entire being: "Why did you kill us, Daddy? It was my birthday..."

"Oh, Abbie-girl. I couldn't help it. The sun got in my eyes." He wept more uncontrollably the more he spoke. "I am so sorry, sweetie. I am so...so soooooooorry..."

⊠ ⊠ ⊠ ⊠

"George! Wake up! George! *George!*" the voice shouted.

After the seventh or eighth call, George Pearson gained consciousness; his pillows and sheets were soaked with his own perspiration and saliva.

He wasn't quite hyperventilating, but he *was* out of breath. And his mouth was arid and pasty.

He squinted and saw his brother at the other end of the living room sitting at his desk smoking a cigarette.

There was an assortment of things on the desk that George observed with blurred vision: notebooks; pencils; different colored pens; highlighters; and stacks of index cards: some had scribbling on them, but most were blank. Sam Pearson had a number of ideas for a new novel.

George took long, deep breaths. He looked around the room conspicuously.

"I put a glass of water on the coffee table for you," Sam said.

"Thanks." George puckered his lips, attempting to give them moisture. He finished the water in a few quick gulps.

"Want any more? I'll go get you some."

George nodded.

Sam retrieved the glass, refilled it in the kitchen and returned – all within a matter of seconds. "Do you want to tell me about it?" Sam asked, placing the glass down.

"What?" George squinted toward the clock above the desk.

"It's five of six...*at night*," Sam said. He walked back toward his desk.

The brothers had gone through this routine before. George would get tanked on cheap red wine, he'd eventually pass out, then he would wake up hours later, typically in the late afternoon or early evening in a tired, somewhat delirious state.

"You don't have to tell me," Sam said, "but if you want to, I'll listen."

A pause. George sat up on the couch. He pulled the black wool blanket off of him. He was wearing just a pair of boxer shorts.

At one time, George Pearson was not a bad looking man. He had fair skin with light freckles and fluffy reddish-brown hair, neatly groomed. Ever since the accident, however, he had let himself go considerably: forty pounds overweight and his reddish hair – now nearly all white – was oily and stringy and came down to his shoulders.

And his younger brother Sam, also fair-skinned with the same hair type, he too was once an attractive man. With his boyish good looks, his wife once told him he looked like Robert Redford. But like his brother, he was unkempt...not necessarily overweight, but not well-preserved either. He was thirty-six and George, thirty-eight, but they both looked and felt older...worn down and tired from the unexpected turns their seemingly perfect little lives had taken.

These two men, who had never been particularly close in their youth, were (perhaps by default) each other's *best* – and in many ways – *only* friends.

"Blood is thicker than water," their mother Meghan would tell them, especially after they'd fight. "When I'm dead and gone, you will both have each other. Savor one another. There's nothing like the sacred nature of brotherly love. *Phil-a-delphia*."

Their mother was born in Pennsylvania and lived in a

foster home in a suburb near the City of Brotherly Love. She was adopted at the age of three by Ben and Chelsea Pirandello, an eccentric couple who owned a restaurant in the North End of Boston.

In 1977, she overdosed (and died) on her prescribed medication. Something used to treat manic depression and schizophrenia. She had the lucky misfortune to be diagnosed with *both* disorders.

Their father Brad Pearson left the scene when they were very young, sometime in the early 1950s, before anyone knew about treating mental illness. He divorced his wife whom he once called "an old nut case not fit to be *anyone's* wife or mother," and a few years later he died of a ruptured appendix at thirty-seven.

The Pearson boys, however, were destined for greatness. As a single mother, Meghan (who went back to her maiden name, Pirandello) made sure of this. Once she admitted to her sons that her only purpose in this life was to give birth to them. "My handsome, successful boys," she would say to them, pointing her finger. "You will both do great things in this life. Mark my words. *Great, great* things!"

And her prophecies rang true. Her oldest boy, whom she nicknamed "Renaissance Man," was number two in his high school class, a star pitcher drafted by a minor league baseball team (he didn't play because he decided to finish college instead), a skilled musician who in college started a three-man rock band called Phantasmagoria, and a gifted biology teacher who eventually became a well-respected educator and scholar in the life sciences.

And Sam utilized his creative talents and ambitions – unlike George, he was not an academic in the traditional sense (he loved literature but was not one to read or write scholarly criticism) – to eventually become a bestselling author.

But now, these two gifted boys were crammed together,

living like sardines in a tin can of a place. All dreams lost.

Sam was presently attempting to write a novel called *Sliced Bread*, a dark comedy about the problems faced by an ordinary man named Harlan Townsend who receives an untimely inheritance; he consequently stages his own death on New Year's Eve to attempt to hide his notorious identity. He also had part of a collection of short stories about teachers called *Go Flunk Yourself*, and another unfinished piece was a play called *Cells,* a series of monologues from three prison inmates who tell their life stories.

Upon occasion, Greek immigrant Yannis Cacoyannis, the main character in Sam's former best seller *Another Life*, would appear before him unexpectedly, projected on the wall like some movie. Writers sometimes speak of their muses – well, Yannis Cacoyannis (who was called John "Bad John" – in Greek *Yannis* means *John* and his last name *Cacoyannis*, oddly enough translates into *bad John*) was what some might call an obtrusive or unwanted muse. According to Sam he was an unavoidable *pain-in-the ass*; at times, he regretted the day he ever penned the character, despite the fact that John "Bad John" was the greatest thing that ever happened to his short-termed literary career.

According to *Another Life*, Yannis Cacoyannis grew up in Turkey, as many Greeks did, and in 1901, when he was eighteen, he and two of his friends, one a Turk, the other a fellow Greek, sailed to America. The men eventually split off from one another, trying to find business opportunities: Yannis learned English quite quickly and was set on starting his own restaurant, but instead found himself working in a factory. He had a tyrannical boss named Hugo Ross who liked to push him around; Ross called Yannis a "stupid grease ball." Eventually, Yannis formed an uprising with other laborers who were also abused by Ross: He eventually killed his boss and was sent to jail where he wrote a manifesto called *Yassou!*

This book became an international manifesto on prejudice and "melting pot" ideologies, and consequently, the Greek immigrant who coined his new name "Bad John," became one of the most notorious political, philosophical, and cultural figures in the early twentieth century. *Yassou!* By "Bad John" was so big, it became what might be called today, an interdisciplinary text: It was read religiously in literary, philosophical political, historical and even business circles. "Bad John" was a confirmed socialist who lifted his ideas from Marx's 1859 book A *Contribution to the Critique of Political Economy*, and *Yassou!* even influenced the works of entrepreneurs like Rockefeller and Vanderbilt.

Although Sam was not Greek, he always felt a strange affinity toward Greek people and their culture. This was most likely the case because when he was sixteen, he became infatuated with a Greek teenage beauty named Kalliope Pappas whom he met at summer camp. To him, Kalliope was the true definition of a muse: in addition to being full-blooded Greek, she was a gifted singer – and interestingly enough, her name, when translated meant *beautiful voice*. In fact, it was Kalliope that served as Sam Pearson's *real* muse while he was writing *Another Life* and some of his earlier short fiction.

It was all so perfect then.

So why was it, that instead of seeing and hearing Kalliope from time to time, it was that quirky, belligerent Bad John that would appear to him as a moving image on the wall – always in a white t-shirt and workman's pants and giving a speech – quoting from his own book *Yassou!* as if Sam were some corporate villain who had never heard these words before? "The American Dream is dead," the Greek would clamor from behind the bars of his prison, his accent strong and proud. "It isn't democracy. It is – what do you call it? – *Fascism*. It is *dictatorship*. And that is why I had to kill Hugo Ross, my friends – to save all of us, so that we can all live in *real* democracy. I know Socrates did not like the idea of democracy, but he was wrong; under the right socioeconomic circumstances, democracy can work, my friends. It *can work*..."

And it was always the same image, the same speech that Sam witnessed, especially when he was hard at work on a new idea. It was as if, ironic as it might have sounded, Bad John wanted Sam – his creator – to *suffer* like he did.

Suddenly George started to sob, but within seconds he composed himself ever so gracefully and wiped the tears off his cheek with his forearm.

Sam put out his cigarette and the image of Bad John faded. "You okay?"

George shrugged. "Fine."

"Want a cig?"

George nodded.

Sam placed two smokes in his mouth, lit them both, then brought one over to his brother.

"Thanks," George said. His head rested on the arm of the couch as he stared plaintively toward the ceiling looking at an image of his dead daughter, Abigail, who (always dressed in that purple dress that he bought for her on her eighth and last birthday) stared at her father with those piecing blue eyes of hers. George couldn't control the tears this time; he whimpered like an injured dog. His muscles seemed to be tensing up again, too; this always happened when she visited him.

Sam kneeled down at the coffee-stained coffee table and patted his brother's hand, which felt cold and dry.

Finally, George spoke in a relatively calm and rational manner as he continued staring up at the ceiling. "I know you mean well," he said half sincerely, half cynically – after all, this was his little brother – "but I don't expect anything from you, Sam. Please, don't bother yourself."

Sam let out some air from his nose that was meant to be a small laugh, but he turned this into a cough instead. "It's no bother, really. I'm just carrying my weight around here. That's all."

George looked at his younger brother again, this time more sympathetically.

Sam said, "We are going to get through all of this."

"Yeah? With what? Our good looks?"

"That's right," Sam said, smiling for real this time. "We'll be out of here real, real soon." His eyes widened. "I've been building up our savings."

"Savings? You clean busses for a living!"

"Not for long," Sam replied, humbled. "I've got a plan."

"Plan," George snickered. "You sound like one of those right-winged product pushers you worship so much."

"Go ahead and laugh. Be like everyone else."

"It's a pyramid scheme," George antagonized. The liquor was still in him.

To George's surprise, Sam, composed, refusing to succumb to his brother's bullying, said, "Maybe you're right, but at least it's something. I don't know about you, but *I'd* like some freedom and peace for once." Despite his intentions, he *was* getting upset. He paused, recomposed himself and gently said, "It's not what it used to be. It's not a door-to-door thing anymore. It's all about finding the right people to build a community with...and to use the products. All I need is to do is find two or three serious people that are willing to help me build a network. Then I – *we* – can be on the road to being free. What's wrong with that?"

"Nothing," George finally said, giving in. He knew his brother was right; not so much about network marketing and getting rich, but the idea of freedom – *that* was the selling point.

Sam picked up a cigarette but didn't light it. "We can make it work." A pause. "At least it'll be a start."

Time passed as both men sat silently, sheepishly, focusing on their own visual projections. Abigail watched George, and George watched Abigail contently. The Greek laborer repeated parts of his speech as Sam watched: "...It isn't democracy. It is – what do you call it? – *Fascism*. It is *dictatorship*. And that is why I had to kill Hugo Ross, my friends – to save all of us, so that we can all live in *real* democracy..."

After a long while, George, still a bit sauced, began saying the following words softly, "In the world with all the others..." He paused, turned his head to look at Sam who shook his head and grinned.

...no one beats the Pearson brothers, Sam thought without skipping a beat. *In the world with all the others, no one beats the Pearson brothers* was a rhyme that George made up when they were kids. They yelled this many times when they used to play razzle-dazzle football with the neighborhood kids in "Little Scotty" Page's yard almost forty years earlier. "Little Scotty" wasn't so little, but they called him "Little Scotty" to distinguish him from "Big Scotty" who was – although shorter and more petite – a few years older than him.

At that moment, the brothers forgot about their respective images on the walls; they chose nostalgia over their present-day hallucinations, focusing back to a familiar scene: Little Scotty's yard. It was a small property outside of a brick duplex that in the fall became a football field and in the summer a baseball diamond. Much of their childhood, it seemed, took place playing sports in that yard.

Blood is thicker than water.

George then quite suddenly jumped forward in time and recalled the day in the high school locker room when he overheard his star pitcher Derek Hamilton make a most inappropriate crack about his dead wife. To a bunch of baseball buddies Hamilton had said that Alison Pearson was a real piece of meat, that he'd even fuck her corpse she was so hot.

If that tall, blond-haired southpaw never said those words – or better yet – never said those words within an earshot of his coach just months after his wife had perished in that head-on collision, then none of this would have been happening. Not like this, anyway.

"What did you say about my wife Hamilton?" To George his own words, as well as Derek Hamilton's surprised look of horror, were just as fresh in his mind *then* as they were the moment they left his lips a few years earlier. Following these words, Coach Pearson's fist crushed the boy's jaw and cheekbone. George sprained his hand, broke Hamilton's face and lost his job all within a few hours.

He was arraigned but never went to court. Conrad and Rose Hamilton never pursued the charges. Rumor has it that Mike Melanson, George's best friend of over thirty years and the chief of police, had something to do with this. On this subject, however, the men never conversed.

George once contemplated what Mike *might* have said: "Try to imagine what you would have done, Conrad, if you were driving home, rounded a corner, got blinded by the sun, then smacked head on into an oncoming car. Not just *any* car, but the one driven by your own wife who was driving your eight-year-old daughter? *On her birthday!* And they *die* and *you* make it out alive with barely a scratch. Think about it. What would *you* do if you were responsible for killing your own Rose and Derek? How would you live with yourself after that? *Huh?* And imagine this: What would you do if you overheard some kid talking about screwing Rose's dead body? I'd smack the little bastard myself. George is my best friend, Conrad. I know no one has the right to use violence on anyone, but just consider the circumstances here for a minute..."

George shook his head, expelling the demons as if they were fleas, got up, and announced that he was going for a walk to sober up.

Sam asked where he was going.

"Probably end up at the Falls," George said. "It's peaceful there."

CHAPTER 5

HOMEOSTASIS

Moira Davis was stringing her Guild guitar, the one her husband bought for her about a decade earlier on their fifth wedding anniversary; even at this time their marriage was already beginning to show signs of deterioration. The author had dropped nearly a grand down on this instrument, money he used from the residuals of his novel.

Moira and Sam were married in May of 1969 (the month *Another Life* hit the big time) and had been separated since June of 1982, nearly two years now. They had not, however, filed any divorce papers; neither one of them was in a financial situation to afford this breach of contract, so they attempted to keep things, to use Moira's words, "simple and civil." Plus, they had a daughter to think about, a daughter they both loved dearly in their own bizarre, arcane ways.

The couple met in Boston in the summer of 1968 when Sam was twenty and Moira was twenty-one. He was an aspiring novelist, already a college dropout, working as a bartender in Kenmore Square in a place called The Circle (which was walking distance to Fenway Park) that has since gone out of business – and she was a budding songwriter who was beginning to build up a relatively impressive musical repertoire by bringing her act into various nightclubs and bars in and around Boston and Cambridge.

One night Moira and her band were playing in The Circle, and Sam bought the sexy young musician a number of gin and tonics. Over drinks they got to know one another; he explained to her that he was writing "the Great American Novel." After a few dates they decided to get a studio apartment together on Commonwealth Avenue, right near the Boston University campus. Moira continued her songwriting career and Sam continued tending bar while revising his soon-to-be literary achievement.

One book reviewer called *Another Life* "a great American novel." Sam and Moira were quite amused. Another reviewer called Sam Pearson "the most significant new voice in American fiction." And yet another critique said this: "Sam Pearson is Sinclair Lewis, Upton Sinclair, Kurt Vonnegut and George Orwell – with a touch of the sublime writings of Thomas Mann – all rolled into one unique voice." On the contrary, one of his few negative reviews said this: "For some reason Sam Pearson is being called innovative. After reading *Another Life*, I beg to differ. His work is nothing more than a rehash of some great literary figures whom he emulates *ad nauseam*. He really needs to stop reading Sinclair Lewis and Thomas Mann! Maybe *then* he will develop his *own* voice."

About a year after the success of *Another Life*, on May 27, 1970, their little girl was born. Both Sam's and Moira's mothers, who had since passed on, had the same name with different spellings: Sam's mother was *Meghan*; Moira's mother was *Megan* – and *Megan* was also the name of Moira's twin sister who drowned back in 1961. So, the name of their daughter was, the couple agreed, predestined. Except they would spell their daughter's name like this: *Maygyn*. This spelling was chosen for three major reasons: first, to give the girl her own identity; second, the first part of her name, *May*, is named after the month she was born; and third, the second part of her name *gyn*, is the root associated with women. This was Moira's idea, but at the time it impressed Sam who, as a writer, always had an affinity for words and wordplay.

Soon after Maygyn's birth, the three of them moved out of Boston and into Sam's hometown Fryebury Falls. He claimed that this would be an ideal place to raise a child, and they would still be close enough to Boston so Moira could continue her musical career. Sam was collecting generous residuals on *Another Life*, so for a couple of years he was able to live strictly off the checks he received in the mail. Plus, he did a short book tour (mainly colleges and bookstores), which helped the financial situation even further.

He wrote his second novel during this period, a speculative piece on the legalization of marijuana called *Dr. Lemon's Potato Salad*. This over-the-top, overblown, outrageous novel didn't cut it, however. One critic, in a most scathing review, said that the book was too much like Thomas Wolfe's *The Electric Kool Aid Acid Test*, even though it wasn't in the least bit like it. Sam's hero was a homeless drug addict by the name of Aaron Edwards who found a portal into the mythical city of Augusta Falls during a pandemic where he grows three strains of cannabis – Jack Herer, Island Sweet Skunk and White Widow – that when liquified and injected into the blood stream reverses the symptoms of the virus.

Apparently, this was not what the public wanted. But why a book by a bestselling author about the legalization of marijuana in the mid-1970s didn't do well, was baffling to the writer and his publisher. His publisher once told him, "Publishing isn't always about good writing; it's about *good timing*." Maybe the public didn't dig the manner of which the story was told, or maybe the public just got sick of Sam Pearson altogether.

Then mysteriously, people stopped buying *Another Life*.

It's as if *Dr. Lemon's Potato Salad*, which Sam thought was twice the book *Another Life* was, somehow blacklisted him. It's as if his short-lived adoring public and flattering critics formed a conspiracy against him – or disappeared completely – or never existed at all. It simply didn't make sense. He *did* get his hands on one review of his second novel, which went like this: "Pure rubbish. Immature. Pearson's overrated first novel *Another Life* somehow got him critical acclaim, but this tripe truly proves what I have been trying to tell people for years: Sam Pearson is no writer; he's a hack, an idea thief..."

Less than a year later, the novel went out of print.

"Just one of those things in this unpredictable and cut-throat business that doesn't make sense, Pearson," his editor told him. "You just have to keep writing. Write another book. That's my only advice. What can I tell you? I still think you're a talented guy. But it's not me out there deciding the fate of literature. Maybe write a mystery...a detective story...something that combines the elegance of Poe's Dupin and I don't know...Philip Marlowe...or Hercule Poirot..."

At this time, Moira's career was also fleeting. Her music, as one critic said, was "too raw...unsavory...dissonant...not musical..." It was as if this promising couple became cursed together. It was as if some greater entity told them: *You are talented...and doomed.*

But it wasn't until Sam emptied their remaining savings (the last of the residual income) into a business opportunity that Moira really began to detest him and the marriage itself.

Sam had explained to his wife about the business plan that would solve their financial difficulties. All they needed to do was convince a few of their friends (they had lots of them – mostly struggling artists who would jump at an opportunity to make money) – to buy motivational tapes, attend monthly pep rallies (this is where they really lost their savings)...and in no time they'd be collecting monthly commissions. *Easy-*

peasy. Sure, it would be a bit of work, but nothing they couldn't handle, Sam assured Moira, especially with both of them working together.

Ah, the irony of it all: Sam Pearson used residual income to pay for something where he would receive residual income – and the end result equaled *no* residual income.

"Have you lost your mind?" Moira thundered. "I think you've gone totally mad! Look what you've done to us. You're worse than a fucking gambler!"

These were some of the things Moira reflected upon while she finished stringing the Guild.

Currently, the songwriter was in two bands. One band was with three men called Laura's Mercedes where she played rhythm guitar and did backup vocals. The other band was a group Moira had formed – a female trio known as The Mad Ones. The other members included a bassist named Angela (who called herself Cheryl) and a drummer named Debra. The name of the band was an acronym. The first letters of their first names, Moira, Angela and Debra, spelled MAD.

Moira scored anywhere from five to ten gigs a week in the Boston area, most of them on Thursdays, Fridays, Saturdays, and Sundays. She took home a few hundred a week, not a lot of weekly income, but enough to live off of. After they split, Sam insisted on paying the mortgage, which constituted most of his income from the bus company.

Moira Davis was a self-taught musician; she couldn't read a note of music, nor did she want to learn how. She was always impressed with those songwriters who could train them-selves; to her, this showed a real aptitude for musicianship. After all, look at The Beatles, she would say. They never used sheet music and they did okay for themselves. To Moira, music was more about *instinct* rather than technique. "Any bozo can learn someone else's music then regurgitate it," she once said to Sam. "Like all those studio musicians...they might as well be mechanics in a garage. Music needs to be a visceral extension of our ecstasy, our bliss and our torment."

Maygyn Pearson listened to her mother strumming on the crisp new strings of the guitar. She could not sleep. Not because it was two in the morning (she was used to her mother coming home late after a gig and staying up all hours of the night drinking beer, smoking cigarettes and rehearsing her music), but because her stomach was getting that sour sensation again.

Knots. Nausea. The sweats.

The girl was all too familiar with the symptoms. She had two major tests in several hours. One in Science and the other in Social Studies.

The Science test covered the Kinetic Molecular Theory, the process by which matter transforms into solids, liquids and gases at given temperatures. Her teacher was the incomparable, eccentric Mr. Morrison.

The Social Studies test covered the rise of industrial America from Reconstruction to the late 1920s before the stock market crashed. Her teacher was Mr. Keaton.

Maygyn knew the material inside out and knew she would ace both tests, but she was nervous, nevertheless. The anxiety, for her, was all part of the process, part of the game, the stimulation. For this eighth grader, schoolwork was exciting, especially when the material was demanding. People saw her as smart – she was at the top of her class – but she was also quite aware of her challenges. She wasn't as quick on the intake as she would like to have been (this, she tells herself, is because her mother continued to smoke while she was pregnant with her), but this just made her work harder. She was living proof, as her math teacher once told her, of Thomas Edison's quote: "Genius is one percent inspiration and ninety-nine percent perspiration." Maygyn never fancied herself a genius – not in a million years – but she *did* appreciate the accuracy of the metaphor.

As she lay on her bed – half listening to her mother's music, half obsessing over the tests – she pictured the questions on the pages. Each test would be similar to the ones she took in both classes about three weeks earlier.

She imagined Mr. Morrison's test: it would be completely handwritten, all the questions in capital letters, the purple ink still fresh from the copy machine in the teacher's lounge. The scatterbrained scientist always ran his tests off just minutes before class; you could tell because the ink smudged easily and the paper always smelled funny, reminding her of the rancid odor of the paper mills that she would smell when she and her father used to drive through Portland, Maine.

And Morrison's greasy, fine hair, his buckteeth and thick-rimmed eyeglasses, held together by electrical tape and always plastered with chalk dust, made him a reasonable facsimile to Jerry Lewis's "nutty professor" character.

About a decade earlier, a student in the seventh grade threatened to put a bomb in the disheveled teacher's car and consequently, each morning before entering school, he would search his vehicle through and through for possible explosives while people in all corners of the school watched and laughed.

But Maygyn felt bad for him. She liked him. Thought he was funny. Quirky funny, which was her favorite kind. When Mr. Morrison got irritated with the class, his retort would be awkwardly defensive and intellectual: "You're all on the verge of insanity! You're all merely *Monerans*, which is just a polite way to call you *pond scum!*"

Quirky science humor. Maygyn would always laugh – and Mr. Morrison knew that her laughs were genuine, that she was the only student to appreciate his wit. In class he would wink at her and say, "You and me against the world, Pearson. No one else understands our great minds!"

Then there was Mr. Keaton. His tests would always be

typed, each section of ten questions labeled neatly: Part one would be the completions; part two, matching; part three, short answers; part four, multiple choice (or as he liked to call them – "multiple guess"); part five definitions; and part six, a challenging application essay worth twenty points. You really needed to understand the history beyond the facts to do well on this part.

Mark Keaton was extremely nice-looking, or so Maygyn thought anyway. And also quirky, but a bit *hipper* than Mr. Morrison. He didn't look like a middle school teacher. He should have been on TV or something. He was tall and slender, had blond hair, piercing blue eyes, long sideburns and a well-groomed moustache. And he always wore a suit – a nice business-looking suit, not one of those furrowed, weather-beaten wool suits with patches on the jacket sleeves that so many teachers wore. And...he was the hardest teacher in the school too.

Maygyn was secretly convinced that Mr. Keaton had the hots for her. It was the way he looked at her with those azure eyes – not the way a schoolteacher and a man of thirty-two should be looking at a thirteen – almost fourteen – year-old girl, she once thought. He also had this way of complimenting her work and study habits. One of her classmates, Woneta Deveaux, would often tease her in the halls: "Who's your Daddy, May? Who's your *daddy*?"

"Gross," Maygyn would say, but deep down she was not repulsed by the thought.

"You'll go a long way in life, Maygyn," Mr. Keaton would say to her. The way those eyes shined and the way those cheeks blushed when he spoke to her. *Man!* And how those boyish dimples stood out when he smiled. *Man, oh man!*

Mark Keaton was divorced; that's all she knew about him.

The girl closed her eyes and tried to imagine Mr. Keaton naked, but once she pictured this – *really* pictured it – the fantasy quickly faded into repulsion and the nausea returned. Then she conjured up the front page of his neatly typed test. To her, *that* was the real turn-on. The nausea turned into butterflies; she always liked the tingling, tickling sensation of butterflies in her stomach.

Man, oh man, oh man!

Moira was writing a new song. Maygyn could tell it was a new one because she recognized some of the signs of her mother's process: brief moments of strumming on the guitar; moments of silence; more strumming; the sound of a beer bottle being slammed down during these silences; loud exhales from smoking; curse words when she flubbed something up; and her voice saying "that's it" when something clicked.

As a rule, Maygyn was not a fan of Moira's music, but there was still something comforting about listening to her mother's creative process from the other room.

She assumed this new song was called "Homeostasis" – a word she recently learned in English class. It meant *balance, harmony, equilibrium*. She liked the sound of the song; it wasn't as heavy and angry sounding as the others. It was a melodic waltz in 3/4 time, and she liked the way the chords went into one another. The verse went from A to A flat to D to E7, then from A to F# minor to D to E7 – then it switched to an A, to a jazzy E+ chord, to an F# minor, and then to a D minor. The chorus – switching its rhythm to an upbeat 4/4 time – used A, E7 and D before resolving itself (creating homeostasis) back to the A. Then she listened to the words and suddenly wasn't liking it anymore.

> *I'm poised outside my blue*
> *The things that I construe*
> *I said, I'm feeling that way without you*
> *Equilibrium here*
> *I balance out the fear*
> *I said, I'm in a world full of fear*

A little bit of homeostasis
Sets my mind so at ease
A little bit of homeostasis
Gets my mind so dust free

Maygyn was convinced the song was about her father. It had to be. *I'm feeling that way without you?* Who else *could* it have been about? The symptoms returned. The knots. Nausea. The sweats. She got out of bed and walked to her desk, picking up the school bag on the chair. It was jam-full of school materials. Everything was in place, as usual. *Complete homeostasis.* Her textbooks were on the bottom of the bag, her five-subject notebook (one section per course replete with a color-coded chart of all her grades at the very end of the notebook; she always had her grades figured out right down to the exact decimal place) on top of the books and on the top of the notebook, five folders, each one a different color for each one of her classes.

Delicately, as if she were handling fragile goods, she took two of the folders out: the green one for Science and the blue one for Social Studies. She took two packets of stapled sheets out of each folder. Before each test, Maygyn would combine all of her class notes and textbook information into one specially designed, manageable "review sheet," which she made in the form of a test, the same type of test she would be taking the next day. After completing the questions and answers, she would study from her own test, memorizing each question one by one until she knew them all. Both sheets combined had well over 100 questions, far more than the number of questions that would actually be on the tests – but she wanted to be prepared. In fact, she wanted to be *over-prepared*.

It was all part of the game she loved and dreaded so much.

While Moira continued to hack away at her song, Maygyn went through each question one final time.

CHAPTER 6

"BEWARE THE IDES OF MARCH!"

Officer Jack Cleary sat in the police cruiser and periodically looked at his reflection in the rearview mirror while he waited for the tape to finish rewinding. The car, a 1981 Ford LTD Crown Victoria, was parked in the center of the very roomy two-car garage. From time to time the cop would find refuge in this vehicle; this was, for him, a haven, a place of escape, a hideaway from the rest of the world, especially from his brain-injured son and that equally brain-injured dog of his.

The gray and white home was the newest one on Brown Avenue, built just seven years earlier, in 1977. It was first owned by a wealthy curmudgeon, an elderly Polish widower named Jerzy Wysocki (who went by J.W.), a six-foot-five native of Warsaw, who very accurately fit his surname which meant 'Jerzy the tall.' Jerzy the Tall, who allegedly escaped from a Russian concentration camp back in World War II (because he spoke German so well, he was mistaken as a German by the Russian soldiers), was a right-winged politician – so right in fact that he adhered to the philosophy that "right is right and left is wrong." He was also one of the key figures who helped with the construction of Günter's Millyard in the 1950s (something he did reluctantly for obvious reasons; Jerzy was a Pole and Günter, a German). Jerzy the Tall claimed to have been personal friends with John F. Kennedy and had a number of fascinating anecdotes about the president's pre-White House escapades, including the affairs. "Kennedy fucked *anything* that moved," he once told someone. One of his favorite stories goes like this: He got drunk at JFK's inauguration and gave the new U.S. leader and his ambassador to the U.N., Adlai Stevenson, hell about their politics. After seven or eight cocktails, he patted the men on the back and announced in slurred speech: "Right is right, Jack. Left is wrong, Adlai. Never under...estimate the power of we...uh...us...conservatives!"

JFK looked at Jerzy and said, "Jerzy Wysocki, what would a goddam *Polack* know about the United States?"

To that Jerzy the Tall said, "I'll drink to that, ya' *Mucker*. Cheers to all parties. Right and wrong!" And with that line he looked over at the radiant Jackie Kennedy and asked her, "Would you like to dance, my beauty?" to which she said, "I'd love to. I never danced with a drunk Polack before."

Moira and Sam loved their old, droll neighbor; he was like family to them. Sam believed what Moira called his "tall tales," because, perhaps he as a fiction writer, *wanted* to believe them. "You can't write that better," Sam would tell Jerzy the Tall. "You should write a book yourself."

They were heartbroken when Jerzy the Tall passed away in January of 1982 from his fourth or fifth heart attack. This was about a year before the couple decided to separate for good.

Jack Cleary, who bought Wysocki's house just a few months after he passed away, now sat in the oversized garage that the old man once used as a workshop and popped the cassette out of the recorder; the machine was, by today's standards a massive piece of equipment, taking up a large portion of the passenger's seat. He took the tape in hand: it read: *Job Interview: Tuesday March 15, 1982, Side A.* This was one of the many hundreds of tapes he had made over the course of his career as a police officer. It was his way of amusing himself while deconstructing the world around him. Any good police officer, he insisted, needed to study his craft – and this he did by discreetly recording as many conversations as humanly possible. He would then review and study these conversations in the privacy of his own cruiser. Although only a deputy in a small town, Cleary fancied himself not just a cop but also a real investigator, like that Lieutenant Columbo from his favorite TV show.

He was on the force for a little over two years. He had replaced Mike Melanson's assistant and number one man, Roger Kaplan, who died back in late 1981 of a rare blood disease at forty-four years of age. The only thing anyone knew about Jack Cleary was that he was formerly with the Boston Police Department, but only on "special assignments" – all classified cases – so it made it impossible, even for Mike Melanson, to track his record.

During his job interview for the position of deputy, Jack told Chief Melanson that he had connections with the F.B.I., the C.I.A. and other secret organizations. He supplied the chief with all the necessary papers and certifications, including high grades at the police academy and a gloating letter of reference from a police commissioner who had since been shot and killed, along with other police officers with whom he had worked. Mike, who had only known small town police work, never thought to confirm the credentials, which would later become one of his worst mistakes. It would be safe to say that a lot of these forthcoming events were a product of Mike Melanson's trust, ignorance, and naiveté.

According to these credentials, Jack Cleary was at the top

of his class at a New York City police academy, a place of which Mike was not familiar. During the interview, Jack told Mike he was shot in the line of duty...*four times*. He made it out alive while a group of his fellow officers were killed in action. He couldn't tell Mike what the case was. That's how sensitive it was and still is. These friends and partners were the best people to speak of his character, he told Mike. And now they were all dead. When Mike asked him why he was seeking out this line of work in little Fryebury Falls, he told him that it was *because* of this "special assignments" case that ended in a bloodbath of his closest friends; he simply could not return to that level of police work; he needed something smaller, safer – for himself and for his teenage boy who, years earlier, had experienced a terrible accident.

At the time Mike thought this was endearing – a horribly tragic story, indeed, but still he respected the officer's need to move on with his son, and he marveled at the fact that his little town could be the place where this talented cop could find solace again.

During the first part of the interview, Jack remembered showing Melanson two of his scars: one on his right shoulder and one on his calf. The blemishes looked like bad burn wounds, all red and purple. If anyone asked why this over-grown bulldog walked the way he did – with one shoulder bent downward, bouncing like a penguin as he moved, and a slight limp that Mike noticed immediately – this was the reason. The last two bullet wounds, he said to Mike kind of awkwardly, were "in a place where the sun don't shine."

Mike, who could never top any of these aforementioned bodily blemishes, thought of the scar on the right side of his abdomen where his appendix had been taken out years earlier. And the second-degree burn on his right thigh – a burn he received from a motorcycle muffler when he was in high school. But that was it. In fact, this poor excuse for a law enforcer never even pointed a gun at anyone. Not for real. Only at dummies and targets. He never *needed* to point a gun at anyone; not in Fryebury Falls. Despite having gone through police academy training, Mike never fancied himself a real policeman let alone the Chief; in his opinion he was just a good representative of the people – an amiable figurehead – and that's why everyone loved him so much.

How all of this would change within the course of just a few short months!

Jack looked at the tape for another beat before flipping it over and putting it in the player. *Side B.* He closed his eyes and continued to revisit that day in March – the Ides of March, no less – when he sat in Mike Melanson's office for the very first time.

"...That must have knocked you for a loop," Mike said, examining the scars on the officer's right shoulder and calf.

"It could have been the end of me right then and there." Jack's voice seemed polished, eloquent even.

Jack tilted the seat back in the cruiser, closed his eyes and smiled.

"So, what *exactly* happened to you?"

"I wish I could tell you, but the nature of the work forbids me to. I know this may not look too good in a job interview, but I'm sure you know all about *police ethics*...even when it comes to protecting the secrecy of other cops on other forces."

Mike said softly, "Of course." But he didn't understand at all. He continued: "So what brings you here to Fryebury Falls?"

"My son." He paused. "John, Jr." Another pause. "I call him J.J." Mike's eyes widened. "In addition to all that action I received in the line of duty, my wife Gail passed away. And when J.J. was twelve, he had an accident that almost killed him." Mike sat, intrigued. Jack cleared his throat. "He...he was thrown off of a building." Mike's eyes widened even further, and Jack became more intense with his delivery. "That's right. One of his peers...he...liked to *bully* J.J. a lot...then one day he pushed him off the edge of an apartment building." Jack paused and cleared his throat again. "We didn't think he'd make it." Another pause. "He's...uh...permanently...brain in-jured. *TBI*." He could tell Mike did not know what that meant and then he added: "Traumatic Brain Injury."

Mike didn't know what to say; his heart fluttered, and he found it hard to catch his breath.

Jack said, "You'd think that would be enough for one person to handle in a lifetime. But then, two years back his mother was murdered. Someone broke into our house. That was quite a blow to him. And me, of course. I was completely devastated. But for J.J...having the brain injury *and* trying to make sense of his mother's..." Jack paused again. Mike felt tears forming in his own eyes. "I was a single father trying to make ends meet as a police officer, which *believe me* is not an easy thing. During the day I took him to a branch of Easter Seals where he spent the day with other brain injured people like himself, and then afterwards I would spend the rest of the day with him. He even came to work with me sometimes. Then I got shot and my buddies were killed. And the *bad guy* got away with a stash of drugs. That much I *can* tell you." Another pause. "After that, I told myself, I just can't do this anymore...not with a son who relies on me so much. But I couldn't give up the work either." A brief pause. "And so, I'm here."

Mike bit his lip. Jack gave him a slight, endearing smile.

As far as Mike was concerned, he was looking at his new assistant! He knew he needed a replacement for Roger Kaplan. *But how could* anyone *fill Kaplan's shoes?* he suddenly thought. Mike was secretly in awe of his interviewee; he saw him as a TV hero or something. Fryebury Falls never had anyone from the city like this. *What would it be like to have a real crime fighter in town, someone with a track record and bullet wounds to show? And what would this crime fighter do in a small town that rarely saw any criminal activity?* Occasionally, there would be a domestic dispute or a drunken brawl, but that was pretty much it. Apparently back in the fifties there was a murder/suicide, and in the sixties, when Mike was a teenager, a former high school upperclassman, a handsome, clean-cut, straight-A student and athlete was convicted of murder: he stabbed his girlfriend's mother to death. There had also been some interesting stories from neighboring towns – prostitution, drugs and murder in such places as Newburyport, Salisbury and Merrimac – but these crimes never seemed to interfere with Fryebury Falls (not at this time, anyway), which as stated earlier, was its own microcosm, its own milieu, its own separate planet.

"Well, Mr. Cleary," Mike said extending his hand (as Jack sat in the seat, he could still picture this moment), "we have all the information we need here. I will call you by the end of next week. I still have a few more interviews to follow up with." Miss Julie told her husband, "*Never* hire anyone on the spot; that's not professional. Don't look as desperate as you really are. No one will respect you that way."

"Thank you," Jack said, standing up and shaking Mike's hand again. "I'll wait for your call. I know I can be an asset to your department." Then smiling, "I've got to go get my boy. I told him we'd go out to dinner tonight...job or no job." He paused and smiled more: "He wished me luck before I left."

Mike smiled. He couldn't imagine *not* giving Cleary the job! And then he heard his own voice: "Welcome aboard Mr. Cleary. You've got the job. We're glad you're with us."

Then he heard his wife: "You *low-down townie*. Such a sucker for sentimentality. You need to grow a pair."

Jack sat up, ejected the tape from the player and placed it gently into the cassette holder, then into the briefcase on the floor where he kept part of his audio collection. He had a dozen or so of these briefcases, all of them jam-packed with alpha-betized tapes that chronicled his life through secret conversa-tions with others.

This particular tape was under *M for Melanson* and a subcategory called *The Job Interview: The Ides of March 1982*. Although not a fan of Shakespeare, when he saw a production of *Julius Caesar* in his school days, he was captivated, perhaps even emotionally haunted by the way the actor who played the Soothsayer cryptically said, "Beware the Ides of March" in the second scene of the play.

On or off duty, Jack Cleary was always a private investi-gator. He carried a portable tape recorder with him at all times. He kept it camouflaged in the breast pocket of his uniform shirt, which he wore religiously, like a priest wears his vestments. Even at home he was rarely out of uniform.

If the tape player, for whatever reason were discovered on him, he had a story to back it up. "It's a gift from my boy, J.J. He gave it to me on my birthday and tells me to carry it with me everywhere I go. J.J. is brain-injured; he was pushed off a building when he was twelve. I don't have the heart to refuse him. He's such a good boy. Sometimes I forget it's even there..."

Up to this point, Jack never had to use the story, but he had always been prepared to tell it. Secretly he *wanted* to be discovered; then he could tell this little anecdote to someone who would eat the words up. Someone like Mike Melanson. After all, a good cop needs to be a good storyteller, a good actor. Like Columbo on TV. Someone who can constantly trick his public into believing he is ignorant while adhering to his own clever hidden agenda. To *catch* criminals, you must *think* like criminals.

Jack Cleary craved entertainment in any form, but for him there was nothing more riveting than being able to capture real life on tape. At times, he wished he could do the same thing with a movie camera or one of those videotape cameras that were becoming accessible. He even had his own idea for a TV series called *Busted!* The idea of the show would be to get people on tape without them knowing it – like *Candid Camera* with a twist – and the twist would be *this*: the peeping tom would never reveal his identity. *Oh, the things he would catch people doing and saying!* A voyeuristic show like this, he realized, could never make it on commercial TV, but maybe someday these cable stations like HBO and Cinemax could feature the show...*uncensored.*

He had an idea to call this type of programming "Reality TV."

When he exited the cruiser, he was suddenly taken aback by the cold, biting breeze, the one with the foul odor. He knew what it was. It was *her*. She had come back again. She appeared at the window at the back of the garage, naked and emaciated, two needles protruding from the veins in her left arm. He could see the backyard trees through her chest.

His heart began to race.

The image looked half old woman, half unrecognizable beast. Her eyes were opened as wide as could be imagined; there were no pupils, only two white and red sockets. Oddly enough, to Jack they looked like two candy fireballs after someone had been sucking on them for a few minutes.

Jack, who had seen this image many times before – always in a different form, however – turned away and sprinted to the door that led into the house.

Inside the minute cubbyhole of a room, J.J. Cleary sat straight up on the old green chair, his arms draped over the dilapidated arms, the fabric ripped from teeth marks. He *needed* to sit up straight...these were orders from his policeman father.

Next to the sixteen-year-old boy, who was abnormally

stocky and tall for an adolescent with a face that looked like one of the circus monsters in that old film *Freaks*, lay Lazlo, a six-year-old black lab. J.J.'s soul mate. The dog was given to him when his mother was still alive, when she and his daddy were living together in a studio apartment in Allston, Massachusetts. There was a definite bond between the two species. In fact, J.J. was like a dog himself. When he got excited, he would pant, and if he had a tail, it would certainly be wagging. He also loved to play with toys like a dog: he was fond of a Luke Skywalker action figure that he would even chew on from time to time. The boy, like his soul mate, would also drool perpetually, especially after a meal.

J.J. was kept in captivity – a kennel of sorts – for a majority of the day. Not physically locked in, but not allowed to leave the house either. He was forced to amuse himself around the clock. When they first moved to Fryebury Falls, Jack would take him to Easter Seals, but he found the staff there to be young and unreliable. Except there was this one person – the manager – a voluptuous girl named Lisa Laribee – whom Jack wanted in many ways. She was beautiful in a corn-fed sort of way (Jack loved them big!), and she was kind and gentle, but also had an edgy sense of humor that was very endearing. Despite the fact that the girl was no more than twenty-three, Jack actually pictured himself having children with her. Normal children. But Jack pulled his son out of the program, because frankly, it was too disturbing for him to be around all these other people with brain injuries, Down's Syndrome, autism, cerebral palsy...it was just all too damn depressing.

So J.J. would stay at home.

The boy was amazingly well-versed in movies. Like Jack he loved storytelling. His favorite programs were the stories about policemen fighting off criminals. He loved these stories because he wanted to be a policeman – just like his father was.

"I have a *Mag-mum* forty-five pistol gun, and with it I can clean your head off," he would say, pointing Luke Skywalker's head at Lazlo, pretending the action figure was a gun and his dog, some dangerous killer.

J.J. always dreamed of being a policeman, but he knew that before he could become one, he needed to learn how to behave himself. He had to remember all the things his daddy ordered him to do on a day-to-day basis: wash his dishes; make the bed; read his books; be creative and keep himself busy and out of trouble; and most importantly...not to bother his father who lived and worked downstairs.

J.J was also responsible for feeding the dog and taking him in the backyard so he could *pee* and *poop*. Jack told his son something about the dog needing to get exercise, but J.J. could never leave the yard, and Jack wanted nothing to do with that "black bitch" – so the two eternal prisoners in the Stagecoach Road Penitentiary remained out of shape.

And if J.J. didn't take care of that goddam dog, that "black bitch," Jack told him, then he would put a goddam bullet in his goddam stupid head!

This threat greatly perturbed the boy. "No! No! No! Please don't, Daddy. I'll take good care of Lazlo and take him to do *pee* and *poop* and clean it with the pooper-scooper and feed him twice a day. I will do it, Daddy. I will do it!"

Nothing frightened J.J. more than the thought of his father killing his dog. Nothing except for those nightmares he would have...every night. Those nightmares of *her*. Always of *her*. And sometimes in these dreams she would have a gun and she would point it at Lazlo's head, pull the trigger, then "clean" his head right off.

But upon occasion the boy would have nice thoughts too. Nice thoughts of escaping jail. With Lazlo. And nice thoughts of the beautiful girl next door. The girl with long black hair, blue eyes and the pretty face he wanted to kiss. What nice, nice thoughts he had of her.

Why does Daddy keep me in here? I am not bad. I am not bad. I am good. I just want to go outside.

Jack, however, would never let his son out of his sight, and for good reason, he would say. "A boy with your disabilities can't go out into the real world without guidance. You know what that means? Without *supervision* (a word J.J. associated with Superman). You wouldn't survive one day out there, boy. Not one hour. You must stay upstairs. I live downstairs and you live upstairs. That's the arrangement. It's for your own good. And it only turns into *jail* when you do bad things. Understand? When you disobey the laws of enforcement that I lay down, you must lock yourself in the closet. In jail. I am your father, but I am also like a warden. Understand? It's all for your own good because I love you, son. Understand?"

Yes, J.J. certainly understood, but he still wanted to go outside. He *hated* being in jail. Hated it more and more each day. One of these days he was going to leave, he considered absurdly, knowing that Jack would never allow for such a ridiculous prospect.

"Lazlo – let's play policeman," J.J said, and the dog who was lying down, perked up and got into a sitting position. He was wagging his tail and panting as if to say: *Yeah, let's play again, J.J.*

He picked up Luke Skywalker, aimed it at the dog's skull and said, "I will clean off your head...*punk.*"

Lazlo snapped at the action figure as if it were a bone.

But then J.J put Luke Skywalker down, thought about what his father said about taking Lazlo into the woods and putting a goddam bullet in his goddam stupid head, and began to cry. He patted the dog. "Nobody will hurt you, Lazlo. Not even Daddy. I will clean off *his* head with a Mag-mum 45 gun if he tries to kill you."

Meanwhile, Jack sat in his cruiser and listened to another tape in his collection. This one was filed under 'D' for Davis, Moira.

Periodically he would look up at the window and see the emaciated half-woman, half-beast staring at him with those candy fireball eyes, judging him for what he had done to her...*and* to the others.

CHAPTER 7

HOLY MERDE!

Adam's room was what some might have called gigantic, atypically large for that of a seven-year-old boy living in suburbia. It even surpassed the size of many a master bedroom, even when compared to some of those prominent waterfront homes on the coast of Hampton and Rye Beach. Yet it still had all the little boy furnishings, and then some: stuffed animals like dogs, monkeys and bears; all sorts of books from Dr. Seuss to The Bobbsey Twins to baseball novels; posters of Red Sox players like Yaz (Carl Yastremski) as well as his favorite player, left-fielder Jim Rice; sports equipment like aluminum bats, baseball gloves, a dozen or more Major League hats, a Nerf football and a real one; and quite the collection of baseball and football cards. He enjoyed sports mostly because his father did; Mike Melanson was quite the athlete in his day: in high school he was captain of the football team and along with his buddy George Pearson, an all-star baseball player.

Although Adam was a Red Sox fan, he preferred the St. Louis Cardinals, the Baltimore Orioles and the Toronto Blue-jays. When Mike asked him why, the boy, a lifetime lover of nature and animals said, "Because I like all the birds on the uniforms and hats." Once he asked his father, "Why do so many teams name themselves after birds? And how come I never heard of a baseball team called The Robins...or The Crows...or The Doves...or The Eagles?"

Mike informed his son that there was a *football* team called The Eagles. "They are from Philadelphia. The City of Brotherly Love." Mike had his own way of educating Adam, and he felt good when he was able to contribute these little facts to the boy, who in many ways seemed to be highly intelligent, something he attributed – inadvertently – to his wife's creative interests. Consequently, Adam was the type of boy who knew Ted Williams' lifetime batting average as well as well as who wrote *Death of a Salesman*.

"And do you remember the name of the team in St. Louis?" his father asked him. At times he would quiz the boy on team names and players' numbers, a game that Adam was good at (The child had a photographic memory, something that perpetually amazed Mike.)

"The St. Louis Cardinals," Adam said, not missing a beat. Then he added, "Both the baseball and football teams have the same name."

Adam was an extremely heads-up child. He was also very accommodating, patient and heartfelt. Even at his young age, he aimed to please his parents. He was what Miss Julie called a mindful "old soul."

Mike loved talking sports with his son even though he knew that deep down Adam's passions lay elsewhere.

Miss Julie, however, despised all sports. She called sports figures "overgrown, overpaid Neanderthals with no concept of the real world."

"What the hell is the point of chasing some ball, or hitting one, or throwing one, or knocking someone down to get one?" she would assert. "And running around fields and stadiums like a bunch of children at some elementary school! *Seriously!*

How does that contribute to our culture and society?"

Mike wanted to ask Miss Julie the same questions about actors and photographers (when his wife wasn't dreaming about being on the stage she was engaged in the art of black and white photography), but he was wise and kept his comments to himself.

Adam wasn't a gifted athlete, but he was moderately competent in baseball. He was a catcher, which according to Mike was one of the hardest if not *the* hardest position in the game. When Adam asked him why, Mike explained, "Because, Adam, they are the leaders in the field. They are responsible for every pitch. You know how important that is? *And* they have the most dangerous job too. Being behind the batter with all that equipment is a major responsibility. Plus, they have to communicate with the pitcher and guide him into throwing the right pitch. Fastball. Curve. Change-up. *And* they have to be on the lookout for base runners stealing. I know you're not allowed to steal yet, but next year in Little League you will be able to. That's why catchers have to be on top of things the entire game. They've got to know the situations *and* be able to act on them quickly and skillfully. Baseball is a thinking man's sport."

Mike loved being a father.

In the corner of Adam's room – on the other side of the queen size bed – were four aquaria all practically adjacent to one another on an oak table: one for his two goldfish, Fred and Barney; the next one for his iguana, Blood; and the next one for his pet rats, Gwendolyn and Cecily whom Miss Julie named after characters in some play.

Adam named his reptile Blood from a kids' book (written by this woman named Deandra who lived *right* in Fryebury Falls!). He once read where a lizard named "Scaley" sucked human blood to stay alive.

On the other side of the room by Adam's bed, there was a

cage that held two lovebirds. He named them Carol and Mike from *The Brady Bunch*. He thought Carol and Mike Brady were the happiest married couple in the world...two real lovebirds.

"If it were only like that in real life," Miss Julie once told her son as she kissed his head. "God bless the impressionable minds of our youth."

And if they were to ever get that cat that Miss Julie insisted on having (to her there were no better companions than felines), it would be named Imogene after her favorite photographer Imogene Cunningham, the only photographer who was able to transform lilies into a symbol of the female body. In Greek mythology, according to Miss Julie, who was always fascinated with the life of the goddesses, lilies were voices of the muses as well as the flowers of purity born from the milk of the Goddess Hera.

If only she could find *her own* voice as a photographer, she often thought on the days when she got bored with the prospect of being an accomplished stage actress.

By the time she left for the TV station, Adam had already been home from school for a few hours. At this time, he was engaged in his favorite pastime, drawing in his sketchbook. He was currently drawing a collage of birds: orioles; cardinals; and two eagles who were brothers. He called them *Phil* and *Del*. The second grader had a real penchant and talent for drawing. Miss Julie's father, the mogul of Najarian Coffee, Adam's estranged grandfather, who according to Miss Julie favored coffee beans over his own family, could also draw well. Maybe this is where he got the drawing genes, the boy's mother grudgingly surmised.

But Adam didn't want to be an artist, not professionally anyway. For as long as he could speak, he wanted to be a veterinarian. "Drawing just passes the time," he would say. "It's my hobby. I want to be a *veta-najarian* when I grow up. That and a bus driver."

Miss Julie adored how Adam mispronounced the name *veterinarian* because the last part of the word – "najarian" – was her maiden name. She didn't have the heart to correct the boy, which was uncharacteristic for this woman who was constantly attempting to get him and her husband to speak eloquently like good actors. Once, when they were all on a road trip, she said this to Mike and Adam: "The capital of Vermont is pronounced *Mo-peel-ee-ay*, not *Mont-peel-ee-er*. That's so common. Come on and say it with me. And speak from the diaphragm."

When Miss Julie asked her son why in God's name a boy with *his* creative ambitions and intellect wanted to drive a bus for a living, a job so different from a veterinarian, Adam replied ever so gracefully, "They're not that different. Both jobs are about helping *living things*, aren't they?"

Ever since Adam learned the importance of loving animals from his veterinarian grandfather – Mike's dad, Lucien Melanson who had been deceased for five years – he wanted to dedicate his life to helping animals. On occasion, Grandpa Lucien would visit Adam, appearing to him in a cloud on the ceiling above his bed.

"Hello Adam. You are making Grandpa very proud. You know that? You are going to be a wonderful veterinarian someday. You have what it takes. Study hard and don't lose that heart of yours. Brains without heart, soul and empathy mean nothing in this business. You hear me, Old Boy?"

Grandpa Lucien made Adam promise not to tell *anyone* – even his father – that he occasionally makes visits from the dead. When Adam asked him why, his grandfather said, "It's our little secret, that's why. You and me, we're very much alike. Dead ringers. Soul mates. We have the same birthday: June 4th. We're Geminis. The Twins. We have intuition and insight that most people don't have or even know about. Your mother, who's also a Gemini, she has that insight too, but not like ours. Ours is stronger. We are a rare breed. I love you. Be careful of the evil forces that lurk. They are out there. They pose as the devil. But you are stronger than that. Don't be afraid. Always remember. Think nice thoughts. Good thoughts. And remember: emotional intelligence – being able to put yourself in someone else's shoes – is the *only* intelligence, Old Boy. I will see you soon. *Real, real soon.*"

Then he would disappear into the roughly textured ceiling, always leaving a vague trace of his countenance behind so that when Adam looked above, he would be reminded of his grandfather's presence.

At about five o'clock, Mike tapped on his son's door, shave-and-a-haircut-two bits style.

"Can I come in, Adam?"

"Yes, Dad."

"Hi sport. What are you doing?"

"I'm drawin' a picture of a horse named Stanley, and a cow named Roy."

When Mike entered, Adam placed the colored pencils down, lining them up next to one another meticulously, like a band of marching soldiers, and stared into his father's funny-looking eyes.

"Can I see them?" Mike asked softly.

Adam nodded. "Yes, Dad."

After a moment, Mike widened those crazy eyes of his, which made Adam think of an actress he saw on TV once. She was in a scary movie about two parents who move into a haunted house with their young son, a movie he has never forgotten for two reasons: first, because the actress with the funny eyes looked quite a bit like her father; and second, the little boy reminded him of himself.

Ghosts and all.

"This is very good," Mike said after seconds of speculation. He looked at the details of the two animals, wondering how in the hell this young person could draw so remarkably well. Although Mike could not draw in the least, he admired anyone who could.

As he stared at the page, one of the horses seemed to move. Roy suddenly turned into a naked cartoon blond girl with eyes that sparkled like diamonds. She looked a bit like Marilyn Monroe. She smiled and winked at Mike.

A jolt of electricity passed through Mike's entire system. He quickly flipped the drawing over and picked up another one. This one, the drawing of the brother eagles, Phil and Del, transformed into two scantily dressed women. He had seen them before. One was a redhead, the other a brunette. Both had piercing blue eyes. They were holding hands and smiling at Mike.

Another jolt of electricity. He threw the drawing down, swallowed hard, then smiled very awkwardly at his son who immediately sensed his father's strange behavior.

Adam asked him if he was okay.

Mike smiled. "Of course I am, Sport."

"One of those twenty-four-hour viruses?" Adam asked.

Mike smiled wider and the air that emitted from his nostrils resembled a quiet laugh. "Probably."

Then Adam said, "Mommy's on TV tonight."

Mike placed his hand on Adam's shoulder. "That's right. You gonna watch it with me?"

"Yeah. Mommy will get mad if we don't."

Mike's smile shifted. "You're right. We don't want to get in trouble – do we?"

"It's last week's show," Adam said in Miss Julie's voice. Mike nodded. "Mommy says you forget sometimes."

Yet another smile, but this one somehow looked more serious than the others. Then a pause. He turned his head. The red head and the brunette appeared as projections on the wall...then they dissolved into shadows.

Mike cleared his throat. "Well, we won't forget tonight. Okay, buddy?"

"Okay, Dad."

When Miss Julie returned home a number of hours later, Mike and Adam were asleep on the couch. *My two boys*, she thought and smiled. She looked at her son who had dark skin like hers, jet black hair, hazel eyes and long lashes that she once said "ladies would kill for!"

Then she looked at her husband's sleeping eyes, which, when closed, looked like anyone else's eyes. Back in middle school, Mike's classmates nicknamed him "Cyclops" after the one-eyed monster in *The Odyssey*, a name that carried over into high school. He never really minded the name; he always took it in stride. But his best buddy George never liked the nickname; he never thought it was funny. He would adamantly tell his other classmates not to insult his friend like that.

Before heading upstairs to change into her nightclothes (a process that took nearly an hour every night) she dropped her Gucci purse on the recliner and tiptoed to the closet, pulling out her 35mm camera.

She turned off the TV and aimed the camera at them.

She was inspired to create!

For Miss Julie the photographer, there was no such thing as a so-called Kodak moment; snapshots were for amateurs. As a professional – or soon-to-be a professional, she kept telling herself – she took *photographs*, not pictures. Just like an actor doesn't practice, she *rehearses*. Those ridiculous oversized, overpaid Neanderthals that run around fields catching and throwing balls, *they* practice!

Each shot needed to be meticulously crafted: angles, lighting and composition all had to be carefully considered. These elements, Miss Julie insisted, could make or break a photograph.

She took her heels off, pulled the antique Hitchcock chair from the wall to the center of the room, rested a pillow on the seat to protect the finish, then climbed onto the chair, trying to balance herself on the pillow that had the tendency to slide back and forth. After a minute or two, she managed to find the right position, then she awkwardly aimed the camera directly over her family: it was the ultimate high angle shot. So visual, so sophisticated, she thought. Her husband was on the left side of the frame and Adam on the far right. In the middle – perfectly symmetrical to the human subjects – was a folded afghan with the word LOVE embroidered on it. *How perfect.*

The title of the piece was already figured: "Love & Slumbers."

But right before she was able to take the photograph, Mike awoke. It took him a moment to decipher the giant image looming over him.

His heart skipped a beat.

"Julie," he finally said. He stretched his chunky arms over his head. "What are you doing?"

"The name is Miss Julie," she reminded him in a loud, throaty whisper. "Don't move, this is a *mah-velous* shot. Close your eyes again."

"What are you doing up there in that chair?" He squinted into the chandelier.

She mimicked him: "What are you doing up in that chair?" Then: "Quiet. I want to photograph you two. Stay where you are, close your eyes and shut up!"

Then Adam woke up. He looked at his father who was staring at the ceiling.

"What time is it, Daddy?"

"Oh, this is just great," Miss Julie said, defeated. "Now the entire spontaneity of this moment is gone. Wasted. *Kaput.*"

Adam followed the voice and looked up at her: "Hi, Mommy."

Miss Julie sighed. "You couldn't just stay sleeping for another moment, could you? The piece is called 'Love & Slumbers' but now I just might as well name it –" Then to Adam: "Mommy is trying to photograph you and Daddy. Will you go back to sleep for a minute, while I get this shot?"

"You were good on TV tonight," Adam said. Then he added: "Even though it was last week's show."

Miss Julie sighed again, unable to refrain from breaking into a smile. "Thank you, darling."

"Why are you up in that chair?" Adam continued.

Mike snorted.

"And just what the hell is so funny, Michael Melanson?"

He looked away.

"Well, I can't work in these conditions. You two are absolutely impossible. *Im-poss-ee-blay*. The one moment my muse inspires me, and you ruin it. *Holy merde!* All I wanted to do was to –"

But as the words left her lips, the pillow slid off the chair and she jerked forward. As she tumbled to the floor, she slammed her left ass cheek on the edge of the chair. The chair capsized, and the camera flew out of her hand in a projectile form and the woman slipped to the floor, her knees breaking the fall.

Mike swallowed his heart, the events of the fall unfolding before him like a car accident in slow-motion – like in a movie or something – and if she made any initial sound of agony, it was masked by Adam's high-pitched squeal, a sound so horrific coming from such a quiet, peaceful child, a squeal that sounded like a peacock.

"Mommy! Mommy! Mommy! Mommy!"

Mike gulped, unable to move.

"*Holy merde!*" Miss Julie said weakly, slowly massaging her calf.

CHAPTER 8

REAL, REAL SOON

The dawn broke as George Pearson strolled down Angstrom Trail, one of the several paths that led from Stagecoach Road to Günter's Millyard. He had been out walking all night – walking up and down Baker Street for hours upon hours, trying to put his life and his delusions into some sort of perspective. He must have walked eight, ten miles, he thought, which felt wonderfully refreshing. His heart was pumping rigorously, like it used to after one of his workouts in the high school gym. Now that it was light, he decided to spend the morning in Günter's Millyard where he would often go to refuel himself. The weeping willows and the waterfall offered him solace. This was his respite. A new inner strength and energy were passing through his body. *Things were going to be okay again*, he thought. *It won't be easy, but I will heal. I will heal.*

The morning dew had collected on the grass, shrubs and dead leaves as he studied the outline and form of the trees in his path, listening with an almost extrasensory perception to the sounds of the insects and birds surrounding him. He heard the idiosyncratic call of the mourning dove, always one of his favorite tunes in nature's soundtrack. The bird had a real musical quality to it...a melodic whistling of sorts; it was like hearing someone playing a flute. *I need to get back into writing and playing music,* George thought with an uncharacteristic smile. *And it won't be aggressive, angry or dissonant; it'll be tranquil, ambient, ethereal – sounds for deep meditation.* It'll be on the same lines as Brian Eno's hypnotic, soporific *Music for Airports,* which he used to play for little Abigail when she was an infant.

Even as a boy, he learned to savor the dynamics of the living, breathing, singing life around him. This inexplicable love of music, biology, pedagogy and baseball appeared to develop inside of him innately, holistically, for there were no musicians, biologists, teachers or athletes in his family. In college he was the front man for a three-person band called Phantasmagoria who wrote ecologically conscious folk rock ballads...songs like "Morning Doves," "Green Party Rebellion" and "Old Sarah (She Who Laughs)."

He looked down at a patch of mushrooms. Phylum name *Basidiomycota.* Then he began thinking of a number of different California mushrooms that he remembered teaching in class: *Boletus edulus, Clitocybe odora* (which always got a huge laugh from the boys in his classes), *Tremella Mesenterica, Verpa conica* and *Amanita constricta* – and when one student jokingly asked about "magic mushrooms," the teacher responded: "For those of you who think it's cool to trip on mushrooms, let me deter you from doing so: Let's look at *Aminita Muscaria,* for instance. They are the ones with the red and white dots. In simpler terms, they're called *fly agaric.* They can put you in shock. Like eating any poison might." When one student (the precocious Ian Murphy who was very intelligent but not a dedicated student) facetiously asked him how he knew all of this, the teacher smirked and said, "I read all about it in the Biology text. You should try it." The student, whose expression changed to a serious tone, stared at his teacher. Then George finished, "*Reading*, Murphy, not the *Aminita Muscaria.*"

George Pearson grinned; he was in his element again...if only for a moment.

But only the booze, he thought discouragingly, could get him there, to that state of homeostasis. Sure, it was the vice that brought forth the belligerent animal in this once peaceful man of the Earth, but it was also, according to him, the "juice of the gods." Coming down from an alcoholic's trip, for a short time anyway (right before the hangover symptoms commenced), was the best part of his odyssey. It was peace on Earth. Phantasmagoria. Homeostasis. A hallucination that enabled him to be in harmony once again with himself and the biological world around him.

A harmony that died along with Alison and Abigail.

When he arrived at Günter's Millyard at around 6:30 am, there wasn't a soul around. Later on in the day, however, it would be overflowing with an assortment of people: old folks who would take their daily walks; the middle school skateboarders ("The Boardheads" as they were appropriately named); young couples doing what they do; and a police officer, typically Chief Melanson, who would patrol the sacred spot for any potential wrongdoing. The Boardheads liked to drink, smoke, piss in the water and fuck their girlfriends in the dilapidated hat mills that were supposed to have been boarded up. The town took pride in Günter's Millyard even if they didn't value the rest of their sordid, dingy little town.

George sat on one of the red benches, the one facing the waterfall. He closed his eyes and began his breathing exercises. *In* through the mouth slowly; *out* through the mouth slowly.

Repeatedly for twenty minutes.

This process helped him to temporarily cope with the

trials of his own being, as the lengthy walks and the drinking did. It was his form of physical and mental escape. Self-therapy. For how *does* one really get over accidentally killing his wife and little daughter? *Seriously.* It's no wonder that he cracked up, became reliant on alcohol, and slugged the kid in the jaw. Amazing that's all he did.

Suddenly he was back in the classroom, teaching again. Room 27. Playing music and lecturing on the wonders of the life sciences. It was one of the classes where he was explaining photosynthesis, a topic that baffled students, especially when studied alongside cellular respiration. There was so much involved in creating the simple reaction that began with sunlight: 6 molecules of water plus 6 molecules of carbon dioxide produce 1 molecule of sugar plus 6 molecules of oxygen. The process of photosynthesis came back to him: *PEP, ATP, NADH, chloroplasts, Photophosphorylation, the Calvin-Benson Cycle, The Redox Chain...*

Ugh, George thought. *How did they stand it? There was so much to it.* He got tired just thinking of such details. But he loved it. Loved every one of those PEPs, ATPs and NADHs, loved it all. And he would marvel at his successes when most of the students could not only pass, but ace, the test on the scientific material. To George it was a teacher's job to facilitate difficult topics. And he was very good at doing this; he *knew* he was.

Then suddenly he was on the baseball field, hitting grounders to his infield, telling his shortstop to do more of a crow's hop when throwing to first base, and teaching his pitcher (the same one he cracked in the jaw) how to improve upon his form. "You're just playing catch with the catcher, Hamilton. Like looking at a swinging watch as someone gets hypnotized. It should be like a peaceful meditation. And you're dancing up there on the mound. You choreograph the steps and create your own ballet...from the wind-up to the release.

If you can't dance, you can't pitch. Understand?" Then the coach to his entire team: "Baseball is not like any other sport, gang. It's a thinking man's game, a chess game, and every one of you is a piece on that board. Baseball is also good theater; you are like actors on a stage showing off your moves. Your own batting stance, pitching style, fielding style, running style. You're performing to an audience who is sitting there expecting good drama. They come to a game knowing the basis of the story, the rules of the game, but you end up entertaining them by *surprising* them with your performance. Baseball is also great storytelling, a great narrative, an archetypal journey where the goal – like Odysseus coming back from the Trojan War – is to return home. Why do you think it's called *home* when you make a run? That, gang, is the *magic and mythology* of baseball."

George had his eyes closed tightly. He could see the events of his past as clearly as when he had lived them...even more clearly, for the visuals in his head were accented with rich colors. He breathed in through his nose and out through his mouth. He was at ease.

When he opened his eyes, Abigail appeared before him the way she always did – in that purple dress she wore on the last day of her life, her eighth birthday.

George closed his eyes and took another deep breath; sometimes she would disappear for a while when he did this.

But not this time. She was still there. Her golden blond hair was long and straight. Her eyes were almond-shaped, a trait George and Sam inherited from their Swedish mother's side, the Lindens.

Abigail was a name Alison always liked; it was her grandmother's name. Plus, she always saw her daughter as a "daddy's little girl" and the name itself meant "my father's joy." One day he nicknamed her "Abbie-girl" and then he never called her anything else.

George and Alison met in a college public speaking class when they were both twenty and got married two years later. They were married for over nine years before the fatal accident.

Abigail's brown freckles blended in perfectly with her fair, smooth, almost pale skin. George looked directly into her blue eyes. She walked up to him, closer and closer until she dissolved, then disappeared inside of him.

George closed his eyes tightly again. He inhaled, his stomach now in wild knots, then he exhaled for what seemed like many seconds.

"What do you want?" he asked.

"I want to help you," she said in the same little girl voice he always remembered.

"Help me with what?" *This can't be you, Abbie-Girl,* he thought. *No way.*

"To help you do what you are destined to do."

"What is *that*?" He never heard his daughter say a word like *destined* before.

"I've been telling you." The sound of her voice was hollower now, and it echoed: "You must *kill the devil* and send him back to hell."

"I still don't know what that means."

"You will, I promise. Real soon. *Real, real soon.*"

A light breeze formed; George knew that Abigail created this breeze. There was always a gentle, fragrant wind that accompanied her visits.

"Mom misses you."

No answer.

"She and I have come back for you. But first you must do what you are meant to do."

George felt an overwhelming euphoric sensation – like hundreds of fingers were lightly tickling his skin – that affected his entire body. He couldn't move.

71

Abigail shot out of him, rising above him. She was soaring through the air over her father for what appeared to be a very long time, the warm, breathy, fragrant air blowing on him like a zephyr. She then swooped down like some bird attacking its prey and dissolved into his head. He felt her moving through his body again.

Moments later she emerged from her father again, facing him directly. He looked deeply into her eyes – they were bluer than ever, hypnotic even.

The sun was getting brighter, the rays making their way through the weeping willow trees. The May morning was already showing signs that it was going to be a warm and humid day in Fryebury Falls.

George opened his eyes to discover she was gone. He was himself again. He listened to Niagara Two. The sun now beamed like lasers through the trees, the light penetrating through the branches and leaves. George blocked his eyes with the back of his arm. It was a heavy, burning light, like the ones he had seen in his nightmares, a relentless flood of sunshine reminding him of the worst day of his life. The sounds of the waterfall gave way to screeching tires, a crash, and shattered glass. He felt a prickling sensation in his face, as if he were experiencing the fragmented glass stabbing him from the inside of his cheeks.

It would not be the last time he would feel this sensation.

Then a minute later, things were peaceful again.

George was nearly sober now. He could tell because he felt like shit. He needed another drink. Badly.

The sun went behind a cloud and a warm, fragrant breeze (different from anything he had felt before) massaged his face, soothing, and eventually curing the prickling sensation of fragmented glass stabbing his cheeks. Then it traveled inside of him, tickling his insides. The hot breath of the zephyr surrounded him on all sides. A new smell accompanied this; it was different from anything his olfactory sense had experienced before. Before long, he was in that catatonic state again.

Then it all stopped. George looked at the waterfall and watched a rainbow form over the waters, color by color. He began to shiver. The wind traveled through him, this time in such an intense manner that he was forced to cry. But he couldn't help smiling as the tears streamed down his cheeks.

"I know it's you, Alison," George said whispering. "I can feel you. I can feel both of you. What is going on? I can't take it. You need to leave me alone. Please go. *Please.*"

After a few moments, they were gone.

Niagara Two's running waters flowed on, and the sunshine must have let up because for the next hour or two George Pearson sat in the shade, transfixed by the imagery and sounds of the waterfall in front of him.

CHAPTER 9

WORLDS APART

Maygyn hadn't been in the bathroom five minutes before the vomiting began. Then the coughing kicked in. The nausea and sweats had finally gotten the best of the girl.

The guitar playing stopped.

"Maygyn? Honey? You okay in there?"

No answer.

Honey? Maygyn thought, kneeling down in front of the toilet bowl, her face practically inside the water.

Again, Moira asked if her "Maygyn honey" was okay.

What a freak, thought the girl. *Honey?* Moira was not a *honey* kind of mother. Well, not generally anyways. The girl knew, however, that in her own eccentric, demented way, her mother loved her. But she was also aware that her mother's musical career came first...before motherhood or any other domestic responsibilities. It always did.

On most of the nights when Moira would drive into Boston for a gig or two, Maygyn would either stay with her father and her Uncle George or by herself on Brown Ave where she would have the entire house to herself until her mother returned home, often very early in the morning. On this particular night, the girl decided to stay at home. The thought of studying in her father's and uncle's suffocating hole of a place that stunk of stale cigarettes, booze, Aqua Velva and body odor repulsed her to no end. And even though Moira despised the fact that upon occasion her daughter would be subjected to that disgusting "child-beating" uncle of hers, she had no choice in the matter. She didn't have custody of the girl. When Moira and Sam split, they agreed, for Maygyn's sake they said, to have "joint custody." The truth of the matter was this: both Sam and Moira functioned better as part-time parents, so the "joint custody" thing was a blessing more than anything.

But Moira still had her terms. To Sam she said, "If that delusional drunk so much as *looks* at her funny, never mind laying a finger on her – I'll kill you *both*!"

Moira tapped on the door with her fingernails.

Go away, mother!

"Can I come in?" Moira asked. Without waiting for an answer, she opened the door, surprised to discover it was unlocked. Maygyn, fully dressed, was sitting on the toilet seat, her hands cupped over her face, her head hung, rocking back and forth just inches above the floor. Part of her hair was sweeping the tile.

The girl took her hands off her face, sat up and glared at her mother in a condescending manner, one that said: *What do you want with me? Go away!*

"Well *there's* the look from hell if I ever saw it." Then delicately: "You, uh, threw up again, huh?"

Maygyn nodded slowly.

Moira took a drag on her cigarette and let out a long exhale, a sort of sigh of relief. Nothing seemed to frighten this woman...but the thought of *anything* happening to her child was simply unbearable. She thought that perhaps this was the reason why she distanced herself from the girl. To protect herself.

When she was a few years younger than her daughter, her twin sister Megan, who was called Meggie, drowned at a summer cottage that her family rented out at Lake Massasecum in Bradford, New Hampshire. It was about 75 miles northwest of Fryebury Falls, off of Route 9, just 10 miles from Henniker. The story went like this: Meggie walked out into the lake, sliced her toe on a rock or something, lost balance, then hit her head on a pile of sharp rocks by the shore. She stood up – almost as if nothing really happened – but must have been delirious because instead of walking back into shore, she walked further out into the water. After only a few steps the very shallow water dropped off dramatically to about eight feet or more; everyone knew about this drop-off and was always warned not to step beyond a certain spot. The irony of it all was that Meggie knew about this drop-off and was also a skilled swimmer, very advanced for her age. But the reality was this: she took a fatal blow to the head and that was that.

And the worst part of it was, if you can imagine: Moira witnessed the entire thing from shore. She watched her twin's head bobbing up and down like a buoy, and every few seconds, Meggie yelled for her sister: *Help Moira. Help me, Moira!* Each time Meggie said these words mounds of water would rush down her throat and into her tiny lungs.

But Moira could not swim; it was always her sister who excelled in such things. In addition to being a fine swimmer, Meggie Davis was very gifted in school, sports and the arts. By the time of her death at age nine, she was a child prodigy of sorts: a straight-A student; an all-star gymnast and softball player; and a classically trained cellist and pianist. And to top it all off, she was the kindest child imaginable. How this young talent didn't have a big head was beyond comprehension, but she *didn't*; she was humble and modest, always giving credit to others – Moira included – before herself. A real old soul.

After Meggie's untimely death, Moira swore that she

would carry on her sister's legacy by immersing herself in a world of music.

On occasion, she would – and this is something she never told a soul – see her dead twin. In lakes. In the shower. In the toilet. At Niagara Two. Any place that had water. In these visions, little Meggie would always be in the midst of drowning, calling out after her sister just like she did on that fateful Tuesday on the Fourth of July in 1961: *Help Moira. Help me, Moira.*

"You might want to brush your teeth," Moira said, looking at the drops of water collecting in the sink, half expecting to see her sister. She was still concentrating on the water droplets for a moment, but then looked intently at her daughter. The gaze was almost too intense for the girl to handle at the moment. "Sometimes after a night of too much drinking, I'd go home puke my guts out, then I'd brush my teeth and feel like a million bucks. *Really.*" She flicked her ashes into the sink.

"I'm okay," Maygyn said. *Why are you telling me this, Mother? Brushing your teeth after puking? What a freak!*

"What is it, another test today? Is that why you're so... *nervous*?"

Maygyn nodded.

"You'll do fine, you *always* do." Another drag.

There was a long pause that made Moira more uncomfortable than her daughter. After a moment, Moira said, "Speaking of puking..." She giggled in a way that embarrassed Maygyn. She took another drag, then burped on her Miller Light. "I was about your age. There was this boy. Wayne Parkinson. Man. What a little hunk. And he studied a lot like you did. All the teachers loved him. We girls did too. Oh, man! He's probably some hot shit lawyer or doctor now." Oddly to herself she mumbled: "He was in the jazz band too. Man..." She had transferred herself back to that time in her life.

Is there a point to all of this, Mother?

As if Moira heard this thought, she continued. "I remember that one of my girlfriends..." There seemed to be a slight hesitation in her voice, Maygyn thought. "...Kelley Clark told me that Wayne thought I was cute or pretty or whatever it was he said. And I said I thought he was cute too. Before long, we went out on our first date. Roller-skating, if you can imagine it. I was *foolish* on those things. And afterwards when we were dating, I remember waiting by the phone for him to call. And I got sick to my stomach; I actually threw up at the thought of him not calling me. Can you imagine *me*, your mother, doing this?"

Maygyn let out a faint smile and shook her head.

"Well, I did. Then one day he *did* call and told me he liked one of my friends. Kelley Clark to be exact – the same girl who told me that *Wayne* liked me." She shook her head and then let out a sigh that inadvertently caused her lips to vibrate. "And then I emptied my entire dinner on the kitchen floor." Maygyn let out a bigger smile – bigger than she wanted to – as if to say: *Oh Mother.*

Another pause. "He was so sweet. Once I told him about your Aunt Meggie's accident and he..." Maygyn's eyes widened. Moira turned away and flicked another ash into the sink. She cleared her throat. Through one of the droplets of water she saw her twin struggling. Faintly she heard Meggie's voice: *Help, Moira. Help me, Moira.* A tear formed. Moira cleared her throat and wiped her eye.

Tell me about Auntie Meggie. You never talk about her. Tell me about her.

Rather suddenly, Moira asked, "So, is there anyone checking *you* out?"

Maygyn looked into her mother's eyes but said nothing.

"Oh, come on! Gorgeous thing like you? There's *got* to be someone. Is there? Someone *you* like? Someone that likes *you?* Tell your mother every gruesome detail."

Maygyn squinted one of her eyes and made a face that Moira could read easily: *I'm not going to tell you anything. You're my mother! Gross. Tell me about your sister.*

"There's nothing like those first romances," Moira continued. "The heartbreakers. They never last, but at the time, they seem so...important for some reason." At this moment, Moira seemed to be talking to herself; she would do this sort of thing after several beers. Then she thought about her first kiss with a boy named Alex something-or-other at summer camp. Cute little thing. Short with muscles. Then she remembered her second kiss (also at summer camp) – this kiss was much more erotic and fulfilling. It was with Tracy Spear, a short, rugged, big-busted gorgeous blue-eyed thing. She looked like a pretty boy. The memory returned to her: when the rest of the campers were participating in their daily activities – arts and crafts, swimming, boating, etc. – the two girls sneaked into the woods to smoke a cigarette together. To Moira's surprise, however, Tracy pulled out a bag of marijuana and a bowl that she said she stole from her older brother's bedroom. The two girls got stoned, stripped off each other's bathing suits, French kissed, then got on the ground with one another and did it in a pile of leaves.

Moira still gets turned on when she thinks of Tracy Spear. *I wonder what Tracy is doing now.*

Moira said, "School is important, honey, but don't forget to live your life too."

What the hell does that mean, Mother? Is going to school not *living my life? Freak!*

"You understand me don't you, babe?"

Freak! Freak!

"I'm just trying to help you. I love you...if you haven't noticed."

Could you be any more idiotic? Shut up, Mother. Just shut

up. We are worlds apart, lady. Worlds and worlds apart. You don't know anything.

Then Maygyn thought of David Marino. President of the eighth-grade class. Short, dark-skinned, black hair, muscular. She heard a story that the gym teacher or one of his sports buddies nicknamed him "Big Arms." He also had a very chiseled countenance – piercing brown eyes, a long ethnic nose and a most prominent cleft chin. Oh, the thoughts she had of him! Wonderful, nasty little thoughts. Thoughts of them sneaking out of school, running under the bleachers of the football stadium and then...

I'm no prude, Mother. Not by a long shot.

In fact, that previous summer – at *her* day camp – Maygyn had her first kiss and was felt up by sixteen-year-old Stevie Wilson who had long rockstar hair and beautiful eyelashes. She didn't particularly love the experience, but she didn't hate it either.

Without any kind of warning, Moira kneeled down in front of the toilet and gave her daughter a hug. Sometimes when their conversations weren't going anywhere – when Moira was obviously trying too hard to be a mother (to make up for lost time, maybe) – a hug would at least break the embarrassing tension.

"I wrote a new song. Want to hear it?"

"Is it about Dad?" Maygyn snapped. She could still hear the words: *I'm feeling that way without you. Homeostasis.*

Moira snapped back in a way that was somehow endearing. "It's about *us*. You and me. A mother and daughter trying to make a go of it even when the odds are against them."

When Maygyn initially asked her mother why she and her father split up (she would get the real story later on), Moira replied, "I'm not in love with him anymore, Maygyn. Nothing personal. It's just one of those things that happens. The *inevitable order of things*, I guess. Who knows? He's not a bad man. And I love him, I suppose, in my own way. I'm just not *in* love with him anymore. Understand?"

Her father, incidentally, had said the same of the situation: "Your mother and I are two different people. *Worlds apart.* We need to separate so we can figure out what we both want. It's unfortunate, but it happens in marriages sometimes. A marriage is no cake walk, sweetheart; I'll let you know that right off. It takes lots of work. And sometimes it can be a downright nasty thing." These words reminded Maygyn of that Ernest Hemingway short story "A Clean, Well-Lighted Place," where the author calls an old man "a nasty thing." So with that rationale, does a marriage eventually become weathered and nasty like an old man does? *Maybe it's really not worth it then,* Maygyn thought.

"Well," Moira said, her hands squeezing her daughter's shoulders, "Do you want to hear it or not?"

Maygyn gave her mother an uncharacteristic smile, then nodded.

Moira smiled back, stood up, kissing Maygyn on the forehead, then gently she said, "Why don't you finish up in here, then I'll play you the song. Be patient with me though. It's still a work-in-progress." With this line, she retrieved her cigarette from the sink, ran a bit of water over it then walked out of the bathroom, closing the door behind her.

CHAPTER 10

KISSIN' COUSINS

"Daddy! Daddy! Daddy, help me, Daddy. Help me!"

The downstairs door opened. The boy was hyperventilating. Lazlo was barking and whimpering.

"Huh? What? What is going on?" Jack said, jumping up suddenly. He had fallen asleep on the downstairs sofa in the basement living room, the room adjacent to the garage. He rubbed his eyes forcefully, yawned and yelled, "Keep that *damn dog quiet* or I swear I'll put a –"

J.J. froze, then looked at Lazlo who stopped barking. It was as if the dog understood what Jack was going to say.

You can't shoot Lazlo in the head, J.J. thought as if suddenly he forgot his current trauma. *I won't let you kill him by putting a bullet in his head.*

Jack continued rubbing his eyes as he slowly walked into the garage. He moved around his car, peaked inside the vehicle, instinctively perhaps, to make sure everything was in order. When he got to the stairway, which was quite the slope (it was very steep, forming a forty-five-degree angle) he saw his son in a shadow.

When J.J. saw his father, he yelled even louder, followed

by more hyperventilating. Then he coughed; it was one of those barking coughs, the kind little kids got after spending hours in a pool or a lake.

"Okay, slow down. Slow down." Jack's words were commanding but still somewhat soothing. "Slow down and start from the beginning." He could now make out his son's features. He got a lump in his throat and a knot in his stomach that was painful, like a cancer crab eating away at his insides. He knew she was present. Jack continued: "And take some deep breaths. Get a grip on yourself, will ya? And none of this 'help me Daddy' bullshit. Understand?"

"Yes, Daddy."

"Okay. Tell me what happened this time."

"Daddy –" The boy started to cry then apologized to his father who hated it when he let himself become weak.

Jack knew what J.J. was going to say.

"Nightmare of the Gail."

"Another one?" Jack replied almost sympathetically, for he knew this was no nightmare. How could it have been – he was seeing her too? But his son wasn't to know this. Then he said softly, "Dreams are not real. They exist only in the mind. They can't hurt you, even though they *seem* real. They're like pictures in a book. That's all." He paused and looked around the garage. "You were watching TV again, weren't you?"

"Yes, Daddy, but you said I could watch –"

"I know what I said," Jack said in a softer tone that momentarily comforted the boy, "but why don't you call it quits for tonight? It's polluting your head. Understand?"

"I do Daddy, but –"

"*Uh-uh-uh*, what did I say about 'buts'?"

J.J. laughed. "That they are filled with shit."

"Right."

"Sorry."

Jack paused, got ready to say something, but instead

pointed his finger up at his son, then dropped his hand to his side and got ready to say something again, but nothing came out.

"The Gail is –"

"Not real," he said, pointing his finger again. "They're just –"

"Full of shit," J.J. said laughing.

"Right," Jack said, letting out a sudden snicker.

By dealing with the situation in this manner – by placating the boy – Jack was protecting his son. If he could make J.J. believe that the ghost or spirit or whatever she was, was just in his imbalanced TBI brain then maybe he wouldn't be as frightened.

Perhaps *both* of them wouldn't be so frightened.

But the truth was this: Jack Cleary *was* petrified. More than that. He felt – absurd as it may have sounded at first – that he and his son were haunted by...or better yet *possessed* by...his late wife. She had come back somehow to seek vengeance on all that Jack had done; this much he knew, and this he dreaded more and more each day.

Jack, in the same quiet tone as before, asked his son, "What did she say to you?" He cleared the phlegm in his throat. The crab continued to claw itself through his stomach. And he tasted that sour flavor...that infected sour mucus taste that always accompanied her presence. "In this nightmare of yours...did she *say* anything specific to you?" He cleared his throat again. Another sharp pain in the abdomen.

"Yes, Daddy."

Very gently, Jack asked, "What was it?"

"She said I'm going to die because of the sins of the father. *Real, real soon.*" J.J.'s eyes widened. "What are your *sins*, Daddy?"

Jack gulped and felt his heart palpitate. He sighed, then

said, "Bad dreams. Okay? They're only...*bad dreams*. Understand?" But he couldn't convince himself that this was true. He heard his own trembling voice: *Bad dreams. She's not real. Not real.*

J.J. stopped his hyperventilating. He suddenly became calm. He looked at his father with that horrific gaze that Jack had seen before: His eyes were bloodshot, looking like half-sucked candy fireballs.

Jack felt her inside of him, clutching onto his insides, and at that moment, while looking at his son (who was at that moment no longer his son), he knew that she was inside of him too. Invading him. Possessing him. He heard his voice speak to her: *Leave him alone. He can't handle this. Goddam you, Gail!*

"I won't sentence you to *The Hole* this time," Jack said diplomatically. "Just stop watching so much TV. That's why you're having these dreams. And don't eat right before bed. Do some reading for a change. And keep that dog quiet, too. I have lots of policeman work to do down here. Now go. And close the door. *Chop, chop.*"

"Okay, Daddy," was the robotic response he got.

The door closed.

Jack remained in that spot at the bottom of the stairs. He looked up at the door and suddenly found himself unable to move. A numbing cold, raw breeze ran through him. His body felt as though it had been shot up with Novocain.

"What do you want with us?" he asked her, only able to speak through his teeth.

"*You*, Kissin' Cousin. We have come for *you*."

Gail released herself from Jack's insides and made herself known by dissolving out of his chest...slowly; he was unable to breathe for a few seconds. She floated serpentine-style to the ceiling, then suspended herself in midair as if she were being held up by a harness. Her long, dirty blond braided hair swayed from left to right like little serpents, and she ejected her abnormally long, narrow and pointy tongue from that orifice of hers. Seconds later, she descended in the same serpentine fashion, swaying in small circular rotations that formed eddies of cold air, still flickering her tongue as she did so, eventually positioning herself directly in front of him.

From afar she looked undesirable, from close-up, she was beyond grotesque. Her face was covered with pock marks. By the time she was in her mid-twenties she had the face of a fifty-year-old woman; and by the time she reached her demise at the age of twenty-nine, she looked elderly. But at that moment she looked exceptionally ghastly – pale and decomposed – and that one-of-a-kind pungent metallic and strangely sweet stench that always accompanied her was worse than ever.

"Don't say that," Jack said. He closed his eyes, scrunching up that bulldog face of his, attempting to cast her out. "Get out! Out. Out!" He opened his eyes, but only found that she had moved closer to him. She was in his space.

"Don't say *what*?" she tantalized.

"That. That...*name*."

"You mean *kissin'*...cousin?" She moved closer; she was almost inside of him again. She smiled, her rotten incisors glowing in the available light.

"Shut up!" he growled.

"Surely," she said in an almost musical tone, "you haven't forgotten those Saturday afternoons in your Uncle Toby's shed – have you?"

Jack's father, Raymond, was the older brother of Gail's father, Tobias (Toby for short).

"You are not here."

She emitted more of that sweet metallic stench into the air, causing the cop to gag. He coughed vehemently, then gagged again, blocking his entire face with his forearm.

"Get...out..."

She snorted; she sounded like a sow in the mud. She dissolved inside him again, entering into the same spot in his chest where she exited earlier. The cold breeze turned icy.

Again, he couldn't breathe, couldn't move. His body had become petrified, literally. Sweat jetted out of his pours.

"To make the remaining days of your life...*un-bearable.*"

"Why?" He spoke through his teeth again.

Gail's throaty whispering voice echoed through his essence, the following words ringing at such a high frequency that he felt as though he would certainly explode. "Because, Jack, every dog must have its day. Every devil must account for his sins."

Jack moved his eyes as he followed the woman's aura – a ring of dusty light illuminated the garage. After this, he felt a squeezing in his chest, the symptoms of a major heart attack, the one he always dreaded. Jack Cleary's biggest fear was getting a heart attack – not so much because he couldn't handle the pain – but because he hated the idea of being out of control. Just like he was now. *This* more than likely explained why he had never indulged in mind-altering substances – and this included even the occasional glass of beer.

But at this instant he endured the crushing chest pain, heart palpitations and numbing, like he was being stabbed with tiny needles through every nerve in his body. With the little energy he had left, he gasped for air.

Jack knew he was paying for what had happened to her on March the sixth, seven years earlier. He had the entire story recorded on one of his cassettes. He had it filed under *G* for *Gail.*

After he had done what he had done with the remains of his wife, he sat in his cruiser outside the pet cemetery and delivered his monologue into the tape recorder, whispering slowly and methodically as if he were a detective in a film noir.

March 6, 1977, around 9:02pm. Gail returned home in

another one of those rages of hers. She had done this many times before, but tonight there was something different about her. The way she looked and the way she was acting, she was obviously laced up on something beyond the juice. She was out of control. Violent. More than usual. She cursed me and the day we got married. She cursed the fact that we were related; she even said she was repulsed by it. It always turned her on before; I couldn't understand what she was talking about. Then she brought up J.J. Blamed him for all her problems. Even before the accident, she always felt him to be a burden. Anyway, she started picking a fight, the way she always did in the past, but on this night, she decided to enhance it with theatrics. She slapped my face, kicked me in the shins, and twisted my...testicles...with those vice grip hands of hers. Then she took the gun from my holster, which was still around my waist, and waved it at me while screaming obscenities. Called me every name in the book. Filthy! She had her finger on the trigger and kept pointing the piece at my head. Said she was going to put me and that kid of ours out of our misery, but then in the next moment, she took the piece, then she opened her mouth and blew her brains out. I panicked. I woke up J.J. who had slept through all the noise and just got him out of the house as soon as possible. I called David Aaronson, my chief, and told him about the situation. He said he would take care of every-thing, told me not to worry, that he understood how unbal-anced she was. He knew I stayed with her only because we had J.J. And he knew what she felt about J.J. And he knew how I felt about my boy, knew I loved the unfortunate little bastard with all my heart. Aaronson is a good man...too bad he was killed three weeks later in that freak accident. Life just doesn't make sense sometimes. I only wish things were normal. *Normal like real people with real families are* normal. *I just want to make a difference in law enforcement. And I want to be a good model for my son who, despite his head injury, needs discipline and direction, which I feel I am giving him...*

The temperature in Jack's body lowered considerably and the heart symptoms subsided. Within a couple of minutes, he could move his body. But Gail was still there. She was facing him now. She transformed herself into a beautiful woman; this woman still resembled Gail but a Gail he had never seen before. No pock marks, and instead of those snake-like braids, she now had long, straight brown hair. And no more stench. There *was* a fragrance, however; it was sweet like honeysuckle...very inviting. Jack was enamored. Turned on. *What was going on?* And when she spoke, it wasn't in a throaty rasp...it was soft and kind of breathy, maybe like a Marilyn Monroe or Ann Margaret. It was no longer Gail. The lovely specimen in front of him spoke pragmatically; she was no longer a spook.

Or was she?

"You are quite the storyteller and performer, Jack Cleary. Quite the imagination. Where did you pick up that scenario – a movie from the forties? The devil takes on many roles, doesn't he? But your facts are a bit skewed, aren't they? Not to worry, though; we are all on to you. We know who you are and what you've done. To me. To Chief David Aaronson. And to the boy who pushed J.J. off of that building. You are going to pay for your sins Jack Cleary. One by one. Real soon. *Real, real soon.* You have made many enemies here. And you will make more."

With this line she rose up, began spinning around in those eddies, then dissolved through the window of the garage door.

For the rest of the night, Jack sat in his cruiser and listened to his tapes, thinking of what that beautiful woman had said to him. He began to cry, and when he closed his eyes, he clearly saw a memory from years ago he wanted to forget, that of him and his cousin Gail naked in his Uncle Toby's shed. Gail was getting ready to ask him to do something he had never done before...

89

Dirty, he thought. *Disgusting, filthy, impure and dirty!*
Then he heard what sounded like a giggle.
It was Gail; she was laughing at him.

JUNE 1984

S	M	T	W	R	F	S
					1	2
3	4	5	6	7	8	9
10	11	12	13	14	15	16
17	18	19	20	21	22	23
24	25	26	27	28	29	30

CHAPTER 11

THE INVALID AND
THE IMAGINIST

"M&M! M&M! *Michael Anthony Melanson!*" the voice screeched from the upstairs bedroom.

What the hell does she want now? Mike wondered. He was upstairs with her not ten minutes earlier with her dinner, her dessert, her camera (somehow it was still in one piece) and her priceless copy of the contemporary drama anthology.

Since her fall, Miss Julie had a number of innovative ideas for creating a portfolio of photographs in her bedroom. She was to call the future book *The Invalid: Perspectives of a Crippled Imaginist.* Since she was unable to solely commit to one art form – she knew she was an artist, but she could never see herself as strictly a photographer, an actor or even a TV personality – she labeled herself an *imaginist.* She once heard someone on TV who referred to himself as an *imaginist.* She couldn't remember who it was exactly – someone who wrote scholarly books and fiction, directed and acted in film and theater, and composed music. A real jack-of-all-trades, master of none. She could still hear the guy's smoky, flamboyant voice when she recalled these words of wisdom: "I create because I must. I can't stop. It's not about being talented or super-skilled in one thing. It's about creating because there is a *need* to create. End of story. I don't want to limit myself and say that I'm just a writer or an actor or a director or a musician. I am all of them. On the charts I may be incompetent in all of the fields, but I do know this: as an *imaginist*, I am the best in the racket."

When Mike left the room, his wife had been reading the end of *Miss Julie* aloud. She was propped up on her pillows, high enough so she could see her face in the mirror. Occasionally, she realized just how beautiful she was.

Into the mirror, she performed, changing facial expressions after each line: "*I can't repent, can't run away, can't stay, can't live – can't die! Help me now! Order me and I'll obey like a dog. Do me this one service, save my honor, save my name! You know what I should do but don't have the will to...you will it, you order me to do it!*"

She was reciting the last scene between Miss Julie and her servant, Jean.

Her left leg was in a brace. Even though the doctor (whom she kept calling Marcus Welby, M.D.; she insisted that the gray-haired man looked exactly like Robert Young in the TV show of the same name) told her the cast was not necessary, that at best she just had a minor sprain, something a little rest would cure in no time, Miss Julie insisted anyway.

"It's my leg – you don't know how much pain I'm in," she said. "I want the works. I can afford it. And I want it."

By "the works" she meant the best of the best – a cast with style and charm. And the doctor, a real humorless man that according to Miss Julie needed to learn the art of laughter, reluctantly signed this rather normal looking cast, *Marcus Welby, M.D.* She also got a pair of maroon designer crutches that complemented her jewel-toned ensemble.

When she walked out of the emergency room (ever so

dramatically, as if she had been in a near-fatal car accident or something) she spoke to Mike in a low monotone voice, which at first kind of frightened him. Then he realized it was just Julie being Julie, or Miss Julie being Miss Julie, he corrected himself. She said, "Well Keyes, you couldn't crack this one, could you? Maybe because the one you were looking for was too close to you. Right across the desk from you." Then to her husband: "Now you say, 'Closer than that, Walter.'"

Mike paused, then said the line to which his wife retorted, "Good boy. Now take me home." She later told him that this dialogue exchange was from the great classic film noir *Double Indemnity*, the movie with Fred MacMurray as insurance man Walter Neff who narrates his tragic story into a tape recorder (while on crutches) to his boss, the prophetic Keyes played by Edward G. Robinson, whom Miss Julie labeled as one of Hollywood's biggest little people. In the film, Neff and the *femme fatale* Phyllis, played by Barbara Stanwyck, plot to kill her husband over an insurance policy. The crutches were part of the murder scheme.

⊠ ⊠ ⊠ ⊠

During the invalid's bedridden days, Mike and Adam became her elected servants. She demanded that her son take a week off from school to assist her – and Mike, despite the fact that he was the town's police chief, needed to be home by three to relieve the young nursemaid of his duties. When he came home at that time, he put Jack Cleary in charge, something he felt safe about doing even though the people in town didn't like him; people never seemed to warm up to Jack and Mike could not understand why. Maybe it was because he was a little too ambitious at times, especially in the humble little crime free town of Fryebury Falls. But it would be during this time when Mike was at home attending to his wife that Jack

Cleary would crack the town's biggest crime: a drug ring.

When he returned to the bedroom, Miss Julie asked him to turn the TV on. "*S.O.S.* begins in one hour and I want to watch myself. And I want you and Adam to watch with me. It's so bizarre – I've never actually seen it. Can you believe that?" Then: "It's last week's show you know."

"Can I get you anything else?"

"Yes, servant," she said snickering, but Mike didn't seem to be amused. "Oh, lighten up, M&M. I was just joking. Don't be like that constipated Marcus Welby." Mike smiled. "There's my handsome man. Now, come over here and read the scene with me. You're going to play the part of Jean again. You're going to help me prepare for an acting comeback." (Then right after she said *comeback*, she heard herself in the voice of Gloria Swanson who played Norma Desmond in *Sunset Blvd*: "I *hate* that word. It's a *return*. A *return* to the millions of people who have never forgiven me for deserting the screen!") She continued: "I desperately need to get back into the theater. *Desperately!* Being held up here for the next few months will give me ample time to rehearse my skills, to sharpen my instrument. I see this accident, really, as a blessing in disguise."

The next several months? Mike thought and got a chill. *You barely twisted your ankle!*

"Someday, I promise you," she kept telling him, "I'll be up there in lights. When this ankle heals, I'll go audition again. And I'll be a free-lance photographer on the side. And I'll publish this book...*The Invalid: Perspectives of a Crippled and Enlightened Imaginist.* Ah, it'll be *mah-velous!*"

Her words seemed sincere enough, Mike thought, but also quite tragic, for he knew that she would *never* practice what she preached. Miss Julie could talk the talk, but when it came to walking the walk, well...that was a different thing entirely. He recalled a previous dialogue, one that always seemed to stick with him.

"Let's go to the city, M&M. I can become an actress like I've always dreamed of. And you can apply for that position in Bean Town. Then we'll wait a few years and graduate to the Big Apple. *Le Big Apple!* I'll be on Broadway where the neon lights are bright, and you'll be a full-fledged lieutenant at the NYPD. It'll be *mah-velous!*"

"I'm not a city cop, Jules. I belong here. In Fryebury Falls. I have a responsibility to this town. A duty."

"It's *dooty* all right," she snapped. "You're such a *low-down townie* with no concept of the outside world. What are you afraid of? Success? It's not like money's an issue."

True; money *wasn't* an issue. Honestly...how many people could get up and change their lives at any moment without worrying about their finances? But Mike Melanson didn't care that he was a rich man – not really. For him, money was not a primary concern, despite the fact that he had more of it than anyone in town could ever spend in a lifetime. When they got married, a prenuptial agreement was never even brought up, even with a dowry worth millions. The truth of the matter was this: Miss Julie needed someone like Mike, a low-down townie with no concept of the real world, because – and this she would never realize about herself – she *too* was a low-down townie with no concept of the real world.

To his wife he said, "I'm not stopping you from pursuing your dreams. I can't hold you here against your will. We live close enough to Boston and...New York. You can fly there as often as you need to." Then, in one of Mike's moments of insight, something that inexplicably happened from time to time, he said: "We're rich enough where we don't *have* to move. Ever think of that?"

It sounded logical enough. They *were* filthy rich. Why they didn't live in a sumptuous place like Beverly Hills – or Italy for that matter – was beyond comprehension. Even Adam could have been accounted for in her absence if she suddenly became an acclaimed Broadway star.

But Miss Julie wouldn't budge. Her excuse: "I won't have my son raised by nannies. Plus, what about *us*? When would *we* be together? You already spend too much time in that stink-hole office of yours. When are you going to get some sense and quit that racket? *No*. If you stay, then I stay. End of story. I'll rot in this town until I die before I sacrifice my family."

Translation: Julie Jill Melanson was afraid of that outside world.

They finished reading the scene together. And although not an actor, Mike performed Jean quite well. He was getting good at reading and interpreting lines because he had been asked so often to perform with his wife. Mike actually quite enjoyed these performances. He felt important, like he was cultured or something. Plus, it was during these times that his high-maintenance partner would remain calm and relaxed. She loved acting, and she loved that her husband was there accommodating her needs. They were holding hands when the scene ended. She asked where Adam was. Mike said he was in his room drawing.

She smiled. "That boy with that *fecund* imagination of his. He's going to do marvelous things in this life. Wait and see. *He* won't stay in this stifling, suffocating, stuffy minute town his whole life, I assure you of that." Then she got this heavy, pressing feeling in her stomach; it was like a surge of gas moving like a juggernaut through her system; it was most unsettling but lasted only a few seconds. Then: "Since I won't be hosting *S.O.S.* for a while, I wonder what Billy will air in this time slot." She snorted. "Hopefully not those abysmal high school dances. Or *worse*: one of those disgusting plays that the schools try to put on. It amazes me what people *don't* know... *holy merde!* How people can be so ignorant when it comes to putting on a play. They think *anyone* can act and direct. *Au contraire!* Not everyone can do theater, you know. Not correctly anyway." She paused, her eyes widening. Miss Julie was in one of her playful modes. "*I know,*" she said, squeezing Mike's hand. "I'll tell Billy we can do the show right here. From the bed. A la John Lennon and Yoko Ono. Wouldn't that be a hoot? We'd have cameras here. What do you think?"

Mike smiled. *What a beauty you are, Julie. I mean, Miss Julie. What a beauty. I love you. Lord only knows why you love me back.*

She squeezed his hand. "Go get the boy, will you?"

He was already halfway out the door when she called him back.

"Will you get me some popcorn? No butter and a splash of salt."

"I know how you like it," he said grinning.

She held up her glass. "And can you fill me up with more Tab?"

He obliged.

She smiled and then said, "Good boy."

Within fifteen minutes, the Melansons were sitting on the bed, Miss Julie sandwiched in between her two boys.

The nine-year-old, who was very protective of his "sick" mother, took a hold of her hand, which made the woman smile. The little boy had a certain magic touch, a healing quality about him. She had, on many occasions, told him that she felt he was very in-tuned with his energy, that he possessed psychic qualities. Julie knew this because she herself was well aware of her surrounding energies and psychic powers – the good and the bad ones – which is why she often said that she went a bit crazy from time to time. And Grandpa Lucien had told him pretty much the same thing...that he could become a great vet someday, a great healer.

With her other hand, Miss Julie took a hold of her husband's massive bicep, which was, impressively, more muscle than flab, and for a moment she forgot about her injury.

The Melansons sat attentively in front of the fifty-two-inch TV until it was time to watch the local celebrity talk about the scandal regarding a former child actor named Bobby something or other. Mike never heard his name before, but apparently he had been in a number of Hollywood films and personally knew stars like Boris Karloff, Bette Davis, Joan Crawford and Vincent Price. He was also the voice in a number of Disney cartoons (when Mike heard this, he tried to conjure up those cartoon girls who were certainly *not* Disney characters). The actor had been a homosexual, one who claimed to have had affairs with Cary Grant, James Dean and Roddy McDowell. This particular scandal involved the alleged homophobic murder of his partner, a likable character actor who was apparently in over two-hundred Warner Brothers films.

Once, Miss Julie did a piece on the notorious rivalry between Bette Davis and Miriam Hopkins. Another story involved the overdose of silent film actor Wallace Reid, which contributed to the Hollywood Production Code in the 1930s. Each week was a different half-hour long story narrated by Miss Julie, replete with a series of publicity stills projected on the screen behind her. Miss Julie donated a little fortune to F.F.T.V., which allowed for advanced studio equipment that Billy Ashburnham would never have been able to afford. Primarily, this equipment had been used to enhance *S.O.S.* with lots of graphics and other effects that weren't really needed for this type of program.

The show began. It was the one from the previous week, her last show before the fall.

Miss Julie was appalled.

"Oh *merde!* I don't look like that, do I? *Yuck, yuck, yuck!* It must be the lighting. And do I *really* sound like that? It must be the sound system. I have to talk to Billy about that. *Abysmal.* And look at my hair! Turn it off, turn it off, I can't take it!"

CHAPTER 12

WHAT GOES UP, MUST COME DOWN

George Pearson sat on the edge of the red bench that over-looked the waterfall. He swore to himself he would be sober the next time he met up with his best friend, but he just couldn't do it. Not this time around.

Every Friday morning, he and the chief of police would meet in Günter's Millyard. In the colder weather, they'd meet at Rodney's Donut Hole in downtown Fryebury Falls.

The men had been friends since they were five. They grew up together in the same neighborhood (on Hill Street, a few miles from Baker Street), played baseball together, went to school together and smoked their first joint together in 1961 in a remote section of the woods known as the Stone Crusher, aptly named because in this location there was a gruesome medieval-looking machine that someone said was once used to crush stones. Nobody ever attempted to move this stone crusher; it's as if the horrific antique belonged there. Over the years, kids had attributed great powers to this stone crusher, like people had done for the waterfall. In fact, it was eleven-year-old Sammy Pearson, who, during one of his many creative moments, gave mythical powers to this rusty old machine. "It's a ghost machine. Back in the early 1900s, the machine was owned by an evil old man named Jeff Krebs. When he died, his spirit inhabited the stone crusher. Then *he* became the machine. And because Krebs was such a horrible old man, he went to hell but was rejected by Satan who didn't consider him evil enough, so he forced him back up to Earth as a demon to roam the woods and abduct and kill little children. After he abducted enough kids, then maybe Satan would readmit him into hell. But in the meantime, old Krebs remained in the woods, in the machine, in the stone crusher, waiting to lure innocent kids into his powers."

In 1959, a young girl was hit by a car and killed on Hill Street. According to the powers of the legend, she was overcome by the force of Krebs. And whenever tragedy hit the little town of Fryebury Falls, some insisted it was because of this demon who lived in the Stone Crusher.

As kids, George and Mike were inseparable. They did *everything* together.

Miss Julie, however, never liked George. Even before he killed his family in that freak car accident, before he struck Derek Hamilton in the jaw, before he took to the bottle and began hallucinating unworldly people and events, something about him didn't feel right with her.

"Anyone *that* perfect has to be putting us on," Miss Julie would say. "There's a darker side to him. And something tragic, too. He will not live long."

Incidentally, Miss Julie had said similar things about Jack Cleary.

"Watch out for him. I've told you before and I'll tell you again, there's something evil about him. He won't live long either."

Miss Julie's insights, her predictions (or *premonitions,* as she called them), would become her most impressive characteristic as well as her worst downfall. She credited these premonitions with what she called her gift. "I have a gift," she would say, "a gift of clairvoyance. If I needed the money, then I'd make a fortune as a medium."

Years earlier she had attended the Erhard Seminar Training Program, which allowed people back in the 1970s to "tear themselves down and put themselves back together again." Or so they claimed. Those who attended the spiritual experience – like actress Valerie Harper and other celebrities – were associated with the epiphany of "getting it." And clearly, Miss Julie was one of those people who would verbosely exclaim, "I've got it!" Then she would add: "But take it from me, being in-tuned to the energy around us is not always such a treat. Where there's good energy, there's also evil energy. And we all want to be careful about knowing too much about our own destinies. That's why I try to shut it out when I can." When Mike asked her once what she sensed about him, she said, "You M&M are an enigma. You carry yourself as this low-down townie, but somewhere within you there is a complicated being that I haven't quite figured out yet. You are a survivor, that's all I know. You are resourceful and possess a quiet, almost silent wisdom. Despite your poor health habits, you will live a long life." Then suddenly breaking the intensity: "That's what I love about you. You're complicated, but you don't know it."

For years Miss Julie had been saying that something terrible was going to happen in a major U.S. city – Los Angeles or New York – in the next twenty years or so. "Not long after the turn of the century, thousands of people will die in a catastrophic event. It will start like the Second World War. Like Pearl Harbor. It'll be the beginning of World War III. But it'll be like no war we have ever known. And then it will be followed by a global pandemic. Like the Spanish Flu at the end of WWI."

When Mike asked her what this so-called *terrible event* was going to be, she said she didn't know details like that. Being clairvoyant didn't mean you had empirical answers, she explained. "It's not about being God. It's about tapping into your surrounding energies and listening to the guides." Then she cryptically whispered, "For instance, I know that something evil awaits me *real, real soon* and it really scares the shit out of me, M&M. And don't get me started about our beautiful little boy. He's an old soul, you know. And you know they say about old souls, don't you? That scares the shit out of me even more." Then with tears in her eyes: "I can't think about it...I just can't think about it..."

Actually, these words kind of scared the shit out of Mike as well.

At one point, Miss Julie compared her skill for predicting things to the great Nostradamus. "I was Nostradamus in another life," she reported.

Nostradamus, Mike thought elusively, *wasn't that an old silent movie that Julie had me sit through once...the one about an old vampire?*

George was wearing a pair of wrinkled blue jeans that had two small rips in the knees, a Montreal Expos cap and a plain gray t-shirt that he had worn for two or three days straight. It was Saturday, the second day of June and even though it was only eight in the morning, the sun was out, and it was already quite hot and humid.

He was transfixed on Niagara Two whose running waters were so piercing that he got a ringing in his ears. This temporary tinnitus transformed into what sounded like chimes or bells. He needed a drink. Or at least a glass of water for now to get that pasty texture out of his parched mouth. He spit on the brick pavement, and from his mouth emerged a titanium white-textured fluid that looked more solid than liquid. In the center of the cloud of saliva there was a dark yellow nucleus, a remnant from his insides that at the time looked quite awesome; he stared at it for a while and imagined this spit being the most profound biological phenomenon of our existence: for that moment he was convinced that he was staring at the formation of the beginning of life on Earth, the "organic soup" as it has been called in Biology texts, the first cells ever created, the catalyst and source of life as we know it. As a biologist, however, George knew it in more rarefied terms, a language he loved to speak: "This primordial soup describes the aqueous solution of organic compounds that accumulated in primitive waters of early Earth, a result of endogenous abiotic syntheses and extraterrestrial delivery by cometary meteoric collisions – many think the first living organisms evolved this way."

Then he looked upward, into the eye of the waterfall and for a moment it became a glass skyscraper that suddenly exploded, and he heard what sounded like the theme to *2001: A Space Odyssey*...then it turned back into the waterfall and then he caught a glimpse of another image through the translucent water. The sunlight bounced off the waterfall and there it was – a perfect little portal of sorts that revealed a myriad of colors, but they were not the colors of the rainbow; they were different forms of the color spectrum...deeper and darker oranges, purples and other jewel tones like maroon, reds and yellows all surrounding a textured azure sky. This transformed into a bright green meadow or field that seemed to expand infinitely with hundreds, maybe thousands of different exotic plants. Off to one side it looked like there was a greenhouse with a Byzantine-like design. And off to another side, a colony of marine creatures – tropical fish and coral reefs all within a massive aquarium. And off in the distance – running toward him – it was Alison, who looked just like she did when they were in college together. He even caught a whiff of that hand cream she used to wear, a scent that always reminded him of her. And quite suddenly, a college-aged George himself appeared in the image, holding hands with the running girl.

George reached up at the waterfall, but as he did, the entire world faded out – dissolved like a shot in a film – and what remained *now* was only the running waters of Niagara Two.

The sounds of water gave way to sound bites of a song he remembered:

> *What goes up, must come down*
> *Spinning wheels, got to go 'round*
> *Talkin' 'bout your troubles, it's a cryin' sin*
> *Ride a painted pony let the spinnin' wheels spin*
>
> *You got no money and you got no home*
> *Spinnin' wheel, all alone*
> *Talkin' 'bout your troubles and you never learn*
> *Ride a painted pony, let the spinnin' wheel turn*
>
> *Someone is waiting just for you*
> *Spinnin' wheel, spinnin' true*
> *Drop all your troubles by the riverside*
> *Catch a painted pony, let the spinnin' wheel ride*

It was that Blood, Sweat and Tears song. A song he always liked. He liked how the band had a unique way of blending two very different genres of music: Rock-n-Roll and Big Band Jazz. He considered the lyrics as he sang the song to himself again and was suddenly moved. He related to the words...metaphors and all. To him, riding the painted pony was exactly what he was doing. Horses, a symbol of virility and sexuality, are painted, or in this case, for someone who always loved to play with song lyrics: *tainted*. He was riding the *tainted* pony while the spinning wheels turn...that is, while life moves on with no remorse. He thought of the lyrics, then the band's name: *What goes up, must come down. Blood, sweat and Tears.*

Story of my fucking life, he eventually concluded sheepishly.

He continued staring into the gushing waters that took the shape of a purple mass: The mass morphed into a purple dress and the dress morphed into a little girl with flowing blond hair and piercing blue eyes.

"Where is your mother?" he asked her. "I saw her through the waterfall a minute ago."

The girl smiled, not answering.

George whispered the following words: "Please leave me alone, Abbie-Girl. *Please.* This is torture. I wish I could take back what happened." He looked down and a tear from his eye dripped like water from a faucet onto the pavement.

> *Someone is waiting just for you*
> *Spinnin' wheel, spinnin' true*
> *Drop all your troubles by the riverside*
> *Catch a painted pony, let the spinnin' wheel ride*

The girl flew above him in a circular motion; her image resembled a cyclone. As she did this, George's vision became blurred; he turned away and looked into the waterfall again. He saw nothing but a series of Venn Diagrams, all different, replete with overlapping colors. Occasionally one of the circles transformed into several images – images of Alison giving birth, images of Alison breast feeding, images of young Abigail coming of age, images of Alison holding young Abigail, images of Alison and Abigail on a family picnic, then of George running with his Abbie-girl on the beach, then more Venn Diagrams that blinded him. He closed his eyes, but the images only got stronger and more rapid. The juxtaposition of the circles and colors and images gave George a debilitating headache.

He got the spins.

Abigail's voice echoed: *Kill the devil...you are the chosen one...real, real soon...we love you...we'll see you...real, real soon.*

He was spinning out of control. Spinning. Spinning. Around and around and around and around...

⊠ ⊠ ⊠ ⊠

There was a hot, steaming pile of vomit on the brick path underneath the immobile body collapsed on the bench. George's head and arms were hanging over the side, all three body parts almost touching the pavement.

This was quite the sight for Mike Melanson, who was carrying two coffees and a bag of doughnuts from Rodney's Donut Hole.

When he saw the body, then the puke, he panicked. *Was he dead? Shit.* Inadvertently, he conjured up Miss Julie's voice: *One day you are going to wake up and go to that man's funeral. I hate to say it, but I can feel his doom.*

Damn you Julie and your predictions, Mike answered.

Mike danced around the puddle of throw-up, placing the cups of coffee and the bag of doughnuts off to one side near a neighboring bench, then went over to his friend and shook him on the shoulder.

No response.

Not today. Not now!

Mike repeated the action, this time shaking George more forcefully, almost belligerently. *Not now. Not today. Please. Please!*

Then he heard a ringing in his ears. Bells. Chimes.

Miss Julie's voice: "Not to say that I told you so, M&M, but..."

"Mike," George said, covering his face with his arms, blinded by the sunlight shining through the willows. He turned on his back, straightened out the cap that was nearly falling off his head, and said, "I must have...dozed off."

"Why don't you come over to this bench? I've got some coffee and doughnuts. Can your stomach handle them?" He helped George get to his feet, straightening the hat on his head. "You're an *elb* today." He was referring to the Montreal logo – the curvy *M* in a fine cursive font made it look like the letters *elb* connected together. This had been something they joked about as kids.

"Better than being a Blue Jay."

"That's for sure. *Canadian*." He handed his friend the cup. "Here, drink this; it'll put hair on your chest."

"It's good," George said, taking several little sips.

"Of course it is. It's Najarian."

George hung his head and said, "I'm sorry, Mike."

"Are you okay?" Mike asked. No apology needed.

"Yeah, I think."

George took another sip of the coffee and thought about how fortunate he was in at least one capacity: having Mike Melanson as a friend. The chief never judged him. At least he never showed it. Actually, both men, even as kids, seemed to always have a mutual respect for one another. Even when they argued, they never *really* argued. To George this was refreshing – refreshing because he could always tell Mike exactly what he was feeling.

"The forces are strong here today," George said. He had told his friend about his recent hallucinations – about Abigail and her visits – but he never got into the actual details – and Mike never asked him to.

Mike didn't answer. He may have not been judgmental on one level, but on another level, it perturbed him to watch his boyhood pal deteriorating like this – to lose all sense of reality

– to be delusional – to speak a language he no longer understood. In a way, however, the chief *could* relate to him. After all, he had been seeing things too. *Outrageous things.* Not just those cartoon images (the brunette and the redhead were still on his mind from time to time), but other things. Visions. Unpleasant ones. Ones that would contribute to his own deterioration in later months.

But the Chief of Police was not ready to reveal any of these thoughts to George...best friend or not. They were just too deranged, discomfiting, disconcerting...

Mike thought: *The forces are strong here today.* What does that mean? *Would these forces be similar to the things I've been witnessing? What would Miss Julie have to say about these forces?* It didn't matter. Mike didn't need to know. All he cared about at that moment was his friend's physical well-being.

George broke the silence. Holding the coffee cup with both of his hands – as if he were trying to keep himself warm despite the humid weather – he said, "It's still hard, Mike." He placed the cup to his lips but didn't drink. "One minute I think I can conquer it...I mean *really* conquer it...cold turkey...but then I'm taken back into that circle. That *fucking*...vicious circle!"

"Finish the coffee; it'll sober you up."

George took a sip. "How's Julie doing? How's her...what is it...her leg?"

"Ankle. She's okay, you know. She's...she's okay."

Although George disliked Mike's wife as much as she disliked him, he said, "That's good to hear."

"I got a couple of Sox tickets," Mike said, pulling out two tickets from the breast pocket of his uniform.

George studied them as if he had never seen baseball tickets before.

"Crowley got some extra ones. He and Adam Bonner

111

couldn't go this weekend." Mike smiled. "They had a wedding to go to." George grinned as he thought about the Fryebury Falls everyman – police officer, church Deacon, Council on the Aging coordinator, baseball coach and umpire and summer camp director – the man who never got married but always did things with this fellow named Bonner, a lawyer who had his own practice in Newburyport, Massachusetts. The poor guy could never become an ordained priest, since his mother had him illegitimately. But he always joked about it: "Sometimes I can be a real *bastard,*" he would say.

"Who they playing?" George asked.

Without saying anything, Mike motioned toward the tickets.

George squinted and even though the print was blurry, he could clearly see that the Red Sox were playing the Yankees. "Shit." He grinned awkwardly. "Maybe someday they'll make the Series and beat the piss out of them. I'd love to live to see that day I tell ya."

"Julie predicts that they'll win the series again twenty years from now. Not just one but a string of them. She said the same thing about the Pats. Imagine that? Be nice, wouldn't it?" Then: "I'll call you tomorrow with more details. I think Julie will be okay for a few hours without me on Sunday."

"She won't be..."

"She'll be fine," Mike said almost curtly.

Then George said quietly, in a melancholy tone, "It must be nice to have someone." He hung his head.

Mike turned away, focusing a second on the pile of vomit that had now stopped steaming.

Silence.

"Hey," George said looking up. "Ted Williams or Roger Maris?"

Mike smiled, looking up. "Don't start."

It had been an ongoing argument since high school, back

in the early 1960s, a few years after Roger Maris hit sixty-one homers in one season, beating Babe Ruth's record of sixty.

⊠ ⊠ ⊠ ⊠

The seniors were on the bench in between innings at their high school baseball game.

George spoke. "You're telling me you think there's a better hitter than Williams?"

"I never liked Williams," Mike said spitting into his glove.

"How can you not like him?"

"He's overrated."

"Overrated?" George's voice carried as the other players and some of the spectators observed the friendly altercation. "Ted Williams is the best hitter this game has ever known. End of story. What kind of Sox fan are you?"

"I am a Sox fan. I just don't like him. He's...arrogant."

"What the hell does that have to do with anything? *Arrogant*! I'm talking about the facts. Williams had 521 homers! If he didn't go into the service – oh, man..."

Mike said, "I like Maris."

"Maris is a hotdog. .260 batting average. 250 homers."

"What are you, *blitzed*? He's got the *record*. When did Williams ever hit 61 in a season?"

"When did Maris ever bat *.406* in a season? Plus, Williams had a lifetime average of *.362*. That's insane."

"*You're* insane."

George sighed and smirked at his friend, then tossed his glove at him. He had to have been pulling his leg! "Hang it up, man!"

⊠ ⊠ ⊠ ⊠

When Mike left, George remained on the bench watching the waterfall. He thought about what Mike's wife had predicted ...that the Red Sox would win the World Series in twenty years. That would make him fifty-eight in 2004.

The bench that he was sitting on was no longer in Günter's Millyard facing Niagara Two; he was now in Fenway Park, in the dugout. The top of the waterfall opened up and there it was: The baseball diamond at night...and in the distance...on the left field side...the Green Monster! And underneath the lights, kicking the dirt off the pitcher's mound rubber, it was *him*...George Pearson in a Red Sox uniform. He was glowing, a bright yellow aura surrounding his image. He sprung off the rubber like a ballet dancer, and released the pitch...a magnificent curveball. The batter jumped out of the batter's box, only to watch the pitch glide over the inside corner, just barely making the strike zone.

"*Stee-riiike three!*" yelled the fat, jolly umpire, who turned to his side, clenched his fists and pulled his right fist in to his chest. It was all a big dance, just like George always told his players: from the way the pitcher winds up, to the way the batter stands in the box, to the way an infielder plays a ground ball or a line shot, to the dramatic style of the umpire's performance; it was all great theater and great storytelling.

As a pitcher, that was one of George Pearson's strengths: he really knew how to hit those corners.

The sound of running water became a crowd of forty thousand fans cheering, emphasizing the two syllables of his name. *Pearson, Pearson, Pearson...*

George Pearson, hypnotized by the world he saw, smiled uncontrollably. He got butterflies in his stomach. There was hope for him after all. How did he know? He *just* knew. It was his own personal truth. He recalled the day back in his twenties when he discovered this truth. It was after the fifth time he read Plato's *Phaedrus*, the ancient Greek dialogue where Socrates and young Phaedrus discuss the significance of love, rhetoric, writing, eros, madness, the soul and...*truth*. To George, truth comes to you unannounced; in its simplest form, it is something you simply *know*. As a biologist, he never simply relied on empirical data; this life science was also innately linked to classical philosophy and spiritual beliefs.

The truth and essence of life.

The cheers subsided into the sounds of rushing water, and then Fenway Park dissolved into the robust waters of Niagara Two.

He was now at peace.

Biological nirvana. Phantasmagoria.

It was time to uproot that hair from the dog that bit him.

Sobriety, damn it!

It could happen. It *will* happen. Today. Right now. Cold turkey...

CHAPTER 13

ANOTHER LIFE

Whenever Maygyn Pearson stayed with her father on Pine Street, her Uncle George almost always remained in his room...hidden like some cat under a bed. He didn't want to interfere. He also did his damndest not to carry on like a drunken ass in the presence of his pretty little niece whom he always had a difficult time facing. Maybe it was because she reminded him of what he once lost, that she symbolized the daughter he never got to see grow up – or maybe he felt in some way she was passing judgment on him, like her mother had done.

Or maybe he was jealous of his brother; after all, he had a daughter who was alive.

George left his door slightly ajar. He stood on all fours as he peered out of the crack, able to see part of the girl's bare leg and her smooth, tanned hand resting on her knee. She was wearing three rings that glowed in the available light; one was green, the other red, and the other silver.

He listened to the conversation.

"...but I want to stay with you. Doesn't that mean anything?" Maygyn looked up at her father who had just balanced his cigarette in the opening of a Coke can.

"Yes, it *does* mean something. It means a lot. But you can't. Your mother and I came to a mutual agreement about seeing you. No custody battles. It doesn't do anyone any good. We've been down this road before, Maygyn. I'm not sure what you're expecting of me. Things are very complicated."

"That's what you always say. *Complicated.*" The girl was impatient. *Stop talking to me like I'm a child.*

"And this is what *you* always say right after you and your mother lock horns." Maygyn looked away. "Don't you think this isn't hard on me? It's not easy...any of it. Your mother and I need to talk about a lot of things...and we're not communicating very well right now. We need...I don't know...a little more time...lots of time...I just don't know."

"Aren't you getting a divorce?" Maygyn was abrupt. *Is this what she wanted to happen?*

"I don't know," he answered, raising his voice more than he intended to. "There's a lot of legal matters that need attending to, and quite frankly, I don't think we're in a position to do that now."

"Can't you just make it work?" She asked this not so much to be hopeful, but in a more matter-of-fact tone as if she had some kind of wisdom on marriage: *You married one another. You had a child together. You have a contract. Why don't you just fucking grow up and take responsibility?*

"May," Sam said, leaning in toward her as if telling her a secret, "Your mother and I are very different. Sometimes – no matter how hard you work at it – it just doesn't...*work.* You can't force something that's not there anymore." He paused and then as if to himself, he added: "Nothing lasts forever..." Pause. "Sometimes it's nobody's fault."

Sam lifted the girl's chin up, making her face him. Gently he said, "You wouldn't want to live here. It's...look around... this is a bachelor pad...it's not a home for...a young woman.

You need a real house to grow up in. And you have that...with your mother." Then he added with a bizarre, crooked smile that did not become him (even though he had a good set of teeth, he had no bite, so when he smiled, it looked as though he had no teeth): "And we still get to hang out quite often, don't we?"

Maygyn looked at her father and then instantaneously turned away. Her father's words "not a home for a *young woman*" bothered her because the truth of the matter was this: she did not *feel* like a young woman. In fact, for going on a year or so, Maygyn Pearson was convinced that in addition to being female, she also felt like she identified with being a male...but not completely. She still felt like she was mostly female, but with a touch – maybe a bit *more* than a touch – of maleness as well. And she knew for sure that she was attracted to boys. It was – to use her father's own words – *complicated*. She knew she was not ready to tell anyone about how she was feeling.

"Look," Sam said after a long pause, "lots of kids have separated parents. It's not the end of the world." He thought of his own father, the abandoner that he was. "And sometimes it's for the best. We both love you. You know that, don't you? But we just don't..." He cleared his throat and went for his cigarette and, before inhaling it, said, "Sometimes it's just for the best."

She scowled. "You smoke too much. Don't you care about yourself? About getting cancer?"

Sam wiped a tear that was dripping down her face. She could smell the combination of stale cigarettes and after-shave lotion on his fingers.

A long pause.

Then: "Dad?"

"Yeah?"

"I have something to ask you."

"Okay."

"I have to know, and don't lie to me either."

"What's going on?"

"Why did you and Mother separate? – *really*?"

He took a second to process the question, and another second to interpret the tone. *What was she asking?* Actually, he knew *exactly* what she was asking.

"I told you before. Sometimes things don't –"

"Come on, Dad!"

"What?"

"The real reason."

The real reason, he thought sheepishly. *Oh, my. The real reason.*

Bad John's voice played in his head: *The American Dream is a facade...a front. It isn't real...*

"I...don't know what you want me to say. Your mother and I...we don't...get along anymore...she..."

"Why?"

"What do you mean *why*, we're? –"

"Is she a *lesbian*?"

Sam looked at the wall. Bad John peeked out from behind the bars of the jail and smiled almost sadistically. Then he disappeared.

Silence.

Sam gulped. He picked up his pack of cigarettes, his fingers fondling the tops of the filters. When he noticed that he was fidgeting – and that his daughter was watching him nervously finger those cigarettes – he abruptly tossed them down on the coffee table. He smiled even more awkwardly than he did before. "You're right – they're going to kill me." More silence. "Where did you hear that, May?"

"I don't like that," she said.

"Don't like *what*?"

"You calling me that name."

"*May?*" She nodded. "Since when? Haven't I always called you that? You want me to call you by your full name? *May-gyn?*"

She shook her head, clicked her tongue and sighed. Then, after another rather long pause: "Is she a slut?"

"Jesus Christ, May," he said waving his hand, signaling for her to keep quiet, but it was really quite pointless, for George could hear everything. In a loud whisper: "Sorry. Maygyn. Right?" A longer beat. Then: "Where are you getting all of this?"

"Did she go to bed with Jack Cleary? Is she with Cheryl Benigni? Is that why you're separated?"

"Stop it!" Sam went for the cigarette this time. The girl was glaring at him. *Oh, Jesus! That countenance!* he almost said aloud. She looked just like her mother sitting there with that *look from hell*: her eyes wide open; her nostrils flared like a bull (it was as if you could look into her nose); and that bizarre, crooked movement of the lips. It was a little Moira Davis! Remarkable, Sam thought, that his daughter could replicate her mother's idiosyncrasies. As a writer he had always been a great observer of people and their habits – like the way *his* mother used to twist her lip to the left and bite down on it as she did her crossword puzzles – or the way his brother George would squint like a cat when he'd listen to people talk – or like the way his geometry teacher would tap his bald head with two of his fingers as if they were drumsticks, a seemingly nervous habit he did even when he wasn't talking.

"Well?" The girl was ruthless. "Lisa Began says she is. Micky Nyman told Melissa Walton that she was a slut. I heard them talking in the halls."

Sam looked outside, blew his smoke toward the window, saw his *Another Life* character smirking at him from outside, then turned to face his daughter who was staring directly at him, and began. "Your mother apparently likes...men and women both. Okay? Is that what you wanted me to tell you? Is that what you wanted me to *confirm*?" He turned toward the window again; he seemed angry, but his anger wasn't directed toward his daughter; it wasn't even so much directed toward his wife at that moment. At that moment it was a general disappointment that manifested itself like a sullen rage. "And as far as any relationships between Cheryl Benigni and Jack Cleary – well, let's just say there's truth to it. I don't know how your friends found out, but I guess we're in a small town and, well, you know how that goes." Pause. He was no longer talking to a fourteen-year-old. He smoked. Absurdly he recalled that quotation from the philosopher Immanuel Kant, the one that he used at the beginning of *Another Life*: "The nice thing about living in a small town is that when you don't know what you're doing, someone else does."

Maygyn was silent.

"Be careful what you wish for," Sam said.

Maygyn remained silent.

And so did Sam.

During this silence, Sam tried to imagine Moira fucking Cheryl. He just couldn't do it. The thought of it could at *least* be sexy, couldn't it? But it wasn't. The truth of the matter was this: he simply didn't find Cheryl Benigni remotely attractive. He found her butch. Rugged like a man. A pretty boy. He wasn't into pretty boys.

Then he thought of Moira and Jack. That backstabbing motherfucker Jack Cleary, who once called himself a friend. A charming guy, a funny guy. A single father taking care of his beloved brain-injured boy after the tragic death of his wife. They had cookouts together, drank together, told stories together. (According to Sam, Jack Cleary must have been invaded by the spirit of Jerzy "the Tall" Wysocki when he moved into the house on Brown Ave, because he, like the old

Polish politician, was a natural storyteller.)

And during all this time, he was banging his wife!

Kill the bastard, he heard his character say in his strong Greek dialect. *Kill him like I killed Dorian Ross. He deserves to die. Do it. I'll show you how. It's easy. Come on. Another life awaits you, Pearson. If you don't do it, someone else will.*

The writer pictured the cop's massacred body as he always did – dismembered and scattered on the garage floor, axed to death by his own hands.

Then another image of Cleary's dead body on the garage floor – tied up and gagged, propped up against the back of his cruiser – not dismembered, but sliced up beyond recognition.

Maygyn still didn't speak. *Was she in a state of shock? Was she angry? Was she relieved that her father told her all this?*

She became nauseous again, worse than ever. She looked away and focused on a black-and-white photograph of a baseball diamond on the wall by the window. The photograph got blurry and then she turned away. Now she was really sick.

She excused herself and went into the bathroom to vomit. When she finally hung her head over the toilet bowl, however, nothing came out. Dry heaves. She closed the toilet seat, then sat on the cover like it was a stool. She looked at the white shower curtain and suddenly an image projected onto it. It was a place. It was gorgeous – dark green lawns, a stream, birds chirping... and then beyond the stream there was something there, lurking in the background. It was blurry for a minute, then it became a shadow of some sort. This black and gray shadow took on no definite shape or form; it was large and looming. Then she heard what sounded like a swarm of bees buzzing. This dissolved into the faint whisper of a deep voice that said, *Someday, but not yet.* Then the whisper transformed into the light sound of a gentle breeze; to Maygyn it sounded like someone breathing.

And then she shivered, like a jolt of electricity had passed through her body. She went over into the mirror and stared at herself intently until her reflection blurred, transforming into the face David Marino. After a few seconds, this image blurred, and then she was looking at herself again.

Sam lit another cigarette, not realizing that he had another one still burning on the top of the Coke can.

George tiptoed out of the bedroom and asked Sam if everything was okay.

"Not really," Sam said. "She knows about her mother and Cheryl. And about Cleary."

"She didn't know before?" George asked.

"I don't know...maybe she did." Sam was still looking out the window.

"She going to be okay in there?"

"Yeah," Sam muttered. "She'll be okay."

George took a cigarette from Sam's pack.

He made an oath to remain sober for the rest of the evening.

CHAPTER 14

PURITY, LAW & ORDER AND PEACE

Jack Cleary watched Moira Davis from the side window in the garage. The window was a glass square that from afar looked like the image sensor of a camera. It was the perfect size for him to spy on his neighbor with those high-resolution binoculars of his. The one drawback to doing this, however, was that he had to position the binoculars in an upward angle because of the height of the window (it was about seven feet high...too tall for Jack to be able to look outside from just standing and not really tall enough where he needed a lift to boost him up); this put a strain on his neck, but in a way he liked it; it was a reminder that he *was* in fact, spying on her...concealing himself from her. It was all worth it, though. The low angle shot actually gave him a better perspective on Moira Davis's parts: her bare feet with toenails painted green (or was it blue?); her leg and knee where the guitar rested; and her hands with those long, narrow fingers. He got butterflies in his stomach.

He couldn't hear what she was playing – it didn't matter, he never liked her music anyway, or the lifestyle that went with it. It was dirty – stank of loud noises, cigarettes, drugs, seedy people...He hated this filth, this sordid world of hers. It was one of Jack Cleary's goals – as a law enforcer, as a father and as a lover – to help sanitize the world around him.

Purity, law and order and peace. Yes, this was his motto, his secret mantra. These three things were long-term goals of his, three missions of leading the perfect life. He *wanted* to live according to these rules, but the odds were against him, and he knew it. They were always against him.

Jack had been married to a junkie, his first cousin, a rotten degenerate and a nymphomaniac who got off on being impure.

Jack got the chills. Maybe this is why he strived for a life of purity. Because of *her*.

When he and Gail first started screwing compulsively in the rafters of his uncle's shed, he became addicted to the wild, experimental foreplay and sex.

So dirty, so filthy. Impure!

Jack became involved with Moira Davis – a very mild version of Gail he once concluded – when she was still supposedly happily married to best-selling author Sam Pearson. Later on, he found out they were anything *but* happy. She had been the one to make the first move. Like Gail did. Like David Aaronson's sixteen-year-old nymphet sister, Petra did. He can still recall the day his partner came up to him – not too long after Gail had overdosed and died – and broodingly stared into his strange, practically colorless eyes and said, "Jack, what the hell is going on with you and my sister? She's sixteen man!" But at the time Jack couldn't resist that exotic black-haired, blue-eyed Petra. On occasion, Gail would remind him of that incident: "Is that why you cut him up and beached him in those trash bags...because he was the man who *knew* too much?"

"I didn't do anything. I haven't hurt anyone in my life.

You're the one who hurt people. Why don't you just leave me alone?"

What was it about Jack Cleary that lured these befouled little temptresses toward him? Did he exude an inexplicable, irresistible, incessant carnality? *Or was he a victim? Did he exude an inexplicable, irresistible, incessant* weakness *that invited psychopathic sirens to prey upon him?*

He didn't know. He didn't want to have to think about it anymore. The past was the past; it was gone. He wanted a good life, a new start. A normal pretty, clean, pristine wife. And he wanted normal children. Three of them. One to represent each of his missions: *peace, law and order* and *purity.*

As he stared at Moira's toenails, he imagined the following scenario: he comes home after a long, challenging but utterly satisfying day of police work. She greets him at the door with a long, juicy kiss (her breath is minty and her face smells of something sweet). She'd be months away from delivering their third child. And from somewhere inside the house, two boys would rush toward him, each of his sons grabbing onto one of his legs and holding onto it tightly. They are so excited to see him.

Jack's eyes remained pressed against the lenses of the binoculars, which were pressed to the window. He pictured his hand running through Moira's reddish, stringy, greasy hair. Then, as he was about to kiss her again, he was startled by the noise: he jumped back and fumbled his binoculars; they fell to the floor.

It was the *ten knocks* from the upstairs door.

The emergency knock.

Lazlo was barking and whimpering.

"Christ," Jack said. He picked up the binoculars and looked through them to make sure nothing was blemished. Luckily, they were intact.

"Daddy, Daddy!"

More barking. More whimpering. The emergency knock again.

"Christ," he repeated, this time louder than before.

"Daddy! Daddy!"

Jack put the binoculars on the hood of his cruiser, then yelled up the stairs, "Open the damn door already!"

The door opened slowly. J.J. stepped out, and even from that distance he could see through the available light that his son was sweating, and his thin, stringy hair was disheveled. He was gasping for air.

Before Jack could yell at Lazlo's barking and whimpering, J.J. said, "Emergency, Daddy. Emergency!"

"Okay, okay," Jack said, suddenly becoming calm and sympathetic. He knew that Gail must have scared him again. He asked him if she was there.

"The Gail! The Gail!" the boy said, still hyperventilating.

"Okay, calm down. Just take deep breaths. Okay? Deep breaths and calm down. Now, tell me what happened this time."

J.J., whose breathing was most irregular, focused on each syllable as he said the following: "She went into my head and then flew out and said, 'You gonna die, J.J. Cleary, just like your Mommy. Your daddy gonna kill you, J.J. Just like he did to Mommy. And he is gonna shoot Lazlo in the head. *Real, real soon.*'"

Jack couldn't speak. He couldn't tell his son any more lies; he couldn't convincingly tell him this was all in his head. *How could he?* She was there. In the house. Inside of them. He could feel her, smell her. The cellar developed a cool breeze.

Jack closed his eyes and just let her travel inside of him.

The chill prevailed, as did the tingling, almost electrical sensation throughout his body. Now he too became violated; he felt something sharp, slimy, moist and warm travel through his prostate, up to his bladder and then into his chest.

Jack closed his eyes tighter, scrunching up his face, grimacing as if constipated, and gritting his teeth so tightly that he felt additional pressure on his temples.

"I am very scared, Daddy."

Jack mustered up enough energy to say to his son, "*Will* her out, son. You need to will her out. Think very hard. Tell yourself that you don't want her here. *Think it.* Think very, very hard. Will her out. *Will her out!*" He continued to cough, as did J.J. But Lazlo was no longer barking or whimpering. The dog had found refuge under the kitchen table; he had lain down and didn't move or make a sound.

"Are you going to clean off my head, Daddy, just like the Gail says?"

Jack gasped and felt his heart skip a beat. A tear squirted out of one of his eyes. "No, no. J.J. I would *never, ever, ever* hurt you. Okay? Understand? *Never.* These are very bad dreams, and you need to will her out. Close your eyes and will her out. She is only in your mind. Okay? Close your eyes and will her out!"

"Are you going to shoot Lazlo for barking?"

"No," Jack confirmed in the gentlest tone he might have ever spoken. "Sometimes I say things I don't mean. I'm sorry."

"It's very cold."

"I know. Just go upstairs now. Okay? It will be better soon."

"Only a nightmare, Daddy?"

"Yes, only a nightmare. This is a big one, but it will go away like the others."

"Yes, Daddy."

"Hey," he said rather tenderly to the boy. "It will be okay. And close the door before you go."

J.J. liked his father's tone. He turned around and closed the door behind him. He was gone.

And so was Gail. Or so it seemed. For now, anyway.

He shuttered. Impurities everywhere! The foul smell still lingered in the air but only as a reminder that she had been there. Or was she still there? What was all this madness? This crazy, ridiculous madness...*what was it?*

Why couldn't she just die for good? Or, Jack thought quite pragmatically, why couldn't *he* just die and start all over again? He would surely make drastically different choices this time around. Undoubtedly. Or were all these things that had happened to him...*were* happening to him...meant to be? Perhaps this was all the inevitable order of things that could not be changed. Destiny. But was there any free will associated with this so-called destiny? Surely, he could make choices to change. To be good. To be decent. To have purity, law and order and...*shit*, what was that other one? The third one? He couldn't think of it.

What was going on inside of him? This all had to be an internal thing...didn't it? Or if Gail really was a supernatural force...a ghost or phantom or something...then what did that ultimately mean? He just wanted to be good. And kind. *What was that rage inside of him?* That rage that drove him to do things he didn't want to do. That rage that controlled him.

He pictured Gail waving that gun at him, then the bullets going right through his calf, his thigh and his buttocks, respectively.

An image of David Aaronson helping him cover this thing up, then a sudden flash of Aaronson peering through him, asking him what was going on between him and his little sister.

Then the trash bags...scattered all over Salisbury Beach... and the gulls picking at them.

He scrunched his face up, trying to expel the demons inside of his head. This wasn't really happening. None of this was real. Why was he thinking these thoughts?

But Gail told him every single bit of it *had* been real.

This was all an anomaly, Jack thought torturously. *Life's cruel trick being played on me.*

How ironic this all was, this dichotomy of feelings, of good and evil, this rage versus the purity, law and order and – he just remembered the third one again – *peace.* Purity, law and order and *peace.*

Why, oh why couldn't he just be free from all the madness? *I want to be good.*

But then as if his thoughts had turned on him and mocked him, he thought of J.J. He pictured the boy sprawled out on the garage floor, a knife pierced through that clueless head of his.

Jack, unable to control the nature of his feelings, wiped tears from both sides of his face. Out of all the pictures in his head, this was the worst one of all. He loved his son. *What was this fucking crazy madness?*

Leave me alone! Leave us alone! Please!

More tears.

I love you, son. I love you. I am so sorry this has all happened to you. I will never, ever, ever hurt you. Never.

He returned to the window, and, as if nothing much had happened, he positioned the binoculars on Moira Davis's feet, legs and knee. Then he continued with the domestic scenario he conjured up earlier before all of this nonsense: His wife Moira, dressed in a stunning red and yellow sundress, was rubbing his cheeks, her hands smelling of something spicy and sweet, a hand cream or perfume. She whispered softly into his ears, her hot breath giving him the chills: "I love being with you, Jack. You're my man. A good man. And so pure and clean. But also pretty damn sexy, too." She kissed him gently on his cheek, little pecks that turned into soft sucking kisses on his cheeks, chin and lips. Eventually, this led to a passionate kiss, her strong and gentle tongue moving around the inside of his mouth like a bread maker kneading dough.

He had to remove the binoculars from his eyes because

they were fogging up the lens with his tears.

Maybe it was time, he thought both reluctantly and optimistically, to visit her, that neighbor of his who months ago told him she was no longer interested continuing with their carnal rendezvous, the neighbor who had told him (and at that time *all* men) to get permanently lost.

"You can't treat people like that," he told her months ago. "I love you."

"Oh, get real, Cleary. Don't make me laugh." But she laughed anyway.

"I won't forget this, Moira," he told her. "You'll pay for this." Then, quite unoriginally: "Bitch!"

He was truly heartbroken when she broke things off.

But calling her a *bitch* and threatening her in this way... that was just the rage talking. It was always the rage...that uncontrollable force from within that drew this man into his world of sin.

He needed to make peace again. Peace within himself and peace with Moira Davis. She *had* to know there was a compassionate and tender side to him, he concluded rationally.

He thought of her in that sundress again as he opened the garage door; he inhaled forcefully and wiped his eyes with the back of his fingers.

The music immediately penetrated him; he shivered. He hated this music of hers. Hated it! It was so – what was it? – *unmusical.* Jack Cleary was no music aficionado, so he really had nothing to compare it to...he just knew that it was a lot of screaming and loud strumming.

That's okay – he could overlook this. He could try to appreciate it. After all, this was the girl of his dreams, even if *she* didn't think so. Once, Jack watched a war movie from the 1950s or 1960s where a girl asked a man why he loved the army so much, that it hadn't been very good to him. To her, he said something like the following: "A man can love something...that doesn't mean it's got to love him back."

Moira Davis might just be that *something,* but according to Jack, there was always hope. Hope for him to turn his life around; even hope for him and Moira to make another go at it.

When Moira saw Cleary approaching her, she stopped playing.

"Why stop?" he asked with a smile. "It sounded nice." He made himself believe this statement. He took a few more steps toward her.

Moira didn't respond. She took out a Marlboro and lit it.

"How are you doing, Moira? It's...been a while."

"What do you want, Jack? What are you doing on my driveway?"

Cold, cold, cold.

"Just came by to say hello." A pause, followed by a new smile, one more pathetic than happy. "I miss you." Another step toward her. He pictured her scantily dressed body covered in that sundress. She really was a beautiful woman, he thought. Look at that body and that face...it was very striking, even if she did have those circles under her eyes. If only she would do away with that lesbian hippy shit...if only she weren't afraid to present herself decently...like a real woman. Feminine.

"Hello," she said calmly. His goofy smile angered her. She wanted to smack him in those fat rosy cheeks of his. Slap him...*hard.* "Now please go."

"Wait a minute, hold on," he said, taking more steps toward her. He was pretty much eye to eye with her. "I'm just saying hello. That's all. I've been thinking about you, and I'm sure you've been thinking about me, haven't you? A little? Maybe?"

How egotistical and pompous this man could be one minute, how puerile the next.

Jack said, "How are things?"

"*Things* are just fine, Jack." She took a drag of her cigarette.

Cigarette whore, he thought, the rage making its way through him. *Dirty, filthy!*

"And how's your...daughter?"

Moira shivered. "My daughter is fine."

"Good to hear." He turned toward his house, suddenly a shy boy approaching the prettiest girl in the class for a date to the prom. "J.J. is doing okay." He laughed, but it wasn't really a laugh; it was more of a strange noise that formed in his sinuses and made its way out through his nose. "He gets a little excited still. He's been having some nightmares..."

"What are you doing, Jack?" snapped Moira.

"What?"

"I thought I made it clear that we..." Then a lot quieter: "Look. We *did* what we *did*. Let's just leave it at that. *Capish*?"

"Goodness," he said. This was an overt effort to control his language, which in turn could help him control his rage. Nevertheless, a rush of blood filled his face. "No need to be hostile. I'm just saying hi. Is that a crime?"

"Cleary," she said and paused for what seemed to be a long time. She called him *Cleary* like a mother would call her son by his full name when she was reprimanding him. "I'm not your fucking *girlfriend,* so why don't we just...*call it a day.*"

These words crushed him. Couldn't she have said something else like *Go to hell* or *Fuck off?* He thought again of her in that sundress; the image he had of her was so clear in his mind that it became torturous. The image quickly dissolved back to Moira as she was. Her countenance, accented by the lines around her eyes, was apoplectic.

Finally, he said, "I didn't say I was your husband." He stopped. Did he say *husband*? Didn't he mean *boyfriend*? Moira closed her eyes and shook her head back and forth.

A man can love a thing, don't mean it's got to love him back.

Jack's heart skipped a beat. Moira's eyes were now open and peering through him. It was as if she, like Gail, had invaded his insides.

Blood rushed to every part of his body, or so it seemed. He pictured those eyes of hers sliced up and plucked from their sockets, blood soaking her face beyond recognition.

Damn it! Damn it! Peace. Law and order. Damn it all! What the hell is that third one again? Peace. Law and Order. And – Damn it!

He was defeated and now had a hell of a headache. To the ground he said, "I didn't mean to start anything."

"Why not just come out with it?" she said suddenly. "Tell me what you really want? Don't play games."

Jack Cleary suddenly pictured the juxtaposition of two mental images: having his way with her real savage-like in the back of his car; and a colorful scene of her, as his loyal wife, greeting him at the door while wearing that sundress she put on just for him. *Man!* He wanted her...*badly*. He wanted her all to himself. He tried really hard to focus on these pure thoughts of her in that sundress but was only able to conjure her naked body. Then her naked body sliced up, dismembered, and scattered on an open field, then on Salisbury beach, stacked neatly in one of the many trash bags lined up on the sand next to the other victims.

But these were only thoughts...weren't they? Sure, Aaronson and all those others were dead, but not because of him. He didn't do it! He *didn't*.

It was insane. Sordid. Disgusting. Filthy!

But he *was* a killer. Wasn't he? That's why he needed to become pure...needed to start over.

No, it's not real. They're only hallucinations.

Whatever it was...it was there. And real enough to be playing games with his mind.

His head felt like it was going to burst.

Moira continued playing her guitar. Jack turned around and walked pensively down the driveway – that awful music getting louder and louder and louder...echoing through his insides...invading him.

A mild wind formed, and he pictured her dismembered body scattered about in a wide open green field. The wind penetrated him. It was that heavy feeling along with the cold. And that smell...that foul, inexplicable stink that lingered in his sinuses like a virus attaching itself to a host cell.

And instead of conjuring up that sundress scenario that had been playing so vividly in his mind, Cleary recalled a previous sexual encounter where Moira was handcuffed to the bed. He was running his Billy Club up and down her body...

The wind picked up again, and through its whistling he almost didn't hear Moira calling after him. He turned around and faced her. With a loud whisper, she said, "Meet me in your basement in ten. We have to be quiet, and we have to be quick. I mean it." She smiled diabolically; he didn't like that look. "Maygyn will be home in less than two hours and there's no way in hell she's going to know about *any* of this. Got it?" Then that strange little smile again.

Jack nodded with no expression. He turned around and headed back to the house. He pictured himself ripping that sundress off her body. She wasn't worthy, or clean enough, to wear it.

I'm not worthy, or clean enough, to be anyone's *loving husband.*

For the rest of the way home, which seemed like a much longer walk than next door, he moped, and in his mind cursed the cards he had been dealt with in this foul, tainted life. But on the good side, despite his purity and peace and law and order jazz, he was still going to get to touch that body again. That had to be worth something.

Purity, law and order and peace – for the time being, anyway – would just have to wait...

CHAPTER 15

GAMES

Friday, June twenty-second, the first day of summer, was another warm and dry day in Fryebury Falls. According to weather reports, Boston was getting hit with intense electrical storms, but the only sign of water in the little town was that of Niagara Two.

Mike Melanson was in his office eating his breakfast – two honey-dipped crullers and a large coffee with extra cream and sugar from Rodney's Donut Hole. He wasn't feeling particularly well that day; another one of those twenty-four-hour viruses was coming on, and to make matters worse, he kept hearing his wife's cursing voice: "It's from too much coffee and those repulsive cancer sticks!"

There were many things that plagued his mind this morning. He was thinking of Miss Julie who was bedridden, but who was, in his opinion, perfectly capable of moving about (He smiled as he thought about how she manipulated that poor young doctor – Marcus Welby – the wet-behind-the ears intern who "didn't know the first thing about a woman's anatomy.") He was thinking of Adam and how he had missed so much school playing nursemaid to his "ailing" mother

(How was he going to become a vet if he kept missing elementary school?) He was thinking of George, his best friend, who was slowly killing himself with alcohol and how he recently backed out of going to the Red Sox game because he simply couldn't face people and the sport itself. (It would only remind him of his baseball glory days, the days that would never return to him.) And he was thinking of his livelihood, his so-called mission in life, his *duty*, (or as Miss Julie called it, his *dooty*) a duty that was becoming far too stressful and complicated. Like all this drug business that was going on in town. For the past several months, Jack Cleary had been nailing drug dealers left and right. In fact, just three weeks earlier, the big city cop cracked a major drug ring right in town. Right in Günter's Millyard.

Mike thought again of those teenagers – those "Boardheads" – who had been desecrating Fryebury Falls' most enchanting microcosm to buy, sell and use drugs. Thousands and thousands of dollars of the junk too. Hard stuff. Smack. And this new type of cocaine that apparently came from L.A. called Crack.

According to Jack Cleary, the dealing had been going on for some time now – even before he joined the force – and this made the chief feel especially incompetent. The king pin or leader of these Boardheads was seventeen-year-old Eddie Price, whom to Mike always seemed like a good enough kid – a bit on the rough side, but still rather quiet and polite.

"It's always those quiet ones," Cleary said. "I call it the *Eddie Haskell Syndrome*."

Who the hell is Eddie Haskell? Mike considered. *I thought we were talking about* Eddie Price.

"Oh M&M," Miss Julie's voice resonated, "What are we going to do with you? We really need to get you cultured."

"This is one dangerous kid," Jack explained to his boss who knew Eddie's father quite well. They had gone to school together, even played ball together in their Little League days. Roger Price was a well-tempered, rather charming fellow. He was the town's mechanic. His garage – Roger's Auto – was the place where everyone in town took their vehicles for maintenance. He was also a certified auto body specialist. On the surface, one may never have referred to this guy as moderately intelligent, let alone a genius, but when it came to automobiles, he was most definitely a genius. He even referred to himself as a surgeon and a cosmetic artist. "I'll take care of your baby...inside and out," he would say, those rosy cheeks and gin-blossomed nose glowing as he smiled. And he would. There wasn't a broken or ugly-looking car in town. Mike didn't know how the guy did it.

A few days after Eddie was arrested by Jack Cleary, Roger Price paid a visit to Mike.

"Eddie ain't no drug dealer, Mike. He's got his problems like the rest of us – his mother and I never could control who he hangs out with – but he don't sell drugs. That Frank Hugo kid, the one with the motorcycle and all them tattoos, the one who got Eddie smokin' cigarettes, I'd look out for *him*. But Eddie, he ain't a bad kid. You know that." Roger was nervous, out of breath, and after a while he was stuttering a bit. Mike thought he was going to cry.

"I don't know all the details yet, Roger. I'm still reviewing Officer Cleary's report. There's some paperwork I've got to sort out here" – paperwork Mike Melanson was still familiarizing himself with...after all, he had never dealt with anything quite like this before.

"And *that-that* Officer Jack Cleary," Roger said, the stuttering getting worse, "He...he should be the one you...you look out for. He's worse than that...that Hugo kid."

Mike listened.

"Did he write in that that p-p-police report that he slapped Eddie crossed the face for sayin' s-s-some remark toward him?" Roger paused, took a few more breaths, then continued. This was strange, Mike thought, because he never knew Roger Price as one who stuttered...he must have *really* been nervous. But the more the guy spoke, the less he stuttered, gaining more and more confidence with each additional word. It was as if he recognized a weakness in himself and immediately worked at correcting it. "Did he also write in that p-police report that he threatened to cut my boy's nuts off and hang them around his neck? Huh?" Roger sniffled as if he had a cold. "I bet that's not there in *that-that* report you got there. *Is* it?" A pause. "Did he write in that report that he...planted them drugs on Eddie?" Roger took a couple of sighs, the kind one takes after a major event has happened, sighs not of anticipation, but those of relief. *There.* He said what he wanted to say to the chief. Although the two men weren't by definition friends – certainly not to the degree that Mike and George Pearson were friends – they were certainly long-time acquaintances who always got along.

Mike said, "Is that what he told you?"

"Who? The cop?"

"Eddie."

"Yeah, that's what Eddie told me. And the boy...d-don't lie. Plus, he's got a red mark crossed his cheek. He may do lots of things he ain't...supposed to do, but he never lied to me. I know my son. He tells me all the shit he gets involved with."

"I see." Mike was trying to be as professional as possible. He was, however, having a difficult time believing all of this. How can a father be so naïve as to think his own son would never lie to him? And what was all of this about Jack Cleary slapping him in the face? Telling the kid he was going to – what was it? – cut his balls off and wrap them around his neck? What a fucking image that conjured up, Mike thought rather absurdly.

"Look, Roger," Mike said, lighting a cigarette. He offered

one to Roger, who told him he was trying to quit. "Jack Cleary is a good police officer. That's why we brought him on. He's a smart, experienced cop and let's just say...well...he's pretty much an expert when it comes to such things. He worked in Boston on special assignments." Mike paused, still unaware what those special assignments actually *were*, but for now, in the chief's mind, his assistant was a skilled narc. Mike continued, speaking slowly and carefully, "I think we've been going too easy on these kids. Actually, I *know* we have been." Pause. "Apparently, Roger, there has been a serious drug problem going on here in town for a long time and to say that Eddie, with the gang he hangs out – that Frank Hugo kid included – had nothing to do with this is being a bit naïve, would you agree?" Another dramatic pause. A puff on the cigarette. "I'm not making any judgments on Eddie. I like him. Always have, even if he *has* gotten into a little bit of trouble here and there. But what I'm saying is that Officer Cleary caught him in the act. Possession. Dealing. Using the drugs. I mean he actually caught the money transaction going down right there in the Millyard. What more can I say?"

Roger was silent.

"Please Roger, see it from my angle," Mike continued. "We are strictly going on facts here. It's nothing personal. He got caught. Maybe he was at the wrong place at the wrong time. Maybe it was the first time he ever did anything like this. But the reality is that he *got caught*. And action must be taken. It's our job. I'm sure you can appreciate that. We can't have drugs like that here." Mike took two more puffs on the cigarette as Roger remained silent, watching the edge of Mike's desk. Mike was on a roll. Although he felt that he wasn't a real cop – not like Cleary was, anyway – he still knew the law and knew how to talk to people. This low-down townie with no concept of the real world was, rather ironically, good with words, a speechmaker, a counselor, a real mentor. Could someone – in a small town anyway – be considered a poor cop but a good chief? Was that possible? Did Mike Melanson fit that old motto: *those who can't do, teach?* Mike remembered this statement outraged his best friend who insisted that teachers needed to be skillful at two major things: first, they had to know how to do whatever they were teaching extra well; and second, they had to know how to teach it to others. To George Pearson, this was the most absurd quotation ever conceived.

Then Roger said, "What about getting his face slapped then? Now I may not know too much on how the law works – that's your job – but I am smart enough to know cops can't go around hitting kids in the face even if they d-do talk back. That's police *brutality*."

"I don't know, Roger. All I know is that under all this pressure people can say lots of things." He cleared his throat. "When they're scared, they are liable to say..." Mike stopped himself as if something inside of him physically halted his next words. He was speaking very well, but for some reason he couldn't continue with this conversation. How could Jack Cleary have hit Roger's son? But *did* Jack use force on the kid? And if so, why didn't he tell Mike? He was hearing stories around town that his assistant had been exercising what many called "unfair tactics." Like the time he threatened bank president Gregory Reardon's position after pulling him over for speeding. The reputable banker and family man insisted that he was *absolutely* driving within the speed limit!

Or the time a woman approached him in Günter's Millyard telling him that her friend, a seventeen-year-old girl named Alyssa Dupree, had slept with Jack Cleary and that the cop threatened to harm her if she told anyone.

None of these complaints, however, ever seemed to surface, which made Mike think they were either untrue or too trivial to investigate further.

Mike knew at least this much: the citizens of Fryebury

Falls had simply not welcomed him yet. Maybe they were still comparing him to Roger Kaplan. Sure, that was it. They were trying to discredit the new guy (who had been there a couple years now), like any little town would attempt to drive out the mysterious stranger who would *never* be accepted as part of the community. It took a lot for a small town to accept change. This thought reminded him of some movie he saw once about a one-armed stranger who enters a town called Black Rock. The stranger is trying to find out something about a man who was murdered, but no one in the town wants to help him. They are hostile toward him; they try to drive him out.

So, Mike Melanson just let these things go; he never even questioned Cleary on such things. The way he figured it – it was a blessing to finally have someone on the force that was capable of making Fryebury Falls a safer place to live. Plus, the chief never really had the skills to handle any real catastrophe.

Jack *did* seem to take things a bit too far, Mike thought, and his methods *were* rather unconventional (for this town anyway), but the fact of the matter was this: he liked the guy from the word go. He was a good cop and from what he saw a good father. *And* he cracked a major drug case!

Roger finally said, "So my boy l-lied? Is that what you're... telling me?"

"I'm not making any accusations, Roger. All I know is that Eddie is part of a rough crowd. Anything is possible. Maybe he was holding drugs for someone. Maybe it was for that Hugo kid. There could be a million reasons. All we know is that he was caught with them on him and according to the police report, something about a sale. And there is nothing here saying that Officer Cleary needed to...restrain Eddie. It would be here in the report. I am convinced of that."

Roger's face dropped. He really looked like he was going to cry now. But he didn't. Instead, he shook his head back and forth, looking, or trying to look into Mike's crossed eyes, which appeared to have been even more disoriented than they normally were.

Softly Roger said, "That son-of-a bitch hit my son. And he planted drugs on him. And you're not going to do anything about it? Well, maybe I need to, then."

Mike stirred in his chair as he watched the back of Roger's bald head. It was as if he heard Roger say: *Man, you've changed, Melanson. Changed. And not for the better.*

When Roger Price left, Mike recalled the man's parting words again, this time on a different level. *Well, maybe I need to, then.* What did that mean? Need to do *what*?

As he sat in the chair, a force on his legs kept him adhered to the seat. He couldn't move. He thought of George whose life would never be the same again because he slugged a teenage boy in the face. What would happen to Jack Cleary if he did in fact hit Eddie Price?

Absurd.

Then Roger's words again: *Well maybe I need to, then.*

The force intensified; it felt like a heavy, small table had been placed on his legs.

An icy chill entered his system, leaving his body numb. Numb as if he had been shot up with Novocain.

He didn't feel like a police officer anymore, let alone a chief. He had a tough realization: for all these years he had been nothing more than a little town figurehead.

What the hell had he been doing all these years?

Another chill traveled through him.

He thought of Jack Cleary and his unconventional methods. But *were* they unconventional? *Were these the methods that Mike should have been adhering to himself?* After all, being a police officer isn't a popularity contest...or it shouldn't be, anyway. But the truth was this: Mike liked being liked. That was who he was. And he liked helping people and being kind to them.

Maybe it was Mike Melanson who was the unconventional one. A feeble-minded, low-down townie with no concept of the real world!

After all, the police academy he attended was nothing more than a game to him. Sure, he learned how to use a gun and he was formally trained to do all those things they teach to potential law enforcers, but admittedly it wasn't exactly the best academy around. It was actually quite a joke. It wouldn't have ranked anywhere near those academies that nurtured real police officers. Like Jack Cleary. No, to Mike it was really all just a game. Even target practice and those situations where he had to shoot at dummies in an obstacle course...that was nothing more than an interactive video game. It wasn't real life. He never had real life training. It was all a game. And being elected Chief of Police...that too was just a game.

They were all games. Games and nothing more.

But was this business with Cleary a game too?

What *was* the deal with his enigmatic assistant? Were these stories about him true?

Or were the citizens of Fryebury Falls a pack of liars planning to secretly run the guy out of town?

Why was Mike so chicken-shit to approach Cleary with these accusations? After all, Mike *was* his boss. Was he afraid of Jack Cleary, super cop par excellence? Was he afraid of really discovering something about him? Or did he just admire the guy? He *was* taken by him, enamored by him. To Mike, Jack Cleary was still very charming; he was like a movie hero or something. And in a way, he was also kind of jealous of him too.

He thought of Miss Julie who had been, for years now, trying to get him to retire. And maybe she was right, he thought seriously for the first time. Maybe he had done his time. He knew when he accepted the job that it wouldn't last forever. Maybe what this town needed – whether anyone wanted to admit it or not – was the firm hand of Jack Cleary. To keep the town clean and free of crime.

He felt the blood rush from his legs to his head, which gave him a heavy headache.

As he was finishing the remnants of his cigarette, he again thought of Roger Price and George. And those kids – Eddie Price and Derek Hamilton.

Did Cleary slap Eddie Price? *Did he?* Did he make all of these threats? Maybe he did. And if he did, maybe there was a method to his madness. Maybe Eddie Price deserved a crack in the mouth. Little drug dealer. Just like that foul-mouthed south-paw Derek Hamilton deserved a crack in the mouth for saying those indescribable things about Alison Pearson after she had been killed. But it still didn't make it right. *Did it?*

Or did it?

A breeze came through the window, replacing the cold chill he had been feeling for the past several minutes, and again Mike's body felt agile. And free somehow. Like he could do anything.

He got up from his chair and walked proudly out of the office and into downtown Fryebury Falls, knowing that there were some personal and professional decisions he needed to make.

CHAPTER 16

ESCAPE

J.J. had fallen asleep on the couch. And Lazlo, the big dog that he was, was also on the couch asleep, sprawled out as if he were human; he was nearly as big as the teenager. Their long day of play had come to a close.

Earlier on, the boy and his dog were playing "Escape." It was a game J.J. invented, one that he would play frequently, with or without Lazlo; it was a game that would one day become – he told himself secretly – a reality. Being a perpetual prisoner was tiresome and boring, so what he would do was this: pretend to lead a massive prison bust, very similar to the ones he had seen on TV. His favorite escape movie involved three guys who broke out of jail then swam across a lake to their freedom. He especially liked the movie for two reasons: first, because it involved escape; and second, the star of the movie was the same guy who played in his favorite cop movie, the one where the policeman warned the criminal that he would "clean off his head" with a Magnum forty-five gun, "the most powerful handgun in the world."

J.J. Cleary would escape from jail just like all these characters did. He would escape into a new world, one where people were kind to him, one where no one would mock him because of his brain injury – a world where he and his father, super-hero cops, would fight off criminals with magnum forty-fives. It would be a world where certain people would not be welcomed, especially his dead mother, *The Gail*. But it would also be a world where certain people *would* be welcomed...like that attractive, dark-haired, blue-eyed neighbor of his.

What he wouldn't *do* to escape to this world! And for J.J. Cleary this place really existed; he pictured it down to every last detail: gardens of red, blue and yellow flowers; big fields with green, green grass; a dog kennel with Lazlo and hundreds of other dogs he could play with and take care of; and lots of room to run around. This place was real; it had been shown to him many times in his dreams. And now it was time to see how he could get there.

For he hated being locked up all day. *Hated it, hated it, hated it!* It made him angry. It brought out the rage in him. He wanted to tell his father he hated it, but he knew that if he did, then Jack would get angry himself – or (God forbid!) put him in "The Hole" again, that minute cubbyhole of a place with no light and little air. "The Hole" was nothing more than an empty walk-in closet, "the jail within the jail" as Jack had called it.

J.J would be put in "The Hole" when he committed what Jack referred to as "an inexcusable and careless offense." And this could include anything from the following: entering the basement without the emergency knock; forgetting to clean his "cell" after dinner; and not taking proper care of that stupid dog of his. J.J wondered why his father let him keep Lazlo if he despised the animal so much. The answer probably had something to do with Jack feeling a bit sorry for the boy; he knew how much the dog meant to him, and as cruel as Jack might have been to his son, he still loved him more than anything. He really did.

According to Jack Cleary, his son needed to be *disciplined, focused and tidy* so that *purity, law & order and peace* could prevail.

"No son of mine will be a lazy slob – brain disability or not," he would say.

The last time J.J. spent three days in "The Hole" – about a year earlier – for taking one of Jack's personal books. It was a book that helped people who had things wrong with their brain, J.J. vaguely remembered. According to Jack, J.J. needed to be severely punished for breaking and entering (he obviously went downstairs while Jack was at work...even though Jack always locked the door leading to the basement and garage) and stealing private property. (*What the hell did he want with that self-help book about peace from nervous suffering?*) As the days passed, however, Jack surmised that the boy couldn't *possibly* have gone downstairs and taken this book. Plus, even though he was slow-witted, he wouldn't have been so stupid as to disobey this house rule...the most important one! But by that time, it had been too late; his son was already three days in "The Hole."

In his dream, J.J. saw Gail again. *Or was it a dream at all?* Lately he had been seeing her while he was awake as well – flying around, passing through doors and floors and the ceiling and furniture – then entering through his head and... *hurting* him.

She was walking up a set of stairs toward him. He was locked in a kennel with Lazlo who wasn't Lazlo at all but more of a big black bear with long fangs, drooling white foam from its jowls. The beast was frightening and made awful monstrous noises – and he looked like something out of a cartoon, but not any cartoon J.J. had ever seen before.

As she ascended the stairs, she would periodically disappear, reappear, then disappear, then reappear...over and over and over again. And she was covered by a thick white and yellow fog. Once he saw a movie on TV about a town overtaken by a looming fog. There was a scene in this movie when the yellow-tinted fog devoured an old woman who was babysitting a little boy. This always frightened J.J.

Gail spoke, reaching out her arms as she continued to appear and disappear on the stairs, her voice echoing throughout: "Come with me, son, before your father gets a hold of you and Lazlo. Before he puts a bullet in your heads. Come to your mother. I love you very much, dear. Very much..."

J.J was shivering in the cage. He looked over at Lazlo who was no longer a fierce black monster. The dog was emaciated, curled up like an embryo on the floor, breathing strangely. Like he had asthma or something. His eyes looked as though they were sewn shut. Then J.J. focused in on the dog's head, which had a big chunk of it taken out...and it was smoking... and flies were covering the wound. The boy looked up and saw an image of his father smiling sadistically as he held a smoking gun. In the same distorted echoing sound, Jack said, "I told you: if you don't keep that dog quiet, I will put a bullet in his brain." Then he pointed the gun at J.J. "Are you next? Want me to put you out of your misery, too?"

Then the boy looked at Gail again who seemed to be getting closer to him, but she only continued walking up the stairs, never progressing, disappearing and reappearing over and over and over again. Her voice whispered: "Your father is a very bad man. Did you know that? And we're coming to get him. He killed me you know. He has killed other people, too. And he's going to kill again. He's going to kill you. And Lazlo. But first he's going to starve you and put you in 'The Hole' forever and ever. He's going to shoot you and Lazlo in the head." J.J saw Lazlo who now looked like a stuffed animal. "Maybe you can help your mommy... *kill* him before he...*kills* you and Lazlo and the others. It's the only way for you to escape..." Then her voice got loud and echoed, but still in that whispering tone: *Escaaaaaape. Escaaaaaape.*

When he awoke, he was panting, and his febrile face was soaked in his own perspiration.

Lazlo began to bark in a way he had never barked before, a bark that might have been heard from Cerebus, the three-headed hound at the gates of Hades. Then he began to whimper.

Gail was flying through the room, and J.J. watched her move in and out of the walls and the ceiling. "Escape," she kept saying as J.J sat there, eyes wide open, hypnotized by those words.

⊠ ⊠ ⊠ ⊠

Within half an hour, Moira Davis was inside Jack Cleary's bedroom, naked and smoking a cigarette.

The bedroom was spacious but haphazardly decorated, therefore producing a stifling ambiance. It appeared that the officer placed the objects – two dilapidated dressers, a green letter writing desk, two chairs (one a recliner and the other, some kind of rocking chair), a number of milk crates and an old bookshelf that reminded Moira of something someone would buy for a couple of bucks at a yard sale – in a circular fashion, almost as if these objects were their own walls. There were no posters or artwork on the actual walls, and to the left of his bed – in a decent-sized walk-in closet – hung his uniform, draped neatly over a couple of hangers as if it had been a three-piece suit. According to Jack Cleary, his attire was a reflection of himself and what he did, so he needed to take good care of it.

"What you need is an interior decorator," Moira said, blowing smoke out the side of her mouth.

Jack, who despised cigarettes and everything else dirty, opened a window and handed her a half empty Mellow Yellow can for her to use for an ashtray. She didn't even ask if she could light up; she knew he didn't like smoking. "I'm not trying to get into *House Beautiful*," he said. "At least it's clean."

"Have it your own way."

"I do." He paused, then asked, "Did you like it?"

"What?" She blew more smoke out the side of her mouth. Jack waved and swatted some of it out the window, then he smiled vaguely.

He repeated the question to her.

"Did I *like* it?" Moira asked. She blew air through her nose, the sniffling sound posing as a laugh. "You make it sound like an ice cream cone or something. Yes, Jack. I liked it. It was *awesome*. You are an animal." She looked away.

"Did I make you...you know...feel good?" He imagined that he was her husband when he asked her this.

"Did I *come*?" she quickly replied. "Is that what you're asking me?" He smiled and nodded. "You were *there* weren't you?"

"I know, it's just that sometimes...you know...women..."

"Women *what*?"

"You know..."

"I've never faked an orgasm in my life, Cleary. I either come or I don't."

Jack smiled in a different way now, lightly massaging his jaw with his index finger.

Then there was a noise of some sort – a *popping* sound.

Moira asked what it was.

Jack's heart raced. "Yeah, I heard it too. Sounded like something from outside. It might be –"

"It came from *inside* the room," she said, looking around. Then she grabbed her clothes and dressed herself as she followed the sound.

"It did? I don't know. I guess it could have been any number of things." He laughed. "The house settling?" Then a little less humorously, "Or a ghost?" He swallowed a glob of spit.

"It came from over here," she said, walking toward one of the dressers.

"No," Jack said, jumping over to the open window. "I think it came from outside."

Moira faced Jack. She was significantly shorter than he was. She looked into those lifeless eyes of his. "What are you so nervous about, Jack?"

"Nervous? Me? I'm not..." Then Jack Cleary transformed into another part of himself, a person he hated, the person who lived a life of fear, the person who was nurtured from childhood by an overbearing, God-fearing Catholic mother, a woman who excommunicated him for living a life of sin, for marrying his first cousin Gail who, in her own way, became yet another emasculating woman in his life. It was no wonder that he became what he became – a person with at least four distinct personalities: the first, a dominating, confident, seemingly fearless and highly intelligent law enforcer; the second, a vengeful, angry man who couldn't control the rage that besieged him; the third, the current one, was nothing more than a vulnerable little boy whose own neuroses and psychoses made him, like his own son, a helpless prisoner in an unkind world; and then the fourth personality, the one that desired to be pure, the one that strived to be clean, the one that wanted a loving family. He would merge in and out of these personalities so quickly that he simply learned how to deal with them on a day-to-day basis.

His heart was fluttering.

Moira fingered the objects on the dresser – keys, key chains, coins, peppermint candies – then a portable tape recorder no bigger than the dimensions of her hand. She palmed the evidence.

And after what seemed like a long moment, Moira said, "You *taped* us?"

Jack was defeated. He shrugged. Then he thought of the story he made up, the one he planned to use if anyone ever discovered the tape player on him, the one explaining that the tape player was a gift from his slow-witted son.

But he said nothing. Plus, this was not the story to use on Moira.

Moira rewound the tape and played it.

"...*What you need is an interior decorator...*"

She rewound it even further, but before she could press *play*, Jack approached her, grabbing onto her arm. "There's no need for that. Come on."

She jerked away from him. "I can't believe you taped us!"

Jack took another step toward her.

Moira maneuvered around one of the dressers as if going through an obstacle course. She pressed *play*. They both listened for a moment, not making out anything except some white noise.

"Well, listen to this." She raised her arm, waving the recorder in the air.

"Give it to me," he said, reaching for it as both of them continued moving through the obstacle course. The way Jack set his room up allowed for many possibilities of moving around the furniture.

"Wait," she said almost playfully. "Not done yet." She continued moving through the obstacle course in a serpentine manner until her back met the wall.

Jack approached her, grabbed her arm more forcefully than before and twisted it, giving her an Indian sunburn.

"Jesus, that hurts! Let go!"

"Damn right it hurts," Jack said, speaking through his teeth, his face turning redder with each breath. "That's private property. Hand it over."

He twisted her arm so forcefully now that she shrieked. With his other hand, he pulled the recorder from her now limp hand. It fell almost gracefully into his own hand.

"What are you going to do with that?" she asked, her back pressed even further against the wall. She was no longer running through the obstacle course. She was panting like a tired dog; then she let out a few smoker's coughs.

"I wasn't going to do *anything* with it," he said, checking the machine and tape for possible blemishes. Then he placed it in his front pocket.

"Pervert!" Moira said, laughing. She was staring directly at Jack who, unable to hold the gaze, looked away. "You don't plan on doing anything with that tape now do you?" Suddenly, Jack's vision became blurred; Moira existed in front of him in a cloud of heavy film. Her voice was muffled, and he got a high-frequency ringing in his right ear that took over his entire being for a number of seconds. "Because I would really be *perturbed* if it got into the wrong hands. Especially my daughter, Jack. I would die. You understand that? I would die."

The subtext of the *I would die* appeared to take on a bigger meaning for Jack Cleary at that moment as a cold chill filled up his insides. *I would die. I would die.*

A delightful little madness, along with another chill, filled his insides.

Jack said, "I don't plan on doing *anything* with it. Nothing. Just –"

"What?"

"Nothing," Jack said, defeated.

Moira quickly slipped on her shoes. "I knew this wasn't a good idea. What the hell was I thinking?" Moira said these words more to herself, making it additionally hard for Jack to hear her. "I can't believe you did that. What an invasion!" She reached out her hand and like a mother scolding a child: "Give it to me...*now.*"

"No." He grabbed his pocket, touching the player through his pants.

"I want that tape destroyed," she said, grabbing at the player.

"Whoa-whoa-whoa," he said ever so playfully, laughing and dancing about. "Is there something in my pocket, or are you just glad to see me?"

"Jesus," Moira whispered, shaking her head. "How old are you? *Seriously.*"

"This is private property." A resurgence of confidence and energy prevailed. Gail had left his body and one of the other Jack Clearys had now surfaced.

Moira then said, in a tone more pathetic than anything, "It would be a real shame if my daughter were to ever get her hands on this. I would die, Jack. Please. If not for me, then for her. For Maygyn. Please, Jack." She gulped. *Was she going to cry?*

For some reason, Jack bought into Moira's request – maybe it was because she said her daughter's name; maybe because one of Jack Cleary's personas (the one that wanted to live a good peaceful life with a wife and normal kids) took over and wanted to purify the filth on that tape. Whatever it was, the cop slowly fingered the recorder from his pocket and when he had it in his hand he ejected the tape, then handed it over to Moira.

"Go ahead, take it," he said, knowing there were many more where that came from.

Moira was stuck, like Velcro, to the wall. She heard a ringing in her ears that sounded like the beeping from a cash register. Her eyes closed involuntarily. In this split second or two she caught a glimpse of her little sister struggling in the water. In that swimming hole. Sinking...sinking...sinking...a puddle of blood swirling like water going down a drain. *Help...Moira...Help me, Moira...*She opened her eyes, focused now on a glass of water on one of the dressers. Then she pictured herself beating the side of Jack Cleary's head with that

Billy Club of his. She looked to the floor, her tone now sullen and melancholy, but she still had that edge to her, the one Jack found both menacing and amusing. She pulled the tape ribbon out of the cassette until a mound of it filled her palm. Then she ripped it all to shreds. Then she threw the cassette across the room.

"You stay away from me," she said quietly.

Jack looked at the sad, filthy creature in front of him. He undressed her with his eyes but instead of becoming aroused he became repulsed as he thought about the time when he first began sleeping with her, when she was still living with Sam. Unsavory little adulteress! But this was the type of woman Jack Cleary was destined to love, wasn't it? He tried to think of her in that delightful sundress standing in their kitchen cooking dinner for him as their kids ran around the house.

He now felt something warm toward the woman standing in front of him. "I'm sorry, Moira. It won't happen again. I promise." He smiled at her and the smile was somehow, surprisingly at that, authentic. Moira stood there for a moment, a bit stunned. She actually believed him. She knew his four temperamental personalities quite well by now, and – even though she may never have consciously recognized it – this was most likely what made this overgrown bulldog so appealing and even attractive to her. Jack Cleary might have been a lot of things, but to Moira Davis he was never boring. In fact, if her husband – with his natural creative talents that was unto itself a turn-on – had a bit more of this unpredictable charisma, then maybe their story would have had a different outcome.

"I'm leaving," she said, pushing herself away from the wall.

Jack backed away from her. "Nobody's keeping you here."

She glared at him for a long moment. "You stay away from me, or I *swear*...I'll... *kill* you." She seemed to regret saying this immediately. Then: "We are *done* Cleary. You hear me?" Then practically to herself: "I should have my fucking head examined."

As she walked out, he smiled and said, "I still had a good time."

Moira stopped in her tracks, but didn't turn around. Jack closed the door.

As Moira walked back to her place, a hot gust of air traveled inside her. She pictured once again that image of the Billy Club clubbing his temples. Then she saw a bullet piercing through his chest, then one through his forehead. Then a machete slicing his jugular – the projectile blood spewing out of him like water from a broken fountain.

There was a metallic taste in her mouth. Her head hurt like never before – like sharp needles jabbing her temples and forehead.

Her vision became blurred, tears forming in her eyes. Then, in an out-of-focus image above her, in a small cloud above her house, she saw Meggie. The girl was dressed in a bathing suit, standing on a beach by a lake.

The little girl walked out into the lake, slowly dissolving into a bright white light that gave way to a small circular-shaped cloud.

Moira wept as she walked into her house. All she wanted to do now was go to sleep.

And Jack Cleary lay on his bed staring at the ceiling, thinking about the afternoon. *Was he pleased, or was he repulsed? Or was he both?*

He closed his eyes and within minutes was fast asleep.

CHAPTER 17

LEAVE SLEEPING
DOGS DEAD

"Morning Mike."

It was Dexter Crowley. As usual, he was grinning crook-edly and proudly, exposing those two or three teeth of his. Dexter had been on the police force (if you can call it such) for nearly as long as Mike had been, just shy of fifteen years. He was fifty-seven years-old, six foot five and naturally skinny. He had one of those metabolisms that even at his age was fast. It must have been a fast metabolism because the guy lived on a diet of doughnuts, Dr. Pepper, cheeseburgers, chicken salad sandwiches and Snickers bars and he never gained an extra ounce!

Mike Melanson never in his life met anyone so blissful, so complacent. He was almost *too* blissful and *too* complacent. According to Miss Julie, Crowley had a promiscuous lifestyle, one that he hid rather well. Regarding his friendship with Adam Bonner, Miss Julie once said, "There's no question about it: they are *definitely* living in sin." But for the first time in his life, Mike looked at his friend (the one who always got him great baseball tickets) and got a lump in his throat. *You're no cop, Crowley. Who are you kidding? You're a joke.* Then he got another lump in his throat. *And a real bastard,* he thought with a bit of a smile, remembering the story Crowley told him about his mother having him illegitimately, a fate that would perpetually disbar the deacon from ever becoming a true man of the cloth. Then grudgingly, Mike looked to the floor. *We're both fucking jokes!*

What the hell constituted law enforcement anyway? What did it mean to really be a successful man of the law? Mike contemplated these questions bitterly as he trudged coyly past the volunteer who was presently eating from a bag of cheese curls and drinking a Coke.

Then he contemplated another series of thoughts. *Drugs. Drugs! Drugs in Fryebury Falls?* Drug *dealing in* Fryebury Falls? Surely, he couldn't have been so stupidly blind to such things. *What did all this mean? What had he been doing with himself all these years?* Sure, people liked him...saw him as a good man, as a man who protected his little town...but could he *really* protect them if the stakes were ever raised? Like this drug situation that had been going on for...*years?*

He sighed. There needed to be changes. Major changes. Within a few minutes, the restless chief left the station and headed over to Rodney's Donut Hole for another cup of coffee. In his mind he was rehearsing what he was going to say to his second in command (*Second in command nothing,* thought Mike. *Cleary was the real cop in town. The* only *cop in town.*) Another long-drawn-out sigh, one that forced his lips to vibrate. Well, the time had come. He needed to have a meeting with Jack Cleary. A talk about small town police work; a talk about small town politics versus big city politics; a talk about police ethics; a talk about drug dealing; a talk about many things.

Man to man.

He told Dex that he was going out for a coffee and that he

would be back soon. He asked him if he wanted anything from Rodney's and then the officer – exposing those two or three teeth again – smiled and held up his bag of doughnuts. "I'm good to go, Chief."

"I'll be back soon," he said.

☒ ☒ ☒ ☒

"Hi Chief," the Turkish girl said to him with a smile.

"Hi, Sevil."

"The regular?"

"Please."

Mike watched the young girl pour the coffee into the white Styrofoam cup. He looked closely at the logo, which was a picture of a brown doughnut with a bite taken out of one side and a brown coffee mug steaming from the top. And in the middle, in the shape of a semi-circle, was the yellow and green cursive font that read *Rodney's Donut Hole*.

To Mike, Sevil (whose name in Turkish meant "beloved") was unusually attractive. *Exotic.* She was short with long black hair, green almond-shaped eyes and a unibrow, an oval-shaped face, a prominent nose that protruded like a ski slope but still complemented her features and large, kissable lips. According to Mike, she would easily – with those strong, pronounced features — translate into a beautiful cartoon character goddess. Sevil Yildiz was only nineteen but had a real sophistication that would allow her to pass for someone five or ten years older. She had worked at Rodney's Donut Hole since she was sixteen while being groomed to work in her family business. She currently lived with her parents (mother Ayla and father Altan) and younger sister Janan (which also meant "beloved") in the town's one funeral home, known optimistically as *The Rising Star Home of Rest*; in Turkish their last name, Yildiz, means "a rising star."

The Yildiz family, incidentally, added a sorely needed multicultural diversity in this otherwise uncultured, WASPY town of Fryebury Falls!

"Busy today?" Sevil asked in that naturally flirtatious manner of hers.

"Trying to stay busy," he said with a half-smile, sipping his rich, tasty Najarian coffee. "And how is your family?"

Sevil, who was quirky, convivial and coltish said, "Just waiting for their next customer."

Mike chuckled and said goodbye to the girl, and walked back to the station.

Back in the office he closed his eyes and pictured the following scene: it was like something out of a Robert Crumb comic strip published in the underground Philadelphia newspaper, *Yarrowstalks*...

Jack Cleary's stocky body shook back and forth in the chair as the sound of giggling filled the office. He was sitting in front of Mike's desk and the two police officers were recuperating from a joke Mike told concerning three prostitutes and an old man.

"Oh shit," Mike said, his laughter now controlled. He let out a sustained "ohhhh" and then after a bit of a pause he said, changing beats, "I just want to tell you, Jack, that you are doing one hell of a job. One *hell* of a great job."

"Well Mikey, we do what we got to do. Right? Like the three whores and the old buck." The men laughed again – tears gushing out of their eyes like sprinklers. Then, as if things suddenly became serious again, Jack said, "Christ, it's not easy locking those little bastards up, but we've got a job to do, a community to preserve. Like I was telling you during my interview, I take lots of pride in wearing this uniform. And pride in Fryebury Falls, too, even though my methods might be a bit un...conventional. I'm working on that. It's a tough transition from city to small town police work. In a way I think what you've been doing *here* is much more challenging than what I was doing in the city."

Mike was intrigued. "Really? How so? I mean...with all those special assignments and all?"

"A lot of that is just brute force, Mikey. Cities are dirty places no matter how hard you try to keep them clean. What you do *here* I admire much more. You've got a difficult job. And the people respect you. You're their hero for crying out loud! Being a big fish in a small town is more admirable than some might think..." He paused, lowered his voice. "They love you and they fear me. I've got to learn how you do it, man. You're a fucking artist. I wish I could do what you do. Except for the little drug episode, which quite honestly happens everywhere, you run a clean and tight ship." He puffed on Mike's cigarette that was resting in the ashtray. He coughed vehemently. "Jesus, man, that shit'll kill you."

"You flatter me. I'm just doing my job, doing what feels natural. It's no secret, really. You could do it too. Just follow your heart and be good to people. That's the key to everything. Be good and kind to people and you'll make it."

Mike sat back in his chair and smiled. Jack Cleary would be just fine, he thought. Just fine. Then he leaned over his desk and whispered, "So tell me. Between friends here. And of course, in the *strictest confidence...*"

Jack sat motionless, intrigued.

Mike continued, "What *were* those special assignments you go on about? You've *got* to tell me. The suspense is killing me."

"I'll tell you sometime," Jack said, grinning like a mischievous child.

"When?"

"My moment of death."

"I see," Mike said, sighing. He too was grinning, but was still disappointed with the response. "Moment of death, huh?"

Jack laughed, slapping his knee. "Oh man, you give me too much credit. You want to know what these special assignments were, I'll tell you." Mike sat back in his chair and Jack leaned forward, the little mischievous child now a skilled storyteller. "Once upon a time there was this little weasel scumbag pimp named Burnham. And once upon a time there was this...teenage girl. 'Lolita Number Two' we called her at the station. Well, Burnham was banging this 'Lolita Number Two,' beating her – she had little black eyes when I saw her – and he was selling her to underground films and shit. The girl looked like she was twenty – *at least*. It was remarkable. A little Traci Lords, you know what I mean?" Mike did *not* know what he meant, but he kept smiling. Jack paused, took a drag off of Mike's cigarette, coughed, then continued. As Jack told the story Mike had his eyes closed, picturing every event and character in vivid detail. What Mike saw was an adult cartoon unfold before his dreaming eyes with a very eloquent first-person narrator helping the story along. Jack's voice and method of telling the story reminded him of the narrator in that movie Miss Julie loved so much...the one about a double something or other. "This Burnham guy we find out later had a file two miles long. And he was this model citizen – one of those guys you couldn't nail. Not at first. He was a popular middle school science or math teacher. Probably where he recruited his Lolita. But we knew he was shady...we knew he was up to no good. It was a long story, but one thing led to the next and one of our boys on the force – my buddy Dave Aaronson (who is now deceased) – he saw this Burnham and 'Lolita Number Two' in the woods kissing. *Pretty freaky shit.* Aaronson had to look twice. Well, he followed the guy back to his house and one thing led to another. He called me for some back up, we did some investigations and lo and behold what do we find but an entire kiddy porn business that *he* – and get this – his *wife* – had been running from their basement! *Fuck-*

ing A! Well, Aaronson and I, we broke into the house while everyone was out and found the goods. Obviously, at the time, we couldn't do anything about it...no warrant, no case. Right? So later that week we snuck in again." He paused thoughtfully: "Is it *sneak* or is it *snuck*? I always mess that up." Mike shrugged. *"Anyhoo –* I planted a shit load of coke and smack, uppers, downers, acid, dust, mushrooms, you name it, then made up some convincing story to a judge to obtain a warrant, and we went in and busted the little pedophiles for the kiddie porn things *and* a drug ring. Double whammie! You know what they say...the postman always rings twice." Mike looked baffled, but didn't say anything. Then Jack said, "You may get away with murder, but rest assured that the postman will come back and get you for the crime in some way...maybe not the way you *expect*, but in the end, you're still going to pay."

"Unbelievable," Mike said.

"And it gets better. After we walked in with the warrant – it was the wife who let us in – we go down to the basement and before long we discover that she is – get this — holding a gun on us. Believe that? And she shoots it. Kills my partner... shoots him between the eyes. And then she shoots at me: hitting me three times. I showed you all the bullet wounds except for the one where the sun don't shine, and let me tell you that one hurt the most. You would think you'd rather get shot in the ass rather than the leg...I assure you wouldn't. A bullet in the ass is" – He paused, then continued – "You ever experience sciatica nerve pain? The pain is unbearable; it radiates relentlessly down your leg right through your ass. Feels like someone is trying to tear your entire bottom half off with a pair of big pliers. Multiply *that* by ten. No, *twenty*. It's like...giving birth!" He smirked and then the men cachinnated.

"That's one *hell* of a story."

"It's been the highlight of my career. I've had other assignments – other dangerous ones – but none quite so...interesting...or painful." He smiled.

"This sounds like a case I read about."

"The story was all over the place. Made some national news show too. *60 Minutes* maybe. And this guy – this Don or Tom Burnham turned out to be one of the editors for that animated porno mag...what's it called...*Foxes in Boxes* or something?"

"*Foxes and Boxes*," Mike said.

"I stand corrected, then. You sure know your animated porno mags, my friend!"

"That I do," Mike agreed.

"Well, hell on wheels! This calls for a beer!"

"Many beers, Jack," Mike said, rising from his chair. "Many beers."

"The first round's on me, boss."

"Lead the way, big shot."

An hour later, when the *real*, live-action version of Jack Cleary was sitting in that chair facing the chief, Mike wasn't cracking prostitute jokes or complimenting the cop on his brilliant police work or listening to any "special assignments" anecdotes or laughing or drinking beers.

"I want to discuss a few bits of business with you," Mike said, staring into the officer's colorless eyes. Mike Melanson's eyes may have been crossed, but Jack Cleary, he didn't seem to have *any* color in his eyes at all; his pupils were washed out, practically translucent like a great white shark. "A few bits of business that you just might find interesting. But first things first."

"I'm all ears."

"Okay." He paused for a bit, thought that he would lose his nerve, but then suddenly mustered up enough energy to go through with it. "Like I've told you before, Jack, I want to congratulate you on a job well done. You've got a sharp eye and good instincts, and those are qualities that I look for in my police officers." He lit a cigarette and offered one to Jack who reminded him again that he didn't smoke. "Drugs are a serious and mean business, and we need to crack down." He paused and exhaled air from his nose in what might have been the beginning of a laugh. "Huh-huh, *crack* down." Jack didn't stir; Mike cleared his throat. "We can't have this sort of thing happening in our town. There are too many people to consider. After all, we are serving them. *We* are the reason why they feel safe to walk the streets or stroll in the Millyard. That's our job...that's the service we provide for our people." Again, Jack did not stir, staring at Mike in a way that made him most uncomfortable. Mike took a puff on the cigarette as if it were an inhaler. "We've got to work as a team if we're all going to play ball together." If Miss Julie could see him now, he thought. She'd be so proud. Low-down townie *nothing*! "We need to stay on top of this drug business; we need to see where it's coming from..."

"I can tell you right now that it's coming from –"

"Hold on, Jack," Mike said so suddenly it startled them both. "Thank you. We'll get to that later." He cleared his throat and took another drag off of the cigarette. Jack looked at the buffoon in front of him and pictured him with a bullet between his eyes (maybe that would straighten out those eyes of his, he thought wanting to crack a smile). "You will have a chance to speak, I promise." The chief gloated. *And maybe later we can go get a beer...for real.* "As I said before, you're doing fine work. That drug bust was a big breakthrough, but I must also add that you went about it in a pretty – how do I say this – *unorthodox* manner? This isn't Boston, and you're not doing any special assignments work – not yet anyway. We have a small-town system in place here, and despite the work you've done in the past (*What* were *those assignments, Cleary? What* were *they?*), well I think you know what I'm getting at. Take that business with Gregory Reardon, the banker..."

The chief took a breath, looked down at his burning cigarette, but chose not to pick it up. He really hated confrontations.

Jack said nothing.

"There have been a number of complaints," Mike continued. "People coming to me about certain...*tactics*...you've been using. I never said anything before because I figured you had it all under control, and I was still hoping that things would settle down while you got used to the way we do things here. *Anyhoo*, I'm not *a custom* to giving speeches. I've only dealt with a few police officers in my life and never anyone like you..." Mike looked at Cleary's leg and was reminded of the bullet scars he showed him at the interview. "A man doesn't make friends that way. You have to ease up on some of these people. Enforcing the law is one thing, but..." He paused; his heart was racing. "Well, you're a smart guy; I don't want to insult you. You get the picture." A longer pause. "And...that's all I have to say about that."

Jack sat staring at Mike for what seemed like a very long time. Finally, he said, "So what you're saying to me is that we're all one big, happy family here?"

Mike sensed the sarcasm but said anyway, "Yes, in a way we are. I think that we'll maintain the law by taking a more peaceful approach to things." He no longer knew what he was talking about anymore. He felt like a principal disciplining one of the school's best students.

Jack lowered his brow. *Is this guy full of hot air or what? What kind of fantasy world is he living in? Take a peaceful approach to enforcing the law? Who is he...Wyatt fucking Earp?* He conjured up another vision of Melanson with a bullet between his eyes. He didn't like this feeling. Then Gail passed through him. He could feel her invading him like metastasizing cancer cells clawing their way through a person's internal organs. *She* was the one who was making him see these things. It was *her* and he knew it.

"Is this all making sense?" Mike asked. The question was heard in a low, muffled echo.

"It does," Jack said, squeezing his legs together, wishing that this insalubrious entity would leave his body. She created a sharp stinging sensation in his crotch. It reminded him of that excruciating urinary tract infection he had back in his early twenties.

"Good. Sounds like we're on the same page then."

"Sounds like you want me out," Jack said, and this retort startled Mike.

"Oh, no. No. You've got it all wrong. No. That is not what I meant at all. I didn't want to give you that impression. I'm sorry. No. Before you came aboard here there was never any real trouble. Some disorderly conduct, a few domestic abuse cases, but nothing we couldn't handle. But this didn't mean that there weren't problems out there. But if things didn't get too messy, well then, I would just look the other way. My philosophy was to 'leave sleeping dogs dead.' That's my motto." Jack was motionless, the tape recorder picking up every word. Was he going to have fun with this conversation later on...*oh brother*! "And this drug case with Eddie Price and the rest of those kids – well, like I said, you've got a good eye for that sort of thing. Good instincts. Better than I do. No doubt from all your special assignments in the city." Mike thought he was starting to ramble. He was losing his main train of thought. He thought of Roger Price who implied that Jack not only slapped his kid but planted drugs on him too. But he shrugged it off. Let's forget about all that. Let's move on. *Leave sleeping dogs dead.*

Jack was confused. "I'm not catching you. Is there a point to all of this?" *Leave sleeping dogs dead?*

This statement got the chief back on track. He took another puff on his cigarette, the last one before putting it out, then said, "I've been doing a great deal of thinking about what

I am going to offer you here, Jack." Pause. "My needs seem to be changing." Another pause. "*I'm* changing. The town is obviously changing – and not so much for the better." An even longer pause. He looked down at the ashtray. No cigarette. He looked over at his pack of Marlboros. "I'd like to spend more time with my family. With my son. I'm sure you understand, having a son of your own. In fact, I was even thinking of coaching Little League next year...Adam will be old enough to play then. Being police chief requires quite a commitment even for a very small town like this."

Mike got up walked over to Jack and put his hand on his shoulder. "What do you say about forming a partnership? Me and you?" Mike smiled, a real one this time, but it still only looked like a constipated grimace especially with his crooked eyes bouncing about his sockets. "We'd make a good team. Or at least we can learn to become a good team. We can learn a lot from each other, I think. And together – with both of our strengths – me with the small town...uh, politics... and you with the city experience – we can eliminate drugs and anything else that comes our way. Together we can monitor and patrol the town. A team. Two chiefs. You and me. You can teach me how to become...a better cop and well, I can help you with...those other things."

Jack Cleary remained inert. Was he hearing all of this correctly? When he played this conversation back later on in his cruiser, would he hear these same words again? *Partners? Two chiefs? You and me?*

"But I've got my conditions," Mike said firmly. "You and I need to be open with one another. We really need to communicate, or this can't happen. And up to now I don't think we have been communicating like we should be. I blame myself for that. But that can change. And no secrets either. I don't want to hear through the grapevine that you threatened someone or smacked some kid in the face for mouthing off."

Jack's forehead scrunched up. Mike put his hand up and said, "Water under the bridge. No need to talk about *anything*. I don't want to know. Clean slate. Beginning today." And then absurdly – this actually made Jack laugh a bit – Mike said, "Leave sleeping dogs dead."

A pause.

"You're a good cop," Mike continued. "I have faith in you. In us. We can put the past behind us and look into the future. If you agree to this, we need to make a public announcement. We've got to go talk with the selectman and Gary White and people like that. I'm not too sure how this all works especially since this is an elected position, but we can find that out. A split position to me sounds ideal. Two is better than one. And if you play ball, I'm sure that the people in town will support you. Even folks like Greg Reardon and Roger Price – well, they're good men. They'll soon realize that your intentions were – and *are* – good." He took a breath. "So, what do you say? Want to think it over?"

Another scene from the pages of *Yarrowstalk:* Mike imagined Jack accepting the partnership. Both men were celebrating in Jeremy's Irish Pub, one of those members-only bars in Fryebury Falls.

"What would I do without you Mikey boy?" Jack asked, downing a Guinness.

"You'd be beating the piss out of innocent people every day," Mike said, sipping on a Murphy's Stout.

"I'll drink to that," Jack said, finishing the Guinness.

"You can have until the end of the month to decide," Mike said. His throat was scratchy; he couldn't remember the last time – if ever – he spoke for so long all at once. The chief was ready for lunch. Or at least another cup of coffee from Rodney's Donut Hole.

A jolt of electricity passed through him.

The two men shook hands, then parted.

Mike Melanson had a good feeling – one of those "premonitions" as Miss Julie would call it – that Jack Cleary would agree to this proposed plan. Mike still needed to figure out how such a thing would happen. But he wasn't worried.

And Miss Julie would be so proud of him when he told her. "M&M – you are a smooth operator, lover boy. What a brilliant idea. What would I do without you, you darling thing you?"

"You'd probably be famous," he'd reply, and they'd both laugh.

CHAPTER 18

LITTLE TOWN BLUES

On Monday morning, June twenty-fifth, Miss Julie was hopping down the stairs on her one good foot pretending to be Ann Reinking. (According to her, Reinking was the greatest of the Bob Fosse dancers – and a genius choreographer.) She especially loved her in *Chicago*: the way her hips and legs swayed...it was elegiac, like a serpent...so sexy, so seductive.

In addition to Miss Julie's dreams of becoming a great stage actress and photographer, she also saw herself as a skilled jazz dancer.

Miss Julie was also quite the aficionado of Fosse's *Cabaret* and the 1979 film *All That Jazz* where the Chief of Police from *Jaws*, Roy Scheider, plays the pill-popping, chain-smoking adulterer choreographer Joe Gideon (and Reinking plays the comely cuckquean, Katie Jagger). In making this association, she imagined, if only for a second or two – and absurdly at that – what it would be like if her husband, the Chief of Police, were a trained dancer: a choreographer prancing through their estate like Peter Pan or Mikhail Baryshnikov and standing in the middle of the living room next to all the leather furniture in his black spandex in a jaunty arabesque. What a preposterous prospect, she thought, laughing, picturing her husband with those chubby legs of his moving to the song "Cellophane" from *Chicago*.

> *Cellophane, Mister*
> *Cellophane, could have*
> *Been my name, Mister*
> *Cellophane*
> *Cause you can look right through me*
> *And walk right by me*
> *And never know I'm there...*

Presently she was listening to an old recording of Liza Minnelli's version of the "New York, New York," written by Fred Ebb and John Kander. She had always insisted that Liza was destined to sing the song, that Frank Sinatra's version didn't have the energy or pizzazz to do it justice: In her professional opinion, Sinatra just *sang* the song – Liza *performed* it. Miss Julie was not a Liza Minnelli fan, however. In fact, she despised her in *Cabaret* where she thought she was too over-the-top; she always thought that Reinking (the beauty that she was, with those stunning, piercing blue eyes and buck teeth that somehow complemented that comely countenance – and ten times the dancer!) would have made a much better Sally Bowles.

But no one belted this song out like Liza. Miss Julie held onto the railing, continued to hop up and down on her good leg and sang along.

> *I want to wake up in a city that never sleeps*
> *To find I'm King of the Hill*
> *Top of the heap*
> *Cream of the crop at the top of the hill*
> *These little town blues*

Are melting away
I'll make a brand-new start of it
In old New York
If I can make it there
I'll make it anywhere
It's up to you
New York, New York

The lyrics couldn't have explained her life better, she thought, seeing herself as Sally Bowles, dressed in black leotards, a black top and a black hat slanted over her right eye.

I want to wake up in a city that never sleeps (instead of this measly little town that *always* sleeps). *I'll make a brand-new start of it, in old New York* (someday – when I get off these damn crutches, I'll go audition again...never mind Boston; it'll be the real place...Broadway itself!).

These little town blues. These little town blues. These little town blues.

This became her mantra, her curse.

As she sang the last part of the song, Miss Julie, who was undoubtedly getting carried away as she continued doing her one-legged hop dance, slipped on the maroon carpet and took another digger, bouncing up and down ever so gracefully, her ass cheeks hitting the edge of each stair as if she were one of those Slinky toys, until she hit bottom.

And it wasn't a *merde* that came from those resplendent lips of hers; it was a fulminating *fuck* instead.

She began to cry and then conjured up the character of Jean from Strindberg's play. She fabricated the following dialogue with the servant. She stared at a pillow on the couch, then delivered her lines: "Oh Jean, help me to my feet and we can flee from this depressing place. We can go to New York. I will become a great star there. Ah yes, the stars are ageless, aren't they? Oh Jean, my love, I've got to get out of this place...I've got these *little town blues*..."

After a moment she heard applause. The image in the Victorian-style mirror above the black leather sofa came to life. It was a curtain call. And there she was...Miss Julie, curtseying in front of a full house of NYC writers, directors, actors, producers and adoring fans. Some were screaming her name while others simply clapped their hands together tastefully as if they were applauding a performance of the "Queen of the Night" aria from *The Magic Flute*, their eyes and mouths wide open from amazement and awe, frozen, as if their faces had temporarily transformed into theater masks.

Then through the TV the face appeared. It was a prominent, typically Russian- looking face, dark toned, nearly handsome in a fierce sort of way – his long dark moustache complementing his long, angular face outlined with straight, neatly-combed salt-and-pepper hair and a black unibrow resting like a caterpillar over his elliptical eyes. When he spoke, it was in an eloquent, piercing tone, the Russian accent prominent but not overbearing.

"That was sensational. You were perfect. I wish Strindberg were here to see it. Bastard as he was, he'd marvel at your performance. Your *motivation*, your *subtext*, your overall concentration and use of sense memory – all wonderful. You earn an *A* in my class. I wish Anton were here to see you. I'd love to act with you myself. In *The Cherry Orchard* maybe. I can see you as Lyuba Ranevsky. And of course, I would replay the role of her billiard playing brother, Leonid Gayev. But *this* role is made for you. You *are* Miss Julie, no doubt about it."

"Stan?" Miss Julie yelled at the TV. Her eyes were blurry.

"Hello, my *Lyuba*."

"Oh Stan," she said, his image becoming more prominent, "I need to get out of here. I'm going crazy."

"Ah, just like Miss Julie. Magnificent. You will get out of here, my dear. *Real, real soon*. I promise. Just put your faith in me like you always have, and you will be the star that you deserve to be. Now, how would you like to attend an audition?"

"Really?"

"Really."

"On Broadway?"

"Where the neon lights are bright!"

"What audition are you talking about?" Suddenly Miss Julie found herself pulling back her hair, combing it with her long fingernails.

"A show being written by a talented new playwright named Jimmy Orlinski."

"Never heard of him."

"Well, my dear, there was a time when no one ever heard of Ibsen or Strindberg or Chekhov or Brecht or...Stanislavski for that matter," he said, laughing. "Believe me, you *will* hear of him. He's going to be the greatest thing since sliced bread – in the theater anyway. Someday he will be mentioned among all the great names. He has a natural knack for character, language and dramatic structure. Like Shaw and Wilde, and he's got a unique style that will be plagiarized by hack dramatists for the next century. Consider this in a Hegelian manner: If the chamber style of Kammerspiel were the *thesis* and Epic Theater (Brecht always liked to call it 'Dialectical Theatre') was the *antithesis*, then Orlisnki's theatre would be its *synthesis*."

"What has he written?" Miss Julie was not yet convinced.

"Actually, he's still writing it. The masterpiece. It's in its fifth draft and as brilliant as ever. It's got Pulitzer and Tony already stamped on it. It's the play of the century and the funny thing is the poor bastard doesn't even know it yet. He thinks it's a failure. Got to love writers – insecure little creatures. Actors too, for that matter."

"What's it called?"

"*Needle in a Haystack*," Stan said proudly.

"That's a bit *cliché*, isn't it?"

"It's *all* cliché, my dear. *All* cliché. Just ask Aristotle. Or Jung, for that matter. There are really only a few stories and a few good archetypes. The secret is what you *do* with these stories and archetypes...that's what truly marks originality. Then it becomes the genius of the Thespians – that's us my dear – to bring the words and events to life. To create real, living, breathing entities. Like what I write about in *Building the Character*. In this world there are only a select few who are destined for greatness. I was a fortunate one, this Jimmy Orlinski is another one and you, my lyuba, you too have been selected to become one of theater's greats. It's the *inevitable order of things*."

Miss Julie got a chill. She smiled uncontrollably as she combed her hair with her fingers again. "Tell me about the play."

"It's a real tragedy. It'll spawn a new movement in the history of theater. As you know theater has been dead for decades now. There hasn't been anything fresh since Brecht. Or maybe Carolyn Churchill and what she did with *Top Girls*. But *this* play is going to reinvent the myths of the stage. It's a one woman show – a twelve act epic – a twenty-four hour tour-de-force. Performed as a series." He laughed. Miss Julie sat there intrigued, momentarily forgetting her pain. "The show is about how a woman relies on heroin and how she locks herself in a room attempting to quit cold turkey. Her name is Je'Nelle Bouvier, a Mormon from Utah. Before long, that name will have as much clout as Nora Tesmond – Desdemona – Medea – Blanche Dubois – Lady Bracknell – Hedda Gabler – Linda Loman – Roxie Hart – *Miss Julie*."

Miss Julie leaned her head back on the stairs.

"Think it over, my lyuba. I'll be back later to discuss it with you further. In the meantime, take care of yourself. Try to stay in one piece."

He laughed and dissolved into the screen.

During her second hiatus as a bedridden victim, Miss Julie was simply impossible. Not only was she extra demanding, but she would also slip into periods of inescapable depression, doing nothing but sleeping and dreaming of the life she didn't have.

Needle in a Haystack seemed so real to her that she could even anticipate the upcoming rehearsal schedule. And Jimmy Orlinski too. The young playwright – he was only twenty-three years old – was tall and lean with short blond hair and round glasses that were a good fit to his boyish, pimply, light-complected face. To Miss Julie he was handsome – not traditionally handsome, for she hated traditionally handsome; to her, men who had those so-called "magazine good-looks" were repulsively banal. A man, to her, needed to have blemishes. This gave him wisdom and character.

When Billy Ashburnham called her and told her he needed to cut *S.O.S.* from the program list (the station wasn't big enough to rely on syndication despite Miss Julie's logic), she became, to quote Mike, "an entirely different creature" – angrier, talking to herself more frequently and obsessively reading lines and monologues from the Strindberg play. She was so detached from everything that Adam became very concerned about his mother's well-being.

One day he asked his father, "Is Mommy going to get better?"

"Of course," Mike responded. "She just needs lots of rest, that's all."

"I mean is she going to get better...in the *head*?"

Miss Julie's metamorphosis began soon after her second fall but seemed to reach its summit on the day Mike ever so proudly told her of his new plan – that he and Jack Cleary would soon become partners – that once all the appropriate paperwork went through, they were going to split their duties *fifty-fifty* – that soon he would be able to spend more time with her and Adam, something she had been begging him to do for ages. He gloated.

"Are you out of your mind?" was her reaction, her voice almost singing the question, each word resonating with impeccable diction that seemed to vibrate right through her husband.

Mike was, to say the least, unprepared for this response. After the initial shock subsided, he humbly said, "I thought you'd be happy. I did it for us. So we could all spend more time together." He hung his head. "So maybe you could start doing some of that acting you've always wanted to do. To spend more time with Adam and his school and..."

"What the hell is the matter with you?"

Suddenly her acting dreams were – temporarily, of course – placed on hold for this new drama before her. *Partners with that snake? Are you out of your mind?* This was as absurd as Didi and Gogo living the same day over and over, waiting for Godot, who would never arrive.

Mike's eyes were still watching the floor. "I don't understand why you're so upset."

"You *really* don't know, do you?"

"No...I don't."

"Look at me," the invalid said. He looked up. "For once in my life I would like to – no, I take that back – I would *love* to see you surprise me. Just once. Just once I'd love to see you make a decision that didn't make you look like a total ass!"

Mike was speechless.

"I can't believe you gave that overgrown bulldog control of the police department. I can't believe it. I just can't! *Holy merde!*"

"What are you talking about? We'll be partners. I didn't *give* him anything. He's a smart cop. Plus, we had a good talk the other day about how he needed to change his ways. I...kept him in line. You should have heard me. I thought a lot about this decision. I don't have to retire, and I'll have only half the work to do. The way I figure it, we can hire someone to replace Jack's position – maybe even someone part time. I think the budget will swing it. You always said you wanted me to retire. Well, this is the next best thing, isn't it?"

"So now we're throwing my money around, huh?"

"What are you talking about?" Mike scowled at his wife. *You are being unreasonable.* And Mike told her so.

"Don't talk to me like that. How *dare* you!" She lowered her voice and talked through her teeth. Mike hated it when she did this. "Your son is in the other room! What kind of role model are you for him – yelling at his mother? How *dare* you!"

Mike experienced the rage. He simply didn't know why one minute she could be so optimistic and happy and funny and the other minute – literally as if someone flipped a switch on the wall or something – she would transform into that other part. That *thing.* That devil. That castrating, unreasonable, paranoid freak. Once, Mike found a book that his wife kept in her side table drawer...something about peace from nervous suffering and another one with the words "manic depression" in the title. He wondered if there was something really up with her. Mike knew little to nothing on manic depression except that it was some sort of disease or condition that caused people to have two personalities...one good and the other bad. Whatever else it meant, he knew that there was something wrong with his wife's personality; there always had been. Usually her rages would not last long and after a short while that good switch would be back on again as if nothing had ever happened. What was strange about his wife – and this he thought about quite frequently – was that she would lose her temper, say horrible things to him or even to Adam, but then later she would be saying how much she loved her family. It was as if she completely forgot what she said earlier. Mike also knew that Miss Julie could not live on her own. There was something very vulnerable and very sad about her, and the idea of anyone leaving her, of abandoning her, would most likely make her go over the edge. *Oh yes*, he had his hands full with that one, but the strange thing was...he loved her. Not because she was a knock-out, either. No, there was something else, something he could not explain. A true unconditional love that simply existed. And deep down, he knew that no one else could have handled her.

Miss Julie continued to insult him and the more she spoke the more he felt the blood rush to his head. He pinched the side of his leg until it hurt, and his heart continued to race and through the open window he saw an image that stifled him. For a moment he felt as though he could not breathe. He coughed. The image flashed before the glass about a dozen times, each flash lasting longer than the previous one, each flash revealing more horrendous details, more complicated machinations.

The image – resembling the rotoscope technique of Ralph Bakshi's *Wizards, Lord of the Rings* and *American Pop* – was of his wife's corpse sprawled out on their bed. She was naked and her body was mangled from open cuts and bruises. There was a combination of red and black blood about her carcass. And her once beautiful face was no longer a face but a series of slice marks with zigzag patterns around her eyes, cheeks and jawbone.

"Close that window," Miss Julie said. "It's getting breezy in here."

And without thinking, like a programmed machine of some sort, he followed her orders. He could feel his heart doing all kinds of little dances in his chest. He felt a tingling sensation in his left arm that radiated to his neck. But then it subsided and his mind returned to that place from before: that place, that other life where he and Jack Cleary were the best of friends drinking Guinness and Murphy's Stout at Jeremy's Irish Pub; that place where he and George Pearson were together, cooking hamburgers, steaks and hot dogs on a grill while Julie and Alison chatted about the arts and other intellectual things that Mike never understood, and Adam and Abbie-Girl were playing tag and hide-and-seek and building forts with lumber scraps.

Why couldn't it be like this? Mike thought. Instead, his wife was losing her fucking mind. *Why was she acting like this? Why was she like this to begin with? Why did he love her so much...why couldn't he just hate her? And why was his best friend drinking his life away, committing slow suicide? And why did George's wife and daughter have to die? And why was Mike so dubious about his role as a police chief? Fucking why, why, why?* And now this new quandary: *Did he make a good decision by offering Jack Cleary a partnership?* Miss Julie certainly didn't think so. But who was running the department anyway – him or his lunatic wife that couldn't hold down a job if her life depended on it? Thank God for that inheritance...

Miss Julie was not finished with the issue. "Haven't I told you that this guy is dangerous? Evil! More than you know, Michael. That's the problem with being cursed with clair-voyance...you know things. You read energies. Whether you want to or not."

Damn that New Age shit, Mike thought. Damn *that "throw yourself away and build up the new you" bullshit. Damn that Nosferatu, that old vampire who predicts things. Damn it all, Julie Jill Najarian. Damn it all to hell!*

Mike caught another glimpse of her massacred body. *What the hell was going on here?* He coughed. He now experienced some sort of hot spell...something quite unfamiliar. This wasn't one of those twenty-four-hour viruses; no, these symptoms were altogether different. Much different. His heart continued to dance. He became immobile, frozen. That jolt of electricity traveled like a juggernaut up and down and side to side and around and around, creating little eddies of nerves inside himself that made him nauseous.

Miss Julie continued: "The man is the devil himself. I can smell it. I can smell evil as much as I can predict it. And it stinks to high heavens, by God it stinks!" She closed her eyes; her body shook. "No! No! You must get rid of him. You must get rid of him now. He is the *devil*. The devil himself. *Evil. Evil. Evil!*"

Mike didn't know what frightened him more – the physical sensations inside of him, those images of her mutilated body or Miss Julie's current state of (*what was it?*) possession? Dementia?

But the thing that seemed to concern Mike more than any of these aforementioned things (*Jesus, what was happening to everyone?*), was that he believed her. He may have despised her approach, but when it came right down to it, his wife had a magic gift, something that couldn't be explained. Whatever she sensed – good or bad – always came true. And this is what scared him about George. That one day – early in the morning before the dawn breaks – he would get a call from Sam informing him of George Pearson's death. He then pictured Jack Cleary as a demon, a devil with bright red eyes. He closed his eyes tightly, trying to rid himself of these thoughts and images while still trying to give Miss Julie the attention she always needed. *Why was he suddenly afraid?* Afraid that his once brilliant idea had now perhaps become the worst decision of his life!

And why am I seeing things? Hearing things? Murderous things, horrible things! But some of them weren't so horrible either, he thought as the picture of the red head and the brunette, those beautiful animated princesses, flashed in his mind, then as an image on the wall above the dresser.

Again, he contemplated: *Why am I seeing these things?*

What is happening to me?

Another flash of his wife's bloody body.

"Are you listening to me?" Miss Julie asked her distracted husband. He looked into her eyes, which were bloodshot and... did they have some kind of glow to them? But as he continued to stare at her, everything seemed to go back to normal.

Or did it?

His heart was racing faster than ever.

Miss Julie continued: "And what about this town? What are people going to say when you propose this ridiculous new...partnership or whatever the hell you called it earlier? What do you think is going to happen? I'll tell you what. Panic and hysteria. You, my dear have just declared war...on yourself!"

Mike had no retort. The only thing he had was a confirmed insight: *I am no longer worthy of this job.*

But there was much more to it than that.

His wife then kicked him out of the bedroom and told him not to disturb her. She was going to take a nap, she said, and dream about worlds more prodigious, more colossal, more baronial than this one.

Mike took this thought with him as he left the room. He imagined his wife standing on the top stairs facing downward. Then he saw himself picking up one of those ridiculous designer crutches and cracking her over the head with it, forcing her to tumble to the bottom of the stairway. And this scene – like all the aforementioned half cartoon, half live action images – could also have come right out of a Ralph Bakshi film.

He sat on the leather stairs of the downstairs living room, staring at the Ansel Adams landscape. He then looked into the TV and saw this image: Julie was grinning the way she did when they both first met in Gary Wyckoff's backyard in Amesbury on Independence Day years earlier. She was the best thing he had ever set eyes on. And he loved her. And for some reason she loved him. Ugly old cross-eyed buffoon that he was.

Her image dissolved into something strange indeed: his mother. The cancer-stricken, moribund woman just days before she died. She was pallid and emaciated...with purple lips; she weakly reached out toward her boy with her frail, fragile, feeble twig of an arm. She was smiling – or trying to, anyway. "I'll see you soon, Michael, but not *too, too soon*. You have a good long life ahead of you."

Then she faded to white, then to black. The TV screen was blank again.

Mike closed his eyes and squinted hard. "Maybe it's time to let it all go," he said, not exactly understanding the entire meaning of these words.

Why in God's name did he talk to Cleary about a partnership? Had he gone mad?

And should he have hired Cleary in the first place? Now he was really beginning to doubt it. His wife was very good at making him see the other side of things quickly.

But Jack Cleary – despite his shortcomings – was impressive. A great city cop. Cleary even began implementing drug tests in all the schools in the area, which was a good idea. It would help eliminate the drug problem, that's for sure.

Alas, Fryebury Falls *needed* Jack Cleary! They may not have liked him...but they needed him. Mike needed him!

The chief closed his eyes tighter, escaping into a scene with him and Jack at a Red Sox game, cheering, laughing, making fun of players and the umpires and drinking beers. But before he could completely engage himself in that moment, he heard Miss Julie's echoed voice: *The devil himself...the devil himself. It stinks to high heaven. Evil!*

Then suddenly, in another internal vision, a close-up of Jack Cleary's bulldog face, grinning sadistically, his nostrils flaring – and inside his reddened eyes he saw a picture of himself bleeding from the head. And surrounding him on all sides was a massive, blazing fire.

He opened his eyes quickly and at that moment understood his plight.

She was right. Once again, she was right. He could feel that she was.

He closed his eyes again, eventually descending deeply into a slumber. His visions and voices transformed into a series of dreams. Good dreams. Peaceful dreams. An eccentric mix of animation and live action.

In the dream he was running for town manager, a job he could always see himself doing. He knew *just enough* about little town politics to make a decent go of it.

He was in front of a crowd of cheering citizens: They were all familiar faces too, but each face looked grotesque, deformed, as if they were all wearing masks made from their own flesh and bones.

He saw George and Sam Pearson who were oddly enough holding hands while drinking something from straws. He also saw Jack Cleary and his brain-injured boy, J.J., who was asleep on the ground with his dog. And he saw his own lovely family who actually looked better than the rest. Miss Julie was naked, and her long hair made her look like Lady Godiva; Adam, who was only an infant, was sucking on her nipple. She was clapping her hands and whistling through her teeth, yelling, "That's my man. That's my M&M. The town manager of Fryebury Falls. My sexy husband! *Woot-woot!*"

Ah, thought Mike finally as he watched over his town like Zeus on top of Olympus, the crowd moving in slow motion, the sounds of cheering subsiding into pure silence: *peace and harmony in Fryebury Falls.*

Then there were two beautiful female cartoon characters – one had orange hair and the other had white hair (alas, it was Jane and Judy Jetson respectively!) – blowing kisses at their lover boy.

Mike took a long sigh and smiled.

Peace and harmony. These little town blues, they are melting away...

It was, to quote Miss Julie, "simply *mah-velous.*"

CHAPTER 19

SOMETHING WICKED
THIS WAY COMES

On the last day of the month, June thirtieth, the weather had reached a record-breaking one hundred and eight degrees, but the relative humidity surprisingly remained low, which made it quite comfortable for one to sit in the shade.

It was a Saturday afternoon and Mike Melanson was outside on his deck watching rather intently the penumbra that took the shape of the right side of his body. The stagnant air was so still that one could hear the eternal roar of Niagara Two through the trees.

On occasion, a rush of wind would sweep through the trees; this appeared to cool things off considerably.

Miss Julie was asleep, and Adam was at baseball practice. It was the boy's last year of Minor League. Next year, if all went according to plan, he would be a Little League rookie.

Mike pictured himself coaching Adam's Little League team. Then he returned to the dream he had a few nights earlier – in full stylized animation form – the one where he had been elected town manager.

"Speech! Speech!" Miss Julie said through cupped hands.

Jane and Judy Jetson were cheerleaders who kept chanting: "We got spirit, yes we do; we got spirit. How 'bout you?"

Mike was dressed in a navy-blue double-breasted suit with a bright red tie and black wing-tipped shoes. He was waving to the crowd, proudly and humbly, with one hand while holding Adam's hand with his other.

"I'm grateful to all of you," Mike said, and when he spoke all remained silent. "Fryebury Falls is a pretty amazing place. And as your town manager I will make it my mission and duty to maintain its integrity."

"It's *dooty* all right," Miss Julie added, laughing. The crowd joined her, cheering and guffawing.

Mike continued, smiling at his most pulchritudinous wife. How resplendent she looked standing there. Like a real goddess. Then he turned his head and pointed: "And I must point out, my good people, that the crime rate is down to practically *nothing* thanks to my former partner and good friend, Mr. Jack Cleary, who is doing an excellent job maintaining *peace, purity* and *law and order*. He's our beloved Chief of Police. You all made the right choice in electing him." He paused, then winked at Jack. "It may have taken him a month or two to get straightened out, but now I think this city bigwig has finally adapted to the ways of Fryebury Falls."

The crowd cheered. Cleary blushed. J.J. clapped his hands and said, "That's my Daddy!" He looked over at former town manager Gary Wyckoff who had his arm around his delectable wife, Beth.

"And to my girl, Miss Julie," Mike continued, "who is currently starring on Broadway in a play called –" He paused, scratching his head.

"*A Doll's House,* you low-down townie with no concept of the real world!" she yelled.

The crowd made a sound that resembled a sit-com laugh track.

"Ah yes, *A Doll's House*. That play by...Henry Gibson."

"*Henrik Ibsen the playwright,* you low-down townie, not Henry Gibson that foolish actor who was in *Laugh-in* with Lily Tomlin and Goldie Hawn. What am I going to do with you? *A Doll's House* by Henrik Ibsen! You know, the play about a liberated woman named Nora who is trapped in the confinements of her own home. She leaves her husband in the end! Slams the door on his egotistical fat ass! *That* play."

The crowd laughed, clapped their hands, and cheered again.

Then the little voice asked, "What about me, Daddy?"

The crowd went silent.

"How can I forget you, Adam?" Mike said, looking down at his son, still holding onto his hand. He grabbed the boy by the hips and picked him up on his shoulders. "Ladies and gentlemen...my brilliant son. Adam Melanson. The artist. The animal activist. And most recently the MVP of his little league team, the Braves. An all-star catcher."

"That's the hardest position in the game," someone yelled out. Mike looked up at Adam who looked down on his father and they both smiled at one another.

The crowd cheered as if the MVP just hit a home run.

The cheering dissolved slowly into the running waters of Niagara Two.

Mike looked up into the window, wondering if his wife was still sleeping, wondering if she was ever going to let him back into the bedroom. She never held a grudge like this before. It was as if he had committed adultery or something. It was ridiculous!

The running waters of the Niagara Two continued.

Upstairs, Miss Julie was having her *own* dreams: neon lights of red, orange and yellow, displaying her name over Radio City Music Hall; moving black-and-white photographs of calla lilies and her theater headshots; a pulsating montage of Jack Cleary's exploding skull, detonating in slow motion, juxtaposed with angelic voices singing something peaceful and indecipherable in the background; of her husband transforming himself into a long-haired, fitly-trimmed dancer, doing moves that only Bob Fosse himself could do; and a gray-haired gentleman who must have been a version of Stan, holding her hand, leading her out of Fryebury Falls and into a portal revealing what looked like a lifelike impressionistic painting replete with all kinds of exotic flowers; and in the center of it all – a Greek-style theater with all the trimmings, including columns and decorative masks that must have been worn when Euripides, Sophocles and Aristophanes were writing their respective tragedies and comedies.

Mike lit a cigarette.

All the peace he sought and attained that afternoon ended prematurely the second he saw that blurred, moving image from afar come into sharp focus.

It was Moira Davis.

She moved quickly, at the pace of a slow jog.

She was barefoot and on a mission.

"Mike!" she called from the top of the street.

"I'll meet you at the end of the driveway," he said, his heart jumping, figuring that there was bad news forthcoming. Otherwise, why would this obnoxious wife of his best friend's brother be there to see him?

If anyone reminded him of his own wife, it was Moira Davis. Why this was the case, he really didn't know. Moira didn't *look* like his wife – not to mention she was practically a foot shorter than the Armenian goddess. But she kind of *acted* like her at times. That must have been it.

"You know what that cocksucker assistant of yours did to me?" Moira pontificated. She hadn't even reached the driveway yet.

Mike motioned with his hand for her to keep her voice

down. He didn't want to wake his wife up. "What's on your mind, Moira?" He said this calmly enough, but he wasn't calm in the least. His palms were sweating, and he rubbed them together as if – absurdly, in this scorcher of a day – he was warming them from the cold air.

"I want to talk to you about Jack Cleary," she thundered. "*That's* what's on my mind."

"What about him?"

"I need to..." She paused; she was out of breath. She had positioned herself so close to the chief that he could smell cigarettes on her breath.

Moira spoke at almost a whisper now, and consequently her breath was now more pungent. "He recorded us...in bed. I found out, showed it to him, told him I was not pleased and then...the next night...he...came over and told me he wanted me again. Even after I told him this would not happen ever again." She looked down and then up at Mike who couldn't have looked more concerned. She continued, "Maygyn was spending the night with her father and he knew this. He cornered me and then pushed his way into the garage. Then he closed the door...and then...well...had his way with me." She breathed on him again. "Against the car. Against my will."

Mike digested the information. He didn't speak for a moment. "So, he...attacked you? In your garage? Against your will?"

Moira nodded as if to say: *Yeah, isn't this what I just said you low-down townie with no concept of the real world?* "Right."

Mike got a lump in his throat and the word "shit" slipped out in a whisper. He heard himself say: *You're not a real cop, Mike. Admit it. You can't handle this.*

Although he tried to fight the impulse of believing such unsubstantiated rhetoric, he *couldn't* fight it. He believed her. Mike Melanson, in his gut, and before knowing anything more, believed what Moira Davis was telling him. Perhaps something else was telling him that she spoke the truth. *Was it Miss Julie telling him? Had some of those premonitions and predictions rubbed off of her and onto him?*

He recalled Miss Julie's words of wisdom regarding Moira Davis: "She's got her problems like the rest of us, but she's authentic. She's real. People don't like her because she'll tell you where the dog died, but deep down she's one of the most genuine souls I've ever encountered. I feel it. And I also feel tragedy with her. A tragic past that has forced her to escape from her whole life, and a tragic future, too. Poor woman. I feel for her, I really do. She's never fitted in with anything she's ever done. She's one of life's most misunderstood humans. But she's resourceful and she knows herself; you can't say that about most people. And that explains her hard edge."

Moira continued, and as she spoke this time, Mike became endeared to her. Quite suddenly, Mike Melanson understood a lot of Moira Davis's tragedy. He wanted to reach out to her somehow, but didn't know how. "What are you going to do about it?"

Mike sighed as if he were blowing out a candle.

Moira bit her lip. As she did this, chewing away at it as if it were some piece of candy, one of those now familiar jolts of electricity passed through the chief. He studied her arms, which were tanned and smooth except for a little patch of hair on the upper part of her left arm connecting to the shoulder. Her elbows, however, were dry and chalk-white and so were her knees, for that matter. For some reason, he imagined kissing that flaky skin. Moira waited for Mike to answer and in the meantime, she asked him if he had an extra cigarette. He gave her one – a Marlboro Red. She smiled thinly...this was her brand, she told him. He smiled back, another jolt of electricity permeating his insides.

Mike began to sweat from his forehead. He shook his head

vehemently, trying to expel the mental pictures he was getting of Jack and Moira against the car in the garage. Then just for a second the same picture dissolved into an image that resembled Max Fleisher's rotoscoped series, *Out of the Inkwell*. Moira asked him if he was okay. He said he was fine, that it must be the heat affecting him. Finally, he said, "I'll have a word with him."

"I don't think you understand, Melanson," she said in a well-composed manner, "I want to file a complaint. And a restraining order." She blew cigarette smoke off into space and then nearly pressed her nose to Mike's face. "I don't want that fucker anywhere near me or my daughter." She paused and swallowed a glob of spit. Then in a real whisper: "He's dangerous. And you better do something fast, or I swear –"

"I will speak with him," Mike said.

"*Speak* with him? Are you telling me that? –"

"Look –" Mike said with an unexpected rage that made Moira jump back a bit, "I believe what you are telling me. Okay?" Then he leaned in toward Moira, this time practically pushing his nose into *her* face, and whispered through his teeth, "But I need to go about this my way if you want any justice to be served. *Okay?* You need to trust me. Understand?"

Moira understood. She looked into the chief's funny looking eyes and nodded slowly like a child being scolded by a parent. Then Mike tossed his cigarette, sighed, and shook his head back and forth. "Christ." He cleared his throat and touched her on the shoulder. "I'm sorry. Are you okay? Are there any – ?"

Moira jumped back again. "No."

"Good." He lifted his hand from her sticky skin.

"And Mike," Moira added. "Please keep this discreet. I would die if Maygyn knew of any of this. Absolutely die."

Mike nodded and contorted his face into a grotesque sort

of comforting smile.

When Moira left, Mike watched her walk away until she could no longer be seen anymore. He contemplated the facts that had just been reported to him. Maybe now he could exercise his abilities as a law enforcer. He had a real case before him. He was actually kind of excited. And the irony of it all was that it was Jack Cleary himself who had brought this out in him.

This attack, this rape (it *was* a rape, wasn't it?) accusation was the final complaint. Not everyone in town could be wrong about him. Let's just face the facts: *no one liked him.* No one, that is, except for Mike himself. Mike had not only liked him...he envied him. Was enamored by him. Was jealous of him. Was even attracted to him...well, in a way that a heterosexual man can be attracted to another man, that is. What do they call it? A man crush? But here's another troubling fact: the guy was a bully. Mike thought about what Roger Price said he did to his son Eddie; he thought of Gregory Reardon the banker; and he now conjured up the rest of the complaints.

How stupid could I have been? And in his own voice he heard: *You low-down townie with no concept of the real world!*

Mike stormed into his house. A new jolt of electricity passed through him. *Damn it, Cleary. RAPE? Are you kidding me? That will not stand. No way. Not in my town. Not on my watch. And to think I offered you a partnership. Man alive!*

Mike Melanson was a paradox of emotions. In the next instant he pictured himself with Jack at Jeremy's Irish Pub, laughing and telling dirty jokes. A tear filled his eye. *I wanted to be your friend. I admired you. Narcotics specialist, nothing. Special assignments, nothing. Big city Boston cop, nothing.* This big shot needed to be confronted...and if what Moira Davis said was true, then Cleary needed to be replaced as soon as possible.

Thank you, Moira. I'm not sure you know what you've

done for me. You have woken me up from a deep sleep. I am a police officer again.

Out of desperation, he told his wife all about Moira's visit. Humbly, he asked her what to do. He anticipated her responses and dreaded them too, but if anyone knew how to give solid advice, it was his Julie. Plus, he knew that putting her in a position of empowerment would help restore her respect for him.

Games. All games.

He broke down to her. The crippled woman said, "Don't be so hard on yourself. I won't let you talk like that about the man I love." She smiled. She was back in full form again!

For extra confirmation, Mike asked his prophetic wife if she thought Jack really raped Moira Davis. Miss Julie took a long time to answer. She was listening to her instincts – those premonitions of hers. Then, she opened her eyes widely, a look that frightened Mike, and said, "I don't know. There is something strange about that visit. I am getting mixed signals. Sort of like – I don't know – lies informed by the real truth somehow. I *do* sense something, though. Something that has yet to happen." She paused and opened her eyes even wider and whispered: "*Something wicked this way comes.*" Now Mike's eyes widened, captivated by this narrator who just so happened to be his wife of many years. "Whatever he has done to her already," she continued, "is minor compared to what I see coming ahead. He's a monster. *And* he has a terrible past. As usual, I'm not sure about all the minute details, so don't ask me, but I do know this: When I think about it, I smell something...*foul.*" Then, contorting her face ever so grotesquely and speaking with a vocal fry said, "*Fair is foul and foul is fair. Hover through the fog and filthy air.*"

Mike got a pain in his abdomen.

Maybe Moira Davis was all talk and none of this was true. And maybe on Monday this whole thing would vanish. Maybe this was all a dream.

Or maybe Jack Cleary *was* a violent man. Maybe he was a rapist.

Or the devil himself, as Miss Julie indicated.

Whatever he was, Mike concluded, he needed to go. Far away and never to return. For good. Mike needed to confront him about Moira Davis and all the other incidents. He needed to tell him that this new "partnership" was not going to happen. *What were you thinking, Melanson? Two chiefs doing the same job? What the hell is the matter with you?*

Mike Melanson was about to embark upon the challenge of his career. And he kept telling himself he was ready for it. Maybe police work *was* in fact his calling. *Of course it was*, he thought to himself, and smiled sardonically.

Jack Cleary, you're going down!

Niagara Two roared like a lion through the trees.

JULY 1984

S	M	T	W	R	F	S
1	2	3	4	5	6	7
8	9	10	11	12	13	14
15	16	17	18	19	20	21
22	23	24	25	26	27	28
29	30	31				

CHAPTER 20

ACCIDENTS

The first day of July was overcast, but still hot and humid. Mike was on his deck and contemplated smoking a cigarette, but couldn't bring himself to light up. Even though it had been several days since Moira Davis had been there, he felt as though he never moved from that position. He looked down upon his driveway, focusing on the contours of the pavement, and within seconds conjured up a rotoscoped Moira Davis who was wearing ripped blue jeans and a tank top. He had a difficult time interpreting the meaning of that uncharacteristic grin on her face, but something about it seemed exciting and perhaps a bit dangerous.

He looked down at the pavement again, in the same spot where Moira had appeared; it had transformed into a stage with two chairs in the center. And the actors: Mike Melanson and Jack Cleary. They were drinking beers together. The men and their beers were glowing in a bright yellow light. The scene had the same animation style from Ralph Bakshi's 1972 X-rated film *Fritz the Cat*, right down to Robert Crumb's idiosyncratic comic book style artwork. For a split second, Mike pictured the movie poster that pictured two anthropomorphic cats – Fritz and a female cat – snuggling with one another. The logo read: *We're not X for nothin', baby!*

Back to the scene:

"So Jack," said Mike. "Moira Davis has informed me that she intends to file a complaint and a restraining order on you. She feels that you...*violated* her. Now I don't believe this to be true. But for the record, I must ask. Did you, Jack Cleary, *rape* Moira Davis?"

Mike looked carefully at Cleary's eyes; they were no longer red and demonic; they were black dots with no pupils.

Jack said, "Christ Mikey. Come on! She's making it all up. She's a performer! You know how she likes to sing and act and play that damn guitar of hers. And you know how she likes to suck down the juice. That night she was drunk. Wanted to get it on. Said she had the *itch,* and I had the club to scratch that itch. So, I got my jollies, put my uniform back on, and proceeded to leave. She told me to stay. I said *no way*. Then she said something like 'I'll get even with you then. You wait and see what happens.'" He put his hands up, then laughed. "I should file a rape charge against *her* for Christ's sake!"

Mike laughed.

"I can't believe this," Jack continued. "Please don't tell me you believe her. You're my partner! *We* are the *chief of police* for crying out loud!"

Mike paced the deck. He finally lit that cigarette and leaned over the deck to watch the second act of the play.

"So, Jack," Mike said, sipping his beer, "What's up with you and Moira Davis? She said you raped her. Did you? Fill me in on the sordid details, you filthy little dog."

"Mikey? You out of your mind? Look, I balled her a few times, then she got all clingy and shit. When I said it was over, she said it *wasn't* over, not by a *long shot*. She said she'd threaten to tell people I raped her. I called her bluff. And she did anyway. That's it." He paused, leaned over to Mike, and breathed softly on him. "I didn't rape her, Mikey." He smiled sardonically, grabbed onto Mike's hand and finished his beer.

Mike grinned. "That's good to hear, Jack. Really, really good to hear."

He walked upstairs to see his wife.

"Are you leaving now?" Miss Julie asked in perhaps the gentlest tone she had ever spoken.

"Yes," Mike responded. "Can I get you anything before I go?"

"No."

"How's the ankle?"

"Hurts." She stretched, then stayed in that position. "Where's Adam?"

"Getting ready for practice."

"Did you think about what I said?"

He shrugged. "I don't know what to think anymore."

He looked at his wife, perturbed by her sloth-like indolence.

Miss Julie asked, "What are you going to do?" She yawned and wiped a bit of drool from the side of her mouth onto her pillow.

"What?" He was startled.

"What are you going to do about this Moira business?"

"I don't know. I'm not very good at this sort of thing."

"Firing someone you mean?"

"*Any* of this."

"You've got to do it. It's your *dooty*." She meant for this to be humorous – this had now become quite the inside joke between them – but neither of them laughed.

"We don't know if he actually did it. Nothing has been proven yet." Mike knew there would be trouble for this response. "Even you said there might be –"

Suddenly Miss Julie coughed, then rubbed her eyes with her knuckles.

"I'm just not cut out for this," Mike pouted.

"You're the chief of police," she said mercilessly. "What do you *mean* you're not cut out for this? It's as if you're afraid of that...overgrown bulldog." She paused, reconsidered what she just said, then gave Mike one of those drama queen horror faces. It *was* overly dramatic, but this didn't mean he liked it any less; in fact, it kind of frightened him. She whispered, "Well you *should* be afraid of him."

A beat of silence.

"I told him we could be partners," Mike said sadly.

"Oh, come on. What are you, *twelve*? Did he sign anything?"

"No." Mike was now looking at the floor.

"Then you don't owe him anything." Then: "Look at me." Mike obliged. "I'm not sure what he *did* or *did not do* to her a few nights ago, but what I *do* know is that if he comes anywhere close to your job, we will *all* be in trouble! *Capisci*?"

"Is this your *premonition*?" Mike snapped.

Miss Julie didn't like Mike's tone. She retorted, "Yes. It *is* my premonition." A beat of silence. Then in a quieter tone: "Look, the quicker you exorcise that demon, the better."

Huh? Exercise the demon?

"Then I can retire," he said almost in relief.

Miss Julie's expression changed again. She took a while before saying, "And become a full-time father."

Then she grinned in a way that actually transformed her face; she didn't even look like the same woman anymore. Then she finally said, "Hey! I'm two weeks late."

Mike's heart sunk to his stomach then back up to his chest.

"We have ourselves another little accident," she added.

Mike's eyes widened, changing his countenance to a grimace that resembled a smile. Then he took a few steps toward the bed, reaching out to her as if he were about to give her a firm handshake.

Enamored by this endearing, awkward gesture, Miss Julie

smiled, grabbed her husband's hand and said, "Nice to meet you, Sir."

"Nice to meet you," Mike said and grabbed her hand tightly. His grimace now became a full-fledged Cheshire Cat smile as the two of them looked at one another for a long moment.

CHAPTER 21

BROTHERS, SISTERS AND RAPISTS

"So what do you think of having a brother or sister?" Mike asked Adam.

The boy sat on his bed doodling in his sketch pad. He didn't look up. Mike sensed there was something wrong with him, but he couldn't place it.

Adam shrugged. He was doing just fine without a sibling, thank you very much.

Finally, after a rather long pause, Mike said, "I hope you know this doesn't mean you're going to be second wheel around here."

"I know Dad," Adam said still drawing on the pad. His tone sounded authentic enough, but Mike still sensed something wasn't right with him. Those damn premonitions. He was beginning to get them too.

"What are you drawing?" Mike asked, pointing to the pad a bit awkwardly.

"Just stuff."

"Blood and Clot?" He said this proudly, impressed with himself that he remembered the names.

"No, Dad." The tone seemed cold. This was not Adam. Not Adam at all. What was wrong with him? Did he really resent his parents having another child? That *couldn't* have been it. Adam wouldn't act like this. *No way.*

Mike inched his way toward his son who was still intent on his work. It was as if his father wasn't even in the room.

Adam put the colored pencil down and stared into the drawing, which was a remarkably competent caricature of his Grandpa Lucien. "You're a good old boy," he heard his grandfather say. Then the drawing winked at him. Then it came to life; the picture became three-dimensional. "Your dad is a good man, old boy, but there is a lot of trouble for him in the future. Things are going to get very hard for you all. *Real, real soon.* So you've got to be strong. He's going to need your love, and most importantly – you listening to me old boy? – he's going to need your *understanding* and *support.* Your empathy. Your emotional intelligence. You are a special lad. You are a natural healer. We need healers like you in our world. I'll be seeing you, my friend. *Real, real soon* now."

Mike glanced down at the pad and smiled. "That's very good."

"It's a Kuala bear and a kangaroo. They live in an outback in Australia."

"Do they now?"

Adam looked up at his father. He wanted to be there for him; he wanted to give him understanding and support, just like Grandpa Lucien had told him. *What was going to happen to Dad?* he wondered and became a bit worried, but suddenly, as if he had recognized himself as the great healer his grandfather told him he was, he became more compassionate. He loved Mike; his father had always been very good to him. And he knew how much Mike loved him. It was a very real love.

"We learned about Australia in school," Adam said. "And we watched some Australian movies, too. One was called *The*

Man from Snowy River. It was pretty good but kind of boring in places."

"Really," Mike said. Then looking back at the drawing, he said, "Well it's very good. Very realistic."

But it wasn't realistic in the least; it was more abstract. It looked like an impressionistic painting to be exact. Like Monet or van Gough. Adam had used all of his colored pencils to color the picture, but instead of coloring the regular way – by moving the pencils up and down and right to left — he used hundreds of little dots to create the colors. It was pointillism without the boy ever knowing what the art movement was. The picture looked a lot like the place his Grandpa Lucien brought him into in his dreams...those wonderful and beautiful places with lots of different animals. That place *inside* the waterfall, he remembered.

Mike continued to stare at this strange colorful picture and made a most embarrassing connection after he turned his head to look at the goldfish, Fred and Barney. The picture suddenly became a glossy centerfold, one of the adult Pebbles Flintstone, the voluptuous supermodel posing for *Foxes and Boxes*, that adult cartoon magazine. Her long red hair was held back by those braids made of white stone and her large red lips on her oval-shaped face were puckered. That surge of electricity passed through him again. Underneath Pebbles the logo read: BAM! BAM! THANK YOU, MAM. GET YOUR ROCKS OFF! PEBBLES, THE FOX WITH THE FIREBOX.

"Are you going to fire Mr. Cleary?" Adam asked.

Damn you, Julie. Why did you tell him? He's a kid!

Mike said, "It's not as easy as all that, Adam."

"Did he rape that lady?"

Mike sighed. "I don't know; that's what I have to find out." And then carefully he asked his son if he knew what *rape* was.

"It's when a man wants to have sex with a lady, and she says *no* and he does it, anyway. Then he beats her up." Then with perfect pronunciation, he said, "It's *misogynistic.*"

Mike just nodded.

Later that day, the low-down townie sat in the Millyard drinking a coffee. The day was still overcast; it had been cloudy for a number of days now, but it still hadn't rained. The tops of the willows had hints of scattered light trying to break through. Mike wanted to hide. Within the hour he needed to face the inevitable.

He thought of George whom he hadn't seen for the past three Fridays. His friend said he wasn't feeling up to meeting him, that his health was failing, that the drinking was taking a massive toll on his body. This, in addition to all the other things in Mike's complicated life, added another weight to this unwanted barbell he now held.

The chief dosed off.

He was awoken by a squeaking sound of wheels on brick. A blurred image of fifteen-year-old Dickie Macy came into focus. He was one of the Boardheads, Eddie Price's friend who had a large head, crossed eyes that were worse than Mike's (he looked like a fish) and a speech impediment. The boy scowled at the chief. "Eddie dint do it. Dem drugs were planted on em by dat bad cop. I saw em put dem in his pants."

Then he faded out, dissolving into the waterfall.

Mike, his heart now thumping vigorously in his chest, got up, dumped the rest of his coffee out and was now ready to play the game he dreaded.

He had made his decision. Jack Cleary needed to be let go!

Did he rape...violate...Moira Davis in her garage? Did he slap Eddie Price in the face and threaten to cut his nuts off and hang them around his neck? Did he fuck that underaged girl, Alyssa Dupree? Did he threaten Gregory Reardon the banker and his family? Did he really find drugs in town? Well, at this point, none of it mattered anymore. Mike Melanson had been smitten by this guy – hell, he was even *taken* by him – but now he knew better. Cleary was just not meant to be a Fryebury Falls police officer. End of story.

And – like a simple little twist of fate, maybe – Mike *was* meant to be a police officer.

That unofficial contract he once spoke about with Jack Cleary would never become official. In fact, as far as he was concerned the entire partnership needed to be annulled as soon as possible.

"Jack, it just so happens that this little arrangement we discussed isn't going to work out. *Never.* You have had me and so many other people in town by the balls long enough. I don't know *where* you came from or *what* you're trying to pull here, but your time is up. You have overstayed your welcome in Fryebury Falls. We don't want you here. You don't belong. You're not welcome. And...you are a sneak, a liar, a brute and, as the record states here... a *rapist.* Two counts! I give you exactly one week to leave town before I press charges myself. And don't think I can't do it. I'm the fucking chief of police, you know! There are a few things you don't know about small towns, *big man.* Go back to your special assignments and get shot in the ass a few more times. And as far as this alleged contract – well, consider it toilet paper to wipe your fat ass with! And here's some more paper I found for you...your *walking papers, fucker.* Now walk!"

Suddenly Mike Melanson had everything going for him again. He was the chief again, and it felt great.

He grinned, closed his eyes, got that jolt of electricity through his body and saw the following scenario unfold: Moira Davis, the rotoscoped cartoon character, was standing outside his office, nostrils flaring like a snorting sow, waiting for justice to be served. Mike zoomed by her like super fuzz and said, "I'll be with you in a moment, Miss Davis."

Then the climax:

"Cleary, in my office. We have matters to discuss." He put

his hand on the blithely ignorant Dex Crowley (whose perpetual rotten-toothed grin transformed into an outlandish look of constipation) and said pointing to himself: "*This* low-down townie with no concept of the real world is going to send *that*" – he said pointing to Cleary who was shaking in the corner from fright – "overgrown bulldog back to hell where it came from. And hold all my calls. And if you get anymore Sox tickets, put my name on it. George Pearson and I are going to see some baseball this weekend!"

Later on in the day, the new Mike Melanson, reformed law enforcer par excellence, would inform those Boardheads that there needed to be a new law and order in this town: "No more loitering in the Millyard. Hear me? And no more fucking your girlfriends in the hat mills. My town is not the House of the Rising Sun! And if I so much as see one joint, let alone hard drugs, then I will personally take action. You think Jack Cleary played hard ball..." But before his thoughts became too much like Jack Cleary – the point was to be an effective law enforcer *without* using a firm upper hand like Wyatt Earp – he said, "Go on home to your parents before I drive you there myself."

And the local hero would go home and prepare for child number two. And *this* time he would explain to that busybody wife of his: "Julie Jill Najarian Melanson, shut your big mouth for one minute if you can manage that. I have decided what we are going to name our child...and I don't want to hear one more word out of you!"

"Okay, Chief!" she heard him say. "I won't argue with a confident man."

CHAPTER 22

A MAN OF LETTERS

Mike Melanson's office was always unbearably stuffy and cluttered; it was an oversized closet with one small window that always stayed open. The office was located on the second floor, and this meant that in the summertime the heat would rise, leaving the entire upstairs stagnant; in the wintertime the heat from the radiator – a massive rusty old thing that seemed to take up half the room – emitted large quantities of hot, dry air that in many ways was worse than the summer heat. The old radiator didn't have any adjustments, so once the heat was on, it was on. In addition to the open window, Mike kept a box fan blowing at all times. One of these days, he had told himself for years now, he was going to get "that heat issue fixed."

The police station was a comparatively small brick house formerly owned by some Rockefeller-type entrepreneur in the late nineteenth century, a real business prodigy named Hadriel Abramson, a savvy fellow who had stock in the railroads, a few federal banks, the carriage industry, the hat industry, motion pictures and some professional baseball club. Abramson – who owned a small home in nearly every U.S state – was a ruthless millionaire with no family. He lived the life of a bachelor, traveling continuously around the country doing business like some door-to-door salesman. He preferred to live in the country or suburbs while making deals in the bigger cities. Apparently, he came to Fryebury Falls while working in Boston (he once called Fryebury Falls one of the best little towns in America). When he died, he bequeathed his home to some political figure who eventually auctioned it off. The town bought it and over time turned the quaint little home into a quaint little police station. The house, despite being owned by a business mogul, was surprisingly dilapidated. Apparently, Abramson liked to live modestly, cutting corners every chance he could get.

When Mike entered the station, it was half past eight and all was quiet... and relaxing... and most importantly... uncomplicated.

Little did he know, however, that when this ninth day of July was over, his life would never be the same again.

He began the day by calling Miss Julie. He felt obligated – as any expecting father would – to check up on his wife's health and well-being. *Is this all really happening?* Mike contemplated from behind his desk. *This is wonderful news, isn't it? Of course it is, Melanson,* he reassured himself. *There's nothing more wonderful than being a parent. And when all of this Cleary business is resolved, I can concentrate entirely on my family.* Then in his wife's voice: "It'll be simply mahvelous!"

But he was still not at ease. No, there were questions that still plagued him. *How was Cleary going to handle getting fired? And what about Moira Davis...what was going to happen with her? Was George on a binge again and was Miss Julie accurate in her assumptions that alcohol would finally do him in? How was Adam handling all of this sudden news?* He seemed different now. *And what about Miss Julie? How did she really feel about being pregnant and going through all of this again?* He remembered her once saying she only wanted one child.

It was all too much, Mike concluded. *Too many things going on. Too complicated. Cognitive overload.* Mike always liked things to be simple and predictable. He liked an inevitable order of things.

The front door opened.

Mike gulped. Sweat formed on his upper brow. His cheeks were flushed and burning. Man was it hot in that office! *Phew!* He adjusted the fan from medium to high, which made no difference; it only made the room noisier. The rusty old blower – at times the oscillations sounded like a hollow, tinny heartbeat – had its own coating of dust on its blades; it was a wonder the thing worked at all.

The sound added to the chaos; he couldn't handle it. He turned the fan back to medium.

He wiped the sweat from his forehead with the back of his hand. He exhaled slowly. His heart – sometimes matching the rhythms of the fan blades – was galloping inside his chest and he touched his cheek with the back of his fingers, feeling the heat of his face through the skin. It reminded him of the times he had too much to drink – and the red cheeks reminded him that his already high blood pressure had increased dramatically.

Footsteps.

One step at a time, up those creaky wooden stairs.

Another stream of sweat trickled down his temple.

Mike got up and before he had time to think, said, "Jack?"

"It's Dex, Chief." Crowley popped his head into the office. The perpetual grin was painted on that aged, emaciated face of his. Someone once told Mike – which he had a hard time picturing and believing – that in his younger days, Dexter Crowley (known as "Stretch") was rather handsome.

The chief let out a sigh, but not one of relief.

Dex said, "How's tricks?"

With this line, Mike thought of Dr. Mark Porzio, former neighbor of his, the gargantuan pompous proctologist who used to ask him how tricks in the police department were. *Tricks.* Mike laughed to himself. He remembered Doc Porzio saying that there was a bunch of assholes that needed attending to. Then he heard his own voice say, "Ross Thurber should be the next asshole you fix." He laughed to himself again. Not because this line was funny; the funny part was watching the fat "asshole" doctor laughing *his* fat ass off as if he just heard the funniest joke ever told.

Somehow these thoughts comforted Mike, if only for the time being.

His mind then shifted to the special assignments cop. In Porzio's baritone voice he heard: *Jack Cleary should be the next asshole I fix.* But somehow, he couldn't get himself to find this one funny.

"Come in and sit down, Dex," Mike said. Dex had never seen Mike so serious before; he straightened out his grin. "I've got something important to tell you."

Mike told Dex as much of the story as he needed to know. Soon afterwards, Dex Crowley left the office a more serious man.

Mike lit a cigarette.

"Jack," he whispered, looking into his coffee cup. "Have a seat. What I am about to say will come as a surprise." He cleared his throat. "Sometimes certain people are not cut out for certain jobs. You agree? For instance, I couldn't do any of those special assignments..." He grimaced and cleared his throat. "Now, Jack. What can you tell me about Moira Davis? Hmmm? She said you raped her. That's a pretty big accusation. Why would she say that, Jack? Why would Moira Davis say that? Huh? Why would she...?"

The downstairs door opened.

Footsteps.

Big heavy steps. They were definitely the footsteps of Jack Cleary. *Thump, drag, thump-drag.* Jack Cleary had a very distinct method of walking. Like a limp. Probably from all those bullets he had in him.

As he walked into the office, Jack fanned the smoke away, induced a cough and said, "You're going to put us up in smoke." Then he thought: *There's no way this smoking can go on. Not with me in this office.*

It was silent for a moment. *Yeah, we're going up in smoke, Jack. More than you know.*

Mike cleared his throat. *Just jump into it. Tell him. Get it over with. No hesitation. Hesitation kills, remember? Like that military philosophy they teach you at the police academy. But they never had any classes teaching a guy how to fire a fellow cop, did they? Why not?*

"Jack," Mike said after a moment. "I'm afraid we have a situation here. Actually a few situations." He paused, looking into Cleary's expressionless face. "We can't go through with what we discussed last week." *Wow, he was already halfway there!* He paused again, perhaps giving Jack the opportunity to respond or something, but the officer said nothing. Mike continued: "I think it would be in everyone's best interest, yours included, if you wrote a letter of resignation by the end of the week...if it can be sooner, that would be appreciated." *And that's it. All the anticipation was now behind him!*

Weakly, he inhaled the rest of his cigarette. Jack sat there, still with no expression, but his seemingly colorless eyes managed to invade Mike's eyes. The chief felt nauseous, as if he were being turned inside out. A new jolt of electricity passed through his system and with this came a frigidness he had felt before. He heard Miss Julie's voice – "*Send that overgrown bulldog back to hell!*"

"What the hell are you talking about?" Jack asked, smiling.

His tone was almost soothing.

"What can you tell me about Moira Davis?" Mike finally said.

"Moira Davis?"

"Yes?"

"My neighbor?"

"Yes."

"What am I supposed to tell you?" Still the voice and tone were very even-tempered, unstressed – but those invasive eyes forced the chief to look down into his nearly empty coffee cup. He could see the swirls of cream floating on the top, making a white s-shape design over the light tan coffee.

"She told me you...uh...*violated* her."

"Really?"

"Yes."

"Interesting."

"Why would she say that?"

"I don't know," he said with a sort of ennui.

"Then this *isn't* true?"

"No, it isn't." The cop didn't budge. He sat in that chair and actually looked comfortable. "Why? Do you believe I...*violated* her?" No expression.

Mike sighed. "I don't know *what* to believe."

"And you were going to... *let me go* me for that?"

Cleary's temperament was – *what was it?* – calm yet threatening.

"It's a little more complicated than that," Mike said. *Damn it, I don't know what to believe! Why are you acting like this, Jack? Why? What the hell is the matter with you? Did you do it? Just tell me. You can tell me.*

"Oh?"

Mike got a heart palpitation. "I've been doing a lot of thinking." He was still looking into the coffee cup.

"My woman's intuition tells me that this meeting isn't

going to be a discussion about my promotion. Am I right?" He was as cool as could be.

"Just hear me out for a minute," Mike said irritably. It was as if Jack should have had more empathy and consideration for the poor guy who was trying to get through this ordeal.

Jack grinned, but somehow did it without moving his mouth.

"I've been doing some thinking," Mike said, his voice cracking a bit.

"You said that before."

"Yes." Mike cleared his throat. "I have come to the conclusion that this combination – this *you and me* as partners deal – co-chiefs of police – whatever you want to call it – well, quite frankly, and I'm even a bit ashamed to say it – I don't think it's going to work. It *won't* work. *Can't* work."

Jack let out a faint grin but said nothing.

"Look, you're a good cop," Mike said. "An excellent cop; I've told you this before. But this town is not the place for you. Since you've been here, it's been one disaster after another. I've tried to put it all behind me – ignore it – whatever – but I can't do it any longer. People don't want you here. I'm making enemies. And I can't have enemies. You understand? Sure, you've done some fine investigative work – you've helped clean up the drugs in town – but that's not enough. There are all these threats people said you made and quite frankly I'm beginning to wonder if..." Another clearing of the throat and then a big sigh that led into a cough. "And now...this...alleged... accusation." He sighed again. "I really wish it wasn't like this, Jack. We could have been good (he wanted to say *friends*)...a good...a good team." He composed himself: "We could have been a good team."

Poignantly, the chief recalled one of his favorite thoughts: the two friends getting tanked up at Jeremy's Irish Pub. The thought needed to leave him now; he needed to mourn the loss, then let it go. Move on.

"But I didn't do anything wrong."

"I didn't accuse you of anything. Hell, I'm not even saying you hit Eddie Price; at this stage, I don't want to know. But there's just too many black marks here. Look: I'm a small-town chief. And there are certain ways we do things here that you have fought ever since I hired you a couple years back. You're just not fitting in, Jack."

Are you hearing this Miss Julie? This is your low-down townie speaking. Then he looked at Jack and heard Miss Julie's words: "He's a dangerous sycophant. A psychopath! You just can't see it because of your inexplicable...*veneration* you have of that diabolical...*Ahhhhh!* Oh, M&M, you are so damn frustrating sometimes!"

He looked into Cleary's colorless eyes and tried to see the red demonic pupils, but he only saw sad human eyes. *The devil himself...yeah right. Good one, Miss Julie. He's no "sicko-fan"; he's just a normal guy for Christ's sake!*

Mike Melanson felt proud of himself. He *was* in fact a real cop. What do you know!

"And that's all I have to say," Mike said.

Jack's grin soon became a disturbing laugh, one that perturbed Mike to no end. "Now it's my turn," he said. Jack took his time to compose his thoughts, but before doing so, he took his recorder from his breast pocket, ejected the tape, flipped it over, pressed record and placed it back into his pocket. "Oh – this is a gift from J.J.," he said grinning.

Mike couldn't take his eye off of Cleary's breast pocket. He then thought about what Moira Davis told him that day she paid him a visit. More electricity through his insides. Mike swallowed a glob of saliva.

"First off, *Chief* – I'm not going anywhere. *You're* the one that's going."

Mike trembled.

"I've got a little story to tell," Jack announced. "Then soon, *everyone* will know about it. Actually, you *already* know the story. In fact, you *wrote* it. You wrote *all* of them." He snickered. "The story is told in a series of letters – twelve to be exact. Naughty, nasty sex letters. All written by a beloved family man, a beloved police chief, a beloved citizen of a beloved little town called Fryebury Falls."

Cleary got up from his chair, his hulking body looming over Mike who was now sinking into his seat. "Have you heard this one, *Chief*? You *do* know what I'm talking about don't you?"

Mike instinctively reached for his cigarettes.

"That's right, have your smoke. You'll need it for the rest of my story. A dirty habit for a dirty old man..."

CHAPTER 23

FOXES & BOXES

The cigarette popped out of Mike's trembling lips and onto his pants, burning a small hole through the fabric. When it reached the skin, he jumped out of his chair, brushing the ashes to the floor.

But this blemish was the least of his worries.

Jack Cleary had him by the balls – and he was twisting.

"You do whatever you need to do to *finalize* this partnership," Jack said. "I'm not going to insist that you jump ship – no, no, that wouldn't be a smart move for either one of us. People love your sorry ass in this town – and I'm going to benefit from that." He walked around the room, pacing menacingly while Mike Melanson became smaller and smaller. "Within the next few weeks, you are going to make a public announcement as originally planned. It's not like I'm making you do anything – this is all your idea, right? And before long, I'll build up a reputation and people will trust me. Once again, it's everything that you've always talked about. I've got it all here on tape if you don't remember. And then when the time is right, when I've established myself as a...*reputable* police chief, then I may or may not – depending on your cooperation in this matter – reveal this little secret to all our family and friends."

Finally Mike said, "You'll never get away with this."

"What's that?" Jack asked with a smile.

"You heard me." The chief's legs felt like metal weights; he couldn't move.

"I'll never get away with *what*?"

"I could bring you up on charges. Breaking and entering. Stealing personal property. That desk was locked! What were you doing in there?"

"It *wasn't* locked. That was your mistake."

"You can't play me for a fool, Jack."

"Then you don't deny that the letters are yours, that they're all in your handwriting?"

Mike waited a moment before asking, "What have you done with them?" He rifled through the middle desk drawer, the drawer that now felt naked with only a few pieces of scrap paper and some unsharpened pencils, the drawer where he once kept the twelve issues of *Foxes and Boxes* – and inside each publication were the handwritten copies of every letter he wrote and mailed to the *Letters* section of the magazine.

Each letter had been graphic confessions of his so-called fantasies, fetishes, voyeuristic tendencies and actual sexual escapades with a number of young girls – not actual girls, of course, but the cartoon supermodels sketched to ecstatic perfection by some of the top cartoonists and animators in their field.

Foxes and Boxes (the magazine that Mike Melanson first picked up in an alley by a dumpster in downtown Fryebury Falls), the rhyming title that obviously referred to beautiful girls and their genitalia, was an underground magazine that allegedly started in the early to mid-1970s when adult animation was becoming a sought-after art form. It was a response to such cartoonists as Robert Crumb who did the X-rated *Fritz the Cat.* It was also a cute, perhaps demented little nod to some Dr. Suess book: *Would you eat them in a box? Would you eat them with a fox?*

The magazine – edited by a group of intellectual college art students who called themselves "The Story Board" – featured a playmate of the month in addition to displaying a number of beautifully-drawn "spreads" of some of the hottest girls ever to be conceived by a pen. Such playmates as Bambi Foxxx, Lacey Lord-Love and Lezzy Borden – would always constitute a majority of the issues, but the remaining portions were reserved for serious art like short stories, poetry, film reviews, literary criticism...and sex letters written by their fans.

Foxes and Boxes took itself and its letter writing clientele very seriously.

Mike Melanson included, whose letters had all been published. The letters were always penned by cartoon character pseudonyms – horny guys like Woody the Pecker – or other fabricated names to complement the playmates: Billy Blueballs, Peter the Pipe Cleaner and Jeremy "The Rod" Rodman.

Whoever said that Mike Melanson didn't have a creative side? It took *plenty* of creativity to conjure up these names and the content of these sexual letters to the editors – otherwise The Story Board would never have published them!

Wouldn't Miss Julie be impressed?

Oh shit! Mike thought rather suddenly. *My wife!* Surely this was not what she meant when she attempted to get her low-down townie with no concept of the real world to open up and become cultured. To become a "man of letters," in a much different way than Sam Pearson became a best-selling man of letters.

Jack Cleary responded to the question: "They're in safe keeping, not to worry." He laughed, shaking his bulldog head back and forth. "Man alive! *Foxes and Boxes!*" He laughed again – this time followed by a comical snort. "Cartoon chicks, huh? I never thought an old fuddy-duddy like you had it in you," Jack continued. "It's always the quiet guys." He didn't laugh this time. He was repulsed. *Even the good guys are plagued with filth*, he thought. *I need to clean things up! Cartoon pornography? What is the world coming to? Doesn't anyone desire the traditional American dream anymore – the simple, loving life of the wholesome family?* The cop had heard of the magazine before but always disregarded it as some joke, as one would disregard the lead story in a tabloid. *Mad* magazine meets *Hustler* type of thing. He never imagined a normal horny guy getting his rocks off to cartoon characters!

Suddenly Cleary's stomach churned. He caught a glimpse of the grotesque Gail – she was part of an animated world not unlike that movie he saw years back with all those disgusting cartoons set to Pink Floyd's music. She was projected on the wall – her long, stringy hair flapping about her pale face, those yellow and blue pock marks, ballooning, festering like little black insects, expanding into something even more grotesque. And before he knew it, those ballooning, festering, black insect-looking pock marks on her face – popped – exploded – the particles of her face coming at him like objects in a three-dimensional film. Cleary's heart squeezed in his chest. He closed his eyes. Then he opened them. And everything was gone.

"What do you want from me?" Mike asked, now defeated, lighting up a cigarette.

Jack, fanning the smoke away from his face, said, "Nothing special. Just what we originally agreed to. Business as usual." He grinned. "You are right about the folks in this town. They haven't exactly warmed up to me, but with this new plan of yours, I'll have a chance to...redeem myself. With your help of course."

"And what makes you think I'll agree to this?"

"Oh, you'll agree. Let's put it this way, Chief. Those letters are locked up in safe keeping. You'll never be able to track them down. One wrong move – I mean *any* wrong move – then everyone in this freaky little town – especially your pretty little family – will know *everything*. You dig?"

Mike put out his cigarette and hunched over the ashtray.

"Good," Jack said. Then he emptied the ashtray into the trash bucket. "And since we will be sharing this little office in this little town, we will be making a little list of rules to keep things clean and tidy." He gently placed the ashtray in the same spot. "You dig?"

Mike, still hunched over, managed to look up at his new partner.

"This does not need to be complicated, Chief Melanson. Remember – business as usual. I never found a thing." They looked at one another for an unbearably long beat. "Now I am going to go home and spend some time with my son. Celebrate my promotion." He turned around and right before he exited the door, he shook his head and muttered to himself, "*Foxes and Boxes*. Man, oh man!"

CHAPTER 24

CONTAMINATION, CRIME & VEXATION

J.J. was watching music videos and eating a peanut butter and jelly sandwich. Lazlo was resting by the boy's feet, holding himself up on his front paws as if he were a cat. He was panting. The video, one he had seen before, showed a singer with long blond hair running back and forth on a stage singing phrases like the following: *Jump back, what's that sound...hot shoe burning down the avenue...I got the feel for the wheel... Don't you know she's coming on to me...*

Presently, the boy was also attempting to read from a novel called *The Twelfth Precinct*, one of many police procedural novels that Jack bought years back at a yard sale. The book was about a group of police officers who were forced to relocate after a gang known as Black Lightning burned their precinct to the ground. Apparently, the gang wanted vengeance on a prisoner who was locked in one of the cells. Although J.J. didn't understand a lot of the descriptive writing (too many big words), he *did* understand most of the dialogue; this was favorite part. At times he was able to imagine himself in the story as the prisoner, a tough wise-cracking guy named

Ethan Stoker. Stoker kept telling the police officers, "One day I'm gonna bust outta this joint – I'll escape, and you'll never find me!"

J.J. rooted for Ethan Stoker. *Escape! Escape!* He wished he had enough courage to say these words to his daddy – then he could actually break out of his jail and enter that new place he kept seeing in his dreams – in that wide open field, holding hands with a pretty blue-eyed brunette who looked a lot like his neighbor, Maygyn Pearson.

Lazlo jumped up, all four of his legs quivering. A cold chill entered the room. J.J., the remains of his sandwich still in his hand, halted. He shivered, expecting to see her enter through the wall, the window or the ceiling, or fly above him – then penetrate his body in the forceful and invasive way she always did. *The Gail! The Gail!*

Lazlo barked.

But no Gail.

J.J. said bravely, "We got to will her out, Lazlo. She's not real. Not real. Only a ghost like in a movie. She can't hurt us." He closed his eyes, then opened them slowly.

After a few seconds, he hyperventilated the way he normally did, but this time instead of being afraid, he was relieved. He was actually laughing.

He had willed her out!

He heard the cruiser pull into the driveway. He looked out the window, relieved to see his daddy exit the car.

The door of the split-level opened on the first floor, which was strange because when he came home, the police officer always went straight for the basement. When Jack entered, J.J noticed something under his arm.

A box.

"Today, we are celebrating my son," he announced as he entered. "I got me a real promotion. You know what a promotion is?" He smiled, not expecting an answer. "It means that as of today, I am the new Chief of Police, that's what it means."

"Isn't Mr. Mike the chief?"

Jack placed the pizza boxes on the table and opened the top one. "Get some plates from the cabinet, a couple of glasses and some Coke from the fridge and dig in. We've got sausage, hamburger and onion. Unless you don't want it of course..."

J.J. smiled. "I *do* want it, Daddy." The boy was quickly gathering the supplies his father had requested.

"Good. And just for your information, Mr. Mike is *not* the chief of police anymore. I am. I'll be working with him for a little while, but real real soon he'll be working *under* me. That means I'll be the boss."

"Are you gonna be arresting criminals?"

"Yes. It's all part of the job. There are already a few criminals that need reprimanding." Jack took a large bite into a slice of pizza. J.J. knew that *reprimanded* meant the same as punished. He should know; he had been *reprimanded* many times in his life. And people who were *reprimanded* often needed to go to jail. He knew all about this process. "Are you proud of me?"

"Very, Daddy."

Silence prevailed as the two Jacks devoured the pizza like forest creatures feasting on a carcass.

"Now listen to me," Jack said with a mouth full of food. "I've got some very important police work to do tonight. I'll be downstairs in my office. That means do *not* bother me. You have to remember, or there will be hell to pay. No TV either. I don't like what it does to your brain." He continued as he chewed his pizza: "And now it's time to think about your future. It's time for you to grow up. Learn some responsibility. You're the son of a police chief now; you need to start acting like one. "

"I want to be a police officer, too."

"That's very honorable, but you have to earn it. And that

begins with you doing all your chores on time and staying *out* of jail. Policemen don't go to jail – they put people *in* jail. You, boy, need to abide by the rules of society. That's the most important thing one can do. And to lead a good, honest, clean life. *Purity, law and order and peace.* Keep reading those books – it'll build up your brain, make you think like a police officer."

J.J. thought of the main cop in *The Twelfth Precinct*. He was a black cop, a rookie. It was his first week on the force. For the first time, the boy could relate to this character instead of the criminal in jail.

"Yes, Daddy," J.J. said proudly with a newfound excitement.

"And stop calling me Daddy! You're too old for that! Call me Chief. You need to begin police training *inside* the house before you go out into that world." Jack paused, looked at his son's impressionable expression – his mouth and eyes wide open with fascination and anticipation – and part of him was enthralled by the kid's vulnerability, by his unchallenged desire to be the ultimate apprentice. And another part of him was repulsed by the pathetic nature of this hopeless animal in front of him, his son, Gail's son. And before continuing with the lecture, he pictured a series of green garbage bags all lined up behind the cruiser ready to be placed in the trunk then disposed of in some remote dump far, far away from everything. The removal of the bags, filled with the remains of his son, David Aaronson, David Wood, Gail, and now Mike Melanson became symbolic of Jack Cleary "cleaning up his act," and removing unwanted debris in order that he may clean himself up and start anew.

Jack shook his head, trying to remove these impurities. *No, not J.J. Not my boy! I love him. Get out of my head. I will never. Never!* He fought back the tears.

"It took me years to get to this point. To be Chief of Police, you must first be a good citizen of the law." The grease from

Jack's second slice of pizza dribbled down his jaw. Then his body became numb. He felt a slippery and greasy invasion from within. And the foul stench. It attacked his lips and tongue, his breast and his genitals. *Put the monster-freak out of his misery, cuzzie. You've got to do it. For his own good. For your own good.*

Jack looked at his son and was overcome by such a poignancy he didn't know what to do. Now he really felt like crying. He pictured holding the boy in his arms, nurturing him, telling him life was going to be okay, that none of this was his fault. *Not his fault!* Then a rush of heat traveled through his body as he envisioned the look on that sixteen year-old bully David Wood's face when he cornered him in the woods behind his house. Jack kicked the kid in the shins, then when he fell to the ground, he jammed his boot into the boy's temple too many times to count until David Wood, the reason why his son was permanently brain damaged, paid for his crime.

Then an image of Mike Melanson, appearing through the half empty pizza box through a trail of red sauce: he was face down on his desk, his blood and brains and skull fragments leaking from his head, holding a pistol – and next to him, a note in his own handwriting:

> *Beloved Family and Friends of Fryebury Falls,*
> *I am sorry I betrayed you. I didn't mean to hurt anyone. I am nothing but a pervert. I can't bear to live on. Forgive me.*
> *All my love,*
> *Mike*

Where had Gail gone? She left him for the time being, and Jack took this time to enjoy his freedom.

Jack continued, "How does this all sound? Think you can handle it?"

J. J.'s heart was racing. He was well on his way to becoming a policeman!

At that particular moment, J.J. Cleary caught a glimpse of the American dream, even if he didn't fully understand what that meant, and he especially liked the way his father was talking to him.

Jack looked out the window only to see the following images: The glossy pages of *Foxes and Boxes* with those disgusting drawings of female cartoon characters' private parts; Mike's letters and his massacred body hunched over his desk with his final letter to the world scribbled in bleeding red ink; J.J.'s corpse in the coffin, his eyes and mouth wide open (*No! No! No! No! Not this! Not this picture*); and Moira Davis, wearing that sundress, handcuffed to the bed, no longer a woman he imagined in wedlock.

All these images were carefully juxtaposed like a montage in an action film – relentlessly torturing him.

Jack Cleary wanted nothing more than to lead a life of purity, law and order and peace.

But he knew that he was destined for a life of contamination, crime and vexation instead.

CHAPTER 25

A NEW LEAF

At about 2:00 am on Saturday morning, the nineteenth of July, Moira Davis returned home from her gig at a busy bar in Kenmore Square called Uncle Salty's Spirits: Laura's Mercedes played at eight and The Mad Ones went on at ten.

After the Mad Ones finished playing, she and Cheryl knocked back a few Grateful Deads until last call. They left a little after one and fooled around in the back of Cheryl's Oldsmobile until about two.

"Come home with me," Cheryl begged, as she nibbled on Moira's lower lip.

"I can't. I've got to get back," Moira said, ending the evening with a long, moist kiss.

"Come on," Cheryl pleaded, "The kid is at her father's, isn't she?"

Moira despised how Cheryl referred to Maygyn as "the kid," but she let it go. "No, I've really got to get back."

By the time Moira reached her driveway, it was nearly a quarter to three. *Thank God Maygyn was staying with her father again this weekend*, she thought.

She knew she consumed too much that evening, more

than usual. It was those Grateful Deads Cheryl coaxed her into having. She never liked Chambord; she should have settled for Long Island Iced Teas instead.

The garage door was already ajar when she pulled her black Fiat inside of it. *What the hell? Did I really leave that open?*

When she stood upright, she felt all the blood rush to her head. The right side of her head ached, and her stomach was sour and growling.

"Jesus Christ, I'm turning into Maygyn," she told her reflection in the driver's seat window. She laughed and drooled. She wiped the spit from her mouth and thought of her pretty little girl. She really loved her. She did. Very much. She just didn't know how to act around her. What to say to her. Little nerdy bookworm.

She made her way to the garage door handle. She paused and scrunched up her face as if the garage door were a person standing there and said, "What the hell you doing open?"

Moira staggered into the kitchen with an impressive poise for someone in her condition.

She went to the faucet, cupped her hands, and filled them several times with water. She was parched.

She rested her head on the table and within seconds fell asleep.

Minutes later she was awoken, startled, her heart racing; she felt stifled. It reminded her of those times when she needed to pull off into a rest area or a gas station to catch a power nap before continuing her drive: she would recline in the driver's seat and moments after she dozed off, she would regain consciousness again only to find herself in a delirious state of stifling panic and anxiety. For some reason, this almost always happened when she became uncontrollably tired. Her body was playing a game with her: it demanded the sleep, but just as she received it, it would violently reject it.

It was that feeling all over again, intensified by the alcohol.

She went back to the faucet and just as she filled her hands with water, recalled a piece of the nightmare. It was that recurring dream where her twin sister remained suspended in the lake, choking on water, panicking and calling for her: *Help...Moira...Help...Moira.* In the dream, little Moira would get closer and closer to her sister, reaching out her hand, assuring her she was going to be okay, that she was going to save her. And Moira would be seconds away from saving Meggie's life. But then something would separate them again, and Meggie Davis would begin to sink slowly – lower and lower and lower while Moira, the helpless little girl, watched her twin perish under the water.

Moira cried, looking at the water pass over her hands. She whispered: "I'm sorry. So, so sorry." She drenched her face with cold water, then composed herself. She leaned her back against the sink and looked toward the window, expecting to see the image again. She didn't see anything but heard the little girl's voice again: *It's okay, Moira. It's not your fault. We'll see each other again,* real, real soon. *I promise.*

Moira cried again.

What she needed was a cold shower to wash it all away. She just wanted to be left alone. "Go away, Meggie," she whispered. "Not tonight, sweetie."

She knew she would feel so much better, she thought in a half-rational mind now, after a good piss and shower. *Clean it all out!* Then she would take four Tylenol, drink a half-gallon of water and go to sleep. And when she awoke, there'd be no hangover. And hopefully no images of her sister either. Moira knew better, however. Little Meggie would always appear to her unannounced; drunk or sober, it didn't matter. And it was always during the times of her greatest tensions. But Moira discovered that her twin would never appear when she deliberately thought about her. *Why was this? Power of suggestion maybe?*

She took a step toward the bathroom and, as she did, was overcome by a breeze, a cold one, as if the house suddenly had air conditioning or something.

She turned toward the kitchen again. A creaking noise; a crackling sound. *Was it the house settling?* There was a weightiness in the air; it was stifling and stagnant. And when she breathed in, her lungs felt heavy.

Another frigid draft. And more crackling this time, like popcorn when it first starts to expand in the pan. Moira's heart was pounding. She felt nauseous and noticed herself sweating – from her forehead, on her upper lip and under her arms.

Moira...help...Moira...help!

She shivered. She got the spins. Another step toward the bathroom.

She stumbled to the light switch.

The instant the light came on, she felt a pressing pressure on her shoulder, an unpainful but prominent sensation that almost always accompanied the visions. The air was still heavy and cold and there was a foul smell about it too. She couldn't place the smell, however. It was like no other. Was there a leak in the basement? Bad meat in the trash? Was it coming from the bathroom? What *was* it?

Moira looked inside the bathtub and then into the sink and whispered, "Meggie...is that you again?" *Leave me alone. Not tonight, sweetie. Not tonight.*

She splashed more water on her face and then drank a few handfuls of water. She belched involuntarily, tasting the sourness of the liquor. More acid reflux.

She looked to her right at the threshold of the door and gasped, practically losing her balance.

"Oh, Jesus Christ, Jack!" she said with a sort of sigh of relief even though her heart was now palpitating. "What are you doing here?"

Then she realized the absurdity of the situation, now

breathing irregularly: Another sigh, but not one of relief. "Jesus Christ, you scared the *shit* out of me!"

"Oh, I'm sorry," he said, his hulking body completely blocking the threshold. "Not my intention to frighten you, Moira." His voice was soft and even calm. He stared at her for an unbearably long time and this perturbed her, forcing her to finally look away. She felt her way to the toilet and sat down.

"What do you want?" Her heart was still bouncing in her chest, but she was somehow more relaxed now.

"Just to talk," he said, creeping his way over to her. He was invading her space; she leaned back as far as she could, both of her arms hugging the back of the toilet.

"There is nothing to talk about. Please leave."

He moved in even closer, making his way directly in front of her. Then he kneeled down and took her hand. "Moira. I wanted to apologize for the other night."

"How did you get in here?" She was starting to shake; it felt like the chills. She was still very intoxicated and this entire scenario was giving her the spins.

"I saw you come home. I knocked a few times. Then I let myself in."

Moira burped; the sour taste of alcohol made her gag. "I am going to be fucking sick."

"I'm sorry about the other night."

"You said that already."

He now rubbed her hand with his other hand. "I don't know what came over me."

"I don't either. I thought I made it clear that we were not going to –"

"I know," he said with a strange little laugh. "But I couldn't accept that, and I guess I thought, deep down, that we still might have a chance." The strange little laugh now became a strange little smile. Moira couldn't have moved if she wanted to. "I love you, Moira."

"You *what?*"

"I love you. Always have. I think we are really good together." All those times he imagined them as a couple and now he was with her, holding her hand and baring his soul. He caught a glimpse of Gail through the bathroom mirror, then continued. "I won't let myself get like that again. I promise. I am turning over a new leaf. I am actually going to eventually become the police chief. Mike Melanson and I are going to be partners for a while, and then I will be taking over. It's everything I dreamed of. Things will finally be good. Perfect. And I am thinking that since we always had a good thing together – more or less – that we could give things a fresh start. A new leaf. *Purity, law and order and peace.* My motto. Our motto." Moira could not believe what she was seeing or hearing. She looked down at her arm, which was being gently caressed by Jack's giant paw. Then, he moved in even closer to her and whispered in her ear, "I love you. I can be good for you." Then he took both his paws and covered her cheeks. Then one of the paws gripped the back of her neck and he closed his eyes pushed her face toward his and gently nibbled at the bottom of her lip.

Moira managed to take both of her hands and push him in the chest. "Stop it! Stop it!" When this did not do anything, she made fists and punched the cop several times in the chest – one blow striking his diaphragm, causing him to gasp. This just caused him to press himself closer to her, and then he opened his entire mouth, completely devouring the front part of her face. Repulsed and claustrophobic, Moira jerked away and managed to give him an elbow in his jaw, and this knocked him back. His elbow banged on the shower door and Moira took this opportunity to scurry past him, and when she reached the outside of the door she turned around, pointed her finger at him and in a scream that might have caused someone an aneurism yelled, "Get out of out here! Get out of

here! Get out of here! Get out of here! Get out of here!" She
was hyperventilating, and it looked as though she was going
to cry.

Jack waved his hand for her to keep quiet. "Okay, okay,
okay." Then he pulled himself up and stood in front of the
mirror and Gail, with her rotten incisors hanging from their
roots, was there looking back at him. Jack must have taken up
half the space of this undersized bathroom.

Moira backed up as Jack exited the door. Before she could
say anything else, he put his hand up and said, "Okay. I get the
picture." In that instant, her fear turned into a rage that
surprised them both. She charged him and knocked him back
against the wall. Now he was sitting against the wall just like
he was in the bathroom. Then he got up, brushed his pants
and moved toward Moira who was moving in reverse with his
every step. Jack went to the front door and said, "I am going."
Then he tiptoed toward this shivering creature and grimaced,
"I am sorry. I just thought we might –"

Moira backed into a wall. "Just go!" she thundered, her
voice vibrating as if she has been out in cold weather.

Jack turned around and exited, and as he walked home, all
he could picture was Moira in a sundress greeting him as he
returned from the police station. "Well, there's my handsome
chief!" Then she gripped his behind with both hands, thrusted
herself toward him and nibbled the bottom of his lip.
"Welcome home, my love."

Gail's laughter and little Meggie's cries gave way to the
running waters of Niagara Two.

CHAPTER 26

METAMORPHOSES

The next morning, Sunday, was a typical mid-July day in Fryebury Falls. The sun was burning in the deep azure skies: mockingbirds, mourning doves and peepers were talking in overlapping dialogues – and Niagara Two could be heard clearly through the trees.

Maygyn got up very early and was reading Nevil Shute's *On the Beach*, one of the several novels she was required to finish for her summer reading list. She loved the characters. Her favorite was the eccentric scientist John Osborne who had a penchant for racing. She had just begun the ninth and final chapter, the one where all the main characters in the Australian community, presently the only survivors of a nuclear war that already annihilated the rest of the planet, would meet their inevitable deaths. To her, the novel was suspenseful. It was a hyperlink melodrama where many characters' lives eventually became interconnected. Years ago, she had seen the film on TV, a black and white movie with Gregory Peck as Dwight Towers – and even more absurdly, Fred Astaire as John Osborne. The cast definitely didn't fit her interpretations of the characters. And the movie itself was one of the slowest moving films she had ever seen.

As she read, she periodically drifted into the worlds of her own writing, specifically a collection of stories called *The Terminals*. The stories were actually more like vignettes – or "slices-of-life" as she liked to call them. She liked short, ambiguous narratives that could be interpreted literally or figuratively: A personal favorite of hers was Hemingway's "Hills Like White Elephants," a story about a man and a woman dining in a Spanish train station who are specifically talking about something that is never openly revealed to the reader (yet, when you read between the lines, it becomes most obvious what they are talking about); Shirley Jackson's off-beat, macabre narrative "The Lottery," which took place in an unnamed small town (which she pictured as Fryebury Falls), was another one of her favorites. What *was* the lottery? What did those *stones* represent? A year earlier she read Sherwood Anderson's *Winesburg, Ohio*, another slice of small-town life. She especially liked "Paper Pills," a very short piece that told the story of a doctor who would write insightful thoughts on scraps of paper. Then he'd crumble them up into little balls and keep in his pocket. The reader never knows why these paper balls are known as "paper pills." What the audience doesn't know, it can make up. *The Terminals* would be like this too – short insightful pieces tracing different characters in different circumstances and time periods, each character connected by one setting: an airport terminal.

Presently she was drafting a story called "It's Raining Frogs" about sole survivors of a religious-based war that ended in a nuclear apocalypse.

Sam's room was neat enough but smelled of cigarettes and toiletry products: shaving lotion, air fresheners, after shave lotion, and the like. Sam always made sure that when Maygyn stayed over she had clean sheets – and anything else that would ensure her comfort. After all – as far as he was concerned anyway – she was a young woman, but little did he know that she was experiencing early stages of "gender dysphoria," a term coined about a decade earlier that had to do the distress or discomfort associated with a person whose gender identity differs from their assigned sex at birth.

He was at the living room desk eating a piece of bread, sucking on a Marlboro Red and scribbling in a notebook. He was writing regularly again. It would only be a matter of time, he convinced himself, before his words would be back in print.

He had a new novel going. The premise involved a professional baseball player turned one-hit novelist named Rupert Bickel who wrote the award-winning *Closets*, a character study of nine people and their *closet* lives: one was a *closet* homosexual; another was a fifth-grade teacher who was a *closet* masochist; and yet another story was about a *closet* artist caught in a repulsive world of conservatives, including his right-winged stepfather who turns out to be a *closet* pedophile. In the story, Rupert Bickle learns to battle the demons of his subconscious while managing his role as a relief pitcher in a professional farm team, waiting for his big break to make it to the Majors by the end of the season.

And now that he was immersed in another novel – one that was less literary than his previous endeavors – he was no longer plagued by the taunting, didactic nature of John Bad John from behind prison bars. Instead, he was able to conjure up a vivid memory of that young, beautiful Greek goddess, Kalliope Pappas, with whom he was once involved.

George Pearson was snoring under his moist sheets that smelled of stale sweat, cheap rye and that pungent odor often accompanying damp laundry left in the washing machine too long. He appeared to be sinking deeper and deeper into the depths of his own darkness – his world becoming nothing more than a Kafka story.

As George Pearson awoke one morning from uneasy dreams, he found himself transformed in his bed into a gigantic insect.

What *would* become of George? It was a fair enough question that both Sam and Mike Melanson perpetually pondered.

One day you'll get a call from Sam with news of his brother's death, he heard in Miss Julie's cryptic tone.

Maygyn was sympathetic to her uncle's condition. Instead of being repulsed by him – like her mother and a number of other folks in town who never knew the whole story – she pitied him. Pitied him because she could imagine him as the popular teacher and coach he once was – the handsome, physically fit, passionate educator who was also a gifted biologist and songwriter. She had seen pictures of him in his younger days. She thought he was very nice looking; it was as if she was looking at a different person altogether. She thought of him in a white lab coat leaning over a microscope, staring into it and explaining to a student the significance of the prepared slide of pond water.

"When I call you all Monerans," she heard him say – absurdly – in Mr. Morrison's voice, "it's not a compliment. It's just a polite way to call you all *pond scum*."

She understood her uncle's plight – understood that at one time he was married to beautiful Auntie Alison whom she recalled very, very vaguely (and on occasion she would take a moment to peer into the woman's soul through an old photo album snapshot). And little Abigail – her cousin — who would never see nine years old. What would Abigail look like now as a teenager? Would she look like her mother? Her father? A combination of both? She remembered (what *was* it, five or six years ago now?) how her father wept when he received the news by phone about the car accident that – in a flash – ended the lives of his brother's wife and daughter.

Sam wrestled with a number of potential titles for his novel. He considered calling it *Foul Play* – a play on the baseball theme, a play on alcoholism, a play on Rupert Bickle's sexual promiscuity and drug addiction, a play on the word *foul* itself, indicating what a *chicken-shit* the character really was and a play on the fact that Rupert may or may not have been involved with an unsolved murder. *More* foul play. Sam concluded that basing a character on his brother would be good writing material.

Sam thought of another title. He arrived with *Line Shots*, a play on the baseball/cocaine themes.

Maygyn continued to read the final chapter of *On the Beach* as a wind swept through her, its Arctic-like temperature giving her a chill, its vigorous intensity nearly taking the book from her hand.

Her eyes were drawn toward the above ground swimming pool, which was located on the side of Peter and Donna Moon's mobile home across the street. In this image she saw splashing. And then she heard a gentle cough, a gargling and then what sounded like choking. Maygyn could already feel her heart racing and beads of sweat collected on her upper lip.

Then another jab of cold air, punching the front of her body. She stood up, squinted, saw what appeared to be a limb of some sort gripping the side of the pool (the limb looked emaciated and deformed like the branch from a rotted tree). Her head suddenly jolted – it was as if some energy source compelled her to move – and for a split second or so, she saw a young, dark and beautiful androgynous-looking girl with piercing blue eyes and a "whiffle" buzz cut; Maygyn concluded that she was about nine or ten years old. The girl was struggling, treading water, she couldn't breathe...

But as Maygyn took a step forward, things suddenly changed back to normal: there was no splashing in the pool; the sun reappeared after napping behind a cumulonimbus that strangely looked like the mushroom cloud at Hiroshima; there was no limb over the side of the pool; and no girl treading water. Nothing.

She felt nauseous.

Sam suddenly stopped writing. Something made him stop. The trailer was stuffy, and he too began to sweat. For some reason, he felt out-of-breath, suffocated.

He walked outside for some air. He felt some sort of presence next to him. Was it Bad John returning? Kalliope? He looked for both of them but there was nothing. A cool breeze formed, and it felt as though something climbed into his body. The intensity of this force brought tears to his eyes.

He continued sobbing until her presence left him. Then as he walked through the woods, he momentarily became John Bad John and in a poor Greek accent recited the dialogue he had memorized: "It isn't democracy. It is – what do you call it? – *Fascism*. It is *dictatorship*. And that is why I had to kill Hugo Ross, my friends – to save all of us, so that we can all live in *real* democracy. I know Socrates did not like the idea of democracy, but he was wrong; under the right circumstances, democracy can work, my friends. It can work..."

He stopped suddenly. "Kalliope? Is that you, *ah-gah-pee mou?*" He pronounced this translation for "my love" well enough, but instead of pronouncing the 'g' as more of a hard 'gh' sound, he pronounced it as a hard 'g' as in the word 'gregarious.'

When George awoke, he reached over his nightstand, picked up the glass with two fingers and drank the remains of the water.

A small fan blew air on his sweat-drenched body. At that instant, there was no better sensation in the world. And no hangover either.

Then he felt her presence; it was a chilly, heavy gush of air that came from the window.

"Happy birthday, Abbie-girl," he said, looking into the mirror. She was wearing that purple dress and blowing out all eight candles on the cake.

The girl transformed into the teenager she would never become, emerged from the mirror, flew across the room, then flew out the window.

He stared at the disappearing apparition as it flew over the forest trees heading toward Niagara Two.

CHAPTER 27

THE MAHONEY BOYS

It wasn't easy for Mike Melanson to confess his sins to his best friend that day in Günter's Millyard. But afterwards, he felt inexplicably liberated.

They sat with their coffees, eating stale doughnuts and sweet rolls. Rodney's Donut Hole had an unrivaled gourmet coffee, but its desserts were, to say the least, mediocre at best.

It was a mild morning on the twenty-seventh of July, a morning that gave promise to another warm summer day in Fryebury Falls.

The two friends looked at one another in self-pity. The childhood pals were now anchored down by the confinements of adulthood.

The child beating alcoholic widower and the perverted police chief.

Men of scandal.

At that time, Mike thought himself less fortunate than George. He bore a heavier cross: At least Pearson's wife was dead. *What was Miss Julie going to say when she found out about this?* The thought of her knowing was simply unbearable.

"That bastard is going to ruin your life," George said. He was half sober at this time.

"He already has."

"He won't get away with it." A hopeless phrase of confidence and they both knew it.

"He *is* getting away with it."

George got a sharp pain in the side of his head. "Is there any way to get those letters?" he asked.

Mike shook his head. "He has them in *safe keeping*...so he says."

"Shit," George thundered. "He can't, *can't* get away with this." He sighed. "And what's all this about Moira? Explain that to me again." Mike didn't try to calm his friend down; it felt good to have somebody on his side.

Mike made a disturbing sound of laughter without changing the expression on his face. "*One false move*, he says, and he'll spill the beans so fast I'll never know what hit me."

Silence.

Mike continued: "But not until he and I have been partners for a while."

More silence.

Then Mike did something very uncharacteristic: he beat himself over the head with his fists.

Seeing this act of anguish conjured up in George Pearson an inexplicable physical sensation: his body began to burn, and from his insides he could feel what felt like hot wax or lava seeping through his vascular system...it was like the times Abigail would travel through him except this time there was something else inside too...something very, very hot...something melting him. And the heat induced a new type of rage inside, a rage that far surpassed the rage he experienced when Derek Hamilton said what he said about his dead wife. No, this time, he wasn't thinking about slugging anyone in the jaw; it was much more than that.

The pain on the side of his head intensified, forcing him to shriek, forcing him to close his eyes. And in the darkness, a prophecy appeared before him. It was his own distorted, melting face taking up the entire frame in his mind. Then, like a camera pulling back from a close-up into a medium shot (while also zooming in, which created a sense of vertigo), he saw this image: He appeared as Death from Ingmar Bergman's *The Seventh Seal*, holding a large foot-long sickle. Then, Death, still holding the sickle, dissolved into a character from the 18th century play *The Intriguing Chambermaid*. "I am stark raving mad!" he said as he raised the sickle over his head – and in one fatal swoop, he hooked Jack's Cleary chest as if the cop were a piece of hanging beef in a supermarket meat locker.

Another sharp pain. This time it was radiating in a semi-circle from temple to temple, arcing up over the top of his skull. The pain was hot. He closed his eyes.

He heard little Abigail's voice: "Hi, Dad."

Then he heard breaking glass. The sound echoed, and the noise was so piercing George needed to cover his ears. The shattered glass continued as he heard screeching tires. Then a crash. Then he saw himself emerging from the car, unblemished, looking over at another vehicle that was crushed between two trees. He walked over slowly and stared at the woman slouched over in her seat, her head stuck to the windshield like Velcro – mounds of blood and gore splattered on the inside and outside of the vehicle. Then at the little birthday girl who was hunched over in the front seat.

A fierce flood of sunlight surrounded the car like a swarm of bees. It burned George's eyes.

Abigail's voice got louder in his head: *It's getting closer now, Dad. Real, real, real soon. It's time to send the devil back to hell.*

Then he saw a flash: it was Jack Cleary looking at him with bloody red eyes.

Do it. Do it. Do it. And then you can be with me and Mom forever. Real, real soon...Real, real soooooon!

"You okay?" Mike, whose voice seemed miles away, asked George. "Got another headache?"

George looked up at his friend.

Those Mahoney Boys must have been acting up again, Mike thought.

Mike remembered that Miss Julie once told him that *Mahoney Boys* was a term used in the 1930s to describe *delirium tremens*.

The things he knew because of her!

"I'll be okay," George finally said, still staring at Mike like a zombie. The pain in the front of his head appeared to subside, but his internal organs were still burning at volcanic temperatures.

It was the rage!

And it only meant one thing.

Do it. Do it. Do it. And then you can be with me and Mom forever.

George heard these words repeatedly.

More heat.

More rage.

He saw another flash of Jack Cleary – this time the police officer was fondling and kissing Alison's face as she lay dead in the car and in Derek Hamilton's voice said, "I'd fuck her corpse she's so hot!"

Fuck sobriety! he thought as he exited the Millyard. *FUCK SOBRIETY AND THIS PATHETIC EXISTENCE!* He hung his head. His body temperature increased. He felt the rage. He pictured himself sticking a knife into the side of Jack Cleary's face, about the same place where his fist struck Derek Hamilton.

So many overlapping voices; it was unbearable.

LEAVE ME ALONE!

But he knew they wouldn't leave him alone. Not until he did what they were telling him he needed to do.

So many voices now; they had become a mad chorus.

Send the devil back to hell!

He told Mike he needed to get home to sleep it off.

He whimpered with no shame all the way down Angstrom Trail to his back yard and into his bedroom where he closed the door and buried himself under a sheet and two pillows.

CHAPTER 28

CASTLES MADE OF SAND

Later on that morning, after George left for a stroll in the woods to obtain the peace he sorely needed, Sam and Maygyn had breakfast. He made her his famous fried egg sandwich with peanut butter. All he had was coffee, a piece of toast and a cigarette. They ate in silence. Maygyn was still spooked by the scene she observed earlier. Lately she had been experiencing what she concluded to be surreal hallucinations. In addition to the image in the Moon's swimming pool, there were other things she had been witnessing. Outrageous, fantastic things like shadows that appeared to follow her, shadows of magnificent geometric proportions: distorted triangles; pentagons; spheres; and looming cylinders. They seemed to be living and breathing entities.

And in addition to the shadows, shapes and the visions of the drowning girl in the pool, she had – now more than ever – been witnessing a giant, all-consuming white, blue, pink, yellow, purple and black rainbow that periodically turned into what looked like lightning bolts – and to this she had no explanation.

Sam looked at his daughter and smiled in a way that made

both of them a bit uneasy. He wondered what she had been thinking with regard to her mother's lifestyle. *Had Maygyn and Moira discussed this? Was his daughter hurt, confused, or angry? Did she need to talk?*

He continued to watch her as she turned her head away. She was eating her sandwich in small bird-like bites; it was as if she wasn't even conscious of eating. There *was* something on her mind, something troubling her. He wanted to ask her, but couldn't bring himself to do it.

An hour or so later, Maygyn, who had returned to the last few pages of *On the Beach,* looked up from the lawn chair and saw her mother walking toward the house. She was barefoot, wearing a pair of jeans and a baggy pink Janice Joplin T-shirt.

Jesus Christ, Mother! What are you doing here?

"Maygyn," Moira yelled, then made her way to the front door. "Sam!" she screeched.

"Hello Moira," Sam said in a breezeless manner as he exited the front door; Maygyn was surprised by his unfazed demeanor. "What can we do for you?"

She was distraught, unkempt and there were dark bags under her bloodshot eyes.

As she got closer, Sam said, "Are you okay? You look...frazzled." He finally had gotten to that state of mind where he could face her without becoming emotional, unlike in the past when the mere sight of her caused him physical and mental grief induced by intimidation, jealousy and disappointment.

"We need to talk – all of us. *Now.*"

"Okay," Sam said coolly. He looked at his daughter and she looked back at him with a glare – that "look from hell" as Moira called it – which seemed to say: *What trouble are we in now?*

Maygyn's sour stomach intensified and was brought on by many things: heatstroke; the empathy she felt for the doomed characters in *On the Beach*; those hallucinations she had been experiencing; her mother's sexuality (was Moira currently sleeping with another woman?); her own identity quandary and this sudden "need to talk" (Maygyn sensed bad news forthcoming).

The three recent encounters she had with Cleary – the original carnal encounter where the cop taped their lovemaking, a follow-up encounter in Moira's garage where he made unwanted advances against the car and the most recent encounter where he had stalked her in her own home and took advantage of her while she was shit-faced drunk – were undoubtedly difficult to explain, even for Moira Davis. She looked at Maygyn and she felt a tear trying to squeeze out; she held it back. Maygyn sensed the anticipated tear and for a moment pictured herself hugging her mother.

Moira smiled at Maygyn; Maygyn smiled back.

When she finished telling them the details, in a rather effective first person narrative replete with description and dialogue, she paused, unable to speak any further.

Sam offered her a smoke, then glanced at his daughter who was getting one of her previous questions confirmed.

As strange as it may have been, they were a couple again – the three of them a family again – if only for a moment.

Moira became silent. She was trembling, shivering in that repulsively stagnant room in the middle of summer.

The family sat cautiously in their seats – each of them facing in opposite directions of one another like statues in a museum. Moira stared at the wall until her vision became blurred.

Then she revisited the time when she and her sister were about ten – about a month before the accident. They were at the summer cottage on the beach at Lake Massasecum in Bradford New Hampshire – the lake where little Meggie would eventually lose her life – building animals out of sand with their mother, the original Megan Davis.

"I'm building a cat," little Meggie said.

"That doesn't look like a cat," Moira said.

"Yes it does! Yes it does! *Mom!*"

Their mother said, "Of course it looks like a cat. It's Meggie's cat. And there's no other cat in the world like it. That's what makes it so special."

"I want to make a sand crab," Moira said.

"And there will be no sand crab in the world like it," Meggie confirmed, smiling. "It'll be special."

"That's right," her mother said.

Moira heard a sound bite from a Jimi Hendrix song, which frighteningly complemented the scene:

And some castles made of sand, fall into the sea, eventually...

Sam looked at Moira's charcoaled feet and as they continued to sit in a brooding silence, he recalled something his wife told him right after they met, which he always thought peculiar: "When I grow old, I want to live in the mountains, smoke a pipe and grow a Mark Twain moustache."

Maygyn, now concentrating on her father's slumped posture, was still suffering from a sour stomach, but she no longer felt like throwing up. Somehow, she was keeping it all together. All she knew was that she had a confirmed dislike for Jack Cleary and she was finding herself being protective of her mother.

"You okay?" Moira asked her daughter.

The girl nodded. "Are *you* okay?"

"I don't know." A pause, then a little smile to her daughter who always had that anxious look on her face: "I will be."

Then Moira looked at Sam and their seemingly blank, inscrutable stare that lasted for several seconds was anything *but* inscrutable, for at that moment they both conjured up the same image: Jack Cleary's bleeding chest, wounded by the bullet of a gun, gurgling on his own blood.

The three of them sat there.
And sat there.
There were still lots of things they needed to discuss.

CHAPTER 29

MR.CELLOPHANE

"Please tell me that this is a demented gag!" Miss Julie exclaimed from her bed. She held onto her womb as if to protect the unborn child from its father.

Adam was sitting on the edge of the antique Hitchcock chair – the same chair, incidentally, that his mother had fallen from months earlier.

"I wish I could," he said to one of the Ansel Adams prints above the bed. He couldn't believe she insisted that their son be there with them. *Why? What did this prove?*

Miss Julie continued to rub her womb. She shot daggers from her eyes at her husband. Sweat formed on his forehead. Writing sex letters to a girlie magazine? To *Foxes and Boxes*? That outrageous parody of a periodical that featured X-rated animation? The magazine that once featured a story called "Inside Pussy: An Interview with Frank the Cat...Brother of Fritz"? *How could she be so irate with something so preposterous?* Surely someone else wrote those letters. Not her M&M! Not her innocent low-down townie...the Chief of Police...the father of her...children. No way! It had to be a demented gag, just like she said.

But it wasn't.

Mike was surprised that Miss Julie, with all her insights, premonitions and clairvoyance didn't predict this one.

"I sense something evil...in your top drawer at the police station," she would have said. "Something dirty. Something raunchy! A work of the devil! Letters! Pages and pages of filth!"

"Why did you do it?" The question was direct enough, but in a much softer, gentler tone – undoubtedly a dramatic tactic used by the actress. *How would this all play out on the stage? How would Strindberg's Miss Julie react to her servant Jean if he told her the same news? How would Nora react to Torvald in Ibsen's* A Doll's House? "There's so much you can learn about life," she once said, "from those naturalistic Scandinavian playwrights...even if Strindberg *was* a misogynist. Like Ibsen, he still knew how to write about real people. And let's not forget Ingmar Bergman who is not only greatest Swedish filmmaker of all time; he is, hands down, the greatest filmmaker. *Period.* And don't get me started on Liv Ullmann – *Den beste!* There *is* no greater actress from here to Norway! Ah, *Persona, The Passion of Anna, Cries and Whispers, Scenes from a Marriage! Vilken Mästerverk!*"

Mike had no answer for his wife; he had no answer for himself. It was just something he did. He never expected he'd get caught. He stood there looking even more intently on the Ansel Adams landscape photograph, making out his son's name *Adam.*

Adam stared at his father's back. He wanted things to be okay. He didn't want his parents to fight; he especially disliked the predicament he was in regarding his father. Miss Julie told him about Mike's misdeed. "It's like taking your pictures and drawing penises and vaginas on them. Or drawing animals having sex with one another! *Holy merde!*"

Eventually – as if time itself slowed down – Mike said in a

whisper, "I'm sorry."

"What?" Miss Julie reacted. "What was that?"

He now turned around to look at Adam who was on the verge of tears, then slowly to his wife who had his undivided attention. She was looking *right through him*. Mike Melanson, like the character in *Chicago*, was Mr. Cellophane. And you could look right through him and walk right by him and never know he's there.

He repeated, "I'm sorry" which wasn't really an apology more than it was something to say to break the unbearable silence.

She didn't respond.

Adam began to cry.

"And there's no need for *this*," she said, pointing to her son. She got up and limped over to the boy. She hugged him. To Adam she said, "We are coming into some very hard times, Adam. Eventually, everything will be okay though. I'll make sure of it. I won't let anything happen to you – *ever*." She looked down at her womb and rubbed it. "You too, Alexis Sage or Spencer Cagney." Then to Mike: "If we all have to do this alone, we will!" A short beat before the accusatory: "Pornographer!"

Mike felt something hot inside his entire system. Burning him from head to toe. It was the rage. A flash of her dead body, sliced and diced on the bed. *Alexis Sage? Spencer Cagney? Over my dead body! You ridiculous over-dramatic little fool!*

At that moment, Mike understood what drove some men to madness.

She glared at him. He too was the devil himself. And with this look she was sending her husband – along with Jack Cleary, George Pearson and all the rest – back to hell. It was all a goddamn conspiracy. Hell comes to Fryebury Falls! Presently, she didn't care *what* happened to him. Years of marriage, one kid, one on the way...*nothing*. In her eyes he committed adultery. And it was unforgivable!

Adam continued sobbing.

"It'll be okay," Mike said hopelessly. "Everything will be okay. Just listen to your mother." He really wanted to hold the boy.

"This is unfair, Michael Anthony Melanson. *Unfair.*" Her voice cracked. *Was she going to cry now?* She appeared to be trembling. She was clasping her son as if to protect him from his father and his cartoon whores. "You need psychological help. Real therapy. I'm not qualified for this licentious behavior. This is," she said, looking over at Adam's melancholy face, "*effing* madness! And if you don't get the appropriate help, then don't count on being part of *this* family!"

All or nothing. Always *all or nothing.* And everything was a scene in a play too. She always thrived on dramatic conflict in her self-contained little theater. At this time, Mike was merely a walk-on part who needed to disappear by the end of the show. Or maybe *she* needed to disappear. But she wasn't going to end her life like Strindberg's character did. But she *could* do what Nora did at the end of *A Doll's House* – leave her husband and slam the door on his sorry ass!

But deep down she knew she'd be afraid to leave him or her home. *What would she really do out in that big world? Who was she kidding?* The only acting and photography that this woman would do would be within her commodious Brown Ave mansion within the confinements of the most minute Fryebury Falls. How she *longed* for the city that doesn't sleep; how she *feared and loathed* the city that never sleeps.

Stan appeared in the mirror. He laughed in that atrocious manner that frightened her so. *Needle in a Haystack, Needle in a Haystack* was all he said. But that was enough. The words said it all. If she stayed in Fryebury Falls another day, that's all she would be. And she knew this.

"Where do we go from here?" Mike asked.

"I told you where you and your demons can go."

Mike's world was ripping apart at the seams. Then he thought about those letters. *No one else knows about them,* he assured himself. *And nobody ever will!* Maybe Cleary was just calling his bluff. But then again maybe he wasn't. And this is why he finally decided to spill the beans to his wife. He just couldn't keep this thing a secret; it was too big of a thing to hide. Too much of a chance of her finding out in some other way.

He needed to preserve his reputation at any cost.

Mike Melanson made a decision. Jack Cleary – he gulped, his heart fluttering as if someone were inside his chest doing a breaststroke kick – was going down! Somehow. Yes! Somehow Jack Cleary would take the fall. Like one of those cartoon characters he admired so much, he saw a light bulb shine above his head. And he grinned.

He thought: *What if Jack Cleary wrote twelve letters to* Foxes and Boxes? And when the chief discovered the smut, Cleary panicked, became defensive and threatened to make it look like Chief Melanson's letters!

Who wouldn't *believe him? Roger Price? Reardon the banker? Moira Davis? The rest of the folks in town that he knew couldn't stand the guy?* They would all – no questions asked – support their chief.

Then later he could earn the respect back from his wife and son.

If only he waited before telling his wife. If only he waited just a little while...

He walked downstairs, then out the front door.

He lit a cigarette, sucking in the tar and nicotine vehemently, as if to punish himself for all his sins.

The final day of July was windy. The temperature dropped down to about sixty.

By the time he arrived at Günter's Millyard and saw

Niagara Two, a large flock of birds loomed above, and the sunshine glaring through one of the weeping willows temporarily blinded him.

The sound of the falls was so piercing his ears began to ring, a high intensity screeching that one would hear after being exposed to loud noises: music at a concert; a car backfiring; a gunshot...

Accompanying the ringing, the birds, downtown traffic and an airplane was the sound of a crowd cheering the four syllables of his name as they clapped on beat: *Mike Mel-an-son, Mike Mel-an-son, Mike Mel-an-son.*

And more cheers. It was like he was at a ballgame.

He looked into the eye of the waterfall and the following scene unfolded before him like a scene from Harvey Pekar's autobiographical, documentary-style comic books, *American Splendor*:

Mike stood at a podium giving a press conference of some kind: "Ladies, gentlemen – friends of Fryebury Falls. We are gathered here today for a special occasion. One we've all been waiting for. The time has come (the walrus said) to talk of many things: We need to form a posse to capture Jack Cleary, formerly of the Fryebury Falls Police Department, who has overstayed his welcome in our town. He has harassed and used brute force on a great number of us." He winked at Gregory Reardon the banker, then at Roger Price who had his arm around his son Eddie. "And he's a liar and a pornographer." Pause. The crowd went silent. "In my hand I have a stack of sex letters that he wrote to *Foxes and Boxes*." Another pause. More silence. Then he raised his hands up and yelled, "Let's hunt that overgrown bulldog down – and cut his fucking balls off!"

The crowd loved this. They roared and whistled and screamed, "Mike Melanson for town manager. Melanson for town manager!"

As he stared into the sky through a billowy cumulonimbus cloud, he could have sworn the cloud itself opened up, creating some sort of tunnel or portal – and from that spot he saw what looked like a green field surrounded by larger-than-life trees or flowers of all shapes and colors. And another flock of birds were flying into it. A gush of sunlight emitted from this place, mostly blinding and hypnotizing the spellbound chief. He was experiencing more of those visions...

What was happening? *What was happening?*

He grinded his teeth, then with his thumb and index finger, he made the shape of a gun and pointed it at the waterfall as he exited Günter's Millyard into downtown Fryebury Falls.

AUGUST 1984

S	M	T	W	R	F	S
			1	2	3	4
5	6	7	8	9	10	11
12	13	14	15	16	17	18
19	20	21	22	23	24	25
26	27	28	29	30	31	

CHAPTER 30

NEEDLE IN A HAYSTACK

"Your husband has gotten himself into a bit of trouble," Stan said to Miss Julie through the bedroom TV. "He's become quite the *unintentional* Method actor, hasn't he?"

"He's a bastard!"

"*Da! Da! Ublyodok!* And let's not forget, a low-down townie with no concept of the real world," he added, laughing. "And quite the unintentional *writer,* too! A real man of...*letters.*" More laughter.

"It's unforgivable. It's over between us." She appeared as though she were going to cry.

"It's for the best," he said unsympathetically, then hopefully: "On a brighter note: Jimmy Orlinski just completed his eighth and final draft of *Needle in a Haystack.* It's a beautiful play. Stark, haunting, deliciously macabre. It's going to win the Pulitzer. He's also going to direct it and he's going to cast you, my *lyuba,* in the lead. It's the *inevitable order of things.* And after the remarkable ten-year run, you'll be able to write your own ticket...*anywhere.* A Hollywood film will follow." He chuckled. "Unless of course you plan to return to that – to use your word – *abysmal* – scandal program. What's it called again?" He paused, then laughed like some mad doctor: "You could do quite the 'inside story' on your own husband now, couldn't you?" He paused again, but this time did not laugh. "Have you ever thought of just dumping him? Excess baggage, my *dear*, will *interfere* with your *career*."

Miss Julie's heart skipped. Yes, the thought *did* cross her mind, but hearing it said like this made her feel ill. She felt a pounding in her ankle underneath the cast.

"Nothing lasts forever, you know. And you certainly won't amount to anything by staying here in this measly little town."

"What about Adam?" she asked, then held her womb. "Or Alexia Sage or Spencer Cagney?"

"*Real* things require *real* sacrifices."

Tears rolled down her face. "What about my babies?"

But the image on the screen dissolved.

Miss Julie jumped out of bed, dragging her injured leg along. She faced the mirror.

She saw her name and the title, *Needle in a Haystack*, in bright neon lights...on Broadway.

"That's okay. We'll do it together. You hear that, Adam? You hear that Alexia Sage or Spencer Cagney? We can do it. Alone!"

Miss Julie moved to the large dresser mirror and looked at herself at an angle. Stan reappeared in an insert on the bottom of the mirror, watching her, smiling diabolically.

"And now presenting Miss Julie Melanson." She cleared her throat. "I mean Miss Julie Najarian. The lead in that acclaimed show *Needle in a Haystack* by Jimmy something-or-other." She was using her breathy *S.O.S.* broadcasting voice.

She rubbed her eyes violently with the tips of her knuckles, giving her face a puffy, swollen look like a middle-aged broad who twenty years earlier was a striking creature but because of substance abuse now looked washed-up. Someone like Liz Taylor from *Who's Afraid of Virginia Woolf?*

She imagined the first scene:

The curtain opened and Alice Cantrell was frantically looking for a syringe. Her home was in disarray. She was literally looking for a needle in a haystack!

She located a push pen, then made a fist with her left hand as she looked at the veins in her left arm. She tapped the veins with her right fingers. The actress grabbed a red scarf from the closet and wrapped it around her arm frantically, continuing to tap on the more prominent veins. Again, she rubbed her eyes with her knuckles, pushing her eyelids back far enough until she could see spots and colors.

She jabbed the point of the pen into her arm, using the end of the pen to mimic a needle going into a vein. She didn't draw blood, but she *did* manage to leave a rather prominent skin blemish by her wrist.

Then she sat on the bed and engaged in meditation – breathing in and out slowly through the nose and mouth. She pictured her heart slowing down, practically coming to a stop. She sank deeper and deeper into this relaxing state; a vision of pure beauty formed: she was naked in the middle of a green pasture with large colorful trees that looked like flowers. A vision she had pictured before. It meant something. It was a real place. It existed. It was another life, a parallel world with a theater-in-the round and all the fixtures that looked like ancient Greece. Where theater began! And there she was. Center stage. Doing what she was always meant to do in life. Performing.

She opened her eyes. She was ready to delve into her scene. And into the mirror, she spoke.

"Where were you last night? I waited for you, you know. Were you out with that cartoon character playmate again? What was her name? Ellen Morgan? You need not lie to me, I can smell her *you-know what* on you."

She tapped her arm and rubbed her eyes. "Well, well – I'm

a junkie and you're an adulterer. Why don't you give me the letters?" And imitating Bette Davis she said, "Give me the *lett-ahs*, Michael. Give me the *lett-ahs*." She rubbed her eyes and spanked her arm. "Look what we've become. You don't want me anymore, do you? I have become nothing to you. Insignificant. Insignificant as a *needle in a haystack*, aren't I?"

She looked at her wedding picture on the dresser, made a fist and punched her forehead. *Ouch!* Then she flung the photo across the room and watched the glass in the frame shatter as it hit the wall. She cursed the photographer. "You never knew how to take photos anyway. No aptitude for composition."

Then she limped over to it, picked up the frame as if it were an injured pet, attempted to collect all the fragmented glass and cut the tip of her middle finger as she did so. A rounded bead of blood formed and within seconds the blood dripped down her finger and into the palm of her hand. She straightened herself up again and faced her reflection in the mirror. She turned her palm toward the mirror as if she suddenly became a traffic cop motioning for a car to stop; the blood, which now covered her hand was dripping down her wrist. Then she turned her hand around and looked at the original piercing; she could no longer see the bead of blood which at first had reminded her of a shiny, red marble. When she gazed at herself in the mirror again, she noticed she was flipping herself off. She clenched her teeth together, growled and extended her middle finger toward the mirror. "Fuck you!" she thundered. Then: "God damn you, M&M! Fucking god damn you!" Then she licked the blood from her hand and like an infant at a nipple sucked the blood from her finger.

From his room, Adam heard his mother crying and cursing. He looked at Fred and Barney, then at Blood and Max. "It's going to be okay." He felt a sharp pain in his abdomen and looked up at the ceiling. "Grandpa Lucien? Are you there?"

There was no answer.

Adam wanted his daddy home.

But Mike wasn't home. Not by choice, but because Miss Julie told him to leave.

"Come back," she said, quite aware of her fastidious, erratic behavior, "after you've cleaned yourself and all that filth!"

On this fourth day of August, burning at ninety-nine degrees with an unbearable relative humidity that made everything heavy, the Chief of Police sat hopelessly in front of Niagara Two.

At the top of the waterfall, he looked at that opening he had seen before. There seemed to be something inside. *What were all of these things he was seeing?* Perhaps he was going mad. He tried to ignore the vision; eventually it disappeared.

He wished he could crawl into a hole – or into Niagara Two itself. To drown himself. Then he could disappear for good. There'd be no Mike Melanson. And no Jack Cleary. Or Miss Julie. Or Roger or Eddie Price. Or the scandal. Or the incriminating letters. No *Foxes and Boxes*. No George Pearson to worry about.

He would be non-existent...insignificant.

Insignificant as a needle in a haystack.

CHAPTER 31

PARANORMAL
RETRIBUTION

The woman emerged from the closet door with a rope in her hand. She followed the boy who was running from her. It seemed as though the faster he ran, the quicker she gained on him. She took slow rhythmic steps...one long, calculated stride each second. And each time she took one of these steps, she yanked the rope.

She was dressed in a baggy police officer's shirt; it was so long it covered her knees. Her bare feet were bruised – all black and blue and some other hideous colors. All of her extremities looked reptilian.

The boy was breathing heavily, hyperventilating under the bed. As he peaked through a dime-sized hole in the headboard, he saw her as one witnessed a subject through an iris shot in a silent movie. She was ascending the vomit green-colored stairs. Every time she hit a step, she would disappear and then, within a second or so would reappear again.

Over and over and over again.

Step. Disappear. Reappear. Step. Disappear. Reappear.

But she never advanced. She kept climbing in what appeared to be slow-motion but never made it to the top.

He used his belly to slide to the other end of the bed where he got up and sprinted to the bathroom around the corner. Although it was no more than twenty to thirty feet, the voyage was long.

He locked the door, sat on the toilet, fidgeted with his hands, breathed loudly and watched the door handle as he hunched over the toilet like an old buck in his rocking chair.

The bathroom seemed as though it were underwater; there was a blue tint to it. And sounds of crashing waves and running water like he remembered at the beach.

After a minute, maybe two, he rose to an erect posture and peered carefully out the window.

She was there on the lawn wearing a long white night-gown, moving in slow motion through blinking lights that made him dizzy: She would appear and then disappear in the darkness. She was getting closer and closer. There was this strong odor too. To J.J. it smelled strange – like metal and fire. He coughed. Then, in one flash, she was right there at the window; her eyes were wide open, and he could see her top teeth that looked like fangs protruding from the blanched powdery-textured face.

J.J. jumped back and he could feel his heart punching through his chest. As he turned around, he saw her emerging from the closed bathroom door; she had a rope in hand. The rope turned into a long black venomous snake with long yellow fangs and blood in its jowls.

His hyperventilating became uncontrollable. He heard high frequency noises that reminded him of a sound effect from some old monster movie. Like that giant fire-breathing lizard, he thought. Or was it the sound of those giant ants made in that old movie called *Them*?

"It will all be over *real, real soon*," she promised. "Come on. Give it up. Close your eyes. You are not meant for this world. I can bring you into *another* world, *another* life. It's beautiful here, J.J." In a singsong tone she said, "And there's lots of pretty girls." Then three dark-haired, blue-eyed beauties materialized; they were naked, they were smiling, and they all looked uncannily like...his next-door neighbor.

The three of them marched in synchronicity toward him. Their blue eyes were glowing like police sirens. J.J. closed his eyes and when he opened them, they were gone.

Gail laughed.

And now a new scene: The bathroom roof suddenly opened up as if it were a convertible. The sky was bright orange and red and looming above was a dark black cloud...and an airplane.

His daddy was the pilot.

And Niagara Two, superimposed over a group of weeping willows, appeared in the back yard.

Gail reappeared through the window. She had the rope.

J.J. looked skyward. "Help me, Daddy. The Gail has a rope!"

The pilot yelled, "Is it an emergency?"

"Yes...it's an emergency!"

"Damn it boy, how many times have I told you not to interrupt me when I'm working? I have unfinished business to take care of." He released a bomb, which exploded in the distance.

"Daddy!"

The plane exploded.

Gail laughed.

J.J. screamed, then cried. "Daddy! Daddy!"

But then Maygyn Pearson – the "real one" – emerged from somewhere. She was wearing that red bathing suit of hers. "Hello J.J.," she said in a whisper, smiling. "I want you to be my boyfriend. Would you like that?" She winked and then licked her lips. The 't' in the final syllable of the word *that* sustained in a sort of vibrating echo sound.

He moved toward her –

Then he found himself back under the bed watching the Gail through the iris shot walking up the stairs. Stepping, disappearing, reappearing, stepping, disappearing, reappearing – tautly holding that piece of rope.

J.J. tried to scream, but he could only muster up a hissing hubbub that sounded like a choking snake, intensified by the gurgling of his own saliva.

⊠ ⊠ ⊠ ⊠

"Wake up, J.J.! Wake up, son! Wake up!"

To the boy, the voice was muffled and sounded far away. When he awoke, he saw his father looming directly over him. Lazlo was whimpering.

"Shut up!" Jack thundered to the dog. Then to J.J., "It's okay, son. It's okay." The muffling sound became crisper.

J.J. looked up at his father who looked blurry. There was something in his hand and at first, he couldn't see what it was. Then his father's hand – now in perfect focus – came right at him, causing the boy to jerk his head. It was the rope his mother was clutching in front of the bathroom door. This sudden movement startled Jack, causing him to jump back. He moved forward again and said, "It's okay." The rope wasn't a rope at all – it was bunched up toilet paper and it was being used to wipe away the perspiration drenching J.J.'s forehead.

"It was just a nightmare," J.J. whimpered, trying to be strong. "Not real. Like in a movie. Not real." There was something different about this nightmare, however. Not so much with the content, but with how he was feeling. J.J. felt as though he were strapped to the bed, that something was pressing down on his febrile body and preventing him from moving. Oddly enough, he seemed complacent there in his bed. Lazlo stood at the end of the bed, knowing something was not right. He kept moving his head back and forth to Jack and then to his bedridden playmate. Finally, he looked at Jack, as if admonishing him.

"What?" Jack said, absurdly, momentarily intimidated by the black lab he despised so much. Then more to himself: "Stupid mutt."

Lazlo barked directly at him. Before saying anything else, he looked at his son who was still looking upward.

Without moving, the boy said, "Are you going to shoot Lazlo in the head, Daddy?"

"What?" Although he heard him, the question was most unexpected.

"For barking loud are you going to shoot Lazlo in the head like you said before?"

"No," Jack said. "I won't ever do that."

J.J. started gasping for air; like before, he was gurgling on his own spit, making that choking snake noise.

Jack wiped the boy's forehead again even though it didn't look like any more sweat collected on his skin. "Do you still see her?"

"Yes, Daddy."

"Will her out like you've done before. Okay?"

"Okay, Daddy." Then the boy mumbled to himself: "Just a nightmare. Not real. Like in a movie. Sins of the father. Coming to kill me. Real, real soon. Real, real, real soon."

"Right," he said. "Not real." But he knew otherwise. Gail was very real, and not only did she exist in the subconscious, but she was also ubiquitous in the waking world as well. She was living proof of what so many people he saw on TV would insist, that homes can be haunted by malevolent spirits, that paranormal activity, ghosts, *really* did exist. Before he came to Fryebury Falls, any such notion of ghosts, spirits, paranormal activity – whatever you wanted call it – would have been immediately disregarded as ridiculous nonsense. He couldn't understand how this was possible, but now after so many hauntings (or would they be called visitations?) from his deceased wife, he was by default a believer. He also knew that she had come for him, to make him pay for what he had done to her and to the others. It was vengeance of some kind, paranormal retribution or spiritual vengeance inflicted upon by this wraith or poltergeist or whatever she...it...was.

"Are you still going to be the Chief of Police?" J.J. asked slowly, weakly.

"That's right."

"And I will be a policeman officer, too?"

"Sure," Jack confirmed, but his method of delivery was much different this time around. Gentler somehow. "Like we talked about before, it's a lot of hard work and you need to make sure you –" Something pinched his stomach. Maybe it was Gail; maybe it was something else, like a feeling he had. "– you abide by the law..."

"And stay out of jail and the hole."

Jack cleared his throat. "Uh, yeah. That's right."

"Daddy?"

"Yeah."

"Am I going to die soon?"

Another pinching of the stomach, except this time it felt like a claw gripping his insides. At that moment nothing – not even the crimes he committed or Gail's intrusions – horrified him more than hearing his boy saying those words in that frail vocal fry. The only thing he could think of was all those times he reprimanded his son and forced him to do time until he learned his lesson, not to mention all those threats he made on the boy's beloved dog. *But why did he do this? He knew that he loved his son more than anything. But did he really love him? Or did he pity him? And when he yelled at him like a warden admonishing a prisoner, was he really just creating an outlet to mask his real feelings?* After all, there were many Jack

Cleary personalities – the one who enforced the law on his boy like that brutish Buford T. Pusser from *Walking Tall*; the one who felt a poignant bond with his unfortunate son; the one that wanted to erase all those past memories and live a quiet, normal life of purity, law and order and peace; the one who led a secretive life hiding from all his sins...

"No. You will get better soon."

"Real, real soon?" he asked hopelessly, using Gail's words.

"Yes. Real, real soon."

Then they both heard Gail saying the same words but with a much different subtext.

J.J. began to shiver, causing his teeth to dance (when he was younger, before the accident, he once described being cold as having one's teeth dance) and he was still looking up at the ceiling with no expression. Jack looked down on him and whispered his name, but the boy did not respond. At this time, J.J. had closed his eyes and within moments was fast asleep; Jack studied the boy's rapid eye movements for a long moment and then used the cloth rag to soak up the new beads of sweat that were very quickly accumulating on his forehead.

CHAPTER 32

ANOMOLIES

The twelve-string guitar rested on Moira's knee as she leaned back on the couch. She rolled her head from side to side, allowing her neck to crack.

August the sixth was humid, and even though she had just taken a shower (her third of the day; ever since her encounters with Jack Cleary, Moira had been taking more of them) she was still dripping with sweat.

She lit a cigarette as she contemplated the jazzy song she was writing about misogyny and empowerment.

The fact that Maygyn was spending a week and a half in Amesbury with Sam's friends Walter and Phyllis Diamond was a good thing, Moira thought. It would give her daughter some sorely needed vacation time before school started up in about three weeks.

Walter and Phyllis, the wealthy entrepreneurs that they were, the "soap sellers" as Moira liked to call them, had acres upon acres of land, a private lake, an Olympic size swimming pool and a house big enough for four families. Yet, in their own way, they were a modest couple. They were the ones who approached Sam regarding this network marketing business while they were standing in a very long line at a discount bookstore, waiting for an autograph from Kurt Vonnegut who just gave a moving talk about his life as a P.O.W. in Dresden.

Moira called the Diamonds, and all other distributors, "mindless conservatives" – but over the years she formed a peculiar liking for them. After all, despite their capitalistic mentality, they weren't catty and pretentious like so many of the other couples in that ugly business were, couples whose primary interests in life were money and God – in that order. But *somehow* this couple (who were, incidentally, anomalies – they had actually seen Moira perform at some bar one night years ago and they were both avid readers who truly loved and understood Sam's critique on modern America in *Another Life* before they even met him), *somehow* they were enough of a paradox to at least make them interesting. And they never had their own kids; Phyllis Diamond would always tell people that she had "poached eggs" inside of her.

Incidentally, a few years after *this* story comes to end – in the summer of 1990 – the Diamonds – on their way to a business meeting to show another married couple "The Plan," as it had come to be known – were sideswiped by a Citgo tractor trailer and killed instantly.

Moira was expecting Sam's company later that evening. Although they were still separated, no legal papers had ever been drawn. Sam Pearson never fell out of love with his wife, and this was the reason why he agreed to come over; according to Moira they needed to discuss how Jack was going to be punished for his crimes. Unbeknownst to her husband, Moira had some very clear ideas as to what she was going to do.

Or better yet, what *she* was going to ask *Sam* to do for her.

But first things first, she thought and began singing "Moving On," a song she wrote with Cheryl. Both women, before officially becoming involved with one another (Moira still insisted that the relationship be kept from her daughter) had been with men. Cheryl once told Moira after a few drinks: "We are the biggest closet dikes in Bean Town. I say it's time you and I come to fucking grips with our repression. We're meant to be together, babe."

If you thought Moira had spunk or a hard-boiled edge, she was nothing compared to her partner Cheryl Benigni – a five-foot two dynamo who kept her jet black hair in braids which barely reached her broad shoulders. She had one of the most strikingly exotic faces Moira had ever known; it was more Greek or Armenian than Sicilian: dark brown, almost black eyes that were like painted saucers in her round pupils; a sloped, pointed nose; soft, gentle, pinkish lips; and a rather prominent chin, sloped like her nose. From afar one could best recognize her from her almost square-shaped frame, which made her appear more masculine than feminine, but surprisingly, as Moira once told her, her medium-sized breasts, rounded hips and wonderfully curved legs (all of these traits most prominent when she was naked) were considerably more feminine than most women. Even her voice, which was always talking tough like a trucker, was high-pitched and nasally. The twenty-nine-year-old woman had the voice of a sweet seventeen-year-old.

Like the Diamonds, she too was an anomaly.

In the middle of the song, Moira saw her twin sister who transformed into her girlfriend. She was naked, sitting cross-legged on the recliner across from her. Cheryl smiled at her and moved her feet and head with the music.

Moira was serenading her girl.

The girl closed her eyes, the vibrations of the music penetrating her entire being.

> *Waking up after so many years*
> *And I'm feeling okay*
> *Breaking up, and finding truth*
> *What can you do? It's the way*

Dreaming dreams, inside the hole
The memories are alive
Ships that pass may sink below
I'm swimming with the tide
Helping hands to relieve the grip
I'm a parting red sea
Central squares appear to change
They form new shapes under me

Moving on...get along...moving on...on and on
Waking up after all these years
Time to say so long
Breaking up after all this time
Then you say, "I'm growing strong"

Dreaming dreams outside the hole
My head creeps above
Ships that pass may rise above
I'm swimming against the tide

Open hands and flying minds
Are waking in the dawn
Spirits fly and my head spins around
And I see you and I we're moving on...

Moira stopped.

Cheryl continued to move her head back and forth, her eyes still closed, and then she dissolved into the chair.

Then another flash of her little sister. Meggie was dressed in a blue and white dress, a gift from their mother for her tenth birthday, the dress Moira always thought looked like Dorothy's dress in *The Wizard of Oz*.

Then the little girl melted away, evaporated into the chair.

Moira got up. A warm, inviting breeze traveled through

the screen door and through her hair and body. It penetrated her being; it was Cheryl inside of her.

Then the wind escaped from her.

Moira stood frozen in the middle of the living room. Her body trembled again, but not in ecstasy; it was a tremble of fear. She trembled at the thought of telling her girlfriend what Jack Cleary had done to her...twice...once in the garage and then again in her bathroom. She simply couldn't tell Cheryl quite yet what had happened. *Why not?* Cheryl would cut his cock off, that's why! And she'd really do it. But she didn't want Cheryl to do *anything*. Didn't want her to *risk* anything. No...that would be someone *else's* job.

She just couldn't tell her about it. Not yet. Maybe later she would. Much later, though. But what was happening *now*, at this moment? She had a feeling that something was not right – that something was wrong with Cheryl. Why didn't she answer her phone for the past few days? Where was she? She tried to conjure her up again; she wanted her girlfriend to travel inside her again like she did moments ago.

And then, as if her mind were being read and critiqued, the phone rang.

Cheryl?

No such luck. It was Sam. He was coming over.

CHAPTER 33

THE INEVITABLE ORDER
OF THINGS

On one of the hottest days in recent years, August eighth, George Pearson took yet another oath of sobriety.

He sat in his room, the fan massaging his sweaty body, which stunk not just of body odor but also of rye. He was naked except for an old pair of running shorts he wore during his coaching days.

He had to face the facts and quit drinking, or he was going to die. Plain and simple. Then he thought: *But would that actually be so bad...dying?* Ever since Alison and Abigail died, he was living on borrowed time anyway; he was always convinced that he died in the accident with them.

He needed to come to grips with himself. *Right now.* He conjured up the saying "get busy living or get busy dying," a phrase that he, upon occasion, would paraphrase to his players when they were playing sloppy baseball: "Get busy winning or get busy losing – but if you're losing, don't do it on my watch!" The words, however, were always said with a bit of endearment, for George Pearson was never the type of teacher or coach that people feared. Not then anyway.

His wife and daughter were dead. That was a fact. And he was a drunk and a social degenerate who had suffered a nervous breakdown. *Wasn't that what had happened to him? Or had he truly gone mad? Like his mother had. Had he in fact become a paranoid schizophrenic...seeing things, hearing things...being seduced and haunted by his own...deceased daughter?* Crazy! *And what about all those other things he was seeing in his bedroom – or moreover, in Günter's Millyard? What was going on? It was madness! Madness! And it all needed to stop. Right now.*

He needed to will it all out, he thought rationally: the alcohol, his Abbie-Girl, Alison, what he did to Derek Hamilton...*all of it!*

"How can you think such a thing?" Abigail asked. It didn't sound like he remembered her. Her voice was hoarse and smoky. She sounded...*older.*

George blocked his ears. He knew the hallucinations became more intense the longer he went without a drink. It had been nearly twelve hours now. And he knew all about the effects of delirium tremens...those bullies called the Mahoney Boys. "Delirium is the disease of the night," a sadistic doctor told him years ago when he spent a night in a detox center in Keene, New Hampshire. "You, my friend, have only seen the beginning. You just wait until you really start sobering up. I'm talking cold turkey. Oh, man! You'll start seeing turkeys all right. Turkeys and chickens and bats and rats coming out of your walls. It's quite the show. Being sober ain't what it's cracked up to be. You'll go back to the bottle when you leave here. They *all* do." When George first arrived at the center, the doctor smiled at him and said, "Welcome to your lost weekend. Welcome to Hangover Plaza."

"How can you think such a thing?" the girl repeated. "You think you can exorcise me like a demon?" A light, fragrant breeze formed; she moved toward him.

He tightly closed his eyes. *Go away. You're not Abigail! You're not my...Abbie-Girl!*

The girl's energy merged into him.

"You don't exist," he said hopelessly, pathetically, knowing his words meant nothing.

"But I do," echoed the voice. "All of us do."

"No," he said, squinting.

"You want a drink, don't you?" The voice was piercing, as if coming through an amplifier.

Sobriety. Sobriety. Sobriety.

"Come on, Dad. Who are you kidding? Once a juicer, always a juicer." Her energy traveled inside of him – the same warm, fragrant wind as before – except this time the air felt sharp like someone was stabbing him from the inside. He scrunched up his legs until he was squatting like a catcher, waving his hands frantically like an ant caught in a pile of ant poison. He felt her entire being and she was suffocating him.

After a few moments, the struggling ant gave into the poison. He cried, but now it was a cry not of panic and anxiety but a cry of acceptance, a cry of – as strange as it may have sounded – of relief. "What do you want with me?"

Her voice was hollow: "You must complete the task we discussed."

And as if he really didn't know – perhaps through his hopes of sobriety, he blocked the thought out – he said, "What task?"

"Jack Cleary."

Silence. The air through his insides no longer felt painful; it felt light and prickly, as if someone were tickling his organs with a feather. It felt...*cleansing.*

"Drink, then kill. With extreme prejudice." She laughed. "Then the three of us can be a family like we're meant to be." Her voice was comforting, assuring, *certain.*

Before leaving him, Abigail told him he had less than forty-eight hours to complete the job. Something to do with that *inevitable order of things*...the way things were *supposed* to be.

And then Mike Melanson, his best friend, would be saved from a lifetime of scandal and humiliation. Once George did his duty, he would get the incriminating letters and burn every one of them...and every copy that Cleary allegedly made too.

George knew he had nothing to lose at this late stage in the game. He would make this sacrifice for his friend.

He would be honored to do so.

He also – apparently – had no choice.

Then the tortured soul would finally be free from anguish as he spent eternity in another life, one that was anxiously awaiting his arrival (or so insisted this daughter of his).

He needed to believe it.

Wanted to believe it.

He took a deep breath, knowing he would no longer fight Abigail's spell, and accepted it all. *But what made him suddenly convert to this madness?* He didn't care to wonder any longer. It hurt him too much to wonder.

And when it was all done, George concluded, there would be peace and harmony in Fryebury Falls once again.

And peace within his own suffering soul.

CHAPTER 34

CARRIAGE TOWN

Amesbury was less than ten miles from where Maygyn Pearson resided. It rested on the Pow Wow River, which emptied into the Merrimack River; it was in the northern-most part of Massachusetts, bordering New Hampshire. The town, although Moira jokingly called it an "insignificant little ghost town," was one of the most historical spots in New England. Aside from the fact that it was settled by Europeans as early as 1645 and then by the town's first town clerk Thomas Macy in 1654 (who was persecuted for harboring Quakers, and consequently sold the home to a man named Anthony Colby) erected the town's (and New England's) first home – it was also well-known for its industries of carriage making and hat mills. Additionally, it was the home to great historical figures Josiah Bartlett (a medical doctor and New Hampshire legislator with twelve kids who signed the Declaration of Independence) and the antislavery advocate/Quaker poet, John Greenleaf Whittier, who in the mid-nineteenth century published the highly successful epic poem, told through vignettes, about a family amid a snowstorm called *Snow-bound: A Winter Idle* and the much shorter "The Telling of the Bees," influenced by the European custom where bees – seen as liminal guides of sorts – would be told about significant events in their keepers' lives like births, weddings and deaths. Sam Pearson quoted this poem in the opening of his most successful novel, *Another Life*.

Trembling, I listened: The summer sun
Had the chill of snow;
For I knew she was telling the bees of one
Gone on the journey we must all go!

Sam's entrepreneur friends, The Diamonds, owned a mansion on Whitehall Road, about a mile from this Macy-Colby House. Each summer, since she was seven, Maygyn would spend a few days with The Diamonds...just as a fun little getaway...something the teenage girl still looked forward to.

It was the tenth of August, and the girl sat in a luxurious bamboo chair in her bikini by the swimming pool. She was sipping an iced tea and reading the first story in J.D. Salinger's *Nine Stories*, "A Perfect Day for Bananafish." It was a well-crafted, bizarre little narrative divided into two parts. The first half involved a phone conversation between a mother and daughter, the latter who was in Florida helping to look after her husband Seymour Glass, a World War II veteran with post-traumatic stress disorder. In the second part, Seymour strikes up a conversation with a little girl on the beach who liked that his name was "see more glass." Seymour Glass explained to the girl that in this world there existed a certain school of fish known as "bananafish" who continuously ate bananas, then went into a hole to die. Maygyn made what she considered to be a clever association with her Uncle George, a contemporary Seymour Glass – once a reputable citizen who had, for reasons beyond his control – gone completely mad. And the way her uncle would look at her too – the same way

Mr. Keaton and other adult men would eyeball her – this was similar to Seymour Glass's questionable behavior toward the little girl on the beach.

Maygyn enjoyed the time she had alone that morning. Her hosts left her alone for several hours, telling her to help herself to anything in the house. "Mi casa es su casa," they told her. On this day, Walter was showing his so-called business plan to a prospective client in Newburyport and Phyllis was meeting the ladies – her "gals" as she called them – for an expensive lunch somewhere in Boston.

The couple chose to build their modest mansion because Walter had been, in his day, a professional baseball player – a second baseman for the Red Sox farm team in Pawtuckaway. He played with them for five or six years but never quite cut it for the majors.

It was truly a utopia, this home of theirs...a paradise. It was massive, wide and had a modern design. Its square frame, along with its extreme angular architecture, mostly constructed of glass, made the place look more like an office building in a 1920s American city rather than someone's home – especially a home for only two people. It was set in the center of a fifty-acre property with rolling hills, perfectly green and well-groomed, leading to a deciduous forest of seemingly endless trees. Maygyn liked the Diamonds but didn't envy them. They were very humble and sincere people who had a lot of stuff but somehow managed not to flaunt it. If anyone deserved to be "stinking rich," it was the Diamonds; they worked for every penny.

From time to time, Maygyn drifted in and out of Salinger, thinking of constructing another vignette for *The Terminals* (a story about a middle-aged woman who, after working years at an airport, meets a wealthy old man who helps her get out of her longtime rut) as well as her own home life. She still didn't know what to make of her mother's lifestyle or what that neighbor of theirs supposedly did to her (part of her thought her mother might have been embellishing the situation). Nevertheless, she still believed her mother; her confirmed dislike for Jack Cleary returned. She pictured her mother being violated by that eccentric police officer, and quite suddenly she felt something rip quickly through her body, something hot and intense.

And she was thinking of something else too: her parents. She knew that while she was away on this "vacation" her parents were going to have what Moira coined as "a talk that they sorely needed to have." *Were they going to finalize their divorce?* There were times when she didn't want *anything* to do with either one of them. She came to realize that her father – a person she admired and perhaps to a degree, worshipped at one time – the one who told her that there was no way she could live with him – wasn't all too great either.

When she closed her eyes, a warm oven-temperature breeze had formed. She held an image of David Marino; he had his shirt off and his chest was ripped with muscles; a little bush of black hair grew out of his cleavage. She imagined holding onto his ripped bicep with one hand while running her fingers through this bush of hair (that "forest chest" of his) with the other. Then she imagined dissolving into him...*becoming* him...becoming David Marino.

Then the breeze transformed, illogically, into a biting, frigid wind. It felt for a moment that the seasons had changed or something.

When she opened her eyes, the world she saw was tinted with a few flashes of striped colors – purple, black, white and yellow; then things got darker. The pinkish-red sun must have gone behind a cloud, she considered. But why was everything so dark? And so cold? And so windy? This was beyond bizarre.

The wind continued and she gave her scantily dressed body a bear hug.

She thought she heard running water – and splashing. *Splashing.* Like she heard and saw in the Moon's swimming pool.

Her ears began to ring. It was a ferocious piercing sound.

She jumped from her chair, knocking the iced tea onto the patio, the glass smashing into umpteen pieces.

Her heart was racing.

The sweats.

Nausea.

The world was like a photograph negative.

She heard what sounded like hundreds of people conversing in the distance.

Where were they? In the forest?

Then: something that sounded like a car back firing, or a plane breaking the sound barrier.

And after a good part of a minute (or was it longer?), it all stopped.

She stood at the edge of the pool, watching her distorted reflection in the water. The azure sky reappeared, and so did the rest of the world. The sun, once again, was shining.

Cold sweat dripped down from under her arms to her stomach.

A new wind formed. It was gentle and mild. Eddies formed in the pool. The whirlpool wiped out her reflection, replacing it for a second with what looked like an image of herself several years earlier. She was treading water, struggling, eventually choking on the water – and the eddies distorted the image and replaced it with a series of smaller, more intense mini-eddies, each one spinning haphazardly clockwise and counterclockwise throughout the entire pool.

Something was there.

Something was going to happen – she could sense it even though she couldn't explain it.

Maygyn's stomach turned sour, worse than before a test.

Something was not right.

CHAPTER 35

LIMBO

The Melanson estate was now segregated...per orders of Miss Julie. Miss Julie locked herself in her bedroom (*her* bedroom, she insisted to her husband, not *his* bedroom...not anymore), Adam was told to stay in the confinements of his bedroom, making sure he kept busy with his animals and drawings and Mike, he resided in the basement until further notice.

It was a finished basement, replete with brown leather furniture, a rug imported from Istanbul (courtesy of Miss Julie's great grandmother who had been a wealthy woman long before her son made his first million in the coffee business), a modest-sized TV set on a stand, a gold-plated card table, a pool table, miscellaneous European artwork and photographs, and an adjacent bedroom. The basement was a luxurious apartment unto itself.

"I won't have you contaminate the house with your dirtiness and sickness. Go clean yourself, *sex offender!*"

As he stared blankly at the television screen, he thought of those incriminating letters.

And then a montage of newspaper headlines flashed onto the screen as if he were suddenly watching one of those old films from the 1930s.

SMALL TOWN POLICE CHIEF INVOLVED IN SEX SCANDAL...

FRYEBURY FALLS POLICE CHIEF MIKE MELANSON – SEX OFFENDER!

CHIEF MIKE MELANSON LIKES NAKED CARTOON GIRLS!!!

He couldn't bear it. There was no place to go, no place to hide, no one to turn to. Miss Julie certainly didn't want him around. Cleary most *definitely* didn't want him around. And soon, after finding about the letters, nobody in *town* would want him around.

"Jesus, Mike," he heard a voice say. It was Dex Crowley. "I am very surprised in you. And disappointed."

Suddenly more voices – all people he knew – were saying similar things to him. *I can't believe it Mike...You had us fooled...What were you thinking? What kind of leader does this? Sex letters to Foxes and Boxes? This is a joke, right?*

Upstairs Miss Julie stood naked in front of the mirror, her face pinkish, puffy and swollen from crying and from madness. Her husband had driven her to this madness – unwittingly of course, for even she knew deep down that he would never deliberately be spiteful, but nevertheless this inexplicable act of – what was it? – Passion? Lust? Stupidity? – made her reconsider *everything*: her marriage; her passion; her *own* stupidity.

She began to recite from the Strindberg play.

Mike could hear each word through the heating ducts.

He listened and wept.

"You've never traveled, Kristin. You should go abroad. See the world. You've got no idea how nice it is traveling by train – new faces all the time and new countries. On our way through Hamburg, we'll go the zoo – you'll love that – and we'll go to the theater and opera too...and when we get back to Munich, they'll be museums, dear, and pictures by Rubens and Raphael – the great painters you know...You've heard of

Munich haven't you? Where King Ludwig lived – you know, the king who went mad...We'll see his castles – and some of his castles are still just like in fairy tales...and from there it's not too far to Switzerland – and the Alps..."

"Lovely, Miss Julie," the Russian voice echoed.

Mike stopped listening. He paced the room like a caged gorilla, huffing and puffing, forcing the blood to his head, making his face red like his cheeks. This made him light-headed. He still had the strength, however, to beat the palm of his left hand with the fist of his right hand, the pointer finger sticking outward, taking on the form of a gun.

He thought of Cleary with two bullets through the eyes. He remembered watching a colorful western once – it had John Wayne in it. In the movie, Wayne's character shoots an already dead Comanche in the eyes. By doing this, he explained to his posse, the soul of this Comanche could never make it to the Promised Land – he'd be stuck in limbo for all of eternity.

Then he jabbed his own temple with his pointer finger until the pain became unbearable.

Adam was facing Fred and Barney, gazing at them in a cool, expressionless trance. His drawings were scattered on his bed. They were sketches of dinosaurs – T Rexes, Bronto-sauruses and Stegosauruses, devouring helpless forest animals like chipmunks and squirrels. One picture was that of a grizzly bear with blood on its paws. Another was of a panther preying on a dog.

He spoke to his pets robotically: "Don't worry. I won't let anything happen to you. I won't let the dinosaurs get you." He paused and looked at the ceiling. "Daddy did pornography. He's in trouble like you said, Grandpa Lucien. Is he gonna get fired from his job?" He looked contently on the contours of the ceiling and waited for an answer.

But Grandpa Lucien didn't appear or respond.

"Kill me too! Kill me!" Miss Julie hollered shamelessly.

"You who can butcher an innocent creature without a quiver. Oh, how I loathe you, how I loathe you. The blood is between us, and I curse the hour I saw you! I curse the hour I was conceived in my mother's womb!"

"Brava, Miss Julie! *Otlichnyy!*" Stan's voice echoed. "*Velikaya aktrisa!*"

Mike was crying.

Adam was crying.

"I've got to get out of here," she whispered. "I'll die if I don't." Then she sang in a cracking voice, "These little town blues...I'm melting away..."

Mike walked outside the basement's back door, lit a cigarette, but couldn't finish it. He threw it into the yard and watched it burn out into the grass. He must have stood there half an hour.

"I've got to get out of here," he whispered.

As he jetted into the woods, lighting up another cigarette, committing to smoke this one down to the filter, he heard a crowd yelling his name. *Was it a crowd gathered to hear him speak about the state of the town? Was he the town manager again, just like he was in all those colorful cartoon dreams he had been having?*

Or was it a riot, a lynch mob led by Jack Cleary and Roger Price, getting ready to execute the pervert and burn him like a warlock at the stake, as if Fryebury Falls suddenly became Salem, Massachusetts in the seventeenth century?

Niagara Two's running waters pierced through him as if someone with a large straw or something was blowing hot air into his already ringing ears.

He needed to terminate Jack Cleary's command once and for all.

And then a most troubling thought entered his mind: He contemplated taking his gun, sucking on it as if it were a piece of licorice or something, closing his eyes, saying a little prayer (to whom he had no idea), apologizing for his wrongdoing and then...

He'd be free from it all. It's not that he *wanted* to die – it's just that he didn't know how to live anymore.

LITTLE TOWN MURDER/SUICIDE! FRYEBURY FALLS' MIKE MELANSON – BELOVED CHIEF OF POLICE – KILLS HIS DEPUTY – THEN PULLS THE TRIGGER ON HIMSELF...

Well, whatever he decided to do or *not* to do, he would be making headlines one way or the other. Alive or dead. If not from a premeditated murder/suicide (Mike finally disregarded this most preposterous prospect), then surely from this embarrassing sex parody thing hovering overhead like a cirrus cloud on the verge of storming.

CHAPTER 36

STUART CREEK

Sam and Moira smoked Marlboro Mediums in the living room of their home on Brown Ave. Legally, it was still their place. For a couple on the verge of divorce, they had managed to work together remarkably well, especially when it came to their biggest responsibilities – their daughter and her well-being and keeping up with their finances, what little they had.

"What are we going to do?" Moira asked, blowing smoke out of the side of her mouth.

Sam followed her lead, letting out a sigh. "I don't know." He really wanted to give her a better answer.

She glared at him with that famous look from hell. "You don't know? Have you been listening to me for the past few days? Did you not hear the part about Cleary attacking me... *twice?*

I hear you, Moira, Sam thought but the thought that was hard for him to let go of was that of her and Cleary going at it again. Then came the image of Moira making it with that Cheryl Benigni. Then, based on Moira's elaborate descriptions, he tried to picture Cleary violating her the way he did in the garage and then a few nights later the way he came onto her while she was drunk in her bathroom.

Gently he said, "Moira, I didn't come here to fight. I came here because you asked me to. For support. Remember?"

Moira was silent. Sam went to the bathroom. The sound of running water from the sink and eventually the flushing toilet conjured up the little girl's voice: *Moira...help...Moira help.*

In the window, the pale-faced girl floated back and forth as if her body were a paper bag being controlled by the force of wind.

Moira began to shake, her trembling body now a neurotic volcano on the verge of erupting. Then she froze. Before long, the volcano spewed into what seemed like thirty something years of built-up tears.

When Sam returned, Moira got up and clung on to him. "I'm sorry. You're not going to leave, are you? I'm sorry." She squeezed his hand.

"No, I'll stay," he said, rubbing her neck and back, first reluctantly, then more passionately. It became a hug. It felt strange, yes, but at that moment there was nothing more natural than the two of them holding one another. For that moment, Sam and Moira were, in fact, one another's soul mates. He never even questioned whether she was being genuine or not – he knew she was.

Then composing herself, she pushed herself away from his hug and wiped the mixture of tears, mucus and saliva from the tip of her nose.

Sam looked at her worn face. She was already starting to age considerably, especially about the eyes: the dark circles and crow's-feet allowed Sam to see what Moira would look like as an old woman. And then absurdly, he pictured that Mark Twain moustache she would talk about.

She squeezed his hand again. This moment brought him back to the day, about a decade earlier, when that record producer named Roland Blithe obsessed with Freddy Mercury, who thought that all rock music should have a classical opera sound to it like Queen's music did, told her that the music she was writing was too harsh, too punky. He defined the punk genre as "moronic noise made by wannabe musicians who couldn't sing or play an instrument to save their lives." And furthermore, he specifically told Moira, "You and your music are too butch. That dyke shit isn't gonna sell records, sweetie."

After Roland Blithe said this to her, Moira had sunk into a depression for weeks, and at one point she even considered swallowing a bottle of pills. It was that moment all over again. Sam had been there to pick up the pieces then and – if necessary – he was there again to pick them up. He'd always been there for her.

Outside, the summer breeze made the mid-August evening serene. The waterfall could be heard through the trees.

Sam kneeled down in front of the couch, hovering over Moira who had suddenly decided to take a rest. He held her arm. She was no longer the foul-mouthed, adulterous siren, that insatiable diva; no, it was as if they never even had a history together. He looked at those reddened eyes with poignancy. And she looked at him. She smiled faintly.

And they didn't fight the impulse.

Sam went through the motions but could not get those pictures of Moira with Cleary and Cheryl out of his mind.

Moira jerked her head back and forth, not once thinking about the person who was actually making her climax.

Then she came.

They lighted cigarettes. Moira said, "Thank you."

He couldn't imagine saying *you're welcome*. Instead, he smiled, nodded his head. They discussed Maygyn and her well-being – how lucky they were to have such a smart and beautiful daughter. A smart and beautiful young woman whom they didn't even know. Worlds and worlds apart. They needed to change this, they agreed; Maygyn needed to, from now on, be an integral part of their lives.

But they had said this many times before.

A bit later, after a series of fragmented conversations (despite their shortcomings, the couple were never at a loss of words when they were together), Moira, who had a major topic on her mind and had been trying all night to find the right time to address it, without any further delay asked, "So do you ever see Stuart Creek anymore?"

"*Stuart* Creek?" *How random, Moira.*

"Yeah. Do you know *another* Creek?" She laughed.

"I haven't seen him in years."

"He lives on Commonwealth Ave – doesn't he? Near the B.U. campus?"

"I wouldn't know. When I met up with him at that jazz club in Inman Square a few years back, right after you and I split, he was still there. But I'm not sure anymore. Why? What made you think of him?"

"Remember the time there was that torrential downpour and we got lost trying to find his place? We ended up going to the Cape. Then we ended up on the freeway and that old twat threatened to summon us to court because we were in the wrong lane. Remember that?"

Sam nodded and half-smiled.

Moira allowed his mind to wander.

"You think if you looked him up, he'd meet up with you again?" Moira asked. "You two were pretty good friends at one time."

Sam squinted: "At one *time...*"

Stuart Creek was Sam's friend who dropped out of college – like Sam eventually did – to become a "real" writer. To him, listening to professors' bullshit of what a writer is *supposed to do* or *couldn't do* in order to write the perfect novel was "the cancer of his muse." Incidentally, early on in his life, he had been diagnosed with leukemia, which would eventually kill him.

Allegedly, Stuart had mob connections.

"Remember Victor DeLorenzo?" he asked Sam one day in his raspy, nasally theatrical voice (he reminded Moira of a Mel Blanc character from a "Bugs Bunny" cartoon). "The one who tried to bang my girl, Tina? *Deader-n-a-fuckin' doornail!* You don't fuck with Stuey Creek, I always say." Then he'd laugh that outrageous, idiosyncratic ignition-starting laugh of his: *ah-ah-ah-ah-ah-ah-ah-ah.* "I'm serious, pal, you need *anything*...anything at *all*...give me a call and me and my posse'll take care of things." Then he'd slap Sam on the shoulder with his gargantuan paw and say, "Can I buy you a beer, man?"

If anyone *didn't* fit the stereotype of a writer, it was Stuart Creek. He was an anomaly of anomalies. Moira once said he looked like a Nazi with his buzz-cut blond hair and blue eyes; he had broad shoulders, large pecs and biceps (he never lifted a weight in his life), spoke like a truck driver, replete with the expletives executed with beautiful diction, and he wrote passionate romance novels – three of which had been published and did rather well commercially.

But he despised reading, called it a waste of precious time. ("Why waste your time reading *goobly-goob* when you can spend the time writing? That's where most writers get it wrong.") He especially hated old literature. "Ever read that *Turning the Screw*, the one about the old, repressed spinster who sees ghosts that are supposed to represent her sexual desires? That's the pits! You can't even understand what the author's saying. Fuck that shit, man..."

Ultimately, Stuart Creek's goal had been to write beach novels. "That's what most people like to read, anyway. Maybe I'm selling out – but hey, who gives a flying rat's ass, right? I'm making money, right? And people know my name. Plus, they're reading some sexy shit in the meantime. Everyone wins! Hell, man, what else *is* there? This literary shit is for the birds!"

His most popular book, *Jolene's Jewels*, told the story of a young girl's passion for a much older man – but the novel, despite his hatred for literary terminology, was really just a metaphor for his own relationship. Apparently, Stuart's girl Tina (whom Moira called a myth; no one ever actually saw or met her) was almost twenty years older than him. When people would ask how his relationship was going, he'd say, "Me and Mom are doin' great, man!" *Ah-ah-ah-ah-ah...*

"Maybe Jack Cleary should get a taste of what it's like on the other side of an attack," Moira said.

Sam sighed loudly. "Do you know what you're saying, Moira?"

Moira nodded mechanically, almost smiling.

"But the guy was always so full of shit," Sam said, not knowing how else to respond. "He was always joking about that mafia shit." A pause. "I think..."

"You still care for me?"

Sam's heart skipped. She asked him again. She knew the answer. He fidgeted. This was insane. She was playing him again, and he knew it.

A light wind came through the screen of the open window.

"I'm not saying we hire him to kill Cleary or anything. That's crazy." Then softer: "Sort of." She continued: "Just a good roughing up."

Time passed as husband and wife brooded in these thoughts.

What *about* Stuart Creek? Sam suddenly contemplated, albeit absurdly. How *would* he approach his old buddy on this insane proposition? And what if Stuart denied? What if he said, "I'm no hit man, Sam. Whatever gave you that idea, man?"

What then?

"Just a joke, Creek," Sam would say. "You've always said you had these connections." Then he would punch him on that enormous bicep and say, "Just fuckin' with you, man. Let me buy you a beer!"

But if Stuart said, "Job done" or "No problem, man" – then Jack Cleary was in for it. He could then hear Stuart say, "I could do more than break his bones. Just let me know. I can make that dickhead *deader-n-a-doornail* if you want."

Sam got chills.

This was insane. Ridiculous. He tried to put the thought out of his mind.

But then he gloated at this possibility. The chills of fear became chills of excitement. After all, Jack Cleary was the guy who had an affair with his wife! And this was the guy who called himself a *friend* while he was boffing his wife! Hell, Sam Pearson even considered killing the *dickhead* himself.

He experienced that rage he once had years back.

A flash of Cleary's massacred body entered his mind.

He looked at Moira's legs and feet, then got hard again.

He wanted to fuck her. Hard. Angrily. He hated that he felt this way. Hated that all of these feelings of love, lust and murder were plaguing him like one evil emotion.

What was happening to him? Why were his insides so hot, as if there was a blazing fire scorching his organs?

He looked again at his wife. She got chills as she looked at his face. It was strong and handsome (that Robert Redford look), like when they first met.

A gust of wind blasted through the screen.

Projected on the wall across the room, it was Bad John from prison: "It isn't democracy. It is – what do you call it? – *Fascism*. It is *dictatorship*. And that is why I had to kill Hugo Ross, my friends – to save all of us, so that we can all live in *real* democracy. I know Socrates did not like the idea of democracy, but he was wrong; under the right circumstances, democracy can work, my friends. It can work..."

"You're right," he said to Moira. "He *can't* get away with this."

Moira nodded her head pragmatically, but inside she was smiling.

CHAPTER 37

WE ARE BROTHERS

The clouds slightly gave out on August the twelfth, producing not a downpour, which the arid town sorely needed, but a heavy mist that later developed into a thick, titanium white fog.

By high noon, George Pearson had already soaked his insides with cheap rye. He was drunker than he ever remembered being – he was *out-of-his-mind* intoxicated. He must have had nearly twenty shots within the past hour.

His vision was impaired so drastically that the world about him was a complete blur, a brooding film of air pressing against his dilated eyes. And his stomach – so sour and acidic that it felt as though daggers of sulfuric acid were pinching, then stabbing it. His fingertips had turned a chalky blue; he was cold even though the humidity was stifling, and he felt himself needing to catch his breath from time to time.

The voices would not let up; it was as if his head were the forum for a party he threw for uninvited guests. It wasn't just Abigail, but all sorts of dead people: some of the voices he recognized immediately and others it took him a while to decipher. But they were all the voices of those who had since passed on.

As time progressed, the voices got louder; all were scream-ing and shouting in overlapping dialogue. The intensity of it was so unbearable, George hit the back of his head with a candleholder in hopes that either the voices would terminate or he himself would perish.

He kept hearing things like the following: *Do it George; Do it, Daddy; Do it for Mike; Have another drink; Kill Cleary; You're the chosen one; It's the inevitable order of things; Drink...it helps with the rage; Join us real, real soon. Make love to me, George...*

And in a chorus of what sounded like a hundred voices singing a nursery rhyme: *The time has come the walrus said: Kill that devil, make him dead. Make him dead. Make him dead.*

Over and over and over again.

Then there was silence. Finally.

Another shot, but most of it missed his mouth and trickled down his face.

Within minutes, the voices returned, slowly dissolving into his mind, then exploding in full throttle again.

And then the rage.

Following a series of primal screams, throaty barks, like that of a mangy dog, and irregular breathing, the former biology teacher, baseball coach, beloved father and husband, hopped around the room as a caged animal would, entertain-ing a laughing group of sadistic spectators who loved watching imprisoned freaks. He was like another Kafka character...the hunger artist from the short story of the same name, driven mad from forty days of fasting.

And he was punching everything in sight – knocking objects off the bureau and night tables – smashing the frame then ripping to shreds a rare and treasured Ted Williams poster from the early 1940s – drawing blood from his fingers and knuckles – listening to more voices talking to him about the *inevitable order of things* – and the rage...

Drink – rage – drink – rage – drink – rage...

Fifteen to twenty minutes, maybe longer, George sat on his bed, spent, so out of breath he thought he would surely collapse.

The time has come the walrus said, the chorus said in musical unison, *to kill that devil, make him dead! Make him dead! Make him dead!*

And then the music and more voices...

What goes up, must come down, Spinning wheel got to go round...

And the images, hovering above him, below him and coming in on him like white blood cells devouring a virus.

Closer and closer.

The faceless image, the woman carrying the aborted fetus, the locomotive getting closer and closer and Abigail (aged sixteen or so – an age she would never see) appearing and disappearing as she walked up a flight of stairs...these were all visions from this recurring nightmare.

He closed his eyes and prayed to the God he didn't believe in, to make it all stop. *Make it stop. Now. Please, God. Stop. Please.*

The ghosts were so close now that he felt them all coming inside of him, choking him, ripping his insides, lighting his heart and lungs on fire...

And again, that smell – that foul and sweet smell. *How could a smell be so appealing and at the same time so... repulsive?*

The right side of his head twitched. He saw that place, that land, the one with the green fields and baseball diamonds and flowers and greenhouses and Abigail and Alison on the rolling hills calling his name...reaching their hands out, asking him to join them.

It was all so wonderful, George thought. He stood strong, perfectly plumb, in the middle of his room, eyes closed, unable

to move, not wanting to move, enjoying all the senses penetrating his being. It was that state of nirvana again. That
phantasmagoria. *Ah, yes...*

*But where had the pain and horror gone? Where were the
ghosts?* They were gone. There was peace within him.

Everything went dark...

⊠ ⊠ ⊠ ⊠

"Holy shit! What the hell happened here?"

George, who was lying flat on his back, head tilted to one
side, resting on his shoulder, legs crossed, white foam
dripping from his mouth, opened his eyes without moving and
said as weakly and complacently as he'd ever said anything in
his life, "Brother...you're back." Then he closed his eyes again.

Sam kneeled down. He looked around rather frantically
for something to wipe George's mouth, which Sam thought –
in a darkly humorous vein – looked like he'd just given
someone a blowjob. He found an undershirt which stunk of
sour sweat and wiped his brother's mouth as if he had been a
mother cleaning a baby's dribble – the semen had suddenly
become infant formula that didn't quite make it down the
baby's throat.

"You were with the bitch of...bitches...last night," George
said, then he attempted to giggle, but this only caused him to
cough. "Did ya...fucka?"

"You need a doctor." Sam held the back of his brother's
neck and tried to lift it. His other hand scooped under his rear,
but the weight of everything made it an unsuccessful attempt.

George coughed again, spewing up more of that white
foam.

Sam jumped back in horror, then he moved toward
George again. "Come on, you got to get up!" He tried to repeat
the action but was unsuccessful again. Momentarily he gave

up. He looked around the ransacked room – the bureau, the holes in the sheetrock, the Ted Williams poster... He got a lump in his throat. His heart palpitated. Suddenly he became quite sympathetic. He asked for the third time, "What happened?"

And with a bit more gusto but still weakly, George sang, "'It's the same old story, the same old song and dance...my friend.'"

"We got to clean you up. You stink. I'll go get some water, sober you up. Some coffee too. You don't look good. You're still foaming at the mouth, man. You should see yourself. Look at you. You're..." Sam jumped up. "I'll be right back."

George made a sound of distress as he attempted to stand. "Whoa – spinning wheels got to go 'round..."

By the time he stood up, Sam had returned with a glass of water and said, "Coffee's brewing." He handed him the water.

"Thanks, nurse," George said, raising his glass as if he were going to make a toast.

Time passed.

"Do you need to talk?" Sam asked graciously.

"Nothing to talk...about," George replied, slurring his words as if he were imitating a bad actor playing a drunk character. "I've been...chosen to take on dah devil." He laughed. "Dah devil. Dah devil."

"What, what are you talking about?"

As if he still didn't believe his mission, he said, "I have been given an insur...mountable." He burped. "Duty. By the...uh... what do I call them? The..."

"The voices?"

"Sure. Dah voices of dah devil. Fuckin' A...dat's fucked up!"

"What are they saying?"

Although George was stinking drunk, he somehow sobered up for this moment to answer his brother as pragmatically as possible. He looked into Sam's eyes, which were bloodshot. He also noticed something else he had never seen on his brother before, crow's feet. His baby brother's crow's feet. "I have been chosen by," he cleared his throat, but this only caused the words to slur more, "Dah voices to...terminate...dah devil. Dah devil." Another burp. "I guess that makes me an angel of some sort, doesn't it?" Sam could smell the alcohol with George's every breath.

Another long pause. Tears streamed down over those crow's feet.

"Don't worry," George said rationally. "I'm not crazy. I just know what I know. I know how it sounds. I think it's fucked-up crazy shit, but I also know it's...the truth. I've come to realize three things now: First, there is no God and there is no such thing as free will; Second...second...we are all governed by other...inexplicable...*things*; and last, third, these *things*...make the rules." Then, changing beats, he said almost in a whisper, "What about you? Have you ever been told what to do by...*anyone*?" Sam looked at his brother dead on. Of course he did. He knew all about the voices...or at least *one* voice, the voice of Bad John. "I'm tired," George said finally. "I can't control them anymore. They've won."

"We can get you some help," Sam said and gulped. "We can –"

"I'm not fucking crazy," George thundered. "I *wish* they were hallucinations, man, but I know they're not."

Silence.

In the silence Sam got chills and heard Stuart Creek's gruff voice: "This would all make a fuckin' great beach novel, man." *Ah-ah-ah-ah-ah...*

Sam's breathing converted into a cry of anguish.

George put his hand around Sam's neck (the action made Sam flinch, for the gentle touch on his jugular seemed stifling, suffocating as if his brother's fingers began choking him or something) and in a tone more peaceful than frightening: "I appreciate all you've done for me." He clenched his fist and pounded his chest with it. "I'm honored you're my blood." A familiar breeze soothed his tension-free face. "You're a saint, Sammy. What can I say?"

"You've said that before. I'm no saint."

George contemplated this, wrinkled his forehead, smiled with closed lips and in his best Jack Nicholson impersonation said softly, "I like you, Lloyd. I've always liked you. Best god damned bartender from Timbuktu to Portland Maine."

"Or Portland, Oregon for that matter," Sam said, completing the line from *The Shining*. Interesting how playful they could both be under the circumstances.

George giggled then burped, "Or Portland Oregon...for that matter."

Sam watched his brother speak; it was as if he could see the actual words floating from his intoxicated lips. Speaking wisdom. George had always been a born teacher – even as a boy. Sam remembered when they were kids and George would design tests for him to take – tests on naming different types of seaweed at the beach (Rhodophyta versus Clhoryphyta...); and tests on baseball players and rules (*Why was the infield fly rule invented? How many lifetime home runs did Ted Williams have?*). At one very brief moment in his life George Pearson was completely in his element. At one very brief moment in his life, George Pearson was living *his* dreams and passions. At one very short moment in *his* life, Sam had done the same. A lot of this can be credited to their mother – who in addition to teaching them that "blood is thicker than water" – also preached to them about the significance of reaching for the stars. She wanted her boys to have everything she didn't. "Do as I say, not as I do" was one of her many mottos.

Sam didn't try to stop his brother, who got up, kissed him on the top of the head and made a stride to the door as if he had never been tanked in his life.

The time had come.

"You really going. In your condition?" Sam's voice was raspy, weak. At that point he understood that Jack Cleary was the devil, that George was going to terminate the devil. *How did he know this?* The temperature in his body was boiling... and something inside of him confirmed this. And George knew that Sam knew.

"Yes."

"Now?"

"Yes."

Sam felt that if he could talk his brother out of doing what he was about to do (*Was this actually happening? Was his brother about to commit an act of murder? What the fuck was this? What the fuck?*), he would have. But his brother's mind was made up. He sighed. Sadness. Relief. "It *does* get tiring, doesn't it?" Sam said. "Life, I mean." He sniffled, wiping a tiny tear drop from his cheek.

"You said it, bro." Then George smiled, saluted his brother, blew him a kiss and said dramatically, "And if I run into any of you bums in the street, let's just pretend we never met."

As boys, they loved *Stalag 17*, the P.O.W. film with William Holden. This was the line that Holden's character Sefton says to the other sergeants, moments before his escape.

Tears gushed down both sides of Sam's cheeks.

As Sam watched George drive off in his brown 1975 Monte Carlo (George had driven the car only a handful of times since the accident – and this vehicle, one he purchased with Alison's and Abigail's life insurance money, barely got any use) he didn't think about trying to make sense out of any of this.

The only thing that plagued him, as he watched the back of his brother's head, difficult now to see because of the mist, was the discernment that he would never see George again. This was something Sam just knew in the same way that George knew he was the one chosen to exterminate Jack Cleary.

As baffling as it all must have seemed to Sam at this time, and without knowing all the details, he began to realize that Bad John was speaking through his brother. He listened to the Greek man's voice as he stood hopelessly by the window: "It isn't democracy. It is – what do you call it? – *Fascism*. It is *dictatorship*. And that is why I had to kill Hugo Ross, my friends – to save all of us, so that we can all live in *real* democracy..."

Eventually the car disappeared over the horizon and into the thickening fog.

Blood is thicker than water.

A picture of little Scotty Page's yard replaced the entire image of the road. George and Sam were playing razzle-dazzle football with a group of neighborhood kids. The play was in progress. Together they sang in harmony: *In the world with all the others, no one beats the Pearson Brothers. 'Cause we are brothers.*

Hike one. Hike two. Hike, hike, hike...

CHAPTER 38

THE JAWS OF LIFE

Once he reached I-95, he picked up speed considerably. George Pearson had the steering wheel in one hand and a bottle of Southern Comfort in the other (he already had enough of the cheap stuff inside of him; he wanted to treat himself to something a bit sweeter for his final act in this heavy life of his). He was now so intoxicated that he didn't even comprehend his own mortality. At this moment he was a racecar deity, alive and confident and on a mission. And Jack Cleary's head was that mission.

He swerved in and out of three lanes, passing Sunday drivers, tractor trailers that honked their obscene brass horns at him, sports cars that were already going twenty over the speed limit, and any other vehicle that prevented him from moving forward. He was heading back toward Fryebury Falls; he had made a special trip fifteen miles out of town to a state liquor store.

The Monte Carlo started shaking. It wasn't meant to go past eighty – and George Pearson, who was flooring the gas pedal, was doing nearly one hundred.

"Better be careful, Dad, or you'll get yourself into another accident. Better watch out for that sun."

When George looked over at his daughter in the passenger seat (she was a young woman; she looked about sixteen or seventeen), he smiled at her.

"I am here to tell you there's been a change of plans." Her face was intense, she wasn't smiling.

"A what?" He tapped his foot on the brake, causing a sudden jerk in his body.

"As it turns out, you are not the one to do the task. Matters have already been taken care of. Mr. Cleary is facing a different destiny. But I am here to take you with me. It's the inevitable order of things, Dad. Your time has come."

"What are you talking about? What do you mean *my time* -?"

"Like I said, matters have been taken care of. You are going to join all of us, finally. Aren't you happy?"

He kept looking back and forth at her and the road, which seemed to be getting smaller and more distorted, more labyrinthine. Highway 95 was turning into...no, it *became* that beach road he had seen so many times before in his dreams. And a fog rolled in. He continued to swerve. His heart raced.

"It's not meant to be, Dad. Not anymore."

"But...the inevitable order..."

"The inevitable order of things has changed. The inevitable order of things is always changing and shifting. You'll find that out soon enough when you join us."

"But...I'm the chosen one. You said so yourself." He said this to her as if she had never been anything but real to him.

She laughed and cupped his face with her hand like a schoolgirl who was whispering gossip to a girlfriend of hers. "I sort of lied about that."

"Are you kidding me?"

"No, I'm not." She was serious again.

"But...Abbie-girl?"

The girl laughed, cupping her hand to her mouth again. "Abbie-Girl is dead, George." More laughter.

George froze.

His heart sunk. He slowed down. He had to inch his way through the thickening fog. He was alone on that serpentine beach road. He swerved as an image appeared in the road. When he looked in his rearview mirror, George was not only startled by what he saw from outside, but also by the look on his own face. It wasn't even him anymore. His face was old and emaciated. He looked like what he would have looked like in fifty years. And that image, the one he had seen so many times of the woman carrying the aborted fetus, she kept appearing on all sides of him.

The girl leaned over, her hands massaged the back of his neck and with a firm grip she pulled his neck, forcing his head to turn...away from the road. He was facing her. The girl turned into his wife and then, morphing into Alison, she kissed him passionately for what seemed like a minute or two.

Her grip was unbearably tight. George kicked his feet, trying to jerk his head back to the road.

Then her hands covered his eyes. Her fingers were pressing so deeply into his eye sockets that he was certain she planned to gouge them out. She kept pressing...and all he could see was an array of colors – massive waves of colors – beautiful colors – reds, blues, yellows...

And more waves emitting color after color...a ubiquitous rainbow.

Then the colors faded into that world of green fields and greenhouses and green baseball diamonds and those flowers that stood hundreds of feet. It was *that* place he had seen so many times before. Abigail and Alison, dancing on the rolling hills, were dressed in white and waving at him, signaling for him to join them. The sun was blazing, and he saw himself in that image with his arm over his eyes.

Little eight-year-old Abigail, back in her purple dress, said, "Come on Daddy. It's pretty here. It's pretty."

Alison said, "Come on my love. Join us. It's been too, too long."

The Monte Carlo was convulsing. Steam emerged from the hood.

He sighed, let his foot off the gas and felt for the brake. After fidgeting, he found it. And as he stopped, the pressure from his eyes was relieved.

The colorful world was gone. And so were Alison and his Abbie-Girl.

The brakes screeched, but this didn't stop the car from running head on into a guarded rail, compressing the front end of the Monte Carlo like an aluminum can crusher.

The second George's head hit the windshield – his head cracking like an egg being pitched against a brick wall – he heard the whispering voices. There must have been a hundred of them, a thousand, a million, an infinite amount...

Because he had been moving so rapidly, the impact caused the car to not only break through the metal guard rail but to also take a nosedive into a twenty or thirty-foot ditch filled with a few feet of running water.

The car did a handstand for a number of seconds, then tumbled forward – then upside down.

George's face stuck to the shattered windshield as if it were Velcro.

He did a rapid somersault. He couldn't figure out where he was in context to the rest of the car.

He could hear himself breathing slowly, mechanically, methodically.

He wasn't dead, though. He was conscious enough to realize he couldn't move any part of himself, especially his face from the fragmented windshield.

His eyes rolled around his skull like little periscopes. The breathing...slowing down a notch.

He heard his heart beating...it was irregular, like the thumping bass line to some song he tried to recall. It was as loud, if not louder, than if his ears were pressed against a speaker at a concert. This music was being experienced from the inside out, the opposite of the way he always remembered it being.

And the blood covered his face as if he had been doused with a bucket of water. *Hot damn, blood* was *thicker than water!* It was bizarre listening to himself gurgle on what he knew to be the salty, metallic taste of his own blood.

He knew he had to be on the verge of checking out; he had been going in and out of consciousness, as if he were taking a series of power naps then being awoken by something startling. Like his own breathing. And he could smell what he assumed was death – dried blood and gore and something else added to the recipe, something more rancid, something inexplicable, something pungent and foreign...

His physical sensation could be summed up thus: he felt inside out, upside down – and frozen, yet not cold. And he felt euphoric, better than any drink or drug he had ever taken. And he felt aware...*super aware* of everything. And although he couldn't actually laugh, he *wanted to* – *wanted to* because he and so many others had actually misinterpreted the journey into death. It was not frightening in the least. It was as natural as living and breathing.

At that instant he truly understood the phenomenon of what it meant to be born and to live and to die. How we torture ourselves with religion and philosophy. The biologist was truly in his element. It's all biology and nothing more, he thought. And biology was not at all what he had been teaching or researching. It was simpler than that...much simpler! George Pearson had finally reached his biological nirvana.

This wasn't just the endorphins working throughout his

failing body; this was something else. It was *everything* else.

"Beautiful, isn't it?" Alison said, appearing from the running water.

Yes, he thought, unable to speak or move. *Yes, it is.*

Through the windshield he saw Abigail, Alison, his mother and groups upon groups of other people who had passed on, at different stages in their lives. They were all there now on those rolling hills on the green fields, reaching out their hands.

The voices spoke in overlapping whispers:

Let go, George...Close your eyes...All the answers are here... It's all so simple, so beautiful, so eternal...it's not what you would ever have thought...Finally you've crossed over...Let go! Let go! Let go...

George tried to move his jaws, those jaws that still had an ounce of life to them, to tell them he understood.

His jaws, however, were becoming lifeless. His face was burning, stinging like frostbite – and the pressure about his head and the rest of him was heavy, heavy from the pressure of the atmosphere.

He felt palpitations not only in his chest but in his entire being. He encompassed all time and all space. He was omniscient...ubiquitous.

A stream of tears – tears of fear and remorse from leaving the world he had known for thirty-eight years, whatever thirty-eight years actually meant; and tears of ecstasy from joining the other world, the *real* world, and as he finally understood: the *only* world.

A sudden wind formed. It was a fan blowing on him. It was a hot, fragrant breath, like that of a goddess, massaging his entire being.

This was it.

The crusty, coagulated blood on his face had already turned a deep black. It had become its own outer mask.

His fluttering heart changed its beat...slowing down...

slowing down...slowing...down...

Double vision.

Blurred vision.

Breathing to a minimum.

Let go, he heard in his head as he watched the crowd through the windshield. They had formed for him a placid mosaic image, colorful like a Roman-designed floor or something.

Through the voices he heard fragments of the Blood Sweat and Tears song:

Someone's waiting...here for you...spinning wheel......what goes up, must come down...spinning wheel...got to go round...

Blurred vision.

Double vision.

Triple vision.

Quadruple...

This is the strangest life I've ever known, he thought, absurdly, recalling the lyrics from his favorite Doors' song "Waiting for the Sun," as the blurred vision converted into sleep.

⊠ ⊠ ⊠ ⊠

It was probably three or four hours before the body was discovered.

Paramedics needed to use the Jaws of Life to pry the mangled body from the car.

When Mike Melanson arrived at the scene of the accident, he watched the men pull his best friend's carcass from the totaled Monte Carlo.

Mike's heart raced, and once he began walking away toward the cruiser, he experienced by far the worst internal gas pains he had ever experienced. He held onto his chest with one hand and the door handle of the passenger's door with the other and gasped for air; there was a sour heavy pressure that felt like what he remembered hearing a heart attack felt like – an elephant sitting on his chest. His best friend was dead and now he was having a heart attack! *Just great!* But before he could think about it any further, the pressure eased up almost completely and his irregular breathing turned into relaxed sighs.

"You okay there, Chief?" he heard the fire chief Dwayne Anderson ask him. Mike looked up, forced a smile and gave him a high Columbo-style wave.

Then at that moment he looked around the accident scene, half expecting to see that deputy of his even though he never bothered to contact him once he received the news. But Jack was nowhere to be found. In fact, for the past several days, there was no sign of him at all. The last time he saw him was that day in the office when that overgrown bulldog extorted him through the letters. The last he knew, Jack was going to concoct a master scheme to solidify Mike's original proposition – the now preposterous idea that they would both be dual police chiefs. But what was really up Cleary's sleeve? If he managed to make this partnership work, what was the master plan? After he established himself as someone the town could finally trust, was he going to *turn* on Mike Melanson? Why couldn't it be Jack Cleary's brains splattered on that windshield? Mike closed his eyes and pictured a round of bullets going through the officer's head. When he opened his eyes, he thought about Cleary who was AWOL as they call it in the military. *Where was he really? Why hadn't he come to the office? Why hadn't he reached out about these two equally outlandish, risible situations?* Sex letters to *Foxes and Boxes*! Co-police chiefs! And both of these ludicrous, harebrained ideas came from the mind of this low-down townie with no concept of the real world, who was – to say the least – over his head. It was all too much. He looked down at his gun and pictured himself sucking on the barrel, then pulling the trigger. It would be traumatic for his wife and son, but it would be quick and then it would be all over.

When he got back on the road, the heartburn started up again, but after a few acidic burps, it subsided. *What now?* he thought as he headed back toward Fryebury Falls. Maybe when he told Miss Julie what happened the things might begin to heal. When he got into town he headed toward Brown Ave, and although he was inclined to drive down the road to see if Cleary was there, he decided against it. He peaked down the street but was only able to see part of the house, and since Cleary always kept his cruiser in his garage, there was no way of telling whether or not he was home.

What now?

He pulled into Günter's Millyard and entered into the serene, enigmatic microcosm of *Paradise Park*, eventually landing on one of the blue benches that directly faced Niagara Two. The running waters were equally piercing and peaceful, creating a soothing, even cleansing, brown noise. He closed his eyes.

⊠ ⊠ ⊠ ⊠

The two teenage boys dressed in baseball uniforms were deep in the woods, leaning on the Stone Crusher, smoking cigarettes. "Don't Bogart it, man," George said referring to the cigarette hanging out his friend's mouth that hasn't been flicked in minutes.

"So what the hell is this thing, anyway?" Mike asked, flicking the ash from the cigarette and kicking the rusty greenish device. "And why is it still here? You'd think someone would have gotten it out of here."

George also kicked part of it. "You kidding? This thing's a fixture."

Mike, not knowing what a fixture was, said, "It doesn't

look like a stone crusher, whatever a stone crusher is."

"Did you hear the story of Krebs?" George asked.

"No. Who's that?"

"He's a soul, man."

"A what?"

"A soul. He lives inside the Stone Crusher."

Mike inhaled, then coughed. "What?"

"Yeah, the story goes like this: It's a ghost machine. Back in the early 1900s this machine thing, used to crush stones, was owned by this scary old man named Jeff Krebs. When he died, his soul inhabited the machine, and then he became the machine."

"What are you talking about?"

"No really, man," George continued. "He was such a terrible man that he went to hell, but apparently he wasn't bad enough because Old Scratch rejected him –"

"Who is this Old Scratch?"

"The devil, man. Satan."

Mike smoked. "Go on."

"So Satan confines him here in these woods and somehow keeps his soul locked in this stone crusher." George kicked it again. "And in order to get back into hell, he had to do deeds to make himself worthy. So he would find little kids and sacrifice them and then *their* souls would be locked in the Stone Crusher with old Krebs to be tortured forever."

"Where did you hear this?" Mike asked.

"It's the legend, man."

"Legends! Bullfeathers, man." Of course Mike didn't believe it, but he was a bit freaked out nevertheless. "But legends ain't true."

George looked at his friend for a moment, raised his eyebrows and shrugged his shoulders. "Just what I heard. Plus, remember Tanya Eaton?"

"Yeah. The girl on our street who was –" George's eyebrows raised again. Then Mike said, "No!"

"You'll never know," George said, knowing that he was goofing on his more naïve friend. Although George Pearson was known to be protective of his buddy, he sure liked giving him the business from time to time when they were together. Years later, he would tell Mike that this story was invented by his little brother Sammie who loved writing and telling ghost stories.

"Well," Mike said, stomping out his cigarette. "We better get going before someone finds us."

"Okay, Copper," George said, stomping out his cigarette.

Mike opened his eyes, looked at the gushing water from the waterfall, then sobbed like a punished child for a full half hour.

CHAPTER 39

J-J DAY

There was a very good reason why Jack Cleary had gone AWOL; for the past several days – in fact, it had been nearly a week now – he had been nursing J.J., who had somehow sunk into a deep coma as he continued to sweat profusely, while breathing very slowly and infrequently. For both Jack and J.J., it had been many days of heavy labor – after all, the dying process was perhaps just as grueling for the adult caregiver as it was for the moribund teenager. When Mike Melanson's mother Wendy – the gargantuan woman who was reduced to a state of unrecognizable emaciation – was in her final moments, the chief had never forgotten what the woman said to her father: "The time has come. I have a lot of work to do." The human body – with all of its ailments that will eventually take us all – is also an extremely resilient machine whose job is to keep itself running until it simply can't do it any longer.

On August 15th, J.J.'s body could not do it any longer; the traumatic brain injury (it would later be identified in the autopsy as a seizure, which was quite common with those who suffered from TBI) finally caught up with him, unless of course something else – something more paranormal like that ubiquitous Gail – took over and killed him. During these days, Jack camped out on the first floor of the split-level, neglecting all of his duties, including his job. And in this time, he hadn't showered, and he ate only scraps of what had already been in the house.

In another corner of the room, Lazlo remained inert, half of his body protruding from under the small wooden dining table: The black lab was noticeably depressed; he had lost all hope after J.J.'s passing. And Jack – who was always so mean to the dog, threatening more than once to put the old canine out of his misery – tried to get him to eat and drink, but Lazlo would not budge; he would only growl when Jack got closer to him. How often the police officer screamed at him, swatted him on the muzzle with a newspaper or a shoe and even kicked him or pulled its tail until he yelped. It wasn't that Jack suddenly had empathy for the dog, but the way he was lying – immobile and breathing funny – reminded him of his febrile boy in the final moments of his short life.

Jack looked for the rag he used to wipe up J.J.'s sweat; it was dried up and crusty and for some reason it was this discovery that caused the officer to lose it all. The last time he sobbed like this – forceful, frequent, violent exhales, assisted by an outpouring of tears – must have been sometime long ago when he was a little kid.

"J.J., J.J.," he kept muttering as he looked at the defunct boy on the couch who actually looked peaceful; he no longer had that squinting, grimacing expression on his face that created wrinkles, which made his already elderly-looking face look even older. The teenager would never have to be frightened again – not of *anything*. Not of Gail's hauntings, not of any memories he might have had being bullied by that David Wood who pushed him off the roof, not of his father threatening to kill his beloved companion, not of having an irreversible disability...

It was strange because ever since that day that J.J. slipped into the coma (the sick boy – whose combination of snoring and wheezing that sounded like an out-of-tune trumpet – simply never woke up after Jack watched him fall asleep), there had been no sign of Gail. For if there was *any* time for that festering incubus to appear to mock him, it would have been now. In his mind, Jack could hear her hollow voice, which continued to torture him: "He paid for the sins of the father, Cuz. We took *him* because of what you have done to *us*..."

An even greater torture, however, was the absence and the silence. He looked again at Lazlo and absurdly thought of the old sayings that dog is man's best friend, and every dog has his day. And then even more absurdly, in Mike's Melanson's voice: "Let sleeping dogs dead." The line was no longer ludicrous; it was perturbing.

Gail was undoubtedly still there because he could feel a pulsating pressure in his temples and there were sounds – buzzing white noise that sounded like a swarm of bees had invaded his insides; it was a type of madness brought on by an unbearable tinnitus.

Now he heard running water, and this led to an image of officer David Aaronson ("What's going on with you and my daughter, Cleary? She's fifteen, man!"), then of his boot kicking and stomping on David Wood's head until the moment he realized he was kicking a lifeless body, then of Gail who fell back onto the floor after getting a bullet in the forehead and then the eye. It wasn't difficult for Jack to surmise that this was the moment of payback, that paranormal retribution for this trilogy of murders that he somehow thought he could escape when he moved to Fryebury Falls – one was in self-defense against his doped up, juggernaut wife who most likely would have killed him if he didn't kill her first; one was through pure rage and vengeance for that hector who permanently disabled his otherwise normal and healthy son, the person, as it turns out, whom he loved more than anyone or anything; and one for being that man who knew too much when he unwittingly bedded a minor, and not just any minor, but the young daughter of his chief.

And this is what he had been running from when he came across little Fryebury Falls. Yes, Jack Cleary had done these aforementioned killings, but to him all of them were justified as misunderstandings. Gail, David Aaronson and David Wood, the victims, were all one-in-the-same. Yes, they were bullies. He never would have done what he did if these individuals didn't provoke things. Fryebury Falls appeared to be an innocent small town where someone trying to redeem themselves could start anew. And each of the deaths – which he instantly regretted after doing – would now be symbolic of that motto of his: Purity (Gail); Law and Order (David Aaronson); and Peace (David Wood). They would exist – a la Caesar, Pompey and Crassus in ancient Rome – as their own idiosyncratic triumvirate.

It would be Gail, however, who would immediately dismantle this symbiotic union through her inexplicable, macabre presence. When Jack came to Fryebury Falls, he had a plan to honor this triumvirate by fighting crime and raising his TBI son to the best of his ability...even if it meant resorting to drastic, even punitive measures to ensure that *purity, law & order*, and *peace* were being enforced.

It seemed like a good enough plan until his deceased wife, his drug-addicted first cousin, appeared to him as a ghost (or was she a hallucination in his delusional mind?) and disrupted this plan of redemption. She had no intention of allowing Jack to not only get away with the murders, but to also prevent him from experiencing any type of bliss or purity or law and order or peace. Incidentally, before he arrived in Fryebury Falls less than three years ago, he would never even have *considered* the possibility that spooks actually existed. It was *here* in Fryebury

Falls where this all began and what would it have been like if he knew that many others – including J.J. and Mike Melanson – also knew what it was like to get these invasive visitations? If anything else, this would surely be another story altogether.

Not knowing what else to do, Jack turned on the TV and left it on the existing channel. Being August 15, it was the thirty-ninth anniversary of the Victory over Japan Day – V-J Day – the day imperial Japan surrendered, officially bringing the Second World War to an end. It was a news editorial or documentary that reviewed these events in history. They were talking about Japan's acceptance of the Potsdam Declaration issued by President Harry Truman, United Kingdom Prime Minister, Winston Churchill and President of China, Chiang Kai-Shek. These three men – yet another triumvirate like Caesar, Pompey and Crassus – made Jack think of purity, law & order and peace.

The story shifted to the public's reactions and celebrations to V-J Day, which included an attempted break-in into the White House, two naked women jumping into a pond at the Civic Center in San Francisco and a massive gathering in Times Square.

Jack sat in front of the tube, half listening to the story and half staring at his son's body. He kept hearing "V-J Day, V-J Day," over and over again, which eventually translated into his mind as "J-J Day."

August 15, 1984. J-J Day. A date which will live – for the rest of Jack's short life, anyway – in infamy.

The story then shifted to the Japanese response to V-J Day, which among other deaths led General Korechika Anami to commit *seppuku*. Another story discussed the fate of Imperial Japan's Army General, Ryūkichi Tanaka, who shot himself in the heart and on his desk, among other things, remained letters to his officers and family. With this minute detail, Jack couldn't help himself from thinking about Mike Melanson's letters, which he now kept safely in his own desk drawer – those raunchy, ridiculous hand-written epistles to *Foxes and Boxes*! Then he thought more specifically about Mike Melanson who, lucky bastard that he was, would never have to pay for his horny little shenanigans. Why? Because Jack Cleary knew that he would never leave his Brown Ave home. And then Jack thought about Moira Davis – someone else he'd never face again. For that matter, he would never have to answer for screwing Petra Aaronson and shooting her father or for slugging Eddie Price in the mouth and planting drugs on him and harassing banker Gregory Reardon and killing his wife and killing that fucking David Wood bully. *That's right*, Jack thought. *Cleary was in the clear*. It was interesting, Jack concluded, that one event like J.J. passing on could affect the fate of so many other things!

Jack, still dressed in his uniform, had taken the gun and holster off while he was caring for his son. Now he retrieved it, pulled the gun slowly and delicately out of the holster and carried it over to the table, kneeled down, pointed the gun at Lazlo who was panting weakly (he didn't even have enough energy to growl or snap at his enemy) and just as he nudged the piece into the dog's skull, the black lab sneezed and this startled the cop. "God damn you," he said and pulled the gun away and leaned into the dog. He then pressed his face into the dog's face, then patted his head back and forth for the next several moments and this seemed to really relax the dog who continued panting.

"I just took Lazlo out to do a pee and poop and I cleaned it with the pooper scooper," J.J.'s voice echoed.

Jack moved toward his son and just like he did with Lazlo pressed his head into the dead boy's face and patted him on the head. He sat down on the bed and held J.J.'s hand in the palm of one hand while stroking it with the other.

The events of V-J Day were still being explained through

still frames, footage and personal commentary, but all Jack could think of now was today's celebration – J-J Day.

Nearly half an hour later, Jack recalled the news program that mentioned General Ryūkichi Tanaka. The police officer pictured Mike's letters scattered on his desk much like the general's letters must have been scattered on *his* desk. He also thought about his own collection of tapes that carefully documented many private conversations. Although he would never get to make another tape, he imagined himself describing this entire week, leading to J-J Day. "J.J. was never given a fair break," he muttered to himself.

Still holding J.J.'s hand, he grabbed the revolver and aimed it at his own heart. At that moment he felt a chilled breeze, saw Gail at the other end of the room looking on in anticipation, squeezed J.J.'s hand firmly and then pulled the trigger.

CHAPTER 40

RISING STARS

George Pearson's wake coincided with Jack Cleary's passing on Wednesday, August 15. People had gathered to pay respects for the former high school Biology teacher and baseball coach who, because of the damage that had been done to him in the auto accident, received, per order of his younger brother Sam, a respectable closed casket at the *Rising Star Home of Rest*, Fryebury Falls' only funeral home run by the Yildiz family – mother Ayla, father, Altan and two daughters, Sevil and Janan. Currently the Turkish family resided in an adjacent room, letting the mourners know that they were there if they needed them. Sevil – who knew nearly everyone because they had been customers at Rodney's Donut Hole – offered subtle condolences to Sam and the others, but when she saw Mike, her beloved chief, she embraced him rather awkwardly, eventually kissing him on the forehead; her lips were moist and cold. She knew he had lost his best friend from childhood.

The casket was a modest pine box and next to it was a table featuring all kinds of photographs. Most of the pictures in this shrine were from George's past, and one in particular captured George and Mike in their Little League uniforms and another one showed preadolescent George and Sam playing in the leaves one autumn day. Yet another photo quite poignantly showed George with Alison and his Abbie-Girl at the beach a couple of years prior to that most absurd automobile accident where he killed the two people whom he loved the most when a flood of sunlight momentarily blinded him.

One might have wondered this: If George Pearson – an otherwise upstanding, gifted man of peace – never belted Derek Hamilton in the jaw (an act from such a gentle man that was perhaps just as absurd and ironic as the aforementioned car accident) then the turnout would have undoubtedly been much greater overall. But since George experienced what he experienced, he will forever be remembered for the last years of his life where he slipped from being a lucky man to a man of scandal and tragedy. And this would be his legacy. Miss Julie told Mike that George unequivocally was paying dearly for some past life sin. "Karma's a bitch," she would say. But what about the years of dedication to his craft of teaching and his penchant for the life sciences and his commitment to baseball coaching, meditation and music? Couldn't that somehow play into this legacy, too?

There must have been a synergy at work on this fifteenth day of August because these were the types of things both Mike Melanson and Sam Pearson were contemplating as they sat with their respective families who for the most part remained nonverbal. Aside from the fact that they were devastated from this loss, they were both – as if in-tuned to one another's inner thoughts and emotions – seemingly more concerned (or maybe *outraged* was a better word?) with the unlucky fate of this otherwise great man. Yes, George Pearson – when you stripped him down to his bare bones – to his DNA – was at the core a purely good soul and had he made a number of different choices in his short life, could *easily* have been a much better version of himself...most likely even famous. And Sam's and

Mike's respective wives – Moira Davis and Miss Julie – created their own similar *synergy* – or might one call it a *dyssynergy* – toward the deceased. This dyssynergy went beyond the disliking George Pearson for the man he transformed into after his wife and daughter died because of him; they were both, in their idiosyncratic ways, threatened or maybe even jealous of not his existence, but of his *essence*; after all, they both knew what really lurked inside of him, that he was a high-functioning, sublime old soul whose fate just so happened to be that of a big fish in a small pond. The two women understood his real potential because both of them possessed an "almost famous" persona themselves – Miss Julie as a renowned stage actress and Moira as an innovative singer-songwriter who was meant to carry on her twin sister's musical legacy. How fascinating and peculiar (maybe even amusing) that all of these people – George, Sam, Moira and Miss Julie – all potential rising stars – were destined to remain there in the *Rising Star House of Rest* as four dead souls who never reached their potential.

And what about the children – Adam and Maygyn? Certainly, one might associate this rising star theme to these extraordinary youngsters as well.

Miss Julie often wondered what force gave her little boy such a profound connection to humanity. Where does one inherit such emotional intelligence and empathy in his pre-adolescence? And if one were to peak into the near future, would they see Adam Melanson as a partner in a veterinarian clinic (just like *Willie Wonka and the Chocolate Factory* actor Peter Ostrum, who just this past year became a vet) in addition to being a respected animal activist while also making his name in the world as a unique impressionistic-like artist? At this time, the little boy who had a tear in his eye not for the deceased but for his father who looked so solemn and sad, sat in a state of melancholia, drawing pictures of ravens and crows.

And what about the budding young woman, Maygyn Pearson? Like her father, might she get a taste of literary fame after publishing one of her collections of short stories like *The Terminals* which might even be optioned and picked up by a major studio? Or would she be a *she* at all? Although this narrative merely touches upon Maygyn's gender identity, might we return to this funeral home in a decade or more to see a twenty-five-year-old transgender man sitting here? In fact, what if Maygyn embraced transgenderism and modified her name to fit her new identity – Maygyn-Daved – a person who identified not as a *he, she* or *they*, but simply as another option altogether – someone with a specific ratio of male and female personas? So, Maygyn-Daved – no longer a cisgender female – would identify as both male and female but not equally and not as a *they/them*: This person would be 75% Maygyn and 25% Daved (this name, which meant "beloved," would be a variation on her classmate David Marino). As she sat there next to her parents, she was still discovering this identity, experiencing a mild form of gender dysphoria that would eventually lead to her "coming out." And what if Maygyn-Daved became a literary sensation that changed the entire world of letters? She would be to literature what Miss Julie Melanson would be to the theater, a performer who broke new grounds with her epic tour-de-force role in Jimmy Orlinski's Pulitzer Prize winning *Needle in a Haystack*.

When visiting hours commenced, the two families had positioned themselves on the opposite ends of George's casket. The Melanson clan was positioned to the left and the Pearson clan on the right, so when people entered the funeral home, they would walk right into this arrangement, making it perfectly clear that these two families were the closest people to the deceased. *The Rising Star Home of Rest* was quite minute but as inviting as any funeral home could be – bright curtains, nice soft lighting and an array of colors ranging from green to yellow. And on the outside of the funeral home, the Yildiz family hung their red and white flag (al bayrak), which featured a crescent and white star; for this family, the symbol of the star became another significant symbolic icon that was aligned to their name and ethnicity.

Ever since George Pearson lost his wife and daughter, which led to instant madness, he never connected again with his world of friends outside of Fryebury Falls, so the visitors on this day were more or less limited to the citizens of the town. A majority of them came within the first hour, beginning with the gargantuan Dr. Mark Porzio, who was dressed in that same extra-large suit Mike always saw him in when he was leaving for the hospital in Boston. The rich asshole doctor wore a noticeably sad face – the expression of a clown – which was equally as expressive as his laughing man persona. When he made the rounds, the middle-aged widower extended his massive paw, which no one really shook and in about half a dozen whispers stated, "Condolences." When he came to Mike, he lowered his head as if ashamed of something he might have done to insult the police chief and said, quite unoriginally, at that: "I am sorry for your loss." Then he cleared his throat, bowed at Adam and Miss Julie and turned to leave. As Sam watched Porzio exit, all he could think of was Charles Dickens. That's it – Dr. Porzio was a living, breathing Samuel Pickwick or maybe Mr. Bumble, the rotund beadle in *Oliver Twist*! Sam, who read *Oliver Twist* at least three or four times recalled an exchange in the novel between Mr. Sowerberry and Mr. Bumble: Sowerberry mentioned something about two women who died the previous night to which Bumble replied: "Coffins are looking up, Mr. Sowerberry!" Then he looked at George's coffin and for some reason snickered. Both Moira and Maygyn looked up at him, and all he could do was smirk and shake his shoulders. This made the two of them break into a smile.

The Melansons' only other neighbor on Stagecoach Road,

the independent filmmaker Ross Thurber who for some outrageous reason referred to himself as the white Spike Lee, was not in attendance. He was most likely in Boston working on his multicultural series called *Commonwealth Ave.* Chances are he didn't even know George Pearson had passed away.

From Brown Ave – the same road, incidentally, where both Jack and J.J. Cleary remained lifeless in that split-level home (it would be another week or so before they were discovered and when they *did* find them, they also found a half dead Lazlo, who was eventually adopted by little Adam Melanson) – the same road where Moira and Maygyn lived – entered Ron and Jean Stevens with their kids, Timmy and Michelle. Dick Melon the banker came alone; apparently, he and his wife Lois – an executive at the Museum of Fine Arts in Boston – were experiencing one of their many separations. "The Bank Dick," as he was called, had an air of melancholic tragedy painted on his face. He made his rounds, kneeled down in front of George's coffin, did a fast cross and then left. Maygyn remembered that when she was much younger, Richard Melon was an all-around fun family man, so seeing him in this state was just about as sad as losing her Uncle George the way she did. She specifically remembered getting a kick out of when one day, while playing with his kids he for some reason did a play on the root *oct* and said words like *October, octagon* and *octopus* by prolonging the short 'o' sound and then pronouncing the 'ct' very dramatically, sounding like he was hawking up a loogie, so *October* sounded like *Awwww-kkkhhh-tober!*

Nearly all the neighbors who lived in the mobile homes on Pine Street where George and Sam resided right up to the end had attended the wake. This peculiar mix of Seabrook Nuclear Power Plant workers seemed to all come collectively as if they got off a bus together. Sonny Willis, Tony Pearce, David Henderson and Jennifer Madsen were all devastated, and they all spent some time chatting with both families; they especially felt for Sam, who, finally overwhelmed by the day's events and the visitors, had already begun to tune out. It's not that many people attended the wake; it was just a heavy energy and presence that followed this group. Miss Julie, who kept to herself more than anyone, especially did not like their energy. She sensed something tragic about one or more of them.

Sonny, Tony, David and Jennifer left, and then moments later came the teachers. The Algebra teacher James Taplan, Fryebury Falls' most eligible bachelor who had a short stint playing for the Dallas Cowboys, came with what might have been a date – a stranger to town – who must have been fifteen years younger than the fifty-something-year-old teacher. She was a petite but very strong and healthy-looking African woman named Eshe, who, despite being an outsider, exuded large amounts of comforting energy. Perhaps it had something to do with the meaning of her name...*life*. As an athlete Taplan always admired George Pearson – before *and* after the scandal with Derek Hamilton – because the two of them – rising stars in their own right – were both groomed to be "pedagogical jocks" – quite the rare breed indeed – at least for this town.

When Nancy Deleuze and Jackie Bamford arrived, Maygyn became intrigued because they were a couple, and this reminded her of what it might have been like between her mother and Cheryl Benigni. Plus, Nancy – another gifted teacher – gentle, funny and emotionally intelligent – had a wonderfully appealing androgynous look that Maygyn found attractive, especially for a much older woman. Her skin was shiny with rosy cheeks and her countenance seemed perpetually blissful and perfectly proportioned, and she always seemed to be smiling even when she wasn't. To Maygyn, Nancy Deleuze didn't look like a man or a woman; she looked like...it was hard to explain...she looked like...*herself*. She really had her own identity.

Then came more teachers! Rebecca and David Gibson –

respective high school English and Chemistry teachers (Rebecca also taught Spanish) – were all dressed up, but they looked like a *different kind* of dressed up; they weren't wearing funeral clothes. They most likely had other plans once they paid their respects. The couple was never able to have kids; Mr. Gibson had a low sperm count and even though he wore boxer shorts for years to try to fix the issue, it never helped. That was okay, though, because they were compatible partners; they did everything together and supported their students by attending plays, fund raisers and sporting events. George always found Becky and Dave to be a bit peculiar, and after the incident with Derek Hamilton they admittedly acted differently toward him – a sort of polite coldness, if such a thing could have existed.

Finally, Travis Bread – the adjunct professor who taught at several colleges – arrived with his wife Deandra and alas, all five of their kids. Maybe the kids – ranging from four to eleven – were there out of convenience. Bread had an engaging presence for a man who only stood at 5'4". He had a large muscular frame and dark skin, and even in early fifties he had a full head of salt and pepper hair, which became him. His face was round and chiseled like a cartoon character – he had a prominent French ski slope nose and a cleft chin like Cary Grant – and he wore round glasses that accented his deep brown eyes. Because of his height, he might not have immediately turned heads, but he was the type of man whose good looks became more obvious the more you looked at him. His wife was the town celebrity of sorts, author of the Newbury-Award winning ghost story, *The Worst Night Ever.* A true rising star who, incidentally, like all the other aforementioned rising stars, decided to pursue a humbler lifestyle. Over the years, she and Sam Pearson had had a few engaging discussions about literature, the creative process and the trials of publishing. Maygyn smiled at Deandra (whose pen name was

Andy K.) when she came in, but was most disappointed when the only exchange went like this: "Well, then there now. Aren't you becoming the real young lady? And so pretty!" It's not that Maygyn was let down with the gender reference; it's just that she was secretly hoping that she could talk to her about her experiences as a writer.

In the midst of these interactions, Miss Julie experienced a headache, which she knew was not any old headache; it had to do with her premonitions. Something was out of balance; she felt little Spencer Cagney or Alexia Sage move around in utero; it was as if her child was communicating with her. Then Stan appeared in the Turkish ceramic tile hallway mirror, surrounded by an ornate blue and orange flowery frame. Because of where she was sitting, she could only see the original Method actor's sharp profile. Then he faded away.

Concurrently, Moira, who had been free from her twin sister's drowning calls for a number of days now, saw little Meggie in that same mirror. She was in the water but no longer struggling; her carcass was floating on the water like a buoy. Moira squinted, anticipating the sound of the girl's voice, but there was nothing. The little girl's image faded to nothing.

Little Adam, who suddenly looked up from his drawings, was pulled in that same direction toward the Turkish mirror and for an instant he caught his last glimpse of Grandpa Lucien whose face was nebulous; eventually he dissolved into the glass. The boy – whom Miss Julie thought shared his mother's clairvoyance (at least this is what her premonitions told her) – knew that Grandpa Lucien was gone for good. It was up to the Old Boy to carry on the old man's wisdom and to stay true to his real self. His grandfather had finally gone back to that place beyond the waterfall; in fact, Niagara Two also appeared in this reflection and at this instant, everyone else left in the funeral home – Miss Julie, Mike, Sam, Moira and Maygyn – simultaneously saw the waterfall. Then they all rather awkwardly grimaced at one another, then turned away.

Miss Julie suddenly felt a few kicks inside of her, and at that moment she took Mike's and Adam's hands and placed them on the womb.

"Wow!" Mike said in a loud whisper. "That is really something. Isn't it, Adam?"

Adam shook his head and smiled.

Sam, Moira and Maygyn locked eyes with the Melanson trio and all six of them shared a blissful, ephemeral moment in time that in their own ways they would all remember for the rest of their lives.

At that same moment, the police chief was thinking about how this ironic twist of fate might be seen as a fresh start for him and his family. Although he did not yet know that Jack Cleary lay dead with bullets in his belly, he got a strong sense – a real Miss Julie-like premonition – that he would never see him again. *How* did he know? He *didn't* know. He just *knew* what he *knew*. Or what he *thought* he knew. After all, he hadn't seen him all week. And if Cleary was in fact gone (maybe he left town), then there would be no more worries. There would be no partnership – no "co-chiefs" – to worry about. There would be no revealing of those letters to *Foxes and Boxes*. In fact, as an extra little twist of fate, when Jack Cleary's body was finally discovered, *he* would be the one associated with those letters, not Mike – especially when discovered alongside that collection of self-incriminating tapes. He looked over at Moira Davis who sensed his stare, and then she looked up at him; they both shared a kind smile that lingered and for some reason did not get uncomfortable. It was as if this look guaranteed that everything was somehow going to be okay. How relieved they would both be when they would eventually discover the news about Jack Cleary! How much easier things would now be! And then Moira and Sam could have a few laughs about the fact that they even slightly considered what it might have been like if that gangster romance beach novel writer, Stuart Creek, with that ignition-starting *ah-ah-ah-ah-ah* laugh of his, made that misogynist fucker Jack Cleary, "deader-n-a-doornail..."

Sam and Moira did not see any projections of their respective visions; instead, they shared a look that for the first time ever, spoke of an unexpected hopeful future. *Things were going to be okay, and before long she would feel comfortable telling her parents about her new identity: Maygyn-Daved.*

Although the Melanson trio did not share this type of intuitive clairvoyance, they too would heal slowly. Miss Julie knew that she had seen the last of Stan, that he no longer served the same purpose as before. She also knew that Jack and J.J. were gone and no longer a threat to their family. She may not have yet known the specifics, but like with all her other premonitions, she sensed a much lighter energy field when it came to the presence of that overgrown bulldog, the devil himself. He would no longer be a threat to her family. Adam's face was buried in a new drawing that showed a crescent moon and a star to the right (alas, he was drawing what looked like the Turkish flag!), Miss Julie was looking at the floor and Mike was leaning against the wall, staring at George's casket and remembering a time he and his best friend were playing catch in his yard while on a break from doing a project in Science on the star system Alpha Centauri, the third brightest star in the sky, which he still remembered being 4.37 light years from the sun. The lab partners eventually ended up doing quite an impressive oral presentation on the subject, earning them a perfect score on their assignment.

When 9:00 pm arrived, Altan Yildiz exited from the side room and asked how both families were doing and if they needed anything else before they closed up for the night and prepared for the funeral the following day. The six of them took one last moment at the coffin, then left the *Rising Star Home of Rest* and continued on with their rest of their lives.

The running waters of Niagara Two were the first thing they heard once they were back outside; the piercing low frequency brown noise emulated a peacefulness, something well-suited for meditation.

SEPTEMBER 1984

S	M	T	W	R	F	S
						✖
✖	✖	✖	✖	✖	✖	✖
✖	✖	⑪	12	13	14	15
16	17	18	19	20	21	22
23	24	25	26	27	28	29
30						

EPILOGUE

Tuesday, September 11, 1984

Although the month of September typically produced the sunniest, most comfortable weather conditions in the northern Massachusetts/southern New Hampshire regions, on this Tuesday, the eleventh day of September, Fryebury Falls was mostly cloudy with a relative humidity of about 75% and the temperature remained in the low seventies throughout most of the day. The town was a sponge waiting to be wrung out and the looming storm clouds held in the heavy air – air that was polluted and trapped – air that was the byproduct of all the aforementioned events that unfolded over the course of these past six to eight months.

It was also Mike Melanson's thirty-ninth birthday. Before the chief headed out for the day, Miss Julie, always one for so-called New Age education, did a birthday reading for her Virgo. The reading was mostly a regurgitation of the personality traits associated with those born on this day. Since George Pearson's funeral, Mike's wife gained a newfound love and hope and upon reflection, considered Mike's best friend a real sacrificial martyr – someone whose death yielded powerful change and healing. Additionally, Jack Cleary's suicide and the unfortunate, still inexplicable death of his teenage son, also contributed to this change. It was as if these two men – one good and one evil – created a new dimension that – perhaps in Hegelian terms where George as the *thesis* and Cleary, his *antithesis* – yielded this *synthesis*, which created – to quote Moira Davis's song – a type of *homeostasis*. Ironically, Jack Cleary's passing may have in fact established the purity, law & order and peace that he was never able to attain in his lifetime.

With all of this said, Miss Julie finally forgave Mike and swore she would never utter anything about a sex letter again. "Those born on September 11th," she told him, "know how to delegate work assignments with the right people." And now that Cleary was out of the picture, this statement could now be a truth. "And here is my favorite one," Miss Julie continued. "September 11th Virgos are loyal, especially with their friends and family." She paused and smiled, knowing that these words were bittersweet since her husband was still recovering from the death of his best friend. *What a sacrifice*, Mike thought in so many words, *lose your best pal and get your family back*.

After finishing his second cup of coffee and his honey dipped cruller from Rodney's Donut Hole, Mike decided to take a stroll into Günter's Millyard, something he would periodically do anyway to make sure those "Boardheads" weren't loitering or sneaking into the old hat mill buildings. Additionally, the small town police chief – thanks to Jack Cleary's savvy police work – was also keeping an extra eye out for any funny business that might have involved drugs. Even though Cleary (Mike was still haunted by those former violent images of Cleary, which he had finally concluded as being psychic predictions that foreshadowed the deputy's fate) went overboard with just about everything he did since he arrived in town over two years earlier, but regardless of what someone like Eddie Price might or might not have done, this birthday boy was no longer going to execute any naivete when it came to his police work. *Thirty-nine years old, now, Mike.*

Time to grow up and play adult!

Just as he stepped into Günter's Millyard, he was held back by that same heavy force he had experienced in his office when Cleary told him he knew about the letters. At that moment the clouds rapidly broke up and a flood of sunlight took over, and right as he blocked his eyes from the rays, he heard the overlapping sounds, which matched the image in the sky: two airplanes that seemed to have come out of nowhere raced through the sky, leaving two thick, titanium white smoking contrails. Both of them took on the form of what looked like two city skyscrapers juxtaposed with a piercing noise that sounded like a mass of people screaming in terror. The tumultuous sound lasted just a couple seconds, transitioning into the fierce and still somehow peaceful waters of Niagara Two. When he looked up into the now azure sky, there were no planes, but Mike did not take this vision lightly. He knew this was some kind of sign, just like the visions of Jack Cleary had turned out to be a sign, but of what he could not surmise.

Mike strolled further into Günter's Millyard and then into Paradise Park, the little utopia that was constructed because of a great endowment by German-American entrepreneur Alexander Günter. The waters of Niagara Two – sounding like a tropical downpour – were noticeably louder the further he entered. He walked through the rows of weeping willows that framed the red, white and blue gravel paths, passing by the greenhouse (surrounded by a most becoming black and white stone wall) and looking at a fantastic chrysanthemum that grew as large as a sunflower. He turned a sharp corner, and this brought him into the theater-in-the-round: Yes, this was the place where Miss Julie wanted to produce the play she had written years back – an all-female adaptation of the medieval morality play, *Everyman* called *A Summoning of Everywoman*.

When he entered this enclosed outside space (replete with white marble stairs, pillars, and that crystal monolith-looking sculpture that to Miss Julie resembled the artifact in *2001: A*

Space Odyssey), he saw a figure sitting in the front row on the bottom step. The figure slowly turned around, and even from afar Mike could read the smiling countenance as if the face had suddenly become a grinning comedy mask worn by an actor. If Miss Julie were present, surely she would have said something like the following: "Look, M&M! It's Sam Pearson playing the part of Dionysus from Aristophanes' *The Frogs*; he's sitting there in Hades contemplating a plan of how to bring the tragic playwright, Euripides (his brother George) back from the dead."

"Mike," Dionysus said softly, but the voice really carried. "Good to see you. How you holding up?"

Mike smiled, then sighed. "Hi, Sam. When does the show begin?" He heard a chuckle as he walked to the bottom step.

"Mind if I sit?" Mike asked, already taking a seat next to his best friend's younger brother. For a moment, both men simply stared at the proscenium. He looked around the entire stage and said, "Julie said she wants to do a play she wrote here. We were just talking about it..."

"Beautiful spot for it," Sam said, not turning his head to face Mike. "The town should really use it. The only problem is the damn waterfall."

Mike nodded. "I know. We need to find a way to turn down that volume."

Then quite suddenly, Sam said, "George loved it here." He turned to Mike. "He always said it was so peaceful. And it really is." He laughed almost to himself. "Waterfall and all." They sat silently for a beat. "Amazing what we take for granted." He looked at the stage again.

"We used to meet here quite often...in the warmer weather."

Sam nodded; he already knew this.

They sat there for the next couple of minutes staring toward the stage; the silence was surprisingly not at all awkward and actually it was rather comforting. Mike and Sam were never close friends, but since childhood they were both quite fond of one another.

"You know what I keep thinking about?" Mike said, breaking the silence. "Ever since George..." Mike lowered his head, the mood switching from a gentle nostalgia to an uncharacteristic melancholia. A lump formed in his throat that caused him to gag and without warning the chief wept. He tried to control the sobs, but the tears came out anyway. His breathing became irregular with his inhaling and exhaling, helped along by some loud sniffles.

Sam turned to Mike and put his arm around him, and Mike's head arched onto Sam's shoulder. The two men shamelessly held this embrace until Mike eventually lifted his head and straightened out. They looked at one another in the eyes and smiled poignantly, then they both faced the stage again.

Niagara Two's running waters sounded like static feedback from an amplifier.

Although they knew each other their entire lives, Sam never knew Mike's birthday and nothing about it was mentioned on this day. After all, it wasn't really a birthday celebration; it had turned into an unexpected memorial.

By this time, there was practically not a cloud in the sky; the deep azure sky had a smooth and shiny texture, as if someone had just painted it. The sunshine flooded Paradise Park in scattered patches. Both men looked to the sky and were momentarily blinded by the sun's rays.

"Did you follow the news about the solar flare?" Sam asked, blocking his eyes.

"Yeah," Mike said. "It was reported as an X-class flare."

Sam turned to Mike and in a more intense tone said, "What was it you were going to say a minute ago...something you couldn't stop thinking about?"

Mike grinned. "The Stone Crusher."

"The Stone Crusher?"

"Yeah."

"The one in the middle of the woods where we used to –"

"Do you know of another?"

Sam snickered. "Damn. I remember that thing."

"We – George and I – were dressed for a Braves game and we were smoking butts out there."

"Really?" He looked toward the stage.

"Yep, smokin' butts and talkin' about...Krebs."

Sam turned toward Mike and sighed. "No fucking shit? Krebs? The man who lived in the –"

"You should know," Mike teased.

"I suppose I should."

Mike pulled out a cigarette and offered one to Sam, who accepted.

"Marlboro Reds. Moira smokes these." Mike actually knew this from one of their recent exchanges, but he didn't know what Sam had told him next. "They started off as a woman's cigarette. Marlboros. Yeah, they had this greaseproof...what do you call it...ivory tip thing that prevented lipstick from smudging..." Then he paused and returned to the previous conversation: "Shit. Krebs. That legend began as a short story I was writing – completely unrelated to anything in the woods...at that time."

"I remember he called the thing the ghost in the machine."

"Yeah, I was a fan of The Police album." It took the low-down townie a moment to realize that Sam wasn't talking about real police. "'Ghost in the Machine' was the working title. Then I changed it to 'The Stone Crusher.' I remember learning about Faust. You know the story?" Mike shook his head. " It's an old story about this old German guy named Johann Faust who was not happy with his life. He makes a pact with the Devil at a crossroads where he exchanged his soul for unlimited intelligence and pleasure. A real hedonist." An awkward pause ensued. Then: "Would you sell your soul for intelligence and pleasure?" Mike had no idea what to do with this question and didn't even bother trying to answer; he only opened his eyes widely, which might as well have been a shrugging of the shoulders. "Anyway, I did my own twist on the tale and somehow it mutated. Then I created the legend of Krebs who died and went to hell but was kicked out by Satan and destined to reside inside the Stone Crusher, luring innocent kids to their death..."

"Then there was Tanya Eaton –"

"Yeah, that was fucked up, man. She was killed on her bike, and I used her death to feed the legend. Pretty gruesome imagination, looking back on it."

"But you made it big. With your book."

"My ten minutes."

Mike did not get this, but smiled anyway. "Are you still writing anymore?"

"On and off. I don't know. I might be all...written out. It might be time for something else."

"I hear ya."

"What about you? Are you all...*police chiefed* out?"

"I don't know," he said. "Maybe."

"You're good at what you do, man. Don't give up." He wanted to say something about Cleary, but he didn't know exactly what, so he kept it to himself.

"So where did you get the name? For Krebs..."

"Biology class."

"What do you mean?"

"At the time I was writing the story, I was taking biology. Not in school. You know...it was one of George's teaching lessons." Mike knew what he meant; when they were kids, George would play teacher every chance he could get. "Well, George was teaching me (and some other kids) all about the Citric Acid Cycle, also known as the Krebs Cycle, named after this German guy. Hans Adolph Krebs."

"That's German, all right."

Sam chuckled quietly. "So, this old German turned into the

legend. Actually, George told me that Krebs – the *actual* Krebs – died a few years back. Apparently, he even taught his students about this Krebs Cycle, but secretly we always knew it had another meaning."

"I remember that some other kids would talk about it, too. Like 'Little Scotty' Page. He got a kick out of it."

"Oh yeah. I remember him. We'd all play ball at his house."

"I wonder what 'Little Scotty' is doing now."

"'Little Scotty' has got to be in his thirties now. Right? Man, oh man...this trip down memory lane is killing me, Melanson."

And then quite suddenly, Sam needed to call it quits. Too much of this nostalgia overload, maybe. He swallowed hard, then said more to himself, "Well, I should probably get back. I've been here a while already." Then directly to Mike: "I still have to go through some more of his shit at the house. If you want to come on over this week and take anything, it's yours." Mike's smile looked more like a constipated grimace; he knew he wouldn't be taking any of George's things. Sam patted Mike on the shoulder. "Thanks for being a good friend to my brother."

"*Best* friend," Mike retorted.

"Indeed you were."

"And how are you? How is your...family? Moira. Your daughter?"

"Under the circumstances...unexpectedly good, I'd say. And yours?"

"Unexpectedly good." Then: "For now, anyway."

"Get what you can take," Sam said, slapping his back.

"Let me know what I can do."

"Do you want to buy a mobile home?"

It was a bittersweet line, and they both knew it.

As Sam stared into Mike's eyes, a large tear ran down his face. He could hear himself saying that line he and George would say from *Stalag 17:* "And if I meet any of you bums on the street, let's just pretend we never met." Instead, he said, "Catch you around." Then he headed out of Günter's Millyard and took one of the paths that would eventually lead him back to Pine Street. Later on, he would eat dinner with Moira and Maygyn. It felt bizarre and rather nice to be playing family again. Despite all of these – what should they be named? – turns of events? – twists of fate? – Sam Pearson and Mike Melanson – both men on the verge of losing their respective wives and children – actually had families to go home to.

A half-an-hour – maybe more – passed very quickly since Sam exited Paradise Park. Mike was an audience member and the creator of the scene that unfolded before him, and this time, the scene did not involve adult animation characters from *Foxes and Boxes* or even cartoon versions of himself and Jack Cleary drinking spirits and libations and joking at Jeremy's Irish Pub. No, this scene flash-forwarded to the beginning of the new century; in fact, it was 2001 just like the date in that fascinating but deathly slow science-fiction movie he watched years back that began with a segment called "The Dawn of Man" where a tribe of hominids in a prehistoric violent landscape discover the Crystal Monolith that enabled them to somehow use a bone as a weapon. He glanced at the granite column sculpture that Miss Julie once called the actual monolith in the 1968 film. Although he couldn't make out all the details of this abstract vision forming in front of him, he *did* hear the sounds of those airplanes from before, followed by a hollow, muffled noise that sounded like claustrophobic screaming. Mike sensed a great looming presence, something dangerous. Then he recalled something his clairvoyant wife had said: "...Not long after the turn of the century, thousands will die. It will be something like the sinking of the Titanic or Pearl Harbor. And it will lead into a plague...a pandemic like the Spanish Flu...all within twenty years." When Mike asked her what this would be, she said, "Being clairvoyant isn't about playing God, M&M. It's about tapping into the surrounding energies and listening to the guides. These guides are the truth."

Why was Mike Melanson – this simple low-down townie with no concept of the real world – thinking these thoughts – and through the voice of his own wife who was speaking to him like a medium? *Why?* Well, because this was all *really* happening. The guides *were* speaking these truths even if part of him wanted to dismiss these feelings as *illusions of grandness*. Then in his wife's voice he heard: "*Delusions of grandeur*, M& M. Say it with me and speak from the diaphragm. *Delusions of grandeur. Holy merde!* We got to get you cultured, my boy!" Then he heard her say this: "That's what I love about you, M&M. You are pretty complicated, but you don't know it. *Yet.* I'd even go so far as to say you have some real potential for psychic abilities. How do I know? Well, because I possess these abilities *to know* such things..."

The birthday boy, a hodgepodge of emotional quandaries, closed his eyes and tried to focus on the present moment. Maybe he, too, had "the gift," as his wife once called it. He sat there with a constipated grimace, trying much too hard to conjure up these special gifts. He really wanted everything to be okay. He wanted Miss Julie to have their second child with no complications; he wanted Miss Julie to forget that there was ever a person named Jack Cleary, let alone a collection of sex letters that had most likely now been associated with the deceased police officer when they were eventually discovered on his desk with that collection of tapes; he wanted Adam to regain respect for him and to realize that "everyone's human" and "everyone makes mistakes" and "everyone deserves a second chance"; and he wanted his unborn daughter or son – Alexia Sage or Spencer Cagney – to love him unconditionally. After all, he would be given a clean slate with this child.

Mike Melanson had a second chance – and he was going to take it.

The surge of electricity that ran through him gave him contradictory sensations – both of them overwhelming vibrations that represented the extremities of fear and love. The two abstract nouns that someone once told him were the two strongest human emotions.

What had all those demented, violent past images of Cleary – and even those horrific violent pictures of his wife – meant? And what were these recent visions and sounds of airplanes and skyscrapers? Is this what Miss Julie meant by having premonitions?

Again, Mike closed his eyes to see if he could somehow locate the answers from within. Like a real psychic or medium. He opened his eyes and looked toward the roaring Niagara Two. Maybe there was something fantastically otherworldly about this enigmatic waterfall.

He searched for these answers for the rest of the afternoon; he even made a special birthday request – to whom he didn't know – to be given the gift of extrasensory perception and clairvoyance, that ability to predict things like that old vampire, Nosferatu, the one that Miss Julie had told him about.

"You've got it!" he heard in Miss Julie's voice, that voice that mirrored the mantra of those who attended that Erhardt Seminars Training, where people "tear themselves down and put themselves back together again."

Then, after a few moments of contemplation, he heard Miss Julie's voice again: "My low-down townie has got it! *Holy merde!* What-a-ya know? He *does* have a concept of the real world, after all! How *mah-ve-lous!*"

Mike was smiling as if he had already "gotten it." For extra confirmation he reached out to what he surmised as being the spirit of Niagara Two – a force he knew to be much greater than any old waterfall – and without saying a word, he asked it if he had in fact "gotten it."

He waited the rest of the afternoon and into the evening as he sat there like someone waiting for a train.

But the roaring brown noise of Niagara Two just kept on flowing as it always did...

ABOUT ATMOSPHERE PRESS

Atmosphere Press is an independent, full-service publisher for excellent books in all genres and for all audiences. Learn more about what we do at atmospherepress.com.

We encourage you to check out some of Atmosphere's latest releases, which are available at Amazon.com and via order from your local bookstore:

Dancing with David, a novel by Siegfried Johnson

The Friendship Quilts, a novel by June Calender

My Significant Nobody, a novel by Stevie D. Parker

Nine Days, a novel by Judy Lannon

Shining New Testament: The Cloning of Jay Christ, a novel by Cliff Williamson

Shadows of Robyst, a novel by K. E. Maroudas

Home Within a Landscape, a novel by Alexey L. Kovalev

Motherhood, a novel by Siamak Vakili

Death, The Pharmacist, a novel by D. Ike Horst

Mystery of the Lost Years, a novel by Bobby J. Bixler

Bone Deep Bonds, a novel by B. G. Arnold

Terriers in the Jungle, a novel by Georja Umano

Into the Emerald Dream, a novel by Autumn Allen

His Name Was Ellis, a novel by Joseph Libonati

The Cup, a novel by D. P. Hardwick

The Empathy Academy, a novel by Dustin Grinnell

Tholocco's Wake, a novel by W. W. VanOverbeke

Dying to Live, a novel by Barbara Macpherson Reyelts

Looking for Lawson, a novel by Mark Kirby

Yosef's Path: Lessons from my Father, a novel by Jane Leclere Doyle

ABOUT THE AUTHOR

Photo by Caron Gonthier

David Gonthier is a freelance interdisciplinary artist, college professor and writing coach with a B.A. in Theatre from the University of New Hampshire, an M.S. in Film from Boston University, and an M.F.A. in Writing from Goddard College in Vermont. He lives in New Hampshire with his wife, Caron and daughter, Shelby. He is a published author of two books on film criticism (one of them being the definitive book on filmmaker Alan Parker). He is also a filmmaker, theatre practitioner, and songwriter who is often featured on New Hampshire radio. *Little Town Blues* is his first novel.